"You're a sweet liar, Megan of Dwyrain . . .

. . . but your eyes deceive you. You love not your husband and married him but for duty." Her captor's callused hand reached forward, twining in the thick strands of her hair to brush her nape. "You need the wind in your hair, the song of the falcon in your ears, the power of a steed beneath you." His hand slid lower to surround her throat in a grip that was as powerful as it was gentle. "You need a man who can tame your wild spirit, a man whose black heart is a match for your own."

"Nay," she whispered, but her lips trembled and her skin, where he touched her, throbbed. "Unhand me! Unhand me now!"

"Oh, I will, little one, but not before you admit it. Say the words."

"I cannot."

"You want me."

"Nay," she cried again as he drew her near, and his lips were close enough to hers that she could fairly taste him.

His smile was that of a devil. "Then prove me a liar," he ordered before drawing her body to his and claiming her mouth with a hard, savage kiss that seared through her blood and pierced her very soul. . . .

MORE PRAISE FOR *KISS OF THE MOON*

"ENCHANTING. . . . Medieval romance fans will take great pleasure in reading Susan Lynn Crose's exciting *Kiss of the Moon*. . . . This fast-paced, well-written novel will bring joy to its audience."

—Harriet Klausner, *The Talisman*

Books by Susan Lynn Crose

Enchantress
Kiss of the Moon
Outlaw

Published by POCKET BOOKS

OUTLAW

SUSAN LYNN CROSE

POCKET BOOKS
New York   London   Toronto   Sydney   Tokyo   Singapore

This book is a work of fiction. Names, characters, places and incidents are products of the author's imagination or are used fictitiously. Any resemblance to actual events or locales or persons, living or dead, is entirely coincidental.

An *Original* Publication of POCKET BOOKS

POCKET BOOKS, a division of Simon & Schuster Inc.
1230 Avenue of the Americas, New York, NY 10020

Copyright © 1995 by Susan Lynn Crose

All rights reserved, including the right to reproduce this book or portions thereof in any form whatsoever. For information address Pocket Books, 1230 Avenue of the Americas, New York, NY 10020

ISBN: 0-671-88534-0

First Pocket Books printing December 1995

10 9 8 7 6 5 4 3 2 1

POCKET and colophon are registered trademarks of Simon & Schuster Inc.

Cover art by Danilo Ducak

Printed in the U.S.A.

❋ Prologue ❋

Wales
Winter 1295

"Hurry!" Megan ordered, her breath fogging in the frigid air as she leaned forward in the saddle. Her horse, a headstrong bay mare with an urge to nip, galloped through the forest as night closed in. "Faster, you beast, faster!" Megan glanced at the sky. Through the bare branches she saw clouds, thick and dark and menacing, ready to spill a shower of sleet over the countryside near the castle of Dwyrain, her home.

At least she hoped it was still her home. Her father might just banish her this time. "Please, God, no," she whispered, suddenly frightened and contrite. Why had she been so foolish as to let her younger sister Cayley goad her into an argument? Wouldn't she ever learn?

"Run, Shalimar, 'tis a good girl you be." The encouragement she gave slid through teeth that chattered.

The wind picked up. Megan shivered. Her gloved fingers turned to ice as she held the reins. The forest surrounding Dwyrain had always been an enchanted place in the summer where she'd ridden, hunted, laughed, and waded in the meandering streams. She'd picked berries and nuts, dug for herbs, and plucked wildflowers and ferns from their stalks.

But this afternoon, only a few days before the Christmas revels were to begin, the woods were gloomy; the dark-limbed trees with their naked branches appeared to be forgotten soldiers guarding secrets that no mortal man dared unearth. How many times had her mother warned her that the forests around Dwyrain were sinister, haunted by the spirits of ghosts, people who had believed in the old ways rather than the lawful teachings of the church?

Megan had always laughed at her mother's silly warnings, though Violet of Dwyrain was not the only one who believed in spirits boding both good and evil. Many servants in the castle professed Christianity and knelt on the cold stone floor of the chapel each day, but clung to the faith of their forefathers—the ancient ways. Even old Rue, the nursemaid, trusted the runes and spells of her elders. Megan had spent years watching her, learning quickly, though knowing instinctively that she should never let anyone realize just how much of Rue's pagan magic she'd planted in her mind.

Gathering her cloak to her neck, she squinted as the first icy drops began to fall. The sky was nearly black, and again Megan cursed herself for her foolishness. Her father, Baron Ewan, would be furious with her and would probably send her to her chamber without food and order her to spend hours in the chapel on her knees while begging forgiveness of the Blessed Mother and Holy Father.

Saints in heaven, why had she been so foolish? Frozen cobwebs brushed her cheeks as she rode, guiding the animal down the narrow deer trail. The mare's quick hoofbeats echoed in the quiet forest. Gripping her hood about her neck with one hand, Megan leaned forward and the horse took the bit, running faster and faster along the narrow trail. "'Tis good you are, Shalimar," Megan cried as a branch slapped her face. They weren't far now, just around the next bend and up a hill and—

The earth seemed to shift. Megan flew forward as Shalimar stumbled.

"Oh!" As she slid sideways in the saddle, leafless branches spun wildly in her vision. The slick reins slid from her fingers as she hung upside down. Her cloak fell over her face and swept the ground. Gamely, the horse plowed forward, limping. "Stop! Shalimar! Halt!" she commanded, scrambling to pull herself back into the saddle. The mare went down on one knee and Megan, barely astride again, pitched forward.

The ground rushed up at her. She landed hard on her

2

shoulder. Pain screamed up her arm and she felt dizzy as she tried to sit up. Shalimar stood, sweating and mud-spattered, favoring a foreleg, her liquid eyes rimmed in white, her dirty coat trembling.

Gritting her teeth, Megan climbed to her feet and made her way to her horse. "What is it, girl?" she asked, but the mare shied and limped farther away.

"Your mount's lame." A deep, soft-spoken voice shook the rain from the leaves of the ivy that clung tenaciously to the trees.

Megan nearly jumped out of her skin. She whirled quickly, her boots sliding in the mud, her eyes narrowed as she squinted into the thicket. "Who are you?" she asked, her horse forgotten, her fingers searching through the slits in her cloak for the knife she had strapped to her belt. "Show yourself."

A soft chuckle followed and an owl hooted from the higher branches of a great fir tree.

"I said—"

"I heard you." A man appeared from the shadows. Tall, broad-shouldered, with a ragged cape that nearly touched the ground, he stepped forward with a noticeable limp. His face was hidden by the hood of his cape, and for a second, Megan shivered in fear. "What are you doing out here alone, Megan of Dwyrain?"

Her throat went dry as her fingers clasped upon the hilt of her dagger. "I—I went riding."

"Ahh. Because of a tiff with your sister Cayley, aye?"

Her heart pounded. "But how did you know? Were you in the keep standing with your ear to the door? Who are you?" she demanded, tossing her wet hair from her face and lifting her chin proudly, mimicking her older brother Bevan. Rain dripped off her nose and chin ignobly and dirt was probably smudged on her face, but she stood her ground, refusing to appear frightened.

"I . . . feel things," he said, looking suddenly vexed, as if he would like to come up with a better explanation, but could not. "Now, let's have a look at your mount."

"She'll shy."

He ignored Megan and spoke softly to the horse. His words were nearly hypnotic, a chant of sorts at which

3

Shalimar, snorting nervously, didn't flinch; not even when he lifted her pained leg and examined it with long fingers that protruded from gloves that covered only his palms. What kind of man was he? The mare, anxious only seconds before, quieted under his hands, and when he reached beneath his cape and withdrew a fat leather pouch, she didn't so much as nicker.

"What're you doing?" Megan asked.

"Shh!" His command was sharp. "You'll scare her." Gently, holding his gloves in his teeth, he applied the jellylike salve, speaking nearly inaudibly to the horse, closing his eyes for a second as he wrapped his fingers around Shalimar's foreleg. The bay didn't move and appeared in a trance.

Rain pelted the ground, creating pools and splashing in icy droplets against Megan's face and cloak. Shuddering, she stepped away from the mystical man. Though she believed that there were powers on this earth that she didn't understand, powers greater than those given to men and accompanied by crown and scepter, powers that were invisible to most and granted to only a few, she felt a jab of fear.

"There now, you may go," the man said, turning toward her. His face was shadowed by his hood, but she saw that his eyes were blue as the sky in summer.

"Who are you?"

He slid his fingers through the holes in his gloves. "'Tis of no consequence."

"A sorcerer?"

His smile was humble. "Would you want to think of me as such, so be it."

Shalimar ambled forward, no hint of her injury visible in her gait. "The horse is healed."

"Aye, but be careful. She's not meant to run on slick trails that are weakened by the burrows of moles and rabbits and badgers. Race her only where the earth is firm."

Megan, always impetuous, couldn't help her wayward tongue. "But you limp, sir," she said, motioning to his bad leg. "Why do you not heal yourself as you have the mare?"

"Ah yes, that." He thought for a second, those intense eyes studying her as if she were a mystery. "My injury is old.

4

From my youth, before I knew how to heal. And it matters not. 'Tis a reminder to me that I am mortal and that there is suffering in the world."

"So you choose to be a cripple?" she asked aghast.

"'Tis my fate." He threw her a crooked grin. "Now, be off. 'Tis nearly dark and the baron is not pleased."

She wanted to know more of this man, this would-be magician. "Please, come with me," she begged. "My father would want to thank you for helping me and my horse. He'd surely offer you a hot trencher of brawn or eel and a cup of wine along with the safety of the castle for the night."

The man's smile was odd. "Nay, child. I prefer the solitude of the forest." At that moment, the owl hooted again and the wizard—for that's what she believed him to be—glanced skyward. Rain ran down his face, but he didn't notice. "Hush, Owain, be patient," he said. The owl ignored him, letting loose another soft call, and the man grinned widely, showing off white teeth beneath a nose that wasn't quite straight. "He's a stubborn fellow, that one."

"You know my name," Megan said as he handed her Shalimar's reins, "but I know not yours."

"'Tis better if you don't."

"Are you an enemy of Dwyrain?"

He hesitated and his eyes looked over her shoulder, to a distance that was of his own making. "Nay, child—now, be gone."

As if rooted to the ground, she didn't move—just stared, fascinated, into his eyes. "You speak with animals."

"I only see into their minds."

"Can you see into mine as well?" she asked.

"Perhaps." His sigh was as soft as the wind. "Is that what you'd like?"

"Nay—aye—I know not."

"Sometimes it is best if we know not what others think."

Shivering, Megan shook her head. "Tell me."

Eyeing her but a moment, he said, "So be it." He removed one glove and took her hand in his. She expected his fingers to be frigid as the sea, but a warmth traveled from his palm to hers. "I see not into your mind, but to the years of your life not yet lived."

"You see ahead in time—you foretell what will be?"

"Aye. 'Tis my curse. Would you like to know of your unborn years?"

She could barely breathe and a part of her wanted to flee, to be rid of this odd forest-man with his gentle voice and knowing eyes, and yet she couldn't let go, for she trusted him. The warmth of his hand, his soothing voice, his trustworthy eyes. Nodding, she braced herself and wished she could stop her quaking, for surely he could feel the trembling that had suddenly afflicted her. "Tell me," she said, her words rushed.

"Aye, then." Closing his eyes, he held her fingers between his two hands. "There will be trouble at Dwyrain," he said, his voice sounding as if it had traveled a great distance through a long, narrow cavern. "Sickness. Deceit. Betrayal."

"No."

"The blame will be placed on you."

She recoiled, but he held her hand firmly.

"You will marry in the next few years at the bidding of your father, but the marriage will be cursed—"

"No, I'll not listen—" she said, but stood transfixed, unable to move.

"Your family and castle will be destroyed."

"Nay, sorcerer, I'll not believe—"

"Only true love will restore Dwyrain and your honor," he continued, his eyes squeezed shut, his head moving slowly, as if he were listening to some higher order.

"Love?" So there was hope. If she allowed herself to believe in this foolishness.

"Aye, but the faces of love are many. Some treacherous. Some deceitful. Some as shadowy as candlelight. True love must be tested, Megan, and yours will come from an unlikely source."

Her insides turned to ice. "How will I know—?"

"The man will be dark-haired, fierce of countenance, unforgiving by nature."

"He sounds like a fiend."

"Beneath his mantle of hatred, he has a true heart."

Megan yanked back her hand. "I believe you not," she said, though a part of her trusted the horrid words. "You are the voice of the Devil."

"I speak only the truth, child," he said solemnly, and a blade of dread sliced through her heart. She wanted to laugh at him, to tell him he was addled, call him a fool, but she held her tongue. Did he not know who she was, who her father was? Did he not heal her lame horse?

Before she said another word, he slipped away, as if in his own mist, through the curtain of rain. Overhead, the wings of a great owl flapped wildly.

"Wait," she cried, but before the word was uttered, she knew he was gone.

Swallowing hard, she clucked softly to the horse, pulling on the reins as she led the beast back to the great gates of Dwyrain. The man was mad, she told herself, not to be trusted—an imposter who performed some sort of trickery. But no matter how desperately she argued with herself, she couldn't cast off the premonition of doom that trailed after her, as unshakable as her own shadow, as dark as the deep waters of Hag's End Lake.

❅ One ❅

Tower Dwyrain
Winter 1297

"Come now, smile, Megan. 'Tis your wedding day," Ewan cajoled, lying on the bed in his chamber. He patted the white fur coverlet and smiled up at his daughter.

Even in the flickering light from the candles, Megan saw the spots of age on his thin skin and noticed that his once-fleshy face had hollowed. In his youth, his eyes had been as clear and blue as a mountain lake, but now they had clouded, leaving him half blind.

"You'll not have to look after me much longer, child," he told her. "My time here is short."

"Nay, Father—" she said, closing the door behind her and hurrying to his bedside. She sat on the edge of the feather mattress and took his cold fingers in her own.

"Aye, and I'll be expecting to see a grandson before I go, a strong, strapping lad as Bevan was," he said. Tears welled in Megan's eyes when she thought of her brother, a year older than she but now in his grave, the victim of the sickness that had taken so many in the castle, including her mother and tiny sister. Megan swallowed against a thick lump that had formed in her throat. She'd heard the gossip, knew that most of the servants and a few of the knights blamed her for the death and destruction that had befallen Dwyrain ever since she'd seen the lame prophet in the forest, and he'd cursed her as well as the castle.

Her father sighed sadly. "But ye'd best not wait too long with that grandson."

"Don't talk such madness," she chided, refusing to believe that her beloved father would soon die.

But 'twas as if he were deaf. "Holt, he will be a good husband to you," he said, patting her hands and smiling without reason, as if he had no mind left. There was hushed talk between his men that he was addled, that the loss of his wife and two children, coupled with his age, had finally caught up to him, that he'd taken one too many blows to the head in the heat of battle in his younger years. "A lucky lass ye be to marry a knight as brave as Sir Holt."

Despair raked sharp claws down her heart. "Nay, Father," she said boldly, knowing this was her last chance to change his mind.

"Do not argue with me."

Grasping his hand more urgently, she whispered, "But Father, I need not a husband—"

"Shh," he said, then coughed loudly, his chest rattling, his body clenching against the pain. "God in heaven," he growled, once the attack had passed. He reached for a mazer of wine on a bedside table. His hounds, two gray hunters, lifted their heads and glared at Megan menacingly, as if she were the reason their master no longer rode wildly through the forests and underbrush, drinking mead, whooping loudly, and flushing out deer, boars, and pheasant for them to chase.

Beneath the dogs' yellow-eyed glare, Megan inched up her chin. Even the snarling beasts appeared to blame her for the ills that had plagued Dwyrain ever since that crippled old sorcerer had sealed her doom with his prophecy and Cayley, whom Megan had trusted with her secret, had told the story of the curse.

"But Father," she pressed on, "remember, the magician said that should I marry this man of your choosing, the marriage would be cursed, and—"

"Shh, child! I believe not in such devilment!" Ewan grumbled, bellowing as he once had, only to end up in a deep, bone-jarring hack. "'Tis against the teachings of the church. Father Timothy said 'twas a trick the cripple played upon you, a trick that toyed with your weak mind."

"My mind is far from weak," Megan said quickly, and silently cursed the priest for his false piety. The man was too swift to point to the fault in others, too hasty to give a tongue-lashing, too eager to see punishment meted out when none was needed. Unlike Father Andrew, a kind and wise man who, during his 12 years as chapel priest at Dwyrain, had always seen both sides of a disagreement, Father Timothy was young and all-knowing, with a glint of pleasure in his eye when anyone was caught in a sin. 'Twas as if he enjoyed watching others explain their sins and beg forgiveness.

"Aye, I know you not to be thick-skulled as Father Timothy proclaims, but I cannot believe in witchcraft and the dark arts. What would your mother, rest her soul, think?" With a deft movement, he crossed himself, as he sometimes did when his thoughts turned to Violet and her early death. Then there were other times when he acted as if he'd forgotten she'd left this earth.

"I know not."

"Well, I'll ask her, the next time she comes to visit," he said, and she looked for a hint of humor in his cloudy eyes, but found none. Nay, he believed that his wife, though dead, walked these halls and that she often carried baby Rosalind with her or spoke of Bevan.

"You trust not the sorcerer's prediction but you speak with Mother's ghost."

"Her spirit," he said, correcting her as he scooted upward on the bed and cleared his throat. The effort caused even more strain on his tired face. "You think I'm addled," he said, glaring at her through foggy eyes.

"Nay—"

"It is my curse these days. The servants act as if I'm not only blind, but deaf as well, and that I have no mind left. The truth is that I do talk to your mother, Megan, and she asks about you. Aye, I know that she is dead, but believe it or not, at times her spirit glides down from heaven to be with me." He clapped a broad hand over his heart. "She was and always will be an angel. My angel."

Megan didn't know what to say; to argue against something he wanted so feverishly to cling to would be unwise. Why cause him any more pain? If he thought he could speak with his dead wife and children, what did it hurt? "Aye, Father. An angel she is."

He smiled beneath his snowy beard. "I'm glad you believe me, child, because your mother, she wants you to marry Holt!"

Megan jumped off the bed as if she'd been sitting on the red-hot embers of Cook's fires. "You tricked me!"

He laughed and the sound echoed in her heart. "No more than that silly prophet did a few years ago. Now, go on, get dressed and, please, daughter, be happy." Yawning broadly, he waved her away.

"I love Holt not," she said, and her father grimaced at the words.

"'Twas the same for your mother and me." At the sharp lift of her head, he motioned awkwardly, as if scattering flies. "I know, I know, you thought differently, but love does not grow easily at times, even with your mother and me. Over the years I became devoted to her and she to me. Love sometimes comes with time, daughter, and you have long to live."

Too long, she thought, *if I am to be Holt's wife.* Shuddering inside, she watched as Ewan closed his eyes to rest. Within mere seconds, he was snoring gently, blissfully unaware of the treachery that was mounting against him, the treason she could feel in the hallways. Like rats scurrying through the rushes, the whispers of betrayal darted through the thick walls of Dwyrain.

"The baron, bless him, is not himself these days," Father Timothy had whispered to the steward months ago as the two men stood beside the miller's cart in the inner bailey beneath the open window where Megan had sat on the ledge. Their voices had risen up to her like smoke from a fire.

"Aye, and it's a sad day," Quinn had responded, shaking his head, his bald pate shining in the autumn sunlight.

"And without Bevan to become the baron . . . Ahh, I fear the worst and pray that a man like Sir Holt will step forward and marry the baron's daughter, Lady Megan, so that the castle will once again be secure."

"Aye. Holt would be a good choice."

Megan's heart had frozen for a second, but she had not believed that her father would insist upon the marriage.

Another time, she'd heard one of her father's most

trusted soldiers, Cawfield, confide in the sheriff, "'Tis a pity, that's what I say, when a man's mind goes. There was a time when Ewan of Dwyrain was a fierce warrior. Who would have thought?" Cawfield had been standing guard and his voice had drifted toward the bakery, where Megan was checking that Llyle was not wasting the flour that he was allotted and that there would be plenty of good-sized loaves of wastel, as Gwayne of Cysgod was visiting. But she'd stopped at the sound of the men and tarried in the rose garden, where Cawfield's voice could be heard clearly over the honks of geese and ducks waddling near the eel pond and the creak of the chain and bucket at the well. "Ewan was a strong leader," Cawfield continued. "I pray that he heals soon."

Others hadn't been so kind. The mason had grumbled, "Who can rely on an old relic with half a brain to protect us?" and Ellen, a woman who tended to the geese, had crossed herself and asked to be delivered from Satan as well as the protection of so weak a lord. Ellen, too, believed that Holt alone could rule Dwyrain as a strong, fair lord.

Was Megan the only one who doubted him?

Aye, Holt was a handsome man, tall and strong, with shoulders as broad as the handle of an ax and sharp features that had caused many a scullery maid to sigh and swoon. He was quick with his wit as well as his sword and had, in the past few years, wormed his way into her father's empty heart. From the beginning, he'd noticed Megan, even when she was but a lass, his dark eyes slitting a little as he stared at her, and Megan had always shivered inwardly, sensing that he was trying to imagine what she looked like without her clothes.

She'd overheard him tell ribald jokes to his men and had commented about one of the milking girls—that he would like to drink from her big tits and do his own kind of milking. The men had laughed uproariously and Megan had thought Holt crude.

And now she would be his bride. A sour taste rose in the back of her throat.

Realizing there was no escape, she closed the door to her father's chamber behind her and swept down the hall, her footsteps muted by the new rushes laid upon the stone floor.

Despite the fires burning brightly in the great hall and the tapestries hung on the walls and doorways, the keep was drafty. Megan felt cold as death. In but a few weeks the Christmas revels would be upon them and she, God help her, would be Sir Holt's wife.

Not for the first time, she considered defying her father and fleeing. Once upon Shalimar's broad back, she could ride swiftly through the gatehouse before the portcullis could be lowered! She would race the mare deep into the forest, where she knew of hiding places where no one, not any of her father's soldiers or even the band of outlaws that resided in the wooded hills surrounding the castle, would find her. Yes, she could ride to freedom . . . ahh, would it were so!

She nearly bumped into one of the seamstresses, who was hastening down the hall with another young woman, but Megan ducked into an alcove before being seen.

". . . doesn't know how lucky she is to be marrying the most handsome man in all of Dwyrain. I would gladly lift my skirts for that one and, oh, to be his wife . . ."

Megan's stomach clenched and she slid deeper into the shadows while the seamstress, a silly, freckled-skinned girl named Nell, paused to lean against the wall. Nell was carrying a white silk tunic with gold brocade and rabbit trim. Megan's heart dropped to the floor, for this was her best tunic, the one in which she was to be married.

". . . if I were Lady Megan, I would lick my fingers to be Holt's bride."

"And what else would ye lick?" Grace, one of the cook's daughters who often worked in the kitchen, asked with a suggestive giggle.

Megan's stomach turned over, and she realized she should step forward and scold the girl for gossiping idly, but she wanted to overhear what the maid would say next.

"Shh, Grace—such a tart ye be!"

A big girl with ample breasts and a gap between her front teeth, Grace flirted often with the soldiers.

Nell rambled on, "'Tis true, the lady loves him not, and all the pain she's brought to this castle is but proof she has not a pure heart. Did ye not hear about the curse that prophet, the lame one Lady Megan met in the forest, laid on this castle?"

"Aye. Everyone in the castle and the villages heard, but I don't believe in prophets or curses of the pagan ones," Grace said, crossing her chest hastily, as if in fear that the very Devil himself might swoop down upon her.

"Well, ye'd better change yer way of thinkin', because since that time there have been strange deaths and evil within the walls of Dwyrain." Her voice dropped and Megan strained to hear. "'Tis all because of her. Had Lady Megan not been out riding that day against the baron's wishes, she'd not have met the sorcerer and he'd not have laid the curse on this castle."

"'Tis not true," Grace said, though there was little conviction in her words.

"Aye, ye can say as much because ye did not lose a brother to the sickness that crept through Dwyrain like a thief and took the lives of many, including the baron's wife, his wee babe, and his only son. Ye remember Sir Bevan, Grace, and don't be lyin' to me and sayin' ye dinna. If ever there was one who could turn a lass's head, he was one." She sighed dreamily, clutching the tunic to her.

"Another one ye would lift yer soiled skirts for?" Grace asked, raising her eyebrow.

"Aye, quick as a cat jumping for spilt cream," Nell said with a laugh as they continued, making their way past the smoldering rush lights.

Megan didn't move. Her eyes were moist, her stomach tied in painful knots when she thought of her mother, tall, stately, prideful but loving, a woman whom everyone in the castle trusted. Violet of Dwyrain. Dead. "God be with you, Mama," Megan said with a sniff, then thought of her brother Bevan, one year older than she and a devil of a boy who loved mischief. He had not been felled by the sickness that claimed so many but had drowned in the creek near Hag's End Lake.

Bevan and Megan had been fast friends, always getting into trouble, forever telling secrets. As he'd grown, he'd been groomed to become baron. "'Tis silly, really," Bevan had told her when they were riding far from the castle one day and they paused to let their mounts sip from a stream. Over the tops of the trees, the towering walls of Dwyrain were visible and Bevan squinted as he stared at them. "Ye'd be a much better lord than I. Too bad ye be younger and a girl."

"You'll be a great baron," she'd predicted and he'd grinned.

"Ye're right, sister. I'll be the best!" Then, yanking on the reins, he'd given a loud hoot, kicked his gray palfrey in the flanks, and raced off across the creek, splashing noisily through the water.

Aye, she missed her brother and tiny, giggling Rosalind as well. Not even 2 years old, with only a few teeth and a silly, bright smile, the baby had succumbed to the dark death that had stolen through the corridors of Dwyrain.

Losing his wife and Baby Roz had been the start of Ewan's ruin, Megan thought sadly, squeezing her eyes shut, remembering her father, strong then, kneeling in the mud and laying roses on the grave of his beloved Violet. He'd wept openly, and Holt had been with him, helping him up, whispering condolences, his hands steady.

Then, only weeks later, the tragedy of Bevan's drowning. Megan had heard her father's hoarse wails when he'd been told the news, then watched his stoic decline as his son had never again opened his eyes.

Before the deaths of family, friends, and servants, Ewan of Dwyrain had been a powerful ruler, one of the most envied of King Edward's barons, a fair man known for his good sense and coarse humor. Now, he was but a shell of the man he'd once been, a husk of that courageous soldier who had ridden into battle against the Scots.

There was a time when no one in the castle had dared defy him, no one questioned his judgment, no one considered going against him. At present, there was malcontent, and the soldiers guarding the gates of the tower were new men, unfamiliar faces who looked to Holt for leadership, or old, tired friends who whispered between themselves that Ewan was addled and ill fit to rule.

Megan leaned the back of her head against the cool stone walls of the alcove and remembered the prophet's words.

You will marry in the next few years at the bidding of your father, but the marriage will be cursed—

"Dear God, no."

Sickness. Deceit. Betrayal.

The sorcerer's words rang in her head as they had been whispered through the keep. True, they'd all come to pass. *The blame will be placed on you.*

Had it not? Most of the servants would no longer look her in the eye. Even some of the peasants avoided her. 'Twas as if she were a leper or worse. She'd been blamed for the armorer's son falling off the north tower, and for the baker's wife delivering stillborn twins—even Bevan's death, from drowning in the creek, was said to have been her fault. It mattered not that he'd been brought back to the castle barely alive and she and the doctor had tried to nurse him back to health, nor that she'd spent hours in the chapel under Father Timothy's watchful eye, praying for her brother's life.

Yet, despite all the horrors blamed on her, Holt wanted her.

Guilt chased after her as she hurried onward, toward her chamber and the cold, brittle fact that she was to become Holt's bride.

"Oh, would I were you!" Cayley eyed her sister with envy and Megan squirmed, uncomfortable in the long silk tunic that had been altered for her wedding.

She wanted nothing more than to shed this finery and ride Shalimar as fast and far away from the castle as she could. "If you want to be me so badly, then you marry Sir Holt," she said, mindful of Rue, the old nursemaid who was fidgeting with the hem of the tunic, her needle and thread working steadily.

"Shame on ye, lass," Rue muttered, but when her gaze met Megan's, there was no gladness in her tired eyes, and she quickly glanced away again, turning her attention and the conversation back to her work. "I know not why Nell could not mend this hem. Look at the way it droops! Sometimes methinks that girl has her head elsewhere!" Clucking her tongue, she worked swiftly.

Cayley pushed aside the window covering. A shaft of pale winter light slipped through the tanned hides and the noisy honks of geese rose up from the yard. There were shouts and the creak of wagon wheels and Megan bit her tongue, knowing that the few straggling guests who hadn't arrived the day before were now filing into the keep.

"Aye, Holt's a handsome one," Cayley persisted as she hoisted herself up to the window ledge. Tucking her knees beneath her chin, she stared down at the inner bailey and eyed the new visitors anxiously, searching, no doubt, for Gwayne of Cysgod.

"A handsome man does not a fine husband make."

"Oh, but it helps! Why not marry someone who is pleasing to the eye rather than an ugly old toad like Sir Oswald?"

"At least Oswald is kind." Megan finger-combed her hair and Rue squawked loudly.

"I spent hours on those plaits! Don't you be undoing them now; all the flowers will fall out!"

Megan cared not. Her worries about Holt were too deep for her to be concerned about the braids that were wound around her head.

Cayley was right, he was a handsome man with his thick brown hair, eyes as dark as midnight, and a quick, cold smile. Strong and able, Holt was considered her father's most trusted knight. He had courted Megan for nearly a year, and in that time, he'd done nothing but swear his undying affection for her and his loyalty to all that was Dwyrain. Yet she doubted him and didn't trust the glint in his eyes when he looked at her.

You will marry . . . at the bidding of your father . . . marriage will be cursed— The cripple's words rang in circles in her head, round and round, spinning ever faster on this, the day of her wedding. *There will be trouble at Dwyrain. Sickness. Deceit. Betrayal. The blame will be placed on you.*

"Your Holt will make you happy, as Gwayne will me," Cayley said dreamily. Always a romantic, Cayley had envisioned herself as the lady of Castle Cysgod from the moment she'd met Gwayne when she was but 4 years old and he a boy of 8.

"Holt is Father's choice, not mine!"

"Shh, child!" Rue hissed, shaking her graying head as she straightened and rubbed the small of her back. "I would be careful were I ye," she said, giving advice as she always had. "The castle walls sometimes have ears, do they not? Holt would not be pleased were he to hear your thoughts."

"He will hear them soon enough," Megan said, for if she was to wed this man, he would find she had her own mind, her own plans, her own life . . . or did she? Her heart sank. Whereas Cayley had forever wanted to marry, Megan had longed for something other than being a soldier's or a baron's wife.

"Here, slip your arms through," Rue instructed as she held up a wine-red quilted surcoat with threads of gold. Megan did as she was bid, including donning a mantle of forest green that was trimmed with gold lace. The old nursemaid trained a practiced eye on her handiwork. "'Tis lovely ye are, Megan girl."

"Aye," Cayley said, frowning slightly, twin little furrows growing in the skin between her honey-colored brows. "You are prettier than I thought you'd ever be."

Megan should have been pleased, but she was not. She'd looked forward to this day as if it were the beginning of her death sentence. She would no longer have this bedchamber to herself. Holt had been given Bevan's room and would share it with her. He was not a wealthy man and owned no keep of his own, but he had sworn to her father that he would take care of Megan for all her life and be true to Dwyrain.

Ewan believed him.

Megan did not.

Without much grace, Cayley hopped down from the ledge. "Think ye this keep is cursed?" she asked, biting her lower lip and running a hand along a bare, whitewashed wall.

Rue snorted. "Ye've been listening to idle gossip again."

"Well, I believe it!" Cayley said, staring at her sister with silent, unspoken accusations in her eyes. "Were it not, Mother, Bevan, and Baby Roz would yet be alive!"

"You blame me," Megan said, the knowledge as painful as a hot knife twisting in her heart. Even her sister had fallen prey to the curse.

"Nay, not you, but surely that monster of a cripple who you met in the forest. I remember that day, Megan, when you came riding into the castle, your skin the color of curdled cream, your eyes round and frightened, as if you'd just seen your own ghost!"

Megan remembered that dark day as well. She'd been scared to death and trembled inside. Late that night, she'd slipped from beneath her coverlet to kneel and whisper at Cayley's bedside. With the light of one lone candle chasing away the shadows of the night, she'd confided in her sister, telling an awestruck Cayley everything the sorcerer had said and done, including healing Shalimar's leg and predicting the dark fates that would befall the keep.

"He was the Devil!" Cayley had said, clutching her fur blanket to her chest.

"Nay, I think not."

"He's cursed us." Cayley sat bolt upright in bed and narrowed her eyes. "I wish I would have met him in the forest," she'd said, as she'd tossed her dark honey–colored curls over her shoulder, "for I would have laid a curse on his own black soul."

"Nay, Cayley, the man was true of heart."

Cayley had snorted her disbelief, and now, years later, as the sand drifted through the hourglass and 'twas nearing the time for her marriage to Holt, Megan feared her sister had been right after all. Dwyrain was cursed and she was the reason.

"Come now, child," Rue said with a sigh. "Father Timothy and Holt wait for ye in the chapel."

"I'm tellin' ye, 'tis a fool's mission we're on," Odell complained, rubbing his back and squinting through the underbrush to the castle rising in the distance. Astride a sorrel jennet he'd won in a dice game, he scowled against the surrounding gloom.

Wolf ignored the older man and stripped off his tunic. Odell was never happy lest he was grumbling. "'Tis something I have to do." Untying the bag he'd brought with him, he reached inside and his fingers encountered the soft fabric of the clothes he'd stolen only a few hours earlier from a nobleman.

"For the love of Saint Peter, man, think. What needs we with a woman? Do ye not remember the law of our band?"

"I made the law," Wolf said through lips that barely moved. He patted his destrier's thick neck and stared at the throng of people moving along the road toward Dwyrain, the fortress he planned to plunder. Limestone walls knifed upward to thick battlements and towers; a wide moat was crossed by a single bridge spanning a river that surrounded the hill on which the castle was built. A town, hidden by walls cut from the same stone, lay to the east, with only the river separating it from the castle. Outside the walls were a few houses and fields that farmers tended, but the tilled land finally gave way to the woods Wolf now called home.

"Aye, ye made the law that there would be no women in our band, that women only cause trouble, that women—"

"I know what I said," Wolf growled, sliding his arms and head through a silky black tunic.

"And yet ye're willing to break yer own rules. For this one? Why? What d'ye want with this *cursed* woman?" Odell asked, blowing on fingers that showed through the ends of his gloves.

"She's not important." His new mantle was black as well, trimmed in the fur of a silver fox. Metal studs decorated his new belt and gloves.

"Not important? Fer the love of Saint Jude, then why take her?"

"Because she belongs to Holt of Prydd," he said, and felt a cruel smile twist his lips as he tightened his belt and thought of his quest. "In that respect, you're right, Odell. She is cursed."

"I hate to be the one givin' ye the news, but in case ye havna noticed, this isna Prydd we're plannin' to enter—"

"Not us. Only me," Wolf reminded him. "You're to wait for my signal then take Sir Kelvin's fine horse"—he motioned to the tawny destrier they'd recently stolen—"and ride back to camp."

"Aye, aye. Wait fer the signal. I know. But I'm tellin' ye, Wolf. This woman—this daughter of the baron—will only bring us trouble."

Wolf didn't bother answering, just stared across the great distance that separated them from the castle. His eyes were trained on the crenels of the north watch turret. Baron Ewan of Dwyrain's standard snapped in the wind, the colors red and gold bright against an ominous slate-colored sky. If ever there was a day for an omen, this was one. But Wolf trusted not in too much sorcery. Aye, he'd watched Morgana of Wenlock talk to the wind and see through a window into the future, and he'd witnessed great healing when Sorcha of Prydd had brought the near-dead back to life again, but he trusted not the dark arts. Nor did he trust God.

Mist was beginning to gather in the woods and would soon shroud his view. Then he'd have to rely on instincts rather than the help of spies within the castle. Somewhere in the surrounding trees, an owl hooted softly.

"There it is," Wolf said squinting hard. One of Dwyrain's sentries, a watchman in the north tower, paused, closed the shutters of the crenel, then opened them again. "'Tis time."

Odell scratched his head. "Time fer what—to open the gates of hell?"

Wolf chuckled and checked the knife he'd slid into his boot. "The marriage ceremony is about to begin." A hard smile crept over his lips as the sound of church bells peeled throughout the valley. "I wouldn't want to be late."

"For the wedding?" Odell asked, rolling his eyes as if he was certain his leader was daft. "'Twill be hours before ye get there."

"I care not for the wedding." Wolf's smile faded and determination clenched his jaw. "But the kidnapping can't start without me."

Wolf entered the gates of Dwyrain easily. No one questioned a well-dressed nobleman on a swift mud-spattered destrier. He appeared tired, as if from a long journey, and rode across the drawbridge and beneath the great portcullis that was raised in the gatehouse. Through the outer bailey without so much as a question from the sentries, he followed others and trailed behind a lumbering team of horses pulling a hay cart. A boy he recognized as Jack, a young hunter for the castle, glanced his way, then went back to sharpening the blade of his knife. Though neither acknowledged the other, Wolf and Jack had met before when poachers had tried to steal from Dwyrain's forests and had nearly killed Jack to silence him. It had been Wolf's sword that had convinced them to take their dead stag and leave the boy alone.

Now, three years later, Jack sheathed his knife, met Wolf's gaze again briefly, then grabbed the reins of Wolf's mount before leading the stallion away.

The chapel bells had rung hours before, announcing that the marriage ceremony itself and the nuptial Mass following the ceremony had ended. Good. 'Twas important that Holt be married. Wolf only hoped Holt loved Ewan's daughter with all his black heart. She was the older of the baron's daughters, and some, including his allies within the castle walls, blamed her for their troubles, claiming she'd brought a curse upon the keep. They were only too eager to help him with his plot and be rid of Megan.

As if he had every right to enter, he half ran up the steps of the great hall and ignored a guard posted at the door, but he was stopped by a tall, lanky soldier with a scraggly red beard and a scar running down one side of his face.

"Excuse me, sir, but have you an invitation?"

Wolf paused and let a small, amused smile play upon his lips, the kind of knowing grin that one of superior birth rains on an underling. "Pardon me?"

The man's Adam's apple bobbed. "An invite, sir."

The knife in his boot rubbed against his leg and he wondered if he'd have to use the weapon. "Aye, from the baron himself."

"Yer name, sir?" the sentry persisted, glancing nervously about. No doubt he didn't want to offend any of Baron Ewan's friends.

"Do you not recognize Kelvin of Castle Hawarth?" another soldier, Sir Reginald, a man who owed Wolf his life, asked. Reginald, big and burly, looked Wolf straight in the eye and lowered his head a bit. "How be ye, sir?"

"Hawarth?" the sentry repeated, dully.

Wolf's gut tightened. "Aye."

"That's right, Wendall, Hawarth. Are you dense as a stone?"

Scarface's eyebrows drew into one thick line of concentration. "But I thought the baron was Osric."

"Aye, 'tis so. And his younger brother—?" Reginald prompted while he sent Wolf a glance that silently told him he'd gladly run scarface through with his sword if needs be.

"Lord Osric sends his best to Sir Holt and Lady Megan," Wolf said, though he nearly choked on the words.

Wendall scowled for a second and then, as if some dim thoughts appeared in his cloudy mind, he nodded slowly. "Kelvin of Hawarth," he repeated, "kindly pass. I'm afraid ye've missed the ceremony and the feast."

"'Tis of no matter—just as long as I can give Sir Holt and his bride my gift."

Reginald's smile was as stiff as a dead dog's leg. Wolf slipped inside to mingle with the invited guests. The smells from the meal lingered, rising above the smoke and chatter, and Wolf's stomach growled at the scents of cooked salmon, venison, and pheasant. It had been years since he'd lived in a castle and the feasts he'd taken for granted as a youth were far distant.

Servants had cleared the room of tables and musicians tuned their lyres, viols, and lutes. Guests in silk, velvet, and fur gathered in groups filled with good wishes for the bride and groom.

Wolf's heart burned with a silent fury and he climbed the stairs to the second-floor landing for a better view of the newlyweds. A loud tapping interrupted the noise. Instruments stopped. Laughter and voices stilled.

On the dais, an old man pounded his cane. He was a tall man, now stooped, with a white beard and hair that had once been red. He smiled widely, though with effort, it appeared. "Please, please . . ." he said, his voice raspy. "Thank you all for coming to this, the celebration of my daughter's wedding. Please welcome Sir Holt, who has been like a son to me and now is truly part of my family." Leaning heavily on his cane, he added, "I only hope their union is blessed with many children and I live to see them. After I am gone, Holt will become the baron of Dwyrain!"

A bad taste rose in the back of Wolf's throat while everyone else in attendance clapped, laughed, and shouted congratulations. Holt beamed and his wife lost some of her color. As she held her husband's hand, no smile curved her lips, despair rounded her eyes, and Wolf was struck by her as he'd been when he'd seen her before. Though she was not as beautiful as the golden-haired one who was her sister, there was a spark to this woman that none other in the great hall held. So why did she appear unhappy? Was she already regretting her marriage vows?

"Now, musicians, play!" the old man commanded.

Immediately, music filled the great hall and the crowd parted. In the middle of the floor, Holt bowed to his bride, his eyes never leaving her face as he began to dance.

She was smaller than Wolf remembered, dressed in white, her dark hair braided with flowers and covered with a fine veil captured about her head with a thin gold band. Her eyes, when she looked at her groom, were filled with a quiet, seething fire that Wolf guessed was more than a hint of her spirit.

So this was the woman who was supposed to love Holt. Wolf had caught glimpses of her riding on horseback either coming or going to the castle these past few months, but never had he stared at her full in the face and never had he guessed her so prideful and gloriously beautiful. Her skin was pale but smooth, her eyes wide and warm gold with thick curling lashes and finely arched brows. White and gold ribbons were wound in her hair and small flowers framed a face far too lovely for the wife of Holt.

Wolf's fists clenched.

Holt was with his new bride. His gaze never left her face, his smile seductive and full of promise.

In his mind's eye, Wolf saw them coupling, Holt naked and dark, mounting this small, white-skinned lady . . .

For the love of Christ, what was he thinking? Cursing under his breath, he stared at the woman. What did it matter how Holt bedded this woman—his wife? As long as the mating didn't happen before Wolf had kidnapped and ransomed her, it was none of Wolf's concern. Slowly, he opened his hands and started down to the dance floor. 'Twas time to meet Megan of Dwyrain.

It's over. I am Holt's wife. For now until eternity. Megan danced on leaden legs, allowing her new husband to twirl her around the great hall. He laughed and whispered into her ear, reminding her of everything he intended to do to her later that night. She shivered, not in eager anticipation, but in disgust.

"Ah, yes, my love," he said, his breath tickling her ear. "You will dance with me alone tonight and show me what kind of woman you are."

She didn't answer, couldn't think of lying with him, of having his hands touch her skin, of letting him pierce her maidenhead to spill his seed into her body. Her stomach clenched and she nearly retched as the musicians played on, the notes of their songs rising like the mist in the morning. *Dear God, help me.*

There was ever the chance of escape. Should she decide that she could not lie with this cur, she could run away, humiliate her father, and . . . and go where?

She felt Holt's lips on her neck, and her skin crawled. "Come, love, at least pretend you're having a good time," he cajoled. "I wouldn't want to get angry," he said, his eyes locking with hers, his fingers gripping her more tightly. "I have a nasty temper when I'm crossed, or don't you know?"

"I remember," she said, tilting up her chin. "I saw you kill the bear cub."

The corners of Holt's mouth cinched tight. "We needed his mother for the entertainment."

Megan had never considered bear-baiting entertainment.

"The cub didn't need to die."

"Of course he did, my sweet. He was distracting his mother. And he suffered not."

Megan closed her eyes, remembering Holt's orders and the mace that came down fast and hard, crushing the mewling, frightened animal's skull. She also remembered the furious roar of the mother bear, how the enraged beast had lunged despite the shackles on her back legs. The chains had slipped and the bear swept forward through the crowd in the outer bailey, swiping her powerful claws and leaving one soldier with deep gashes on the side of his face and severing the arm of the miller's son just below his elbow.

"Now, now, you hunt," Holt reminded her. "I've seen you with the carcasses of pheasant, stag, and boar."

She lifted her chin. "I kill not the young, nor the mothers of the young."

"So noble," he mocked. His chuckle was deep and

throaty. "I'm going to enjoy you, Megan," he said, his eyes sliding down her body. "In every way."

"And I will detest you forever."

"Ah, ah, ah. Be careful what you say," he said, his eyes gleaming malevolently. "I wouldn't want to have to punish you tonight, on our wedding night." But the smile that curved his lips suggested otherwise, as if the anticipation of hurting her was somehow exciting and pleasured him.

A shiver of fear slid down her spine and she saw her father, smiling proudly, lifting his hands, asking the guests to join them in their wedding dance. Within minutes, the hall was filled with other couples who jostled and swayed, some laughing, others more serious—men and women dressed in finery, celebrating what should have been the happiest day of her life.

Several men cut in on her dance with Holt and Megan was relieved. Holt, enjoying himself, danced with other ladies, and Megan endured the smiles, congratulations, and sweaty hands of new partners. She was about to make good her escape upstairs to her room when a deep voice asked, "May I?" to her partner, and before she could think twice, she was being swept around the chamber by a handsome stranger she didn't recognize.

Taller than Holt by an inch or two, he was built strong, with wide shoulders and trim waist. His movements were quick and sure. When his gaze touched hers, the breath in the back of her throat caught, for his eyes were an intense shade of blue that cut to her very soul.

"Lady Megan," he drawled lazily.

"And you are—?"

"A friend of Holt's," was his reply, and she noticed that his hands were not soft, but callused, and in the cleft of his eyebrow was a battle scar. He was handsome in a rugged, dangerous way that surprised her, and his smile, when he showed it, was crooked and secretive and scared her more than a little.

"Have you no name?" she asked, and he laughed, holding her closer than she thought was necessary. Yet she didn't draw away—the heat of his body was distracting in a wicked way.

"None that you'd know."

"But if you're a friend of my . . . my . . . Sir Holt's—" she couldn't say it. Holt was her husband but she could not speak the word, would not let it trip from her tongue.

"Come," he whispered into her ear so softly she wasn't certain she heard it correctly. "I have a wedding gift for you and your husband." He guided her to a spot near the door where a bit of a draft moved the tapestries.

"Now—?" She glanced around, eager for a chance to leave, though uncertain.

He pulled her behind the curtain.

"Now," he said against her ear and she tingled inside. What was she doing letting this man, this stranger, touch her so familiarly? He leaned forward as if to kiss her and she told herself to step away, to slap him for being so bold, but she couldn't. To her surprise he clamped a hand over her mouth.

Her body convulsed.

She tried to scream. What was happening? She fought, struggling, but he had one arm, strong as an oak log, wedged under her breasts, the other hand pressed over her mouth.

"Do not struggle, m'lady," he said with a sneer in his voice, "and your family will not be hurt."

She bit down hard on the callused hands, but they didn't shift one little bit.

"If you fight me," he growled, "you seal their fates and your precious husband, sister, and father will be killed. Slowly and painfully."

She went limp in his hands and Wolf felt not only a stab of regret for scaring her and lying to her, but a new emotion as well—jealousy that this woman could love a bastard such as Holt of Prydd. With the cord tucked around his wrist, he quickly bound her hands. She cried out at the injustice of it, but he didn't have time to argue with her.

As he dragged her down the steps, smiling when he noticed the sentries missing from their posts, just as he'd planned, he heard the first shouts from the great hall. No more time.

Not only his horse, but hers as well, was waiting near the cistern. "Climb into the saddle and say not a word. As you can see, I have friends here, friends who have dispensed with the guards and stolen your horse. If you breathe too loudly, I swear, I will have them destroy all that you love!"

He removed his hand from her mouth and she opened hers, only to shut it again. He helped her into the saddle, then climbed onto his own steed while holding fast to her mare's reins.

As the doors of the great hall burst open, Wolf dug his heels into his mount's sides and the stallion took off, racing like the wind through the outer bailey, hooves clattering on the drawbridge.

The feisty mare kept up, her nose at the stallion's flank, her legs a blur. Wolf slid a glance at his prize and her eyes met his for an instant. He expected hatred, or fear, but saw neither. Instead, in that heartbeat, he noticed a glint of triumph in her gaze.

Almost as if she'd been expecting him.

❦ *Two* ❦

Dear Lord, did you have to deliver me into the hands of an outlaw? The wind tore at her hair, yanking off her veil and pulling free the plaits and flowers. Tears stung her eyes as Shalimar galloped furiously to keep up with the stallion. Mayhap she should have been more precise when she'd sent up prayer after prayer asking for deliverance from her marriage, seeking a way to escape the horror of being Holt's wife. But was this man—this savage scoundrel dressed in black—the answer to her pleas? Would God play so cruel a trick upon her? Surely not!

"Halt!" Holt roared from the steps of the keep; his furious voice carried on the wind and followed them. Megan's blood turned to ice. "Guards!" he yelled. "Where the hell are the bloody guards?"

Megan hung on for her life.

"For the love of Christ," Holt thundered, his voice fading in the distance. "Stop that man! Kill him if you must. He's stealing my wife!"

The horse turned and Megan's hands, tied as they were, tightened over the pommel of Shalimar's saddle. Mud spattered upward, staining her tunic as the dark sky cracked open. Rain and sleet slid down her back and pummeled the ground. Darkness crowded over the valley as the horses raced onward, galloping madly along the road. If only she could grab the reins, twist Shalimar around, and somehow elude her captor as well as her husband's guards. Looking ahead, she saw only the outlaw's broad back and his long black mantle sailing in the wind.

Behind them, she heard the shouts of men and thundering of hooves. Hazarding a quick glance over her shoulder, she imagined she saw the flickering lights of torches as Holt's men gave chase. Her heart drummed as wildly as the horses' hooves and yet she didn't know which was a worse fate, being kidnapped by a criminal or being caught by her husband.

My husband. What a horrid, blasphemous thought. She shivered inside, thinking that if only she knew the outlaw's intentions were honorable, she would thank him for helping her escape. But what noble man steals another man's wife on his wedding day?

The demon rode on, kicking his huge mount's sides, pulling at Shalimar's reins, making the little mare gallop at a breakneck pace. They sped frantically down the road, splashing through puddles, careening around corners, sliding through wagon ruts. Faster, faster, faster! Shalimar was breathing hard, struggling to keep up with the longer-legged warhorse, and 'twas all Megan could do to stay astride the game mare.

Think, Megan, think! she told herself as the cold air tore more flowers from her hair and billowed her tunic over her jennet's rump. As thankful as she was to this criminal, she could not trust him. For all she knew he planned to rape, maim, or kill her.

For weeks she'd thought her fate—that of marriage to Holt—was her doom. She'd nearly collapsed at the altar when Holt had slid the ring on her finger and said, "In the name of the Father, and of the Son, and of the Holy Ghost, with this ring, I thee wed."

After the nuptial Mass, Holt had received the kiss of peace from Father Timothy and passed it on to her. She'd nearly been sick. She'd been certain no fate would be worse than being tied to him for life. But this . . . this could be a swift and certain death.

She had no choice but to escape the madman who had single-handedly, it seemed, stormed through the guarded gates of Dwyrain, attended the celebration uninvited, and stolen her away right from under her husband's nose.

The road forked and her captor pulled up short. Shalimar skidded to a halt and Megan nearly toppled over the mare's head. Somehow she managed to stay in the saddle.

"Where are we?" she demanded, for she'd lost her bearings in the dark.

Still holding on to the reins of her mount, he frowned at the ground. Rain dripped down his face, plastering his dark hair against his skin. His horse stomped impatiently, as if eager to be off again. "Damned flowers," he muttered under his breath, sidling his horse next to hers. Once close enough, he reached down and raked his fingers through the tangled strands of her hair.

"Ouch!"

"Be quiet!" Yanking mercilessly on the remaining braids, he stripped the blooms from her tresses.

"Stop! What're you doing?" she cried, attempting to urge her mount away from him. His grip on the mare's reins was stronger than the armorer's vise. Shalimar sidestepped and Megan ordered, "Stay away from me!"

"Hush, woman!" he ordered. "I have spies in the castle; they would slit your husband's throat if I were but to give the command."

"You have no power!" But she trembled to think that all the deceit and betrayal she'd felt within the castle walls had been because of this man, this devil with the harsh, rugged face and cruel threats. Was he the reason that Ewan's knights no longer felt honor-bound to their pledge of fealty? Had he undermined and stripped the baron of his authority? "You scare me not," she lied. If only she could wrest Shalimar's reins from his fingers and ride . . . where? Not back to Dwyrain, not as Holt's wife, so where? "My father—"

"Your father is an old, foolish man who has put his faith and command of his army in a traitor."

"A traitor—?"

"The man you call husband, the man with whom you will soon share a bed and with whom you will bring forth children," he said, his lips curling in disgust.

Megan hoisted up her chin. "You know naught about Dwyrain—"

He laughed, and the sound was wicked as it echoed through the valley. "You're as blind as Ewan!" Leaning closer to her, he said, "If I know naught of Dwyrain, how did I capture you, eh?"

"Bastard!"

"At your service, m'lady."

"Pig!"

"Curses from a woman who would marry Holt of Prydd."

"Nay, Holt is not of Prydd," she said, bristling, then wondered why she was defending a man she did not trust.

In the darkness his gaze slid down her body and she sensed that he was seeing beneath the folds of mud-spattered velvet and silk, through her mantle, tunic, and even her chemise. "'Tis a pity that you should waste yourself on such a man."

"At least I am not a thief, a highwayman who steals and robs and pillages and . . ."

"And what?" he prodded, his voice low.

"Rapes," she whispered. "Or murders."

This time there was no bark of laughter, no sharp denial. "Think what you will, woman," he said. "'Tis of no matter to me." His gloved hands ripped through her hair again and she yanked her head away.

"Stop it!"

"Then take the flowers from your hair," he demanded urgently. "Give them to me! Now!" His lips pressed into a thin, hard line and he glanced over his shoulder as if expecting Holt's soldiers to appear from the shadows at any second.

"My hands are bound."

"By the gods, Odell was right," he growled, and picked— more carefully now—the petals from her hair.

"Who's Odell?" she asked. "And who are you?"

His smile was evil in the darkness. "Tonight I'm Kelvin from Castle Hawarth."

"And tomorrow?"

His gaze found hers and his stare was so baldly sensual, so intense, she gasped. Even shadowed with the night, his chiseled face was cruelly handsome. His eyes, a deep shade of blue, were guarded by thick black lashes and brows.

His nose was crooked, his smile wicked. "I'll be your keeper, *m'lady,*" he said in a voice so low she scarce heard it over the pounding of icy rain.

"Nay! No man keeps me!"

He laughed, the sound wicked. "Not even your husband, or so it appears." Satisfied that the dried blooms were free of her tresses, he gave a sharp order to his horse again and took the east bend in the road. His tireless destrier charged along at a furious pace, and poor Shalimar, her coat already flecked with lather, had to race to keep up with him. As they thundered down the road, the kidnapper dropped the flowers from his gloved hand, sprinkling them on the ground until there were no more, then he pulled the reins on his mount and again rounded on her.

"Well, m'lady, 'tis time to give up your mare."

"What?"

"A fine animal she is, but methinks it would be best if she were set free."

"Nay, Shalimar is a good mare and not yet spent—" But her horse was breathing hard, lathering, and was in great need of a rest. "If we could but walk—"

"And let Holt catch us? I think not." Before she could argue any further, the captor lifted her deftly from the saddle, swung her astride his own horse, dropped Shalimar's reins, and slapped the mare's rump hard with his hand. With a startled squeal, the fiery jennet bolted, hooves flying down the east path until she was swallowed in the darkness.

"Good." Her captor was pleased.

"Are you daft?" Megan cried, trying to climb out of the saddle. She kicked and fought, slapping away his hands though hers were bound, calling out for Shalimar, but the man held her fast. Her heart filled with sudden fear. Without her mare, Megan had no chance of escape. Now she was completely alone with this beast of a man, this criminal, to be forced to do his bidding. He could ransom her to Holt, sell her, or have his own way with her. She swallowed hard, refusing to be defeated, keeping her despair at bay. "My horse is worth much—"

"I care not," he said swiftly, one strong arm circling her

waist, the muscles of his forearm resting hard and firm beneath her breasts, his iron grip clenched tight around her wrists as he held her tight against him.

"But the ransom—"

He clucked to his horse and headed deep into the forest, away from the road, where the darkness was so thick Megan couldn't see. Branches slapped at her face and her back was pressed hard against her abductor's chest. Along with the rain, his warm breath tickled the back of her neck, and his smell, so like the forest, enveloped her. The horse plodded on through the undergrowth and the demon said not a word.

The sound of men's voices, still far away, whispered through the gloom. Through the bare branches of oak and yew, she spied flickering lights, the torches of Holt's soldiers casting odd points of illumination as they searched for her. As if sensing she might cry out, the outlaw's hand clamped over her mouth again.

Her mind spun in wild, frightening circles, but she would not give in to the fear that threatened her. She could not trust this man. Surely her fate with him would be as bad as it would have been with Holt, but at least she was past the sentries and could find her own means of escape.

Without Shalimar, she reminded herself, and felt a great loss.

She heard a night bird call and Wolf stiffened. From his throat came a like cry.

A signal. So there were more of them! Her heart sank. Escaping one man would be far easier than fleeing a band of cutthroats and ruffians. She shivered and the man pulled her more closely to him. His muscles were solid and she felt the shape of his knee and thigh pressed intimately to the outside of hers. She sat tall, trying to keep her buttocks from pressing against his crotch, but the task proved impossible. The saddle was confining, and they were wedged together close enough that she felt the rub of his breeches against the silk covering her rump.

"You'll be caught," she warned him when the lights had faded and the sounds of the soldiers' voices no longer reached them.

He laughed.

"And tortured!"

Again the soft, amused chuckle.

"Then hanged."

"And will you watch?" he asked, his breath feather-light against her ear.

"Aye!" she lied, for in truth she could not watch a man— any man—swing from the hangman's rope. If the rogue were captured and returned to Dwyrain, she would plead for his life.

"My father will not stand for this."

"Your father has lost control of his castle."

The words were true and rang like the dull chimes of death.

"You will be hunted down like a wounded bear."

"By your husband?" he asked, and she felt her spine stiffen and her chin lift.

"Aye."

"Good. 'Tis what I want."

"Who *are* you?"

"Can you not guess?" He leaned forward, whispering into her ear, causing a naughty little thrill to slide down her spine. "I, m'lady, am the embodiment of your husband's worst fears."

"Which are?"

"That he will be forced to pay for the sins of his past." He yanked on the reins and suddenly, over the drip of rain and soft thud of hooves, she heard the sound of water rushing through the forest. A brook splashed wildly as it cut through the trees. Her abductor let his mount drink for a few seconds before pulling on the reins again and urging the big horse upstream.

"You are Holt's enemy."

"Aye."

"Are you not worried that you, too, might be forced to face your own sins?"

His laugh was without humor and the warm arm surrounding her ribs pulled her even tighter against his chest. "Worried?" he repeated, his voice soft. "Nay, m'lady. I long for that day."

* * *

Rage and humiliation burned in Holt's gut, eating at him as hungrily as new maggots on a carcass. Icy sleet poured from the sky, creating mud and muck in the inner bailey as Holt waited in the gatehouse, his ears straining for the sound of his men. He only hoped they'd caught the blackguard who had stolen Megan. When his soldiers brought the fool back, Holt would take personal pleasure in whipping the bastard until his back was raw and bleeding, then have him hanged.

Who was he? Holt wondered, and his conscience pricked with the faces of enemies he'd made during his life. Aye, they had been many, but usually weak men or meek women who had seen the dark side of his temper. None of them would follow him here. So who would dare defy him so openly? *Who?*

His teeth gritted. All his carefully laid plans had changed. Instead of bedding Megan and basking in the glory of becoming the next baron of Dwyrain, he was standing in the driving rain, trying to conjure up the face of the cur who had deceived him.

Holt had been dancing with the scandalous Lady Peony, elderly wife of Baron Griffin, when he'd noticed the stranger in black—a tall man who caused more than one pretty female head to turn.

Within seconds, the stranger with the fierce countenance had taken Megan as his partner, twirled her about the floor, then as suddenly as he'd appeared, vanished with Holt's new wife, leaving Holt alone in the middle of his own wedding celebration.

Holt had thought at first his mind was playing tricks with him, for his greatest fear had been that Megan would refuse to marry him, but after the ceremony when the ring was securely around her finger, he'd let down his guard, actually enjoyed the feast and music. Only later, when he'd finally understood that Megan had been abducted, he'd shouted out and then he'd heard the gasps, whispers, and titters of the guests.

"Is this some kind of joke?" Lady Peony had asked, her eyebrows lifting in delight.

"I know not," Holt had grumbled and she'd thrown back

her head and laughed, an ugly braying sound not unlike that of a donkey.

"What? What happened?" Ewan had searched the great hall with his pathetic blind eyes. "Where's Megan?"

"She's been stolen away," Baron Griffin had surmised.

"What?" Ewan had leaned heavily on his cane.

"Holt's bride has disappeared." Sir Mallory had eyed each guest with suspicion.

"Disappeared? You mean she left, don't you? But with whom?" another woman, whom Holt did not recognize, had asked. Her mouth had rounded in delighted horror.

"The stranger in black, did you not see him? Those eyes, so blue, and his visage . . . oh, my." Cayley had looked to the doorway as if hoping to see the cur again.

"Like the very image of Lucifer!" Father Timothy had proclaimed. "He must be brought back!"

"How thoroughly and utterly romantic!" Cayley had said with a sigh, and Holt's men had all laughed and made jokes about his first night as a husband with no wife. Speculation had run high that the man was Megan's lover, that she'd expected him, that even now they were off in a private hideaway. His blood curdled to think of how he'd run outside into the rain, hearing the fading clatter of hoofbeats as he yelled to his lazy men to give chase.

Now, hours later, he still felt the sting of humiliation on his cheeks, the hard bite of betrayal. Guests and servants alike had gossiped and laughed at his expense and his wrath was greater than he ever could have imagined.

When at last his soldiers returned, they came with the bad news that the outlaw had evaded them deep in the forest.

"So you found her not?" Holt said, cutting through the litany of excuses made by his knights—Dwyrain's *best* men—for returning to the castle without his wife or her abductor. What a pitiful lot!

"Aye, we lost them," Sir Mallory admitted, his moustache dripping with rain and mud, defeat evident in his eyes as he tried and failed to meet Holt's stare. He was holding the reins of his horse when a page came by and gathered them, leading the sweating, lathered beast away.

"How?"

"We followed their trail," the soldier admitted, opening

his palm to show a few wilted and dried blooms. Another soldier handed Megan's bridal veil to Holt. "Hoofprints and flowers from m'lady's hair. They took the fork that leads to Prydd, but . . . there were many tracks because of all the guests traveling through the rain. We found only the lady's horse, grazing alone in a meadow at the edge of the forest by St. Peter's Abbey."

"Did you search the surrounding woods?"

"Aye," Mallory said, "and the abbey itself, though the abbot was not pleased. We searched until our torches failed and the fog rolled in."

"And what of the dogs?" Holt asked, barely holding on to his temper. He should have ignored his guests and taken off after his wife himself. As it was, he looked like a fool, yet again trusting these thickheaded farmers who called themselves soldiers.

Mallory shook his head. "The hounds were useless. Once they found the horse, they knew not what we wanted."

"God's blood, you're fools! The whole lot of you!" Holt's voice resounded in the gatehouse and he threw down the muddy wedding veil in disgust. This was to have been his wedding night, when finally he would not only bed the woman who had teased his mind for years and caused his cock to become stiff as granite, but, being married to Ewan's oldest daughter, he would by rights inherit all that was Dwyrain. Taking off one glove, he slapped it against his hand, thinking hard, trying to understand the way of the outlaw's mind. "Have you any thought as to who the rogue was?"

"He claimed he was Kelvin of Hawarth."

"Kelvin of Hawarth?"

"Aye, younger brother to the baron, Osric McBrayne."

Holt squeezed his eyes closed and counted slowly to 10. Ewan saw these men as dedicated, good-hearted, and loyal, but in Holt's estimation, they were lazy mental midgets and cowards. Not a brave, smart one in the lot. "The man was not McBrayne's brother. He's an outlaw, I'm certain of it." The sky opened up, and rain sliced to the ground in heavy curtains of water. Holt, already chilled to his bones, saw no reason to stand outside. "Come to my chamber," he ordered, striding swiftly away.

In the great hall, he came upon a page and ordered wine to be sent to his room, but his thoughts lingered on the man who had so baldly stolen his wife. The criminal's face had been vaguely familiar when Holt had spied the man in black dancing with his wife. Tall and dark-haired, he'd twirled Megan on her feet until she was breathless. Holt had been about to reclaim his bride's attention when he'd noticed the stranger and Megan slip into the shadows and then quickly away.

His anger burned savagely within him.

Megan might have helped hatch the plot to humiliate Holt, for she'd made it plain that she married him unwillingly. Would she go to such lengths as to plan a false abduction just to avoid his bed?

'Twas possible. Earlier in the week, Holt had come across her in the hallway after one of her visits to her father's chamber. Holt had tried to touch her and she'd shrunk away as if he were poison. "Leave me be," she'd ordered, anger flaring in her eyes.

"Ah, Megan, I cannot. Asides, we'll be wed soon and—"

"And I'll be your wife in name only," she'd said proudly, her chin mutinous, her eyes blazing with a fire that brought his damned cock to attention. He couldn't wait to tame her, to force her to open her legs and mouth to him, to make her want him as much as he wanted her. He'd make her beg for him, tie her to the bed and touch her all over with feathers, allow some of his men to watch her surrender. But no one else would have her. Nay, they could look at her long-legged body, see the pink nipples of her high breasts, lust over the thatch of curls where her legs met, watch as their bodies joined, but only he could press his skin to hers and spill his seed in her unwilling body.

"You'll want me so badly you'll beg me to bed you," he'd told her in that hallway, and she'd slapped him. Her palm had burned an imprint on his skin and he'd grabbed her arm. "Rough ye want it, lass?" he'd growled into her ear. "Then rough 'twill be."

"You'll rot in hell before you touch me!" She'd pulled her arm away and run down the hallway. He'd been so hard with wanting that he'd slid into a dark alcove and slipped his hand into his breeches to ease the ache. No one had seen him gasping there, imagining entering her body, seeing her mouth wet with desire as she kissed and touched him. He'd bit down hard at his release but he'd been unable to stop from whispering her name in a desperate voice he barely recognized as belonging to him.

No, he would not be denied.

The page brought in a pitcher of wine and several wooden mazers, which he left on a tray near the hearth. As his men shuffled in, looking like whipped pups, Holt wondered what kind of soldiers they were. He glared at the sodden lot of them, spineless men warming their backsides at the fire, causing steam to rise from their filthy clothes. "No one steals my wife," he said slowly as he unsheathed his sword and stared at the firelight gleaming against the sharp-edged blade. "No one steals my wife and lives to tell about it. Find out who the bastard is and hunt him down. Kill him if you have to, but my wife's safety and her virtue will not be compromised!"

His gaze roved from one sad soldier to the next, and he smelled their fear. They were frightened of him, which was good. He could use their trepidation to his advantage. Holt ran a finger along his blade, pressing hard enough that a drop of blood showed on his skin. He spread it slowly over the steel and saw each man swallow a sudden knot in his throat. With a smile meant to be cruel, he said, "Do not fail me, lads."

Wolf was beginning to wonder if his plan to humiliate Holt was as clever as he'd first thought. When he'd heard that his enemy was planning to wed the daughter of Baron Ewan, Wolf had finally decided that fate had smiled on him, giving him an opportunity to belittle and disgrace the man he'd hated for so long. He'd thought only of the kidnapping, and then of the ransom, giving not too much consideration to the woman herself. He had heard that she was headstrong and that she'd been blamed for much of the pain in the house of Dwyrain, but he cared not and decided she was the pampered daughter of a rich man, a woman stupid enough to marry one of the vilest snakes in all of Wales. In his estimation, Megan of Dwyrain deserved her fate.

He hadn't expected to see a beauty and pride in her that

appealed to him, nor had he thought that holding her so closely to him while astride the horse would cause him any worry. As it was, he was distracted by the warm, female scents of her and the feel of her skin so close to his. Her hair tickled his nose and his arm felt the soft, supple weight of her breasts. Despite himself, that male part of him that was always giving him trouble responded, and to his disgust his member started to swell.

"We'll stop here," he said gruffly, when the evidence of his desire could no longer be hidden.

"Here? Why?" she asked as he slid to the ground, sinking into thick mud. The sleet had stopped, but the forest was chilled and shimmering in raindrops. Only a few stars dared wink behind a thick bank of clouds.

"'Tis as good a place as any." He helped her from the saddle, then reached into his boot, withdrew his small dagger, and sliced through the ropes that bound her wrists.

She gasped at the sight of the blade flashing silver in the night, then swallowed hard. "Where are we?" she asked, rubbing her wrists and stretching her fingers.

"Not far from the camp."

"Why have we stopped?"

He eyed her in the darkness, her white tunic nearly glowing. Even with dirt smudged on the fine fabric, she was beautiful, too beautiful. "'Tis a wonder we weren't seen," he said, gruffly, noticing the long column of her throat and the proud point of her little chin. Angry with himself, he motioned to her dress. "But there was no time. Now, before we get to the camp, you needs wear something more . . . more common."

"Such as?" she asked, clearly uncertain of his reasoning.

"Such as these." Reaching upward for the bag he'd tucked behind his saddle, he untied the straps that had held it securely, then tossed the sack to her.

She caught it easily and loosened the drawstring.

"The clothes will be too big, but they will have to do."

She slid one hand into the open sack and withdrew plain men's clothes, brown leather breeches and long tunic, the colors of which weren't visible in the night.

Hesitating, she lifted her curious eyes to his. "Why?"

"Your dress is like a beacon, white as the moon on a dark night!"

"But we outran the guards."

"It matters not," he said, eager to be off again. Being alone with her was dangerous. "Just be quick about it."

Stubbornly, she shook her head. "I cannot!"

"Aye, you can and you will, m'lady," he said, watching her lips purse in mulish denial. "Or I will do it myself."

"You wouldn't dare—" she said, and he took a menacing step forward.

But instead of skittering away, she stood her ground, and when he brought up a hand to untie the ribbons at her throat, she didn't flinch.

"Do not touch me," she whispered, but her breath was as ragged as the night, her pulse fluttering wildly below her ear.

His own heart beat a desperate, tremulous rhythm.

"Then undress yourself."

Silently she defied him.

"Bloody hell," he muttered and instead of loosening the ribbons, he slit them through.

The fabric gaped and Megan's hands fluttered nervously. "Leave me be."

"Put on the men's clothes."

"I won't be ordered about like some kitchen wench who—oh!" He cut the ties again, pieces of the ribbons floating to the ground, and the thick velvet fabric parted farther to expose the swell of her breasts, white in the slight moonglow, heaving in mute fury. Ah, they were beautiful, soft and round and large enough to fill his palm, but he didn't let his eyes rest on their plump, unwitting invitation too long. Instead he lay the blade of his weapon between them to the next set of ribbons. "Shall I go on?" he asked, his voice but a rasp.

"Nay!" she whispered, and when his gaze reached hers again, he saw her rage, but there was more in her indignant stare, more than ire and mutiny. Unless he was mistaken, he recognized desire, hot and wanton, steal fleetingly across her face. "You're a true bastard of the lowest order."

"Aye, m'lady. Now, at last, we understand each other."

Muttering under her breath, she snatched up his bag of

clothes, stalked off to a nearby tree, and started to disappear behind its thick trunk.

"Come back here," he ordered.

"But you asked me to change."

"How am I to know you won't run off?"

"To where?"

"I'll not be spending the rest of the night chasing you down."

"I swear I won't."

"I dare not take the chance." Silently, he followed her until he could see her beneath the empty branches. She was working feverishly, quickly removing her mantle, surcoat, and tunic, stripping off the white velvet, standing in only her chemise. His gaze fastened on the cleft of her breasts, dark and dusky and deep, and his blood heated as she bent over to step into his breeches and pull them over long, supple legs. Tying the length of twine about her small waist, she was able to keep the breeches from falling to the ground, and then she struggled into his tunic, the shoulders far too wide, the sleeves and hem much too long.

"Better," he said, and her head snapped up.

"You watched me!" she cried.

"Aye."

Tossing her hair off her face, she advanced upon him. Lightning crackled in her eyes. "You have no right to do this," she accused.

"I touched you not."

"Only with your eyes."

"No harm came to you."

"Yet." Dark hair spilled over her skin, and he felt a tug on his heart, a tug that he could not afford.

"As long as you are with me, Megan of Dwyrain, you are safe." He sighed and looked into her eyes. "This I pledge you."

She nearly laughed. "So now you're the noble outlaw, are you?"

He reached forward and strong fingers curled over her tiny fist. "Make no mistake, woman, I am not noble. My intentions for you are far from pure. That you are married to Holt would not stop me from bedding you if I so wanted and you agreed."

"Agreed?" she sputtered, her breath catching. "I would never—oh, for the love of Saint Peter! When my father catches you, he will skin you alive and then lay hot coals on your bare flesh."

"And your husband, what will he do?"

She stopped suddenly and stared at him as if pondering a puzzle she had not yet considered. "He will come after you," she said finally, her voice flat, her teeth sinking into her lower lip. "And, I believe, Sir Kelvin or whoever you be, he will kill you."

Cayley's knees and back ached as she knelt on the cold stones of the chapel floor. Through the open window she heard the sound of the soldiers returning and the creak of wheels as guests left the castle.

Upon Megan's disappearance, her father had collapsed and had to be carried to his chamber. Cayley had stayed at his bedside until the doctor had arrived, then Father Timothy had asked her to join him in prayer for her father's health and her sister's safe return. Cayley, who would rather have been riding with the soldiers searching for Megan, had spent the past few hours on her knees, whispering prayer after prayer.

Candles burned around the altar, their flickering flames reflecting on the portraits of Christ and the Virgin as the priest walked softly around the chapel, his prayer book open in one hand, a rosary clicking in his pockets.

Guests came and went, stopping long enough to cross themselves and whisper their own quick requests to God, but every time Cayley climbed to her feet, Father Timothy laid a patient hand upon her shoulder and searched her face with soulful eyes. "Let us not give up so easily, my child," he'd said, and she'd resumed her position, wondering how much pain she had to endure. "God is listening." Cayley wished He'd listen a little harder.

Cold, tired, and worried, Cayley wanted desperately for her father to awaken in good health. She also needed to know what had become of her sister and why neither Holt nor his soldiers had been able to find Megan and the scoundrel who had abducted her. Cayley had caught a glimpse of the man in black, his bearing resembling that of a devil, and a handsome one at that. Biting her lip, she said another quick prayer and chastised herself for her wanton thoughts, for the truth be known, she thought the stranger far more interesting than Sir Holt or her own beloved Gwayne of Cysgod, the man she'd sworn she would marry years before.

There was something about this ruffian that suggested he could make a woman's legs go weak and her heart pound in a strange and heady cadence. Aye, the outlaw was Satan incarnate; Cayley crossed herself with renewed conviction and prayed.

"That's better," Father Timothy said, laying a hand upon her bent head. His fingers touched her hair and lingered a second too long against the back of her neck. "Surely God will answer your prayers now."

She hoped so.

Nearly an hour later, the doctor announced that Ewan had awakened.

"Never again doubt the power of prayer," Father Timothy said, thankfully relieving her of her prayer duty. On aching legs, she hurried up the stone stairs of the great hall, past guards who had been stationed throughout the keep and were ever vigilant for spies or thugs or strangers. "A bit late," old Rue had said, silently motioning to the guards. "Why close the stable door once the horse has escaped?" But Holt had ordered the men to watch over everyone in the castle, and no one was looked upon without suspicion.

Passing so quickly by the rush lights that they flickered in her wake, Cayley slid through the door of her father's chamber. Only a few candles burned near the bed. A fire was lit, but it had burned down earlier and now there were only red-gold embers glowing in the grate.

"News of your sister?" Ewan asked hopefully, his dim eyes sparking for a second.

"Nay, Father, the soldiers found her not."

He sighed wearily. "Then we must pray for her safe return."

"I have prayed all the long night," Cayley said, sick of the tiresome supplications to a God who was deaf this night. Discovering mossy chunks of dry oak in a basket near the door, she tossed two dry logs onto the fire. Sparking hungrily, greedy flames crackled and hissed over the new fuel.

"Holt believes that there are those soldiers and servants who are unfaithful to me," Ewan said as he adjusted the furs on his bed with his bony hands. "He claims that the outlaw who invaded our keep had spies within the castle, men who helped him steal your sister away."

"I know not," Cayley said, though she'd sensed a change in the castle these past few months.

Somehow, Cayley thought as she walked to the window and watched the clouds part to show a sliver of moon, the magician was responsible for her sister's abduction as well.

Frowning, she sent up one last prayer. "Keep her safe, Lord. Please, keep her safe."

The tunic was scratchy and far too large and every one of her bones ached as the first gray streaks of dawn lighted the eastern sky. They had been riding for hours and Dwyrain was miles behind them, somewhere far to the south. She'd not spoken to the outlaw since catching him watching her step into his clothes. Never had a man seen her in such a state of undress; the thought bothered her.

His mount was lagging as they climbed a steep trail that crested a ridge and then eased down to a valley near a winding stream. On the far shore of the brook was the glow of a fire.

"Your camp," she said, dread clamping over her heart.

"Aye."

Laying a hand over his, she drew up on the reins. "Why did you do this?" she asked, wanting an answer from this silent man before she had to face those who called him their leader.

His eyes were dark and the lines around them proved that he, too, felt the strain of the long ride. "I came for you," he said, and she felt the jump in her heartbeat, no doubt visible at her neck. Nervously, she licked her lips, and he watched the motion. "I stole you away because you are Holt's bride."

"Why not before the marriage?"

"'Twould not have been the same."

"Because, in truth, this had naught to do with me."

"Aye."

"So I am but a prize with which to barter."

His jaw became hard as iron and she caught a glimmer of regret, leading her to believe that she was seeing a glimpse of another man, one he'd been long before he'd taken the life of the outlaw. She guessed from the conversation they'd had while dancing, the way he'd fit into the skin of a nobleman so easily, the few words they'd exchanged in the forest, that hidden beneath his ill manners and roguish ways was an educated man, one who might be able to read as well as command, one who was shrewd in the ways of the forest as well as in the running of a castle.

Again she asked, "Who are you?"

His smile was positively wicked. "Wolf."

"You took the name of a beast."

He lifted a shoulder.

"And why do you hate Holt?"

"Because he once rode with Tadd of Prydd."

"Tadd of Prydd is dead," she said and felt a tremor of fear.

"Aye."

Her mouth was suddenly dry as sand and her fingers curled into nervous fists. "You killed him."

Wolf's eyes flashed. "I sent him to hell where he belonged."

So he was a murdering rogue. God in heaven, why did she feel safe in his arms? Why had she no fear for her life or her virtue? Why did she feel that she could trust him? Though she'd never met Tadd of Prydd, she'd heard from her father that Tadd had been a cruel leader who met with a well-deserved and painful end. At Wolf's hand.

"I have no argument with you, Megan. Nor with your father. Only Holt, your husband, is my sworn enemy." He eyed her and frowned. "What know you of him?"

"Only that he had been in my father's service for years."

"And before that?"

She shook her head. "'Tis as if he has no past."

"That's where you're wrong, m'lady," Wolf said, tilting up her chin so she was forced to look into his eyes. "What he doesn't have is a future."

"Because of you?"

"Aye." A muscle jumped in his jaw. "Now, before we

meet my men, I think you should know that we have a rule that there are to be no women in the camp."

"Then what of me?" she asked, eyes narrowing.

"You will dress, think, and act like a man. You will do nothing to distract them. They are to think of you as one of them."

She tossed her glorious mane of hair. "Well, I certainly have the clothes for the part."

"But 'tis not enough." Was there regret in his voice?

She turned to look ahead. "What more could you want from me?"

"Only this, m'lady," he said. "Forgive me." She felt him grab her hair in one hand and then, quick as a starving dog on a shank of meat, he withdrew his knife as if intending to slice the long tresses in one swift swipe.

"Nay!" she cried, her hands flying to her head. He hesitated, his weapon upraised. "You black-hearted beast!" she cried, trying to slide out of the saddle while his arms, strong as new steel, held her against him. Tears of fury burned behind her eyes but she would not give him the satisfaction of letting them spill. "You have no right to treat me this way. No right!"

"'Tis only hair," he said.

"*My* hair. You have no right. . . . Please do not cut it."

"But 'twill grow."

True, it would grow, but the humiliation, the idea of him taking a part of her without so much as asking, burned hot in her soul. "If you do this, I hope you roast in hell!"

"No doubt I will, m'lady," he said, sheathing his weapon and sighing as he let her long hair fall free. Clucking the horse forward, his eyes dark with self-loathing as they approached the camp, he said again, "No doubt I will."

❋ Three ❋

Megan bit her tongue. She wanted to rant and rave at the devil who'd captured her, to kick and scream at him, but she didn't say a word as they rode into the camp. 'Twas better if he thought she was meek and frightened.

A sharp whistle broke the morning stillness as Wolf's horse emerged from the forest. The outlaw's camp was little more than a clearing by a small stream with several dirty tents and a few wagons scattered around a fire pit.

"I was beginnin' to think ye'd been caught," a thin, short man with a shock of gray hair grumbled. "About time ye decided to return."

"Were ye worried for me, Odell?" Wolf said with a mocking grin that caused the shorter man to blush.

"Me? Worry?" Odell spit on the ground as Wolf swung from the saddle. Before he could help Megan to the ground, she hopped off the stallion's back and stood a distance away from him, her hands still bound, her hair wild about her face. "'ell's bells, I never worry!"

"Then why were ye askin' about him every time there was a noise in the woods?" another man, with only one good eye and a patch over the other, teased.

"For the love of—" The thin little man eyed Megan curiously as he changed the subject and said to Wolf, "So this is yer prize," narrowing his eyes as he scratched his head and studied her with a frown of distaste. "Ye gods, what are we going to do with 'er?"

Most of the men edged closer, forming a half-ring about them, and Megan managed to meet each set of curious eyes with her own stare. A sorrier group of outlaws she never wished to see!

"This is Megan of Dwyrain," he said as the men gaped at her. "She is our guest and—"

"Guest?" she repeated, stung and unable to quiet her tongue. "You call me a guest? Was I invited? Did I have a choice of whether I would come with you?"

"Shh—" he said, his blue eyes glinting as the morning mist began to rise.

"Was I treated as a *guest* or as a prisoner? Were my clothes not taken from me? Was I not forced to ride into the forest?" Rage seethed through her and though she knew she should clamp her lips together to appear meek and frightened, she couldn't stop the tirade that came from deep in her soul. "Were not my hands bound and my horse whipped so that it would run off?"

"Ye let a good 'orse get away?" Odell asked, his voice edged with concern.

"I had no choice."

Again Odell spit, this time in disgust, and Megan, though she knew she shouldn't say another word, couldn't keep her jaws clamped together. "If this is how your leader treats a guest, I would hate to think what he does with a prisoner!"

By the time she was finished, Wolf's expression was deadly, his hands clenched in tight fists, and his bold jaw was jutted and rock hard. "I promised I would not hurt you, Megan," he said with slow measure, each word pronounced as if it was to be the last she would hear in this lifetime, "and I always keep my word. I ask that you do the same."

"You have ripped me away from my home, dragged me away from my marriage feast, and forced me to ride with you here, wherever we are."

"Have you been whipped?" he asked through lips that barely moved.

"Nay." She shook her head and her wild curls brushed her shoulders.

"Beaten?"

"No, but—"

"Raped?"

Her breath caught for a second. "Nay," she whispered.

"Bound except for your hands, which were set free when I knew I could trust you?"

When she didn't answer, he lifted a dark brow. "Nor were you gagged, hauled about like a sack of grain, or touched in a familiar manner. You, m'lady, have been treated as my guest. However, should you disobey me or make trouble with my men, then you will be treated as a prisoner." He pressed his face close to hers, near enough that she could see the angry streaks of gray in his blue eyes. "I mean you no harm, Megan of Dwyrain, but you will do as I say or suffer the consequences."

"You have no right—"

"And as for your husband, if you love him, then you must know that I will do anything in my power to destroy him."

"But why?" Megan asked, her eyes searching his face. What a puzzle he was—gentle one moment, cruel the next.

"Because he did the same to me. Now—" He looked up and found his men, quiet for once, staring openmouthed at the two of them. "Is there nothing to eat? We've been riding all night and our *guest* must be starved."

"Robin caught us some rabbits," Odell ventured. "And there's pike from the stream and bread we stole from . . ." His voice drifted off and he cleared his throat. "Let me get the fires going."

"But first, introductions," Wolf insisted, naming them each to Megan. Odell, the older scamp who wondered about Wolf giving up her house and was tossing dry leaves and twigs onto the warm coals, looked harmless enough, though she wouldn't trust him with the truth. The others—Jagger, who appeared tough and mean-tempered; Peter, with only one eye; Bjorn, blond and muscular; as well as several others. Last in the group was Robin, a boy of no more than 12 who could only stare at her and swallow hard, his Adam's apple bobbing like a leaf upon a rippling stream. His face, beneath a thatch of dark hair, turned three shades of red when at last he spoke, and upon saying her name, his voice cracked. The rest of the men laughed and made great sport, but the poor lad ducked away hurriedly, finding an excuse to slip into the privacy of the forest.

Odell had already constructed a spit over the glowing coals, and soon two rabbits were roasting, sending the scent of sizzling meat through the naked trees and bracken. Megan's stomach growled and she heard a great flapping of wings in the branches of an oak tree overhead. Looking up, she spied an owl seated near the trunk, its neck twisted so that he could view her.

"Well, I'll be buggered," Odell muttered. "Look who's back!"

"He's been here before?" Megan asked.

"Aye, lately." Odell raised his eyes up at the huge bird. "'E's a bother, if you ask me. Bad luck."

"That's an old wives' tale," Peter put in, but he, too, glanced up at the bird in vexation. "All he wants is our breakfast."

"Sorry, 'e'll 'ave to be cookin' 'is own. I'm not wastin' my time sweatin' over an open fire for some bloody damned bird. Go on," Odell yelled, raising his hands and flapping them wildly. "Shoo away, ye overgrown pigeon. Off with ye!"

The owl only blinked and settled his head into his neck feathers.

"Ah, who cares about ye anyway," Odell complained, turning back to the charring meat, frowning as the grease drizzled onto the coals.

"Come," Wolf said, once the men had gone back to their tasks. Some hunted, some whittled, some sharpened weapons, others gathered wood or tended to the horses. One man was carefully cleaning the blades of daggers and swords, and the boy, Robin, cast several nets into the stream.

"Come with me," Wolf ordered, then led her to the largest tent situated near the forest's edge. "This is where you'll be sleeping," he said and Megan heard Odell, from the fire pit, give a snort of laughter.

"Whose tent is it?" she asked, but she knew the answer.

"Mine."

Her silly heart fluttered. "And where will you be?" she asked, lifting a dark brow and crossing her arms under her breasts.

His smile was that of a rake and her pulse thundered as he

said, "I'll be outside, m'lady, guarding the door, but if you try to escape, then I'll be forced to sleep inside with you to make sure you stay until your husband comes for you." His gaze touched hers and she lost her breath. "Where I sleep— how close to you—'tis all up to you."

"Who was the outlaw?" Holt demanded of the commander of Ewan's troops, a tall gaunt-looking soldier who never smiled. Connor was his name, and he had no family and no friends; he was a solitary sort who kept to himself. He gave a few of the men the willies. But the tall man was smarter than the rest of the lazy scum that were supposed to guard Dwyrain, and Holt needed his help. Now, Connor was checking the chain mail that had been cleaned and was hanging on pegs in the armory. "And don't tell me the rogue's name was Kelvin McBrayne, for I know better."

"Nay, he was not McBrayne," the guard said, fingering the tiny links, the metal clinking softly. "He looked more like . . . well . . . 'tis not possible."

"What?"

"Years ago, I rode with Strahan Hazelwood at Abergwynn, and the younger brother to Baron Garrick was a hotheaded lad who was eager for battle." Lost in private thoughts, Connor moved from the mail to a wall of swords, the finest in all of Dwyrain. Old Ebert, sitting on a cask near the door and fixing links on another mail tunic, watched as Connor picked up a sword and tested its blade. "This boy, Ware, disappeared in one of the many battles at that time. Rode his horse over the cliff and into the sea. Never heard from again. Thought to be dead."

"And now resurrected?" Holt sneered.

Connor lifted a shoulder. "I know not, but the outlaw who came so boldly here knew how to act the part of a nobleman. His bearing, 'twas much like Garrick of Abergwynn."

Holt turned this information over in his mind. A rogue nobleman, but why would Ware of Abergwynn have any grudge against him? They'd never met, and Holt was certain Megan's abduction was aimed at him rather than Ewan— elsewise why do it on the wedding day? "This man—this outlaw—Ware or whoever else he may be, has spies within the castle walls."

Connor's head snapped. His fingers tightened over the hilt of the sword. "Spies?" he said, but Holt guessed it was not the first time that particular thought had crossed Connor's fertile mind.

"Elsewise how could he have got in alone?" Holt lifted a small sleek dagger with a bone handle, testing its weight. It fit well into his palm. "'Tis your job, Connor, to ferret out the spies, find who they be, how they know the outlaw, and bring them to me."

"What if I fail?"

"Do not."

"What if I discover them, but their tongues will not be loosened?"

Holt turned slowly and faced the thin man. "There are ways to convince a man to talk. Some men do not do well with pain, others are more likely to speak if they think a loved one may be seriously maimed, still others can be convinced by bribery or by desire for a woman. I care not how you find the truth," he said. "Do whatever it takes and you will be rewarded."

"With what?"

"What is it you want?" Holt asked, expecting to hear an exorbitant sum.

"A woman."

"Is that all?" Holt was relieved. Women were easier to part with than gold.

"Not just any woman, Sir Holt," Connor said, his eyes slitting in eager anticipation. "I want the daughter of Ewan."

Holt's temper flared and he grabbed the soldier by his throat. Shoving him hard against the wall, knocking over a cask of sand, he growled, "Do not test me. Megan is mine."

"'Tis not Megan I want," Connor said, laughing despite the strong fingers at his throat. "Nay, 'tis the second daughter, the one with hair of gold."

"Cayley."

"Aye. If I find the spies in Dwyrain and they lead to the return of your wife, then I want the lady Cayley."

"As your wife."

Connor's nostrils flared. "Nay, m'lord, I want her for my whore."

". . . to be robbed of yer wife on yer weddin' day." Red, one of the guards stationed at the door of the keep, was eyeing the peddlers, farmers, and hunters riding into the castle while observing some of the late-staying guests who were leaving at last. Red had always had an ear for gossip, so Cayley, on her way to her father's chamber, tarried in the hallway, listening to what the men were saying behind Ewan's back. "'Tis a shame, say what?" Red continued, speaking to a tall soldier with eyes as flat as the stones on the keep's smooth floor. "To be thinkin' all day that you'll be weddin' your wife and then to have her snatched away so some outlaw can 'ave his way with 'er, and don't try and tell me that the lady's virtue will be intact when she returns. She's a pretty one, eh, and what man with blood flowing through his veins wouldn't want a go at 'er?"

"You think she was stolen to become an outlaw's whore?" the tall man said in a raspy voice that caused Cayley's skin to crawl.

"I'm not sayin' that was the reason she was taken, but I'll be bettin' my last piece o' gold that someone besides Holt bedded her last night."

"If so, that someone will pay and pay dearly," the taller soldier replied. "Holt will not stand for it."

"Aye, Connor," Red agreed. "And methinks 'e might blame 'is wife as well. Even if she put up a fight and the man raped her, Sir 'Olt's not a forgiving man."

Cayley's stomach turned over, and she again prayed that her sister was safe.

Shouts filled the air.

"Who's at the gate?" Red asked.

"Maybe the outlaw's been caught."

Cayley's heart beat like a madman's drum.

There was a loud cry from the sentry and both soldiers rushed down the steps. Cayley, her blood cold as the bottom of the moat, slid out from the shadows and hurried through the open door and down the wet steps. Her boots sank into the mud of the inner bailey, but still she ran forward.

Soldiers were dragging a half-dressed man up the path leading to the great hall.

"Call for Sir Holt!" one of the knights ordered Red. "We've got a man who claimed he was attacked by the outlaw!"

"So you're Kelvin of Hawarth," Holt said, tearing off a piece of bread and handing it to the blond man his men had found wandering through the forest not far from the castle. Nearly naked, half frozen, his lips blue as midnight, he'd been discovered by two of Holt's men who were looking for the outlaw."

"Aye, my older brother is Osric, the baron, and Sheena is my niece," he said, shivering in the great hall. He sat on a bench near the fire, warming his back through the blanket that was wrapped around him. A proud man, and impetuous, he was embarrassed as he told his tale. "I was on my way to the wedding when a bastard jumped me, put a knife to my throat, gagged and stripped me, then tied me to a tree. All the while he's doin' this, he's thankin' me for the fine clothes and invitation to the wedding. Jesus God, I thought my life was over!"

He paused to chew the crusty bread. "Hours later, in the black of the night, an old man comes up to me, tells me I'm lucky not to be dead, and steals my horse, leavin' me in the freezin' rain. I started walking, probably in circles mostly, and didn't find the road until this morning."

Holt scowled as he cut a piece of cheese with the cruel little dagger he'd taken from the armory earlier. "You knew this man not?"

"Nay, never seen 'im before in my life, but before I left Hawarth, the sheriff warned me of bands of thugs raiding the roads. There's a man they call Wolf, dark of hair, with a split eyebrow, who is the leader of a group of cast-outs. They say the men know each other only by a name they chose and no women or children are allowed in the group. The men are fiercely loyal to Wolf, the only one of the lot who can read, a man who some claim was of noble birth but was cast out for some past sin."

"Think you that you were the victim of this Wolf?"

Kelvin took a bite of the cheese, then washed it down

with a long swallow of wine. "Aye," he said with a crisp nod. Wiping his mouth with the back of his hand, he scowled. "Shamed me, he did. Left me to rot, though the other member of his band—at least I think the old bugger was one of the thief's men—did release me and only steal my horse. A wicked one, that, with an evil cackle that sounded like it came from the bowels of hell." Shuddering, he looked Holt square in the eye. "I scare not easily. My brother claims I'm too bold and reckless for my own good, but that night alone, strapped to the base of a tree wearing naught but my braies, hearing bats and owls and all sorts of creatures scuttling through the brush, I was scared, let me tell you. What if some beast had come by, or another murdering thug? I had not my sword or hands that I could use. Helpless, I was, and 'tis a feeling I'll not want to have again any too soon. Even after the old one cut me loose, I was near naked. If I ever come across the black-heart who did this to me, I swear I'll run him through and take God's punishment."

Holt believed him. The man felt as humiliated as he did. So Holt gained another ally in his fight against the outlaw. "This time I will go after him myself," Holt said. "You may ride with me if you like, but make no mistake, we will not return empty-handed."

Kelvin grinned. "Aye," he said. "If you can spare some clothes and weapons, I'll gladly hunt down the bastard."

"Are ye hungry?" the lad, Robin, asked her. He was fair of skin with freckles all about his face, round blue eyes, and teeth that were far from straight, but his smile was true and the blush that stained his cheeks caused Megan to return his grin.

"Aye, a bit."

In truth, she was starved. 'Twas evening. Darkness had collected over the land, bringing with it a soft mist and quiet fog that hung close to the ground. Though she'd done little but explore the camp while thinking of ways to escape, she was hungry again. The charred rabbit and fish had been hours ago and though she'd been offered a goodly portion, she'd barely touched the burned, tasteless food. Odell lacked Cook's spices and sense of timing, though no one else acted as if it mattered. The men had devoured the tough meat as if the food were a great feast, and Wolf, while he'd sliced off a shank of rabbit and eaten it with his knife, had watched her, apparently amused at her distaste for the meal.

Since then, she'd barely seen him. He'd been in one tent or the other, off riding or talking by the stream with his men. There were many questions asked of him, along with sidelong looks cast her way from each of the men. 'Twas more than obvious that many of the band resented her. Others, like charming Robin, were eager to make her acquaintance.

Wolf had not insisted she be bound. All he had asked was that she stay in the camp in his sight. When the time had come for her to relieve herself, he'd walked with her into the woods and waited on the other side of a copse of trees until she was finished. 'Twas awkward and embarrassing, but better than having her wrists or ankles tied.

The men in the camp were an odd lot, solitary sorts whom she suspected were outcasts either by their own choice or the choosing of their loved ones. Cutthroats, pickpockets, robbers, or murderers, she knew not. No one, as far as she could tell, discussed his crimes. Past lives were never mentioned, another rule of the band. Just as there were to be no women in the group, there were also no secrets shared about crimes, homes, or loves.

"Tell me about your leader," she said to Robin after he'd brought her a trencher of beans and fish that again was burned. Wolf caught her eye as he spoke to the tall blond one—Bjorn—then turned back to his conversation.

The men ate at will. Whenever their job was finished, they stopped by the fire where Odell offered up his pitiful fare. Wolf had barely eaten but he was unable or unwilling to stop long enough for a meal. There were no prayers of thanks sent to God, no formality whatsoever.

Robin sat on a stone next to hers by the stream. "Wolf took me in."

"You mean stole you away from your mother," she said, eating with her fingers as Robin did.

"Nay, I have no ma," Robin said. "She died birthin' me."

"Oh . . . I'm sorry."

He lifted a bony shoulder. "'Tis no matter. I lived with me uncle and aunt until they died of the sickness and then Brother Anthony, he wanted me to work with the monks at the abbey, but . . . well, I took to stealin' and the sheriff caught up with me. If not fer Wolf, I woulda been cast into the prison at Hawarth."

"But Wolf found you."

"Aye. I know not how, or why, but he kidnapped me right from under the jailer's nose." Chuckling at the thought, Robin ate hungrily.

"Have you no family?"

"Not since me auntie died." He had the reverence to cross himself, then polished off the remains of his trencher. When she paused after a bite, he pointed at her uneaten portion of beans. "Will ya be eatin' that, m'lady?"

Megan shook her head. Though she wasn't finished, she could see that the lad was still ravenous and she remembered Bevan when he was but 12 or 13. It made no matter how much he ate at mealtimes or that he stuffed himself until he belched loudly, her brother could not get enough food to last him from one meal to the next. "Please, if you would finish it for me," she said, handing him the remains of her trencher. "I would not want to offend Odell."

He grinned widely and within seconds, beans and stale bread had disappeared. As he licked his fingers, smacking his lips, she tried to ask him a few more questions about Wolf, but the boy had nothing further to add and went off in search of more scraps. 'Twas obvious that this ragged band's leader was as much a mystery to his men as he was to her.

She should hate the outlaw, despise him, loathe him. For the injustices she'd been made to suffer at his hand, she should be plotting to turn him in to the sheriff herself.

Washing her hands in the icy depths of the stream, she glanced over her shoulder and watched as he walked between the tents, the light from the campfire casting gold shadows upon a hard face that was rigid and unforgiving and battle-scarred.

She had to remind herself that he was a black-heart, a man who should be flogged for snatching her away from her father. But a part of her wasn't convinced, the small, feminine part of her that found the rogue attractive and appealing. That traitorous female part reminded her that were it not for Wolf, she would today be a virgin no longer, in more than name the wife of Holt, perhaps already carrying his child. The thought revolted her and her stomach, laden with Odell's tasteless fare, threatened to purge itself.

For saving her from her marriage, she was grateful to the demon, although she had to make good her escape; if not, he would ransom her back to her husband and she would be worse off than before she was kidnapped.

She'd steal a horse. Wolf owed her one for setting Shalimar free, so she'd take his best steed as well as some food and these clothes he'd given her, tattered and large though they be.

Plotting her escape, she stared into the water's inky depths. She tried to see her image in the black ripples, but the campfire's light barely gave her enough illumination to view her pale face surrounded by wild, untamed red-brown hair. She'd hardly pass for a boy, but then she didn't have the bearing of a woman of noble birth. She pushed a shank of unruly curls behind her ear and turned her head to the side.

"So here ye be."

Wolf's voice startled her and she jumped, losing her balance and half falling into the brook. She caught herself with her hands, but created ripples that distorted her image. He was on the far side of the creek, one boot propped against an exposed root of a willow tree, his back resting against the trunk, arms folded over his chest, his dark clothes blending into the night.

"You scared me."

"Because you wandered too far from camp. 'Tis dark and not safe for you alone."

"Oh, don't tell me," she mocked, rising to her feet and wiping her hands on the long hem of the tunic. "You fear I might be abducted by some outlaw who would steal me away and demand ransom for my safe return?"

His laugh was cold as the night. "You're a sassy one. 'Tis no wonder your father wanted you married off."

"Back to that, are we?" she said, frowning as she wondered what demons plagued this man who had so boldly stolen her from her father's castle. "Tell me—why do you hate Sir Holt?"

"What know you of him?"

"Very little."

"But you agreed to marry him and plan to live the rest of your life as his wife." He made a sound of disgust in the back of his throat.

"He has been loyal to my father—"

"He would cut out your father's heart like that," he said, snapping his fingers.

Genuine fear gripped her insides. "Nay—" she said, but her protest was weak.

"Fear not, m'lady, I'll have you back safely in his arms before a fortnight passes—"

"No!" The word slipped out before she could think, and she had to bite her tongue to keep from speaking her true thoughts, which, she was sure, this outlaw would turn against her.

"Want you not to return to Dwyrain?" he asked, and the wind picked up, riding on the current of the stream.

"Aye, but—"

He waded across the creek, mindless of the depths of the icy water that swirled and splashed about his boots, his gaze fastened to hers as if her eyes opened deep into her soul. Oh, what a fool she was. She should not let this man have the tiniest glimmer of what she thought. 'Twould be dangerous for him to know too much about her, to give him that power.

"Why did you agree to marry Holt?" he asked, his voice low.

"'Tis no concern of yours."

"Why?" he said, climbing up the short bank to stand in front of her. He was nearly a head taller than she and he craned his neck downward to stare deep into her eyes. "Do you love him?"

Her throat closed in on itself.

With one clenched fist, he propped up her chin, forcing her to look into his blue, blue eyes. Shadowed in the dark, they glimmered for a second with some deep and strange emotion that touched her before it disappeared. "Tell me."

A new emotion, one she couldn't name, started deep in

her chest, causing her heart to drum and her pulse to pound and her breath to catch. Though she knew she was making a mistake by confiding in him, she admitted the truth. "Nay, I . . . I love him not. 'Twas my father's wish that I marry Holt."

"And you agreed?"

"I had no say."

His eyes narrowed thoughtfully, as if he didn't believe her. "I've heard of you, Megan of Dwyrain," he admitted, his face so close to hers she saw red-gold pinpoints of light—reflections from the campfire—in his eyes. She stood as if rooted to the earth, unable to move, unwilling to protest. "'Tis said you have a mind of your own, that you do as you choose, that you ride in and out of the castle gates without a guard whenever you so desire."

"Not always."

"I've seen you myself, while I was waiting for my chance to steal you away."

"You were watching me?" she asked, thunderstruck. How long had he sought and plotted his revenge?

"Aye."

Anger took control of her tongue. "You are a fiend!"

His smile was touched with self-condemnation. "So I've been told." He studied her again and she wanted to squirm from beneath his scrutinizing eyes. "Your father gives you much freedom, many choices, pampers you and lets you hunt in the forests and ride far from the castle gates. Yet you say he chose the man for you."

"What concern is it of yours?" she snapped, unable to stop seething. But what reason did she have to hide the truth? If his revenge was against Holt, mayhap 'twas better if she admitted that she, too, trusted not the man she'd taken as her husband.

"Yea, 'tis true," she said, pursing her lips. "But my father is no longer young, nor well. He talks of dying and meeting my mother and brother and sister soon in heaven. He fears that my other sister and I will be able not to care for ourselves, that we need men to protect us."

He snorted as if the thought were that of a simpleton. "Thinks he that you are weak?"

"Nay, not just me. All women."

Wolf laughed. "Not always and surely not you."

She favored him with the hint of a smile as he rubbed his cheek where she'd slapped him earlier that evening.

"Father wants a grandson. He decided that because I had no suitors that pleased me and was not hasty to accept a proposal, he would pick a husband for me."

"So he chose Holt."

"Aye," she said, sliding him a glance. "He chose Sir Holt because of his bravery and loyalty and courage."

"Then Ewan must be deaf, mute, and blind as well as stupid," Wolf said. "Your husband is a weak coward whose only loyalty is to himself."

"He is not my husband," she blurted, then bit her tongue.

"Nay?" Wolf mocked. "Did you not stand up at the altar and pledge yourself to him?"

"Aye," she admitted, feeling weak. Squeezing her eyes shut, she gritted her back teeth, remembering how soft her voice had sounded, how difficult it was to say two simple words. "I do" had come after tense, silent moments when Holt's nostrils had quivered in rage and her father had pleaded with her mutely, his cloudy eyes beseeching hers.

"Then are you not his wife?"

"Yes!" The horrid word echoed through the forest.

Instead of being pleased, Wolf was vexed, his mouth blade-thin, his lips flat against his teeth. "'Tis a pity," he said, "for this husband of yours will do naught but give you pain."

"You know not," she accused, but his eyes were dark as the black waters at the bottom of a well. "Tell me," she whispered. "What is it you know of him?"

Wolf stared at her as if about to say more, then changed his mind. He glanced at the sky, black and starless. "Come," he said gruffly. "'Tis time for sleep."

"You know something of my husband."

"Many things."

"Yet you will not tell me."

"Ask Holt," Wolf said angrily, "about Tadd of Prydd and the fisherman's daughter."

"I'm asking you."

"Oh, for the love of Saint Peter. Come, woman, you tire me." His skin was stretched so tightly over his face that his jawbone showed white and his eyes had darkened to an evil, murky color that warned her she was wading too far into treacherous waters.

Even so, she could not hold her wayward tongue. "But I needs know—"

"When the time is right," he bit out, fury rolling from him in waves.

She begged him to tell her more, but he refused and took hold of her hand, pulling her behind him, dragging her toward his tent. Several men working around the campsite sent curious glances her way as she argued with him. There were whispers and laughter and she imagined she was the subject of their ribald jokes and meaningful knowing glances. Her cheeks burned with color as he pushed her into his tent then closed the flap behind them.

The space was small, but in the light from the campfire she saw not only the pallet in the center, but also a chest and two sacks, one she recognized as holding her wedding dress. Several tools were stacked near the doorway and she spied a hand ax and a coil of thick rope.

Whirling upon her, he planted his hands firmly on his hips and stood between her and the doorway. "Never!" he said, his voice without compromise, his nostrils flared. "Never again defy me in front of my men."

"Why not?"

"It shows a lack of respect."

"But stealing a bride on her wedding day does not?"

Muttering a curse, he yanked on her hand and twirled her against him. Before she could break free, both of his arms held her in a grip that threatened the air in her lungs. "Do not challenge me, Megan." His voice was low, his lips nearly brushing her temple as he gave her a tiny shake. She could barely breathe, and as the light from the campfire seeped through the walls, she met his hard glare with a mutinous stare of her own.

"Do not order me about like some addled scullery maid."

"I have treated you well."

"You—you have treated me with only contempt."

His eyes drifted to her lips and she quivered in anticipation. They were alone in the dark, standing near the edge of a single pallet covered with thick furs. Megan counted her heartbeats and watched as his throat moved.

"You—you promised that I would sleep alone," she said, suddenly mindful of her virtue.

"Aye, and I keep my word," he said as her breasts rose and fell against the hard wall of his chest.

Her pulse was pounding in her head and when she licked her dry lips, he groaned then dropped his arms from her quickly, stepping back. "Mother of God," he whispered, running both his hands through his black hair. "What kind of woman are ye?"

"A captive," she said, her voice breathless.

"If I'm not here with you, what's to prevent you from sneaking away?"

"I would not—"

"Do not lie, Megan. You've been planning to escape since you first arrived. I saw you eyeing the horses and searching the woods. You've watched the men in the camp all day and even this night, hoping you'll discover where the sentries are posted and who they be."

Swallowing hard, she mentally kicked herself. How had she been so obvious?

He reached into a bag on the floor and withdrew a length of soft cord. "Give me your hands."

"Nay."

A muscle worked at the edge of his jaw. "Would you rather I force you?"

"Please, Wolf, do not bind me," she pleaded, and he hesitated, his eyes searching hers, his lips folding in on themselves.

"And I would have your word that you will not try to escape?"

"As God is my witness," she said, hoping the Lord didn't strike her dead for the lie.

He looped the cord through both his hands, stretching it tight. "Then I'll give you a choice, Megan of Dwyrain," he said slowly. "You can sleep alone with your wrists bound. Or—"

"Or?" she repeated, her heart knocking crazily, the air in the tent suddenly too heavy to breathe.

"Or I will make my bed in here with you and you can sleep unbound." One of his dark eyebrows lifted insolently and she quivered inside at the eager gleam in his deep blue eyes. "So tell me, m'lady," he urged, snapping the cord again, "what will it be?"

❋ *Four* ❋

Blankets tossed over his legs, Wolf leaned against the trunk of a tree and stared at his tent. His men were scattered about the fire, some in temporary shelters of their own, while others, the few who could stand no walls, were curled up as he was, beneath the shelter of a tree, the hilts of their swords and knives in their closed fists. Heath, Cormick, and Dominic slept fitfully, as if they'd spent too many years in closed dungeons behind iron bars. Guards were posted, their eyes searching the darkness as, ever vigilant, they tended the fire and walked around the edge of the camp.

Wolf was certain Megan would try to escape. Would he not attempt the same if he were the one who had been abducted? No small cord around his wrists would stop him. Nay, he didn't blame her for wanting to return to her home, even if it were to share a bed with Holt of Prydd. His stomach turned at the thought and a new emotion, one akin to hot jealousy, crept through his blood. He didn't like the feeling, for he prided himself on his solitude, for his need for no one else, especially a woman.

So she would try to escape and he would catch her and then he would end up sleeping in the tent with her, on the same pallet, under the same furs and blankets with her breathing softly in his ear, her body warm and comforting.

'Twould be hell. Even at the thought of it, his lust stirred. He'd been long without a woman, and none had touched him as had this one with her condemning golden eyes and tongue as sharp as a fine dagger's blade, this woman Holt had chosen for his bride. Saints in heaven, 'twas his curse to lust after his enemy's woman.

He'd planned to cut her hair, hoping to make her appear more manlike, to disguise her if they were accosted by Holt's men and also so that she would be less attractive, less feminine, so as not to distract his men or himself. But he had not been able to go through with it, and 'twould not have mattered, for hers was a beauty that was not bits and pieces—eyes, hair, lips—but all-encompassing. He attempted to force his thoughts to a different path, but his wayward mind would have none of it. He could not concentrate on plans for moving the camp, or hunting for the next meal, or training Robin with a sword; no, his mind was determined to settle on Megan, with her wide eyes the color of honey and red-brown hair spread out around her face. The curls were thick and rich and he wanted to bury his face in their scented strands and lose himself in the wonder that was this woman.

Yea, the thought of sleeping with her held more than a little appeal. He dug the heel of his boot into the ground as he remembered the few glimpses he'd caught of her breasts, pale and full, her nipples dark, ripe spheres beckoning his touch. He'd seen the length of her spine as she'd shed her wedding dress, the gentle valley that curved to split her small, round rump.

Stifling a groan, he shifted, damning his manhood that had sprung to life at the thought of coupling with her. How glorious 'twould be to join his body to hers, to thrust deep into the warm well of her womanhood, to collapse on those soft, welcoming breasts.

Aside from the pure physical comfort he would receive, Wolf considered there to be no greater humiliation for his old enemy than for Wolf to steal Holt's wife's virginity. Even if she were not a virgin, 'twould be an insult of the highest order for a hated adversary to take her before she could lie with her husband.

Smiling in the darkness, Wolf savored that particular thought, but an old, unwanted streak of nobility, one he hadn't been able to discard no matter how hard he'd tried, wouldn't allow him to attempt to seduce the woman.

Though she was a fool for marrying Holt, his intent was not to hurt her. His grin faded. Such a simple plan was suddenly complicated. He should ransom her now rather than wait. For though he enjoyed the thought of Holt twisting in the wind, not knowing where his bride was—whether she was alive or dead—keeping her was dangerous, not only because of the threat of Holt's men finding them, but for other reasons as well—reasons that touched his heart and frightened him. In a few days . . . then he'd contact his old enemy and ransom the feisty woman.

He picked up a stick on the ground and idly shredded the bark from the softer white wood. Robin had offered to stand guard at Megan's door and now, seated near the flap, his arms crossed over his knees, his head lolling, he was falling asleep. With a snort, the boy shook his head to awaken, but within seconds his head was falling forward again.

Robin wanted so much to be a man; he was eager to prove himself and would someday make a challenge for the leadership of their outlaw band.

Wolf understood a boy's need to be considered an adult far better than anyone, including Robin, could know. He, too, had been a young eager pup, ever ready to take command of Abergwynn, the castle he'd left long ago in the life he'd shed.

Now, obviously, Robin was fascinated with Megan, the first woman the lad had seen and spoken with since Wolf had saved him from the jailer. Wolf knew the emotion. 'Twas all he could do to keep his hands off her and see that his men, a randy, vicious lot, did, as well.

One of his men, Simon, had once bragged of taking a woman by force and Wolf's justice had been swift. Within seconds he'd knocked away Simon's weapon and pressed the blade of his sword to Simon's long, skinny neck. Simon had been tall and strong, his face pockmarked, his eyes never warm. He'd had arguments and fights with some of the men, and so it was with no regret that Wolf had stripped him of his clothes, horse, and weapons; banished him from the band; and left him, tied and bound, naked as the day he was born, screaming obscenities in the middle of a town to the east of Erbyn.

Simon had sworn vengeance, spitting and kicking and vowing to slice Wolf to ribbons, but Wolf had not worried. Simon was a coward, a bully who loved to prove he was stronger than those weaker—especially women.

Wolf had no stomach for rape and he would not let any of his men near Megan for fear that they might not be able to control themselves around a woman. There would be brawls and harsh words, all because they would want her attention. 'Twas the way of men—the curse of being born male. Even young Robin was already smitten.

This was one plan he hadn't thought through well enough. Was he not as bad as his men—mayhap worse? Though he would defend her honor to the death rather than see her taken by force, was he not, even now, planning her seduction? The thought of making love to Megan over and over again was a welcome balm, and he felt that if given enough time, he could seduce her. But seduction thought out so carefully, planned without her knowledge, was probably not so much better than forcing her. Even though stealing Holt's wife's virtue would be great revenge, a way to further humiliate his enemy, and it appealed to Wolf's sense of justice for the rape of Mary, he couldn't, *wouldn't*, abuse Megan thus.

Disgusted, he tossed the shredded stick aside and wiped his hands. Force and rape were what had driven him to become an outlaw in the first place, though Megan knew nothing of his past. 'Twas years before when he was just beginning to be a man, during the time when Strahan of Hazelwood, his cousin, had nearly succeeded in stealing Abergwynn from Wolf's older brother, Garrick. It had been Wolf, known as Ware in that other lifetime, who had been left in charge of the castle while Garrick was away. Ware had never doubted his ability to command and his own pride and foolishness had been his downfall. He'd lost control of Abergwynn to the enemy and then, while he and his best friend Cadell were fleeing for their lives, they had been chased to the cliffs rising high over the sea. Rather than surrender, Ware had chosen death, urging his mount over the edge of those sharp bluffs and hurtling into the blackness wherein Cadell had already fallen.

He'd thought he was dead when he awoke in a fisherman's hut and the sweetest woman in the world, the man's daughter, Mary, pressed cool cloths to his head. Her hands were soft, her eyes trusting, her lips pink and always turned into a kind smile. She whispered words of encouragement and told him that she'd never lost faith, that she was certain with enough kindness and prayer he would awaken.

He was in love with her from the moment she'd asked him how he felt. He'd blinked his eyes open and even in his fuzzy vision her image had smiled down on him. "I knew you'd wake up," she said in a voice as soft and pure as the first light of dawn. "God would not take one so young and handsome."

She'd tended to him and he'd strengthened, living with her and her father, Alan, learning how to sail and fish, how to read the storms gathering in the distance, becoming accustomed to the gentle swaying of the boat. 'Twas easy to shed his other life, to leave his past and his shame on the rocky shoals beneath the cliffs of Abergwynn. Though his memory returned, he hadn't been able to face his brother. Aside from the guilt of allowing his family to think him dead, he was content and in love—so innocently and completely in love.

He had planned to wed Mary, but before he was able, Tadd of Prydd, cruel firstborn son of Baron Eaton, had ridden through their village and altered the course of their lives forever. Mary, while selling fish in the market, had unwittingly caused Tadd to notice her, and after only one glimpse of her, he'd decided that he would claim her—not for a wife, nay, but for a night's sport and pleasure.

That evening, Tadd and a few cruel-faced soldiers burst into their tiny hut. Swords drawn, expressions murderous, they slammed the door shut behind them and waited for their leader's command. Tadd's face was red from ale. He drew up a stool, smiled evilly, and announced that he wanted only a few hours with Mary, then he and his men would be on their way. He'd pay the fisherman for his trouble, but Mary's father, a man of uncommon strength of character and faith in deliverance from the Lord, had refused, placing himself squarely between the soldiers and his daughter.

"You're being foolish," Tadd warned him, as Ware, too, tried to intervene.

"Leave here," Ware had ordered, but Tadd was quick and armed. His sword struck swiftly, cleaving Ware's eyebrow and knocking him into a watery darkness where he couldn't move.

Tears streaming down his leathery face, Mary's father tried to rescue her, and for his efforts his arm was severed at the elbow by Tadd's sword, in a swift blow that left him howling in blind pain. He fell to the floor and Ware, barely conscious and lying in his own blood, thought Alan dead.

With all his strength, Ware struggled to his feet, but the blackness overcame him and he fell again. No amount of prodding could urge his pained muscles to support him.

Mary's horrified screams rang in his ears, and through damaged eyes, he saw murky images of Tadd moving toward her. Ware screamed but no sound came from his mouth. He tried to climb to his knees, but his legs were no longer under his control. The darkness was like a warm cloak, offering to blind him from the pain, but he fought the urge to give up the battle. Desperate, his own ragged breathing filling his head, he scrabbled for Tadd's sword, which the bastard had discarded as he'd untied his breeches. Eyes gleaming, Tadd stalked Mary, who was on the floor, trying to back away, her hands and feet failing her as they slipped in her father's blood.

"Please, m'lord," Mary had pleaded, tears streaming from her eyes, her body quaking. "Do not do this."

"'Twill be pleasant, girl. You will enjoy it."

"Nay, I cannot—"

"Ah, but you will," Tadd said smoothly, then turned to Holt. "Hold her!"

"No!"

Ware grasped for the sword but his muscles would not move. The shadowy fog threatened him again.

Tadd's breeches fell to his ankles as Holt wrested Mary to Alan's bed.

No! No! No! Ware's mind screamed, but no words passed his lips. *Merciful God, help her! Let me save her! Do not let this happen!*

The floor was sticky with his blood and Ware stretched,

only to be swept away again, but he wasn't so far gone that he couldn't hear her horrifying, bloodcurdling screams or the smack of flesh on skin as Tadd slapped her.

I'll kill you, I swear on my life that I'll kill you!

Holt held her arms over her head while Tadd, undeterred by her kicks or screams, mounted her, grunting in pleasure, his fat white rump jiggling as he rutted hard and fast, undeterred as she screamed in pain. Ware was powerless. He swam in and out of the darkness that was his mind while a leering Holt pinned Mary to her father's bed.

Gritting his teeth, he climbed to his knees, crying a hoarse, "Get off her, you sick bastard," and received a sharp kick to the face from one of the soldiers.

With a cry, he finally lost all consciousness. When he awakened, he realized that again he had failed, just as he'd failed when he'd lost Abergwynn to Strahan. But this was worse—this was not a castle; not a moat, and walls, and locked gates. This was a woman's very soul, her heart. His shame was immense.

When finally he could pull himself to his feet and stagger over to her, he found his Mary, his beautiful, sweet, loving Mary, cowering in a corner, holding a bloodied blanket over her bruised body and allowing no one to come close or touch her. Trembling, spittle and blood collecting at the corner of her mouth, her eyes round, her face bruised, she mewed like a helpless, frightened kitten, then hissed and scooted away when he'd tried to touch her.

He'd found more blankets to cover her ripped clothes and her battered body, but though he'd tried only to help her, she'd been afraid to look at him, nor would she ever speak to him again. That day Tadd and Holt had robbed her of more than her virtue; they'd stolen her mind as well. Her father survived long enough to take one last voyage with his daughter. Alan had refused to let Ware join them, and they didn't return. A storm as savage as the wrath of God swept into the town, and Ware waited. With each day that passed, his transformation continued, and when he hadn't seen Mary for over a month, he knew she was gone from him forever.

That was the day that Ware, no longer of Abergwynn, became Wolf the outlaw, a rogue who trusted no man and asked no questions of those who chose to follow him. Having lost all his faith in God as well as trust in his fellow man, he'd given up what few possessions he had acquired and had stolen away to the forests, where he could live life alone and would make no friends.

Eventually, he'd met up with a few tattered wanderers who, like himself, had pasts they could not face, and as their numbers grew, Wolf became the leader. He alone could read, and he, though not as large as some of the men, was more agile and quick and ruthless with his sword. No one challenged him. And no one ever admitted to rape unless they wanted to incur Wolf's legendary and excruciating vengeance.

For the past few years he'd been satisfied with his vagabond, criminal life.

Until now.

Until Megan of Dwyrain had disrupted all his carefully laid plans. He'd had the satisfaction of destroying Tadd of Prydd and he'd thought that ruining Holt would only add to his vindictive fulfillment, but he hadn't considered that he might be attracted to the woman whom Holt had wed.

"Mother of Moses," he grumbled as the damp fog laid in closer about the camp. He should have killed Holt and been done with it, but he'd wanted to wound his old enemy in other, deeper ways. Death was too easy; he wanted Holt to suffer not only the indignity of losing his bride on his wedding day, but of having to search for her and appear the fool when he couldn't find her. Holt would be the laughingstock of everyone at Dwyrain, servants, guests, freemen, and soldiers alike. The news would travel to other castles and baronies as well and Holt's name would command no respect.

Then Wolf would kill him. But not before.

So what of Lady Megan? What was Wolf to do with her? He'd thought that ransoming her would solve his problem, but the very idea of returning her to Holt was unthinkable. There was not enough money in all of Dwyrain's treasury to change his mind. So he was stuck with her.

That particular thought brought an unlikely smile to his lips.

* * *

Jovan the apothecary was a short, stooped man who liked gold. Where he squirreled all his money away, Holt could only guess. Jovan wore tattered rags, his hut was a hovel, his horse, barely skin and bones, was a sorry hack with a back so swayed it appeared broken. Whereas some men liked money for what it could buy and spent their gold on fine clothes, jewelry, or women, Jovan hoarded his gold pieces jealously. He found pleasure in owning gold, not in considering what he could buy.

But it mattered not. All Holt cared about was that Jovan was greedy and knew how to keep his mouth shut.

"So we do business again," he said as Holt entered his shop. He hunched over a dirty bench, with a mortar and pestle, his knobby fingers working steadily as he ground some bitter-smelling leaves into a paste. Only one candle burned near him; Jovan would not waste precious wax just to save his eyes.

"Aye." Holt dropped a small leather pouch on the bench. The flame of the candle flickered and Jovan could barely take his eyes off the tiny parcel. His tongue rimmed dry lips and his hands faltered in their work. With a cough, he set the mortar aside.

"And you want the same herbs?" Jovan asked, his eyes gleaming with the thought of a nice, fat payment.

"Yes, the same."

"The price has gone up."

"Not much, old friend," Holt said, eyeing the dusty jars of roots, berries, and leaves.

Jovan reached for the leather pouch, but Holt grabbed hold of his bony wrist. "We understand each other, do we not?"

"No one will know, Sir Holt," Jovan said.

"I was not here."

The apothecary smiled, showing off spaces where there once had been teeth. "I know you only as a knight of Dwyrain, now husband of the baron's daughter. Soon to be baron." Was there the tiniest bit of amusement in his tired old eyes? "I will say that you have never visited my shop."

Holt allowed himself a smile and let go of the old man's arm. "Take it," he said of the pouch. "Just make sure your blend is stronger than the last. I have not much time."

Jovan snorted as he unwrapped the pouch and saw the gold. Quickly, he snatched the purse in a clawlike hand and stowed his prize deep in the folds of his dusty tunic. Surprisingly agile, the old man climbed onto a ladder to reach a high shelf with a hidden door. From the cupboard, he withdrew a clean jar. "I thought ye might be needin' this," he admitted, smiling as if he thought he was clever. "It has no taste and will go unnoticed if dropped into food or ale." He handed Holt the bottle and their gazes collided, each sharing his part of a private secret, each knowing that he couldn't trust the other.

"Two drops, no more than three, at each meal," Jovan cautioned. "Elsewise ye'll bring suspicion on the cook."

"The man is old already and dying."

"Aye, but he's the baron. He will be watched."

Holt felt an evil grin slide over his face. "I know," he said. "'Tis I who will see that Ewan of Dwyrain is cared for."

Jovan chuckled and the sound was cold and without any soul. "Then his fate is sealed, and you, sir, will soon be the new baron."

"That," Holt said, "is the idea."

Again Jovan laughed. He rubbed his hands together. "I only hope that I will be rewarded."

"'Twill be done," Holt said, thinking how easily it would be to get rid of the old man and find his stash of gold and silver. But he could not kill off the apothecary for a while, not until he was certain he didn't need Jovan's help in murdering his enemies.

Megan knew he would be waiting for her. As surely as the sun would rise in the east in the morn, Wolf would expect for her to attempt to flee. She had no choice but to try. Silly as it sounded, she was afraid that if she were to stay she might lose her foolish heart to the handsome criminal with the rough edges and hidden nobility. Worse yet, he would ransom her, not to her father, but to Holt, her new husband. Spittle collected in her mouth at the thought of her husband, and she knew she could never return to him.

The cords binding her wrists were not tight, and it was a simple matter to scoot off the pallet and slide over to the side of the tent where she'd seen the tools and the small ax.

Silently she slid the cord over the blade, sawing until the twine broke free and she was able to use her hands again.

She wondered where Wolf had positioned himself and decided that he was probably sleeping near the door, so her best chance of avoiding him was to slip out the back. Carefully, she felt around the bottom of the tent, where the cloth walls were stretched tight. There was no room for a snake or mouse to slide through, but with her ax, she could cut a slit in the tent and . . .

She felt him before she saw him. Though she'd not heard the flap move, she sensed his presence.

"I wouldn't," he said.

"Wouldn't what?"

"Come, Megan, act not like I'm a fool. You are not the first prisoner I've kept."

"And I thought I was a guest," she mocked, turning to face him in the blackness that was the tent. Could the man see in the dark? Did he have the hearing of her father's dogs?

"'Tis time to sleep." His voice was soft and patient and she wanted to crumple into a heap rather than think him kind. His hand reached for hers and she wanted to yank her fingers away.

"Do not touch me," she said, walking the short distance to the pallet. "Leave me alone."

"Nay, Megan, I stay."

"But you can't!"

"'Tis my tent."

"But—"

"My camp, my rules. Lie down, woman, and argue not. I'm tired and have no patience left." He dropped her hand, snagged a rug from the bed, and sat on the ground, propping himself against the bags.

"The men, they will think that we . . . you and I—"

"What matters what they think?" he said around a yawn. "They are not gossiping old hags who will tattle to your husband."

She tried a new tack. "I won't be able to sleep with you in here."

"You weren't sleeping before."

"But I'll . . . I'll be restless."

"Not I," he said, stretching one arm over his head. "Now, either you lie down alone right now, or I'll come over to the bed and lie with you."

Her throat turned to dust at the thought of him sleeping next to her, his arms holding her against the hard contours of his body, his breath warm as summer wind against the back of her neck.

"'Twould be pleasant," he said.

"Nay."

"Once again, Megan, you have a choice."

Reluctantly she lay down, thinking she couldn't sleep a wink with him so close. Her thoughts would run wild, her mind spin in restless circles, her heart pound with fear. She dragged a fur around her body and within minutes her muscles turned liquid and she closed her eyes, not to open them again until the first light of dawn had broken over the hills to the east and the inside of the tent was filled with a gray light.

He was already awake and watching her, his blue eyes trained on her face, his expression less harsh than before. If anything, she saw puzzlement in his gaze rather than hatred. She blinked and the ghost of a smile played upon his thin lips. "Aye," he said, rubbing his beard-stubbled jaw. "You slept nary a wink."

Feeling foolish, she sat upright and held a fur blanket to her chest as if to cover herself, though she was fully dressed in his clothes.

"Everyone here in the camp earns his keep," he said, rocking to his feet and standing. She'd forgotten how imposing he was, how his mere presence filled the tent.

"Aye."

"Peter looks after the horses, Jagger tends to the weapons, even young Robin hunts and fishes."

"And what do you do?" she threw out.

"Capture fair maidens." His eyes found hers and she caught a tiny glimpse of his inner fire, a passion that he deliberately hid. "When I've caught all I need, I lead these men and also work with them. Whatever needs be done, whether it's gather supplies, bind a wound, fix a ripped tent"—his gaze slid away to the spot where he'd found her standing, ax ready to slice through the walls—"or tend to the horses."

"You have something you want me to do."

"Aye. Do you cook?" he asked. "Some of the men have complained about Odell's fare."

She nearly laughed. "Is that so?"

"Aye, but Odell, he's touchy about it. I thought I'd ask him to let you help out."

"I know not if I could do much better."

Wolf snorted and a smile danced through his eyes. "Surely you could do no worse."

The next four days were much the same, though Odell grumbled about having a woman help him with the meals. At first she was allowed only to gut the rabbits and squirrels or pluck feathers from the birds that were killed, but once Odell discovered that she worked well and hard, she was allowed to help cook. They had only a few spices to work with and there were few herbs that grew in the woods in winter, but with a pinch of salt and pepper, purloined from a peddler who was riding near Erbyn, Megan was able to add some flavor to the meals.

The men, except for Robin, who ate anything offered him, appreciated her efforts, and some of the wary and suspicious glances she'd caught before became kind looks of appreciation.

She was allowed to go on a hunt and surprised the men, including Wolf, with her aim. Jagger, usually tough and mean-tempered, grudgingly nodded his approval when she felled a small boar.

"I knew not ladies could shoot," he said, sliding her a confused glance.

She smiled and handed him his bow, for she was not allowed to carry her own quiver or arrows. "I knew not outlaws had a sense of humor."

Even crusty Odell accepted her, though he was worried about Holt's soldiers finding their camp. But Wolf was not so foolish. He had spies throughout the forests and nearby towns who tracked Holt's whereabouts.

"He's with his men near St. Peter's," Jagger announced

one day. "And an unhappy lad he is." Smiling as he tore apart a moist piece of dove, he sighed contentedly and sat on his heels. "There are two soldiers who ride with him who are as intent on hunting you down as is Holt," Jagger went on. "One I know not, a thin knight with lifeless eyes and brown hair that kinks. Goes by the name of Conroy—nay—"

"Connor," Megan said, a rock settling in her stomach. Connor was a lone man who watched everything and kept quiet. His eyes were empty, but he stared at her often, as if not seeing her.

"Aye, that's it, and the other is Kelvin McBrayne. 'Tis said he took offense to being tied nearly naked to a tree, then having his horse stolen."

"And a fine destrier he is," Odell said with a cackle. "'ell's bells. Kelvin, 'e shoulda been 'appy we left 'im with 'is pitiful life."

"How so you know so much about who's with Holt?" Megan asked, wiping the grease from her fingers.

"I get close. Hide with the horses or in a nearby tree, just out of the campfire's light."

"He's foolish," Wolf said. "Takes chances."

"Ye get the information ye want," Jagger pointed out and helped himself to another thick breast of dove. "Odell, 'tis a fine meal ye're servin' tonight."

"Be thankin' the lady," Odell said, but smiled just the same.

There were no prayers offered up, no hint of Mass, no mention of God, though some of the men carried charms for good luck and spoke under their breaths of omens. Brave souls when faced with an enemy, they feared that which they could not see.

"I heard from Odell that some old lame witch put a curse on ye," Robin said one day. "Odell, he listens to all of the gossip in every town we pass through." Robin was at the creek, frowning, as his net had unwoven and a particularly large pike had swum away. The past few days, he'd been moody and had avoided Megan, sending her dark looks when he thought she could see him not. Now, at her arrival on the shores of the creek, he scowled. With agile fingers, he attempted to repair the damaged net.

"No witch—a prophet, mayhap, or a sorcerer. He healed my mare's leg."

"And cursed ye and yer castle, too. That's what 'tis said."

"So it would appear," Megan said, motioning with her fingers for him to hand her the net. "Dwyrain suffered in the past two years, and aye, everyone blamed me." She worked with the string, but it was frayed badly and would not hold together. "Have you more?" she asked, fingering one of the dirty, ragged lengths.

"Aye."

"Run and get it and I'll fix this."

He did as he was bid and was soon back, sullenly watching her weave the string into a simple net.

"Ye sleep in Wolf's tent," he finally said.

"Aye." So that was what was bothering him.

"Yet ye are not his wife."

His wife. How strange to think of Wolf married and yet . . . a part of her saw some woman reaching past his hard skin, finding the inner man, the kind man behind his mask of hate. "Nay, Robin, I'm not his wife, nor do I sleep with him."

Grunting in disbelief, he took the net from her hands.

"Believe what ye will, Robin, but Wolf and I, we touch each other not."

His eyes narrowed on the net, but his mind was on other things. Wiping her hands on her tunic, Megan rocked back on her heels to meet the boy's concerned gaze. "What is it?"

"Are you not married?" he asked, staring pointedly at the ring on her finger. "To another man—this Holt of Prydd?"

She nodded. "'Tis my misfortune, I'm afraid." In haste, she worked the horrid gold band from her finger. It had been uncomfortable from the moment Holt had placed it there, a constant reminder of her mockery of a marriage, yet she'd not removed it, feeling duty-bound to wear the cursed thing. Now, however, she felt no such need and deftly tossed the tiny band into the stream. It sparkled in the sunlight before dropping into the clear water and settling between two rocks.

Robin stared at her as if she were mad. "'Tis worth something," he cried. "'Tis gold."

"I want it not. If you find some value to it, you may have

it. 'Tis yours, Robin, all you needs do is go and fetch it, but I will never again wear it. Nor do I ever want to see it again."

He swallowed hard and stared at her, as if she were some creature he couldn't possibly understand.

"Now, let's see about your net, shall we?"

"The net . . . oh . . ." Once the string was tied and the net strong again, they dipped it into the stream where the water pooled and promptly caught a frog swimming just under the water's surface. Robin grabbed him from the net, but the slippery creature croaked in protest and struggled away, leaving the boy and Megan to laugh at his quick, ungainly escape.

They didn't notice Wolf standing behind them, watching their antics from a thicket of oak. "Robin," he said, and the boy nearly jumped from his own skin.

"Aye?" The boy's flush was hot and red.

"Help Peter with the horses. We're moving the camp."

"Tonight?" the boy grumbled, holding the dripping net against his tunic.

"Aye. Holt's soldiers are headed this way and we want not to be surprised."

Megan's heart dove. The thought of seeing Holt again struck hard, but then she'd found a happiness here as Wolf's captive. The men treated her with respect and she was beginning to know each of them, from Odell, the sharp-tongued liar, to mean-tempered and daring Jagger. Peter, with his one eye and level head, was a kind soul who trusted horses more than he did his fellow man. Bjorn, strong and handsome, was rumored to be some kind of bastard prince, and young Robin reminded her of her brother Bevan when he was young. Then there was Wolf, the leader, a man outwardly cruel and arrogant who willingly defied the law, yet who was blessed with a kinder side he kept hidden. Wolf, who saved a young boy from the jailer; Wolf, who swept her away from a husband she hated; Wolf, who carried a secret that weighed heavily on his heart; Wolf, the man who guarded her each night, sleeping near her but not touching her, holding her prisoner and yet protecting her as well. Aye, he was an appealing man, and it crossed her mind that if she gave in to the desire that awakened whenever he was near, that if she dared kiss him or touch him or make love to him, she would have cause to have her marriage to Holt annulled. But as much as she wanted her freedom from her husband, the thought of actually lying with Wolf frightened her. 'Twas dangerous to become emotionally entangled with a criminal.

Megan helped break camp by folding tents and lashing them to poles to be pulled by some of the horses. There was but one wagon and another small cart for supplies and weapons.

Wolf insisted that they travel at night, avoiding those who traveled by day.

She packed the rugs and fur blankets, lashing them to the pallet. Would she ever see her beloved father again? Or Cayley—would she be able to laugh and argue with her sister? Or ride in the fields surrounding the castle?

That part of her life was over, for even if she did return to the keep, she would have to face Holt as his bride, unless she could persuade her father and Father Timothy or the abbot that the marriage should be annulled, that she could not possibly remain Holt's wife.

She grabbed the bag holding her clothes, the white tunic, red surcoat, and green mantle, then bit down hard on her lower lip as she drew the string that would secure her bag. Surely Holt would want her not if she were no longer a virgin. Would he not cast her out as his wife if she'd lain with another man? And would coupling with another be worse than being married to him for the rest of her life?

Her gaze strayed to Wolf kicking dust into the campfire. Her pulse pounded in her temple. Could she give herself to this man, this black-heart, if only for a night? Her mouth turned to dust at the thought of his touch, warm against her skin, the pressure of his lips as they claimed hers. Her blood heated and she looked away.

Losing her virtue to him would not ease her burden. The clouds shifted, blocking out the moon, and she remembered the crippled prophet's words. Could this man Wolf, leader of this band, be the destruction of Dwyrain as was prophesied, and if so, would she really lose her heart to him?

❈ *Five* ❈

"Aye, they were here," Connor said, eyeing the soggy remains of a campfire and deep ruts from a heavy wagon. Bootprints and hoofprints were visible in the mud by the stream. "If not the outlaw Wolf and his miserable band of cutthroats, then someone like them." Bending down, he examined the crushed grass and rubbed a few wet blades between his fingers.

"How long?" Holt asked from astride his muddy destrier.

"Less than a week since they left. The fire is cold, but it looks only a few days old." Connor glanced up at the sky, where the clouds were beginning to part, and a few weak rays of sun shone on the glen tucked in the woods. "My guess is that they stayed here for some time—see how some of the grass is yellow there where it was covered for days, maybe weeks, with a tent? This camp was left only because we approached."

"Then we are close?"

Connor rubbed his jaw, scratching the short whiskers that covered his chin. "I think not, but I'll send men to inquire. They can ride from house to house and see if anyone saw a group of men and horses and one woman traveling."

Kelvin of Hawarth climbed down from his steed and stretched his muscles. His complaints, as the days and nights had stretched into nearly a week, had become louder and more annoying. "'Tis a wild goose chase," he said now, walking stiffly to the stream and splashing water over his face. "This may not have been Wolf's camp." Giving a short, humorless laugh, he added, "'Twould not surprise me if the cur had this place and others like it made to look like the men were here."

What a fool, Holt thought. Kelvin, so anxious to do battle with Wolf when he'd been brought to the castle, now was more than ready to return to the warm fires and fine food of Hawarth. "Wolf is clever but has neither the means nor the men to carry out such a plan."

"Has he not? What about his spies at Dwyrain? Do ye know who they be or how great their number?"

Holt's fingers clenched over the reins of his mount. "I will find them all, flush them out, and punish them. Doubt me not—before I get through with them, they will tell me everything they know of Wolf."

"If the castle is still under the baron's rule." Kelvin threw out his hands. "Mayhap the kidnapping of the lady was but a ruse to lure you and your best soldiers away from Dwyrain so that either Wolf or someone he conspires with can overtake the keep."

"Nay, I think not—" Holt said, then bit his tongue when he saw Connor's reaction. The man's blank eyes darkened just enough to worry Holt.

"What he says has merit." Connor walked slowly along the bank, his eyes searching the shallows. "Why not?"

"What would an outlaw want with a castle?"

"What would he want with a man's wife?"

Holt knew a moment of fear. 'Twas true. Wolf could have enticed him away from Dwyrain only to capture the castle for his own use when Holt and his best soldiers were searching through the woods. Though Wolf had but a small band of men, there were spies within the castle walls, spies who could turn against the guards in the keep. Even those sentries could not be trusted, not fully, for their first allegiance was to Ewan, and as long as the old man lingered, there was the chance that his mind could be turned against his new son-in-law.

"Aha," Connor said and waded into the stream. He reached into the water as if he planned on catching a fish with his bare hands, but instead plucked a piece of gold from the streambed. With a cold smile, he turned and plowed his way out of the water. "Methinks, Sir Holt," he said, grinning evilly as he extended his fist, slowly opened his fingers, and showed the tiny gold band in his wet palm, "your wife is not honoring her wedding vows."

They traveled three nights, stopping in the forest during the day only to rest, always moving to the north. Megan was beginning to wonder if they would ever stop for more than a few hours so that she would have enough time to sneak away from Wolf and his band of loudmouthed, bad-mannered, yet good-hearted men. They were a sorry lot, though happily so, and Wolf, the black-heart, was a hard, dangerous man she wished she'd never met. She was always nervous and wary around him, but fascinated as well. His smile was captivating, his wits were sharp, and his gaze, ever restless, never moved too far from her, as if he expected her to bolt at any minute.

Though it had been nearly a week since she'd been abducted, he refused to trust her, insisting on sleeping near her, never letting her out of his sight except for the nightly meetings around the campfire when the men gathered together, whispering among themselves. Megan couldn't hear what they were saying, but knew that it involved her and her fate, for often one of the men would frown, cast a glance in her direction, and argue under his breath.

'Twas unfair to be treated so; she could do nothing but plan her escape.

The best time would be during the day, when the men were resting and Wolf, as was his custom, took one man, usually Bjorn, and rode ahead, searching the countryside, looking for a new hiding spot. Often Robin and Jagger went hunting and Odell was busy tending the fire and spit, but he always found jobs to keep her busy. She hauled water, washed the few pots they had, cleaned fowl and fish, or helped sharpen the cooking knives. She considered stealing one of the sharp blades, but Odell knew his few weapons and pieces of cutlery. Before she could find a way to sneak away from the camp, Wolf always returned and trained his suspicious eyes upon her once again.

On the fourth night, they veered from the road and continued on what appeared to be an old deer trail, slogging through muck, easing the wagon through the trees with torches as their only light. The horses shied, and Megan shivered in the wind as she rode upon a gray jennet and held on to the saddle pommel. Her hands were free, but the reins of her horse were firmly in Wolf's hands as he drove to the remains of an old chapel tucked near the bend of a river. The water moved swiftly, a dark, wide ribbon that tumbled over steep cliffs, creating a waterfall not 20 yards from the back door of the ancient church.

"'Ere?" Odell grumbled. "Ye expect us to make camp 'ere?"

Wolf's smile was a slash of white in the darkness. "And what's wrong with it?"

"It's falling down around us. We'll be lucky if the roof don't give way and crush us!"

"Here we have a choice. At the last camp, we did not. Those who want to sleep inside may; those who favor tents or the bare ground can do as they wish."

Odell, upon the destrier he'd stolen from Kelvin of Hawarth, edged his mount forward and raised his torch high so that a pool of flickering light fell upon mossy stone walls. Ivy climbed up what had once been a great fireplace but now was a pile of rubble, and beams, charred from a great fire, held up only a portion of the roof.

"Looks like the Devil himself was 'ere," Odell said and crossed himself swiftly, one of the first signs Megan had ever seen that some of the men concerned themselves with God.

"We make camp here," Wolf said, and though a few of his men grumbled under their breaths, most climbed off their tired mounts, stretched, and hurriedly went about constructing the tents and a fire.

"We'll be inside," Wolf said as he slid from his saddle, and Megan hopped to the ground. Her muscles ached from hours in the saddle and she saw no point in arguing. "Odell's right—part of the old chapel is unsafe, but there are rooms where the roof is intact and the walls strong, and 'tis warmer than outside."

"You know this place well?" she asked, eyeing the blackened rafters that creaked in the wind.

"Well enough," he said gruffly, then ordered his men to bring his pallet, rugs, and bags to a corner room with a small window and a spot where another fire had been lit. The floor was stone, the walls solid, the ceiling appearing steady.

Through the window, she saw sparks from the fire drifting toward the sky and she realized how alone she was with this man. Oh, she'd been in his tent with him each night, but the walls were only thin cloth and she'd not felt so distant from the rest of the men. But here, in a chamber, they were more removed from the outlaws who gathered in their tents around the fire.

"You're not pleased."

"I hate being a prisoner."

"Is it so bad? Have you been mistreated?" She heard him stake out a place near the door. "'Twill not be forever," he said, and she thought she heard a smidgen of regret in his voice, but it could have been her mind playing tricks on her. "Soon enough I will return you to the arms of your beloved Holt."

"When?"

"Shortly I will send a note for your ransom, then you will be returned safely to Dwyrain."

Her stomach clenched at the thought of facing Holt, but she held her tongue and slid out of her boots.

A yawn escaped him, and in the darkness she saw him wrap a fur rug around himself and prop his head against the bag holding her clothes. "Now that he has tasted of bitter disappointment, I'll only too gladly give him back his wife in exchange for gold."

Her insides froze. "Gold? So that's what this is about. Money." She said the word as if it tasted bad. "You're nothing more than a common thief."

"Not so common, m'lady," he retorted sarcastically, his hooded eyes trained on her, his smile as dangerous as the predatory beast for which he named himself. "But, aye, I am a thief."

Holt took aim at the stag's chest and the great heart beating within, pulled back on his bow, and watched as his arrow, usually true, veered away from its target, thwacking hard as it landed in the soft white bark of a birch. The startled buck fled, leaping high over a hedge of brush and disappearing through the forest.

None of his men said a word. What they thought didn't spring to their lips. As the best archer in all of Dwyrain, Holt should not have missed so clear a shot, but he was bothered, his mind elsewhere than on game. He'd sworn he wouldn't return to the castle empty-handed, but he had no choice. Out of supplies and without new information as to where the rogues had fled, spending more time in the forest was useless. And he had to return to the castle for fear Wolf's intentions were to take over the keep.

"Bloody hell," he growled, seething inside to think he'd been bested by a cunning criminal who had stolen his wife and no doubt bedded her as well. As a painful reminder of her faithlessness, he wore her wedding ring on his fifth finger.

Kelvin and Connor had convinced him to return to Dwyrain and wait for word of ransom. The winter air was tinged with ice, frost lay on the ground, and the outlaws' trail was as cold as death. The Christmas revels were soon upon them, and Connor believed that each day away from Dwyrain was another day for the outlaw to take over the castle. Connor . . . an odd one. Deadly. A man who would be brutal to Cayley.

As the stag disappeared into a thicket, Holt motioned for his men to move on. He'd leave Connor with a few men to keep looking in the forests and towns, ever searching for the elusive outlaw and stolen bride. Holt would return to Dwyrain and become baron, for certainly the poison he'd had Nell slip into Ewan's wine would be taking its toll, and the old man, already ill, would be perilously near death, if not dead already.

Half the men continued on their quest. The other half, some of whom would later return to the search party with more supplies, returned to Dwyrain with Holt, but as the horses drew nearer to the castle, Holt's fury mounted.

Megan's ring burned against the skin of his finger and he argued with himself. Whether she was with him or not, he would inherit the castle. He was her husband, and though he suffered a few insults and raised eyebrows and unkind jokes, he would still be baron. Those who opposed him would be silenced forever. If he never saw Megan again, 'twould not matter.

Except that she had escaped him. He'd waited for months to have her serve him, to see her naked on her knees, to force her to do his bidding. He'd savored thoughts of the wedding night and dreamed of how it would feel not just to mount her but see her surrender to his power. For nearly a year she had avoided him, argued with her father about his courtship, defied him at every turn, and he'd waited, somewhat impatiently, because he'd known in the end he would win.

And he'd been thwarted. By a scar-faced outlaw who acted as if he delighted in Holt's humiliation. Why else had there been no demand of ransom?

They plodded on for hours, and at the final bend in the road, the trees parted and Holt caught his first view of Dwyrain in nearly a week. Tall and proud, a giant that swelled from the very earth on which it was built, the castle was one of the finest Holt had ever seen. When he'd left Prydd years ago and come into Ewan's service, he'd silently vowed that someday the keep would be his. He'd started by being of service to the old man, proving himself worthy, using his brains, brawn, and skill to gain Ewan's trust.

And then there was Megan, beautiful, haughty first daughter of the baron, second in line to inherit the castle. Only Bevan stood in Megan's way of inheriting all that was Dwyrain. Fate had cast Holt a great favor in the form of the sorcerer's prediction. Even now as he rode through the brittle-cold afternoon to the gates of Dwyrain, Holt smiled. The prophet's words, foretelling that so many would die, that there would be great pain and loss, destruction and deceit within the castle walls, that Megan would be blamed, had all been too good to be true. Aye, the prophecy had come to pass, but Holt had felt no qualms about hurrying it along a bit.

Bevan's reckless nature had given Holt an opportunity to poison the lad while he was recuperating from a nasty spill off his mount and near-drowning. By killing Bevan, Holt had removed Ewan's son as the final obstacle to Megan's inheritance, and from there it was only a matter of convincing the old man that no one would want to marry her. By the gods, it looked as if that pathetic cripple had been right, and had cursed her.

It took little to persuade some of the servants and a few of the more superstitious knights that she was the reason for the illness that swept through the castle. Had not it been foretold? And when any misfortune befell the castle or those who worked there, it was a simple matter to remind the victim or his family that there was a curse on the keep.

The only part of the prediction that worried him was the piece concerning the marriage being cursed and something about restoring Megan's honor only through true love or some such pig dung. Not that Holt believed in the prophecy; it was just a convenient ploy to use against the simple minds in the castle.

He heard the sentry's shout and the blast of a trumpet announcing his return. Soldiers scurried over the wall walks and Holt smiled to himself. Let the little people hurry to serve him. 'Twas his destiny.

First, he'd show his respect, visit Ewan, eat a hot meal, drink wine, and then find himself a willing wench who would take his mind off Megan. At least for the night.

"You found her not?" the old man asked from his bed. Unable to rise, he hardly moved, but sighed loudly, disappointment etched across his brow. He was ill; the herbs were working their magic and Holt could barely suppress a smile. He was so close to becoming baron, he could feel it; the promise of death hung heavy in the air.

"Nay, the outlaw eluded me." Holt crossed the room and sat on a bench near the fire, warming his backside as he silently willed Ewan of Dwyrain to die. "I left Connor with some men and will send others with supplies to join them soon. But I did not want to stay away from the castle too long in case there was a demand for ransom or . . ." He let his voice drift away.

"Or what?"

"Well, or news of Megan."

"News?" Ewan said and his lips compressed. His washed-out gray color paled even more. "What kind of news?"

Holt sighed and plowed his hands through his hair. "'Tis possible that this outlaw, the one they call Wolf, is an enemy of yours or mine. It might not be money he's after."

"What then?"

"Perhaps her virtue."

Ewan closed his old eyes and shook his head in vehement denial. "I think not."

"Or her life," Holt added, and his father-in-law physically jerked, as if his ancient heart had stopped beating for a moment before jolting into rhythm again.

"Nay, she's alive," Ewan gasped. "I cannot lose Megan, too, not after the others . . ." His old voice faded.

"I pray she's safe," Holt said, but his voice sounded full of doubt.

"You must find her!"

Holt's eyes slid away. "I'll do what I can, m'lord, but I cannot promise."

"You must!"

"'Tis not that easy. There are spies within the castle walls—those who would betray you and follow the criminal."

Jaw clenching beneath his beard, Ewan said, "Then flush them out, Holt. Find out what they know. Mayhap they can tell you where the cur is holding my daughter!"

"As you wish," Holt agreed, then walked back to the bed and offered Ewan his cup of wine. Smiling inwardly, he watched as the old fool drank a long sip, then slid back between the linen sheets. Ewan's eyes closed and Holt wished him dead. It would be so easy to smother the man, as he was already weak, but as that thought chased through his mind, the door opened and Cayley entered.

"You found Megan not?" she asked, casting a worried look at her father's sleeping form.

"Nay, the blackguard eluded us."

"A pity," Cayley murmured, crossing herself.

"Aye, that it is," Holt said as Cayley walked to her father's bedside and laid cool fingertips to his forehead. He didn't move.

"He gets worse with each day. I thought that if Megan were to return he might recover a bit . . ." Sighing, she brushed a strand of white hair from his forehead.

"He is near death's door," Holt whispered, wishing he could find a way to push the baron through that black portal just a bit sooner.

* * *

The moon was high, the campfire mere embers, and Megan knew she had no choice. If she were to escape, she had to leave now while Wolf slept peacefully near the door. Quietly, she slipped from his pallet and across the room to the window, where, with one final glance over her shoulder to see that he had not moved, she hoisted herself up and slid through the opening. She landed with a soft thud on the frozen ground and slowly edged her way around the old chapel. Two sentries, shoulders propped against trees, stood near the clearing where the horses were tethered. Though their backs were to her, she could not get past them and steal a horse as she'd hoped. No, she would have to make her way on foot and hope that by the morning's light she had put enough distance between herself and the camp to elude Wolf.

Her heart squeezed at the thought. There was a foolish part of her that longed to stay with him, to trust him. *You are addled,* she told herself. What would she want with a criminal, a man always on the run, a man who lived by his own rules? Rather than dwell on the dark turn of her thoughts, she crept to the river's edge and decided to follow it upstream, keeping to the banks until she came to a crossing, either a shallow spot where a road splashed across the current, or, if she was lucky, to a bridge. Sooner or later she would come across a village or a traveler who could direct her toward Dwyrain.

And what then? Give up? Live as Holt's wife? Nay! She'd plead with her father and Father Timothy or the local abbot to have her marriage annulled. *Why?* So that her father could insist she marry another man, one no better than Holt? What other options did she have? Life in a nunnery? Or could she find a hut where she could grow and sell herbs and mix potions as she'd watched Rue do?

"Oh, bother," she muttered under her breath as a cloud passed over the moon and the night grew dark. She picked her way carefully, slipping on rocks, holding on to branches and roots that grew out of the bank, and telling herself she was glad to be rid of that wild group of cutthroats and thugs. She was better off away from them, including grumpy Odell and sweet Robin. Now she wouldn't have to feel Wolf's intense eyes on her, nor would she have to train hers away from the unforgiving lines of his face—masculine, rugged, and sensual. When his eyes sought hers, she felt as if hundreds of butterflies filled her stomach. Her heart pounded so loudly that she was certain the entire camp could hear it. When she felt his gaze on the back of her head she had to force herself not to turn around and search his face for just a tiny bit of nobility that she was certain was visible in his unforgiving countenance if only she knew just where to look.

As if it mattered. Now she had to walk to the nearest town, steal a horse if needs be, and hurry to Dwyrain before either Holt or Wolf found her.

The clouds parted again and the river glimmered silver in the wavering moonlight.

"Did you really think you could escape so easily?" Wolf's voice, the merest of whispers, reverberated through the canyon as well as her heart.

Whirling, she saw his dark form sitting insolently on a mossy boulder not 10 feet from her. "I . . . I was thirsty and wanted a drink . . ."

He laughed so loudly she jumped. "A drink?"

"Aye."

Clucking his tongue, he shook his head. "Is the water better here than down at the chapel?"

"I thought—"

"You thought you could escape, that you could elude me and . . . what? Walk the entire distance back to Dwyrain this night?" When she didn't answer, he stretched to his feet, a tall man looming in the darkness. Slowly he advanced on her. "Come, Megan," he said gently. "'Tis cold out here."

"As if you care for my comfort."

"I do," he said, though his tone was tinged with mockery.

"Then return me to Dwyrain."

"All in good time."

"For the right amount of gold."

"Aye," he said, and the smile left his voice. She felt his gaze move to her lips. "Why else?"

"I know not." She was quivering inside and was afraid it

wasn't from the wind that cut through her clothes as it tore down the valley. No, her trembling was because he was close to her, so close that the toes of his boots touched hers.

"Come inside."

"Nay."

"You would defy me?" There was a hard edge to his voice.

"I will not be ordered about like a slave!"

"Mother of God," he growled under his breath and one hand reached forward to clasp her upper arm. "If you haven't yet noticed, Megan, I'm not a patient man!"

"Nor I a patient woman."

"Get back to the chapel and be thankful that I don't put you in chains—"

She gasped and tried to draw her arm away. "What kind of beast are you?" she said, fury spurting through her veins. "You drag me away from the castle against my will—"

"Liar." The word was spoken so softly she barely heard it, and yet it echoed through her heart over and over again, repeating itself and mocking her. He dragged her closer to him, so close that even in the night she saw the breeze move through his hair and the reflection of the moon in his eyes. Her traitorous heart beat faster. "You wanted to be free of the castle," he guessed, his breath caressing her face as he stopped in front of her. "There was a part of you that longed to soar away from all the thick walls and responsibilities."

"Nay," but the lie tripped on her tongue.

"And freedom isn't all that you want," he said, fingers nearly punishing in their grip, moonlight splashing over the ruthless planes of his face. "There is more, much more," he said, and a cold sweat beaded beneath her hair at the suggestion in his words.

"More?"

"'Tis the reason you flee now." His fingers became more gentle and she saw his throat work.

"Which is?"

"Me. You're afraid of me and what your heart is telling you."

"I know not what you say—"

"Liar." Again that damning word. "You feel it, too, Megan," he said.

"What?"

He was so close she smelled the lingering scents of smoke, leather, and the earth all mingling together and causing her pulse to pound. "The wanting."

"Wanting?" she repeated, feeling silly.

"The wanting between a man and woman." His breath fanned her face and she felt his heat through his fingers—hot, hungry, pounding.

Her skin prickled in anticipation, though she could not give in to the wanton thoughts that heated her blood. True, she'd thought fleetingly of seducing him, of finding a way, any way, to have her marriage annulled, but she couldn't so callously cast away her virtue to this . . . this criminal. "I want you not," she lied, trying to deny that which had caused her so much pain. "I'm married—"

"Aye, to mine enemy." His eyes were a dark blue, the color of the sea at midnight, and his face, handsome though it had once been, showed the ravages of battle, a scar that cleaved one eyebrow, a nick on his ear that was visible when the wind tossed the hair from his face. The Wolf, they called him, and so like that frightening beast he was.

"I—I cannot."

"But you will," he said, as if the knowledge had been with him since her capture, as if he'd planned to bed her before she could even lie with her husband. She swallowed hard and his gaze drifted to the circle of bones at the base of her throat. "You're a sweet liar, Megan of Dwyrain, but your eyes give you away." One callused hand reached forward, twining in the thick strands of her hair to brush her nape. "You need the wind in your hair, the song of the falcon in your ears, the power of a steed beneath you." His hand slid lower to surround her throat in a grip that was as powerful as it was gentle. "You need a man who can tame your wild spirit, a man whose black heart is a match for your own."

"Nay," she whispered, but her lips trembled and her skin, where he touched her throat, throbbed. "Please," she said, then cleared her throat. "Unhand me."

"Oh, I will, little one, but not before you admit it. Say the words."

"I cannot."

"You want me."

97

"Nay," she cried again as he drew her near. His lips were close enough to hers that she could fairly taste him.

His smile was that of a devil. "Then prove me a liar," he ordered before drawing her body to his and claiming her mouth with a hard, savage kiss that seared through her blood and pierced her very soul.

She wilted against him, her body having a will all its own. His hands splayed over her back and beneath her clothes, her skin tingled, ready and anxious. She didn't cry out when he pushed her against the trunk of a tree and fit his body intimately to hers. She felt his heat, his need, the soft throb of desire that ran from his veins to hers.

His tongue tickled the seam of her mouth and she opened to him, thrilling as he groaned and rubbed against her. Wild, hot, and decidedly sinful thoughts ran through her mind as his fingers slid lower to cup her buttocks and hook around her leg, jerking forward so that her thigh surrounded his.

"Megan," he growled as he lifted his head and let out a long, quivering breath. "God in heaven, you are a temptress." His eyes glazed as he dropped her leg and gasped for breath. She nearly stumbled, but he caught her. "Come, this is madness!"

"I cannot, will not—"

"I'll not hurt you, little one, if that's what you fear."

"But—"

"Trust me," he whispered, and she wanted to—oh, how she wanted to believe. In her mind's eye, she saw herself staying here with this man, envisioned what life would be without the comforts of the castle, the warmth of her family. He kissed her again, so soundly she could barely breathe.

When he lifted his head, he stared at her long and hard. "Mother of Moses," he whispered.

She expected him to take her in his arms again, but he stepped away, holding only her hand. Disappointment welled in her heart, and her legs were as strong as Cook's pudding when she tried to walk. He half dragged her back to the chapel and she couldn't stop her heart from racing at the thought of the night alone with him, the night stretching ahead. Not that she could kiss him again, not that she would let him touch her, not that she would . . . At the bend of her thoughts, she bit her lip and followed him through the door, across the cold stones, and then gasped as he pulled her down on the pallet with him.

"I'll not sleep with you—"

"You have no choice."

"Nay. I'm married—"

"An excuse, m'lady."

"Wolf, I cannot—" But her protests were silenced by a kiss that burned through her body.

When he lifted his head, she felt him shudder. "Sweet Jesus," he said, as much a prayer as a blasphemy. "Now, Megan, do not move. Just lie in one spot. I will lie here with you and I will hold you close so that you do not escape, but I will not touch you in a way you do not wish, and we will sleep. Within days I will send a messenger with a ransom demand and soon you will be home to face your father or your husband."

She swallowed back the urge to cry out that she'd never return to Holt.

As he climbed beneath the covers, he kept his fingers around her wrists, and turned his body so that it was behind hers, fitting intimately against her curves. Her back was pressed against the wall of his chest, her calves brushed his shins, and her buttocks fit in the crook of his waist and crotch. Closing her eyes, she felt his manhood, hard, wanting, nearly quivering as it was pressed against her buttocks, but he didn't move, just held her close and tried to sleep. She didn't dare even twitch, afraid of what one small movement might cause, certain the simmering heat in her blood would spark to life. Never before had she experienced true wanting—the hunger between a man and woman—but right now she understood that desire all too well.

Holding Megan against him, Wolf gritted his teeth. Her body was warm and fragrant and he wanted to bury his face in her locks and make love to her until dawn.

Sleep eluded him and images of her, naked and willing, filled his wayward mind and caused his eager member to harden and swell. He'd been a fool, dallying with the woman, teasing Holt, keeping her rather than ransoming her right away. But the money had been of no consequence; Holt's humiliation had been the prize.

Now the situation had changed. Keeping Megan with him was not so much punishment for Holt, but sweet torment for Wolf. He couldn't look at her without wanting, couldn't speak to her without wondering what it would feel like to lie with her, couldn't hear her footsteps without his heart tripping a little more quickly.

He must be mad. What would he want with a beautiful, feisty tart with a tongue like the sting of the whip? Why did the woman fascinate both him and his men? He saw how easily she flirted and how half his soldiers were willing to do her bidding. Even mean-tempered Jagger smiled when she was around, and Robin—the boy was smitten.

'Twas strange how most of the men accepted her, though they had a solid unwritten law that no woman could be a part of their band. Some of them appeared half in love with her, others amused by her, still others restless and prone to fighting, like bucks interested in a single doe.

The sooner he was rid of her, the better for all—and Holt's money could be put to good use. But the thought of returning her to his enemy, the idea that Holt might take some of his fury out on her, the merest inkling that Megan would lie with him, caused a burning in Wolf's guts, a painful jealous heat that kept him awake as he held her small wrists in his hands and felt the rise and fall of her chest against his knuckles.

Why not bed her? Why not seize his ultimate revenge against Holt and strip her of her virginity, not brutally as Holt had allowed Tadd to rape Mary, but slow and with care, making her quake with wanting, feeling her go limp and hot with desire? She would be supple and willing, and oh, the sweet rapture of it.

He squeezed his eyes shut and clenched his body against the vision of her lying naked and pure beneath him. No, he could not soil her, could not defile her, could never make love to her, as she was another man's wife. And yet he wanted her, with an aching lust that stormed through his blood and clamored in his brain. Her rump brushed his cock and he thought of the sweetness of entering her, of hearing her pant against his ear, of listening to the sweet moans from her lips.

She wasn't what he expected. She claimed she loved not Holt, and Wolf clung to that thought, though he damned himself for caring. *Oh, Megan. What am I to do with you?* She touched a dangerous, rebellious part of him, a part that caused him to second-guess his plan. Strong and determined, she claimed to want to return to Dwyrain, yet he sensed the hesitation in her voice, that a part of her would like to remain free of castle life, away from her responsibilities.

Though she was a prisoner with the outlaws, she had no castle walls that bound her, no duties to perform as Ewan's eldest daughter, no Mass to attend. She had found a new kind of freedom, and she embraced the nomadic life as Wolf once had before he'd become jaded and tired of moving from one spot to the next, forever looking over his shoulder while outrunning the law.

There was a time only a few months back when Wolf had been offered his freedom, when he'd met his family at Abergwynn, but he had yet unfinished business with Holt. Once through with this, he silently swore to himself, he'd give up his black-hearted ways and return to Abergwynn, which was all well and good, but what would he do with Megan? Could he really ransom her back to a husband he knew to be cruel and ruthless?

She sighed softly and he felt his cold heart of stone begin to crack.

❈ Six ❈

Holt's hands curled into fists. He wanted to bash the sheriff's thick skull against the wall in the great hall. Servants cast worried glances his way and shuffled hurriedly from the room, hiding behind tapestries, as they wanted no part of his wrath. The two men who'd come with the sheriff stood near the door like trained dogs, not saying a word, not accepting the wine that Holt had offered.

"The man is an outlaw," Holt said slowly, as if the dolt hadn't heard correctly. "And he stole my wife. I want him and his pack of criminals found and brought back here, and justice served."

"I know, I know," the sheriff, a doddering old fool named Herbert, agreed. He belched into his cup of wine, then took a long gulp. Holt wanted to strangle him for sitting on his fat rump when he should be off chasing thieves and kidnappers. "Wolf's been a pain in my arse for a long time as well. I've got my best men tracking him down."

"Do they know where he is?"

Herbert scratched his head and scowled. "Nay, but he's a slippery one, that Wolf is." He finished his cup and eyed the wine jug longingly. "How's the baron? Heard he collapsed at the wedding celebration."

"'Tis true. Losing Megan has nearly killed him," Holt said, gladly shoving some more guilt onto the corrupt sheriff's conscience.

Herbert turned his eyes away from the wine. "And where

does that leave ye? If the baron dies, will ye, as Lady Megan's husband, become the new lord?" He rubbed his palms on the front of his dirty breeches. "A sticky problem, eh? Since your wife was stolen away before ye bedded her." Struggling to his feet, he cast one last baleful glance at the wine, then snapped his fingers to the two guards he'd brought with him. "Worry not, Sir Holt. We'll find the rotter." He marched out of the hall with surprising speed for one so heavy. His two soldiers followed without a word, treading after the old fool blindly. For a second Holt experienced the sharp pang of jealousy. Would any of the soldiers guarding Dwyrain obey him without question? Fight to the death?

As Herbert had so pointedly reminded him, the castle was not quite his. Should Ewan die, Dwyrain by rights would fall to Megan, and, as her husband, Holt would inherit the castle, but since the marriage had never been consummated, it could be easily annulled. If Megan were found dead before the old man gave up his ghost, the castle and lands would revert to Cayley, and then Holt would be left with nothing. All his plotting—years of scheming and allying himself with Ewan—would be for naught.

Snarling at a page to bring him more wine, Holt refused to be thwarted. There was blood on his hands already, and the poison he was slipping into the old man's cup was slowly working.

He didn't mind hurrying Ewan to his grave more rapidly than nature intended. But he couldn't be foolish enough not to make sure that he inherited the castle. If it fell to Cayley and she married Gwayne of Cysgod . . . By the gods, it looked as if he might have to find a way for Megan's younger sister to meet with an accident.

That particular thought wasn't pleasing. Killing women was difficult because of the joy they could give a man. Fingering the hilt of his knife, he frowned. Nay, the answer was not to take Cayley's life. He had promised her to Connor, but there might be a more permanent solution. Why not double-cross Connor and marry her off? This thought appealed to him. However, right now he had to find Megan and that damned outlaw.

* * *

Near the morning fire, Wolf talked in low tones to his men, pointing emphatically to Bjorn before spying Megan as she carried a basket of herbs she'd collected near the creek. Several heads swiveled her way and ears burned a bright red at her approach. She'd never before intruded on one of their meetings, meekly allowing them to discuss her and her fate, but she was tired of being treated as if she had no say in what was to happen. She dropped the basket with a thud and it landed at Odell's feet.

"What's this?" she asked, plopping down on the cold ground where the men squatted. Several had knives and were drawing in the dirt, as if making maps.

"We're discussing what to do with you," Wolf said, his eyes burning with fury at her indignation.

"Without talking to me?" She let her eyes rove to each man.

Jagger cleared his throat and sheathed his knife. Bjorn's smile widened, but he found interest in cleaning his fingernails with his blade. Odell muttered under his breath and stoked the fire with a long stick, and Robin's eyes slid away. Only Wolf held her stare with an intense glare that nearly made her flinch.

"So what plan have you chosen, hmm?" she asked, defying the leader of these men.

"Ransom." Wolf rocked back on his heels. "We just haven't decided how much."

"No? I think 'twould be easy."

He raised his split brow, inviting her to continue.

"How about thirty pieces of silver?" she asked, then dusted her hands, stood, and whirled, storming away from the fire toward the chapel.

"Ouch," Odell muttered. "That stings a mite, don't it?"

Bjorn had the nerve to laugh and Wolf, seething, couldn't resist rising to the bait. He followed after her, catching up with her at the ruins and dragging her inside. "I thought you'd want to return to your castle."

"Did you? And what of my husband? Did you think I wanted to see him again? Did I not tell you that I married for duty? You know I love Holt not!"

His jaw clenched so hard it ached. Her face, fresh-scrubbed with water from the river, turned up and her tangled hair fell around cheeks flushed with color. Her fists were curled as if she'd like nothing better than to batter his chest and her eyes, the color of light ale, snapped fire.

"My father will find you, Wolf," she said. "And when he does, he will have no mercy on your black soul. 'Twill be as if hell itself were unleashed on you!"

"Your father is not the man he once was," Wolf said, refraining from telling her that he'd learned only this morning that Ewan of Dwyrain was gravely ill. Jagger had ridden late last night to meet with spies in the castle, and the word was not good. Ewan, after collapsing just after Megan's kidnapping, had become inattentive and confined to his quarters. The priest and Cayley visited him often and he was bedridden, surely dying. By rights, Megan should be with him, to ease his suffering and to be within the castle when he died, so that she, or Holt as her husband, could rule the keep.

"My father will not rest until I am safely returned."

"And your husband?"

She shuddered visibly, her skin turning pale. "I will talk to Holt," she said.

"And say what? That you changed your mind? That you were marrying him only as an obligation and now you feel no need? What?" he asked, unable to resist moving closer to her and watching her lips. They trembled slightly and her pulse, so visible at the open throat of his old tunic, fluttered.

"I have not decided."

"Time is running out," he said, and the irony of his words reflected in her eyes. Their time together was fleeting as well.

She was the first to look away. "So that's it, then. You'll send a messenger to Holt."

"Have I not promised as much?" Guilt sliced through his heart at the tightening of her mouth. What would her fate be with the man who had held down a sweet maiden while another raped and used her? How could he ever release Megan to such a beast? He'd once thought that Holt's humiliation would be enough to satisfy him, but he'd been wrong. Now, because of Megan and his fear for her, Wolf wouldn't be satisfied with less than the bastard's death.

He reached forward, tracing the slope of her cheek with the tip of his finger. "I meant not to hurt you, Megan."

"Ha!" But she quivered beneath his touch.

"I wanted only to wound Holt."

"Nay, Wolf. 'Tis more than that. 'Tis not only the wounding you wanted, but also the savoring of your vengeance." She stepped away from him and shook her head, her red-brown curls brushing her shoulders. "Whatever it is that makes you hate Holt so, you nourish it, feed it, keep it alive. You delight to think that you thwarted him, that he is vexed because you are cleverer than he, but you will not be satisfied to return me to him. Whatever this rift is between you two, 'twill not be mended by gold coins." She shoved aside his hand and looked up at him with disdain. "Money will not ease your pain, nor will causing Holt a smidgen of humiliation. Nay, this—whatever it is—that festers in you will be cleansed only by your death or his."

The truth of her words cleaved all hope he bore of purging himself of his burden of hate. Had she not voiced what he had already considered? She turned away from him, but he grabbed her arm, spun her to face him. Without another thought, he held her fast, as if afraid she would disappear, then captured her mouth in his.

"No," she whispered, but opened her mouth to the pressure of his tongue. Small and yielding, her body fit against the harder contours of his. Her mouth was sweet, and Wolf's mind swam with hot images of making love to her. He pressed harder, shoving her back against the wall, one hand reaching upward to feel the weight of her breast. Even through the coarse fabric, he noticed her nipple harden, and a part of him lost all control. He reached beneath the hem of her tunic and soft chemise to her warm, waiting flesh.

"Wolf," she cried as his fingers scaled her ribs slowly, laying siege steadily. Her breathing was rapid and shallow, her mouth an open invitation as he kissed her.

The swelling between his legs was hard and hot and needing release. He skimmed her nipple with his fingers and she sighed into his open mouth.

Lord help me, he silently prayed, but he couldn't resist her sweet temptation and he lifted the coarse tunic over her head. Then, through the thin fabric of her chemise, he touched her with urgent fingers. Moaning, she leaned closer as he kissed her eyes, her neck, her throat. His blood thundered in his ears. Surely he was crossing some forbidden line, and in so doing, damning them both, but he couldn't stop.

"I . . . I cannot," she insisted, trying to push away, but he was strong, and as she twisted from him, he slid his arms around her, his hands cupping both her breasts as he held her close to him, and he kissed the back of her neck, leaving a trail with his tongue. Through his breeches his hard, stiff member was pressed against the valley of her rump. "Wolf, please—" she murmured, and he turned her again, looking into her eyes, searching her face before he kissed her with all the passion that seared through his blood. Her resistance was without conviction, and soon her arms wrapped around his neck and she was clinging to him, her breasts rising and falling beneath the chemise, her mouth such soft, sweet wonder.

He dragged them both to his pallet, and there, nestled in the furs, she gazed up at him, her eyes filled with surrender as his heart beat a wild, primal cadence. Slowly, he untied the ribbons of her chemise, parting the light cloth, exposing exquisite white flesh.

With a finger, he rolled the fabric back until both her breasts were visible, straining upward, a slight image of tiny veins beneath her skin, her glorious pink tips hard and wanting. He thought she would blush or turn away, but she stared straight into his eyes, and when he lowered his head and brushed a feather-light kiss across one sweet bud, she sighed deep in her throat. "This is wrong," he growled, and again the dark nipple puckered expectantly.

"Aye, we cannot."

"We mustn't," he agreed, but lowered his mouth around the sweetness of her skin and touched his teeth and tongue to the ripe, willing mound.

With a cry, she arched her back and he caught her, big hands splaying over the curve of her spine, holding her tight as he suckled, like a hungry babe, wanting so much more, feeling her tremble with her own desire.

"Wolf," she cried, and it was more a plea than protest. His groin was tight and he thought only of lying with her, of thrusting into the warm, moist haven that was hidden between her legs, of coupling with her far into the night. Still kissing her, he moved, rolling atop her, spreading her legs with his knees, gazing down at her naked breasts and beautiful flushed face. It would be so easy to love her . . .

And then what? She was married to Holt, a woman pledged to another. In that instant, that small flame of nobility, the one he'd tried so desperately to extinguish, sparked in his brain and he knew that he could never have this woman; no matter what, she was married to another man. No matter that Holt was his sworn enemy, no matter that she'd never loved him, no matter that she'd never lain with him, 'twas a sacrament he couldn't break. With all the effort he could gather, he rolled off her and away, landing on his feet and swearing roundly.

"For the love of Christ, what am I to do with you?" he asked, breathing hard, squeezing his eyes shut, pinching the bridge of his nose as he willed the wild heat roaring through his blood to cool.

"I thought you were going to ransom me," she said saucily, though she was dying inside. What had she just done? Nearly given herself to this man—this criminal who had told her that he was sending her back to her husband for a few coins?

Shame colored her cheeks, but she stiffened her spine as she tossed on the old tunic and shook her hair off her face. "If you're going to sell me, Wolf, be done with it!"

"I told you, 'tis not the money."

She tied the strings at her neck and said, "I believe not a word you say." A tic developed under his eye, and she should have felt some sort of satisfaction for vexing him, but the truth of the matter was that she was wounded inside. She'd never felt such longing, such craving for a man, and the way she'd acted like a hot-blooded wench, writhing and wanting him to lie with her, brought fear deep to her heart. 'Twas not wise to give a man such power. 'Twas not wise at all.

"Father . . . please, wake up," Cayley said softly as she took Ewan's hand in her own. She knelt in the rushes by his bed. His two hounds lay next to him, their ears perked, their suspicious eyes trained on her. Each day, Ewan appeared weaker. His skin was cool and paper thin, his eyes mere slits.

"Has . . . has Megan returned?" His voice was but a rasp, far from the loud bellow that used to announce his arrival. It had been long since she'd seen him stand without a cane or heard him tell a ribald joke, which had always earned him an elbow in the ribs from his wife.

"Nay, there is no word of Megan, but Rue told me that you refused your dinner."

"I have no hunger."

"Please," she pleaded, but his eyelids closed again and he drifted off, as he did often when she visited. His breath was so shallow it barely ruffled the soft hairs of his moustache. She couldn't imagine life in the castle without him. Who would she turn to? Who would perform the duties of the lord? So many people depended upon him, and she loved him with all her young, willful heart. *Please, Father, do not die. Stay with me here at Dwyrain. I have no one else. . . .* And that was the sad truth. If Ewan died, then her only family was Megan, the sister with whom she'd spent so much time arguing and fighting. Even the love of her life, Gwayne of Cysgod, no longer visited. There were ugly rumors that he was betrothed to someone else and Cayley felt disappointed, but not the great heartrending sorrow she had expected.

With all the trouble in the castle, she felt as if the very walls of Dwyrain were tumbling in upon themselves, just as it had been foretold by that snake of a prophet. If only she could have one chance at that pathetic worm of a man, she'd spit in his face and curse him to hell. He was the reason for all of the trouble at the castle, not Megan.

Please, Lord, see her safely home.

The terrifying thought that Megan might already be dead crossed her mind, but she pushed the idea firmly aside. Megan was too strong, too stubborn, too cursedly defiant to die. And surely the outlaw did not steal her from within the castle walls just to kill her. Or did he?

Nay, she wouldn't believe it. When she conjured up the face of Wolf, for he was now blamed for the kidnapping, she envisioned strong, forceful features, a countenance set by fierce determination, a powerful enemy, but she did not consider him a murderer. And soon he would be found. Holt wouldn't rest until he was flushed out and captured.

She should have felt a flicker of hope in those thoughts, for she had once trusted Holt, believed in him as her father did, thought him a capable leader and honest man. But lately, she had discovered her first misgivings. He surrounded himself with men she did not trust. Connor, a knight who kept Holt's counsel, was a hard-hearted man with eyes that missed nothing, and Kelvin of Hawarth was a simpleton who appeared to enjoy other people's suffering. Jovan, the apothecary, was reputed to be a miser who would sell his own daughter's virtue for the right price, and Cayley had seen him once in Holt's company.

Holt himself was more than troubled and worried over Megan's disappearance. In his agitation, he showed another side to himself.

"Oh, Father, you must wake up and take your place as baron," she said, desperation and fear clutching her throat. For the first time in her life, Cayley felt as if she could rely on no one but herself, and that feeling scared her half to death. Were the situation reversed and she the one captured, Megan would have known what to do. Megan had always called her weak, and now, finally, Cayley understood why. She didn't have the first notion how to help her sister.

There was a soft knock on the door and one of the dogs growled low in his throat. The other lifted her nose aloft, sniffed the air, and snarled. Cayley, who had been kneeling at her father's bedside, climbed quickly to her feet just as Father Timothy entered. One look at the bed and he sighed, crossing himself as he said a quick prayer for the baron's recovery, keeping a wary distance between himself and the sharp teeth of the hounds.

"He is no better?"

Cayley shook her head. "Nay."

"Mayhap 'tis his time," the priest said as he moved closer, and one dog leaped to his feet. With lowered head, the fur on the back of his neck bristling, the male growled a low warning. His mate, a bitch with dark spots, pulled back black lips to expose her wicked fangs. Her eyes never left the priest's soft throat.

He swallowed and his tongue rimmed his lips nervously. "Must the dogs be kept in here?"

"'Tis what Father wants."

"But they are dangerous and should be chained outside near the gate."

Cayley never had much cared for Timothy. "Mayhap you would like to take them to the gatekeeper."

The priest's thin lips drew tight, as if a drawstring had pursed them. "Mayhap one of the guards should slay them both."

"My father would not be pleased."

Father Timothy offered her a patient, tenuous smile. "I was only joking, child. These beasts shall stay with the baron. Now, let us pray," he suggested, and though his words had a soft, even cadence, the thin man who was baron did not move beneath his blankets and the hounds who guarded him never gave up their tense, growling vigil.

The priest was in the middle of the third decade of the rosary when the door swung open and Holt strode in. He stopped near the fire, surprised to find anyone with the baron. Father Timothy, unhappy about being interrupted, motioned Holt to close the door and fall to his knees as the priest continued his litany. Cayley shot a glance at her brother-in-law and her heart turned to ice. How had she ever thought him handsome or kind?

Strong he was and possessing an authority few questioned, but there was a menacing cruelty about him she hadn't noticed before. 'Twas as if she'd been blind and some angel had touched her eyes and given her sight.

When the prayers were finished, Holt helped Cayley from her knees. "Your father, did he awaken?"

"Only long enough to ask about Megan," she said just as the sentries gave up a shout. There was a pounding on the door, which flew open, and one of the guards, breathless and smiling, snapped to attention in front of Holt. "The sheriff and some of his men have returned," he announced.

Cayley's heart knocked in anticipation.

"They've located Wolf and my wife," Holt said, his eyes flaming with triumph and vengeance.

"Nay, m'lord," the guard replied and Holt's jaw turned to granite.

Cayley bit hard on her lip.

"Why have they returned?"

The guard slid a glance to Father Timothy. "They found a man in the woods, a sorcerer lurking about the forest of Dwyrain, a man who limps."

"The crippled prophet?" the priest asked, a look of fear sliding through his eyes before he straightened his spine.

"Aye."

Holt's face grew thoughtful. "Bring him to my chamber."

"Should he not be chained and locked in a dungeon? He's nothing but a heathen," Father Timothy protested.

"There's time for that later. First, we needs discover what he knows."

Cayley started to follow the men out of the room, but Holt, hearing her footsteps, stopped at the door and turned on her. "This concerns you not, sister-in-law."

"It concerns me greatly," she argued. "He may be the man who cursed Dwyrain, and if he is, I want to be the first to condemn his soul to eternal damnation!"

❧ Seven ❧

"This is the sorcerer who cursed Dwyrain?" Holt said, eyeing the pathetic creature the guards held in the gate-house. He was tall and thin with the coarse, tattered clothes of a beggar and a mud-colored cape with a hood that had been yanked from his head. His hair was lank and uncut, his beard a scraggly uneven growth hiding his chin. His hands were bound and shackles hobbled his gait, but he appeared calm and fearless, mayhap even a simpleton.

"Cursed?" the man said, and when he looked into Holt's eyes, the would-be baron felt certain fear. This man was no weakling as he'd first thought, and his soft-spoken voice was deceptive—the truth lay in his eyes, cold and blue as a clear winter morning. "I cursed nothing."

Cayley, who had the nerve to defy Holt, strode up to the captive. "Are you not the sorcerer who met Megan in the woods two winters past?"

The man's smile was crooked and self-deprecating, indicating the kind of humble intelligence that caused a tremor of fear to pierce Holt's heart.

"Aye, I came upon her in the forest. Her mare was lame."

"You healed the horse and cursed us all!" Cayley cried, fury twisting her face. "Mother, Bevan, even tiny Roz—" Flinging herself at him, she began to batter him with her fists and Holt didn't stop her. If this man were as powerful as was believed, then he could shield himself from her blows, untie the ropes that bound his hands and feet, and stop her, but he didn't. Instead he stood proudly, unflinching, and didn't say a word as she cursed him and flailed mercilessly at his face and chest.

"By the gods," Reginald muttered under his breath. "Has she lost all sense?"

"Cayley—" Holt finally restrained her, but not until most of the fight had left her and she was sobbing pitifully, tears running from her eyes, her throat so clogged she could barely speak, her pain raw as the wind that tore through the outer bailey. "Take her away," he said to several of the guards, and she fought them off.

"Unhand me!" she cried.

The guards stopped for a second.

Holt's fury grabbed his tongue. "I said, 'Take her away.'" Were all his men so soft they wouldn't restrain a woman? God's eyes, he was surrounded by fools. Pitiful fools. Soon, he would take care of this stubborn woman. Cayley was fast becoming a thorn in his side. The sooner he got rid of her, the better.

"Don't touch me! I'm still the baron's daughter."

The man held prisoner said in a voice as calm as deep water, "Megan is safe, Lady Cayley."

Holt's gut twisted. "Know you where my wife is?" he demanded, new rage burning through his blood.

"Nay, only that she's safe." The prisoner's face was so untroubled Holt felt another sharp jab of fear. The man should have been furious for being restrained, resentful that the hellcat of a woman had attacked him, or, if not angry, then afraid for his very life that he was to be held in the castle to which he brought such tragedy and pain. But he was serene, as tranquil as a lazy summer day.

"Where is she? Who is she with?"

"'Tis only a feeling," the strange man explained.

"So you don't *know* she's safe? 'Tis but a *sense?*"

"Aye." The man's gaze moved to Cayley again. "Be strong."

"You lying bastard!" Cayley cried. "You know where she is! You—" Two guards clamped powerful hands around her arms.

The sorcerer stepped forward as if to help her, but he

nearly tripped, his bad leg dragging a bit. A soldier yanked him back and he fell to the gatehouse floor, cracking his head against the worn stones. Cayley gasped, and Holt felt nothing but loathing and fear for this pitiful excuse of a man.

"Throw him into the dungeon," he commanded, "and when he wants to tell me more about where I can find my wife, bring him to me. Otherwise, leave him to rot. No food, no water, nothing!"

Cayley shook her head. "You cannot—"

"You're the one who condemned him to hell, m'lady," Holt sneered. "I'm just carrying out your request."

"Nay—"

"Take her to her room. Place a guard at her door."

"You cannot restrain me."

"You're not in your right mind, I'm afraid," Holt said. "Do not fret, Lady Cayley. 'Tis for your own good."

Megan watched the boiling water steam and thought longingly of a warm bath. Snow was drifting from the dark sky and a cold wind whistled through the surrounding trees, causing their dark, leafless branches to dance eerily. Feeling alone, she shivered. Wolf had left the camp. Again. There were days when he was gone for hours. Sometimes he rode alone; other times, some of his men accompanied him. She was never asked or allowed to ride with him, nor was she told what he did. But when he left, one guard was always asked to watch her closely, and no matter how she flirted with the man or complained of needing time to herself, she was never alone for a minute. No one wanted to incur Wolf's wrath should she escape.

She was surprised how the camp changed when Wolf was away. The men were more silent and brooding, and she felt as if something vital, the heart of their small group, had stopped beating. Even Cormick, the kindest of the lot, was in a foul mood.

"Fool," she muttered under her breath as she plucked the feathers of a goose unlucky enough to have been on the wrong end of one of Robin's arrows. These days, the boy was always off hunting, trying to avoid her, as if sensing that she and Wolf had grown closer.

She dipped the carcass into a pot of boiling water, soaking all the quills and pinfeathers as she'd seen some of the serving girls at Dwyrain do. Working swiftly, she plucked the wet feathers and dropped them into a bucket. Her breath fogged in the air and her fingers grew numb, but she didn't complain. Jagger and Cormick spent hours chopping wood; Peter, brushing the horses and cleaning up after them; Robin, sharpening knives; and others cooking, cleaning, shoring up tents, tanning hides, and mending or polishing weapons. Each man worked hard and complained only a bit now and again.

As the wet feathers stuck to her hands, she glanced at the slate-colored sky. Surely the Christmas revels had begun at Dwyrain. 'Twas that time of year when the castle would be decorated with holly and ivy, and the Yule log—the trunk of a great tree—would be dragged by horses from the surrounding woods and hauled into the great hall to burn for days. Music, wine, dancing . . . she missed it, and thought often of her ailing father. And yet, would she return? If she had no threat of her marriage to Holt, would she think of Dwyrain as her home?

Surely Wolf would send a messenger soon with ransom demands, though he hadn't as yet, and he was cross most of the time, snapping at his men and ordering her about as if she were his servant. He'd taken his post at the door of the chapel, and had never kissed her again. After the day when they'd nearly made love on his pallet, he had not touched her and kept his own counsel. The men had begun to mutter behind his back, remarking on his black mood, and sliding worried glances in her direction.

The day before, Jagger had once questioned him about the ransom and Wolf had leaped to his feet, grabbed his dagger, and demanded to know if the big knight was asking for a fight. Jagger had held up his hands and backed away and Wolf, his jaw working in quiet fury, reminded everyone in the camp that he gave the orders.

Odell had been amused, Robin wide-eyed and frightened, Peter disgusted, and Bjorn ready to take on either man who became victor.

"This is your fault, ye know," Odell had whispered to her later when they were alone. She had been adding chunks of wood to the fire and trying to avoid the smoke while Odell was skewering three skinned rabbits for the spit.

"Mine?"

"Aye. Wolf's got a woman on his mind. Like as not, 'tis ye."

"How can you tell?"

"'Tis easy. Wolf is usually a silent man who leads with a low voice and a strong fist. Of late, he's been moody, growling at the men, expecting perfection, and there's a dark look in his eyes all the time." Carefully, Odell placed the crossbar over the forked sticks that held the meat over the flames. "Anyone who stumbles across the Wolf's path is likely to get a tongue-lashing, if not more. 'E's spoilin' fer a fight, 'e is."

"I don't see how you can blame me."

Odell made a sound of disgust in the back of his throat, then spit into the fire. "Do you not see it?" Gray eyebrows lifted as flakes of snow drifted from the leaden sky. "The way 'e looks at ye, m'lady. I've been with Wolf a long time— years—and I've never seen his expression like this afore." He lifted his hood over his head. "Tell me this, why do ye think 'e's takin' so long to ransom ye, eh? He puts the whole camp in danger—not that we care, mind ye—by keeping ye here, and yet he does nothin' to change things. I'm tellin' ye, it ain't like Wolf."

Now, she finished plucking the bird, then singed its skin in order to remove a few stubborn quills. The task was nearly finished when she heard the thunder of horses' hooves resounding through the forest. Megan's heart soared and she looked up to see Wolf's steed galloping through the underbrush. But the smile on her face vanished when she realized that Wolf wasn't alone and saw the blood on his face and hands. He was holding Robin's slack body, and as the horse slid to a stop, Wolf, still carrying the lad, leaped to the ground.

"Boil more water. Hurry!" Megan ordered Odell as the men gathered around. "Find me some cloth—"

"Bring his pallet into the chapel," Wolf yelled at Peter.

"Dear Lord, what happened?" Megan asked, her eyes settling on Robin's pale face as they hurried into the old building.

"Robin nearly killed himself trying to slay a bear. The animal was wounded and had knocked Robin's quiver to the ground when I came upon them." Peter, hurrying, lay Robin's pallet near the fire and gently, Wolf placed the boy on his bed. Robin gave a soft moan, but his eyes didn't flutter open and he was white as death.

Not waiting for anyone's approval, Megan bent over the boy and lifted his bloodstained tunic to reveal a jagged, bloody rip near the boy's waist. Deep claw marks dug into the flesh but did not slice to his organs. Blood, sticky and hot, was smeared across his white skin. "Hand me that bag," she ordered Peter as she motioned toward the sack wherein her white tunic was hidden. As Peter tossed her the bag, she sent up a prayer, then catching the sack, she opened it, withdrew the tunic, and began ripping it into strips. Peter and Heath built a fire in the chapel where the roof had given way and Odell carried in a pot of near-boiling water. Smoke curled upward through the opening in the rotting thatch and snowflakes drifted into the room, only to melt as they met the heat of the fire.

Please, don't take this young one's life, Megan silently prayed, remembering all the other times her prayers had gone unanswered.

"Now, Robin," she said gently, "you just hold on. We'll tend to you and see that you get better."

Wishing she had the herbs Rue used, Megan soaked some of the strips of silk, then washed the blood away. "Find a needle and thread," she said. "Dominic was mending earlier." Within seconds, she was stitching the wound, hoping the torn flesh would hold, worrying about the blood that continued to flow. She wrapped his torso in the lengths of white silk, and prayed that they would not stain scarlet.

Wolf watched her work in silence, listening to her talk to the boy who could not hear her, noting that she tore up her wedding tunic as if it were already rags. She was efficient and calm, ordering the men as if she expected to be obeyed, stitching confidently, without qualm, offering all of herself for the boy's life—just as Mary had given him his own life back so many years before. 'Twas funny, he thought, for after Mary had disappeared, he'd told himself he never again would care for another woman, never desire one as he had her.

Now, because of Megan, all of his promises to himself seemed foolish and so easily broken.

"Why in the name of the Virgin would he go after a bear?" Odell asked, scratching his head.

Wolf's eyes trained on Megan. "Mayhap to impress someone."

"Me?" she asked, her fingers never stopping their fluid movements.

"The lad was seeking the lady's approval."

"No!" Megan shook her head. "Why would he do anything so foolish?" she asked, but blushed, as if she heard the truth in his words and felt a sense of guilt that he might well be right.

"Because he is smitten with you, *m'lady,*" Wolf said, anger causing the blood to rush from his face, and he shot a furious glance at the outlaws gathered in the decrepit chapel. "As are half the men in this band."

Several of the men visibly started at his accusation and Jagger appeared about to argue, but spying Wolf's white-lipped fury, he had the good sense to keep whatever was on his mind to himself. Jagger cleared his throat. "Methinks you bring us ill luck, Megan of Dwyrain."

"Ahh, then mayhap we're even," she shot back, though her eyes were fixed on Wolf. "You've been the curse of my existence for nearly a fortnight."

"And you'll be mine to the end of my days," he muttered under his breath.

A tiny hole ripped in her heart, but she pretended it didn't exist and went about her work as if she felt no pain, as if his words didn't have the strength to wound her.

When she was finished and the boy was resting, she glanced up at Wolf. "Now, what about you?"

"I'm fine."

"I think not. Lift your tunic."

"What? I'll not—"

"Lift your tunic, Wolf, for you are the leader of these men and they depend upon you." She motioned to the crowd of his followers, who were lingering in the room. "Yea, even I am forced to rely on you, though I detest it."

"Do you?" he said, his eyes narrowing as he lifted his tunic, and she saw his wounds, not as deep as Robin's, but nasty cuts from the swipe of a powerful paw. The slashes across his skin from the day were not his first. Scars of all sizes cut across his dark skin.

"You've been in your share of fights."

"More than my share."

"And flogged as well," she guessed.

His mouth curved into a half-grin that caused her stomach to tighten. "More than once."

"Why?"

"I'm not good at taking orders."

"And what of this?" she asked, running a finger along the cleft of his brow.

"A gift from Tadd of Prydd, so I forget him not."

"'Twas then that you met Holt."

"Aye," he said, his voice sounding far away, as if it were in a cavern, and his face turned fierce, the way it always did whenever Holt's name was brought up.

"Sit," she ordered, and with only a slight hesitation, he did as he was bid, glaring at his men as if he expected some of them to make comments about him taking orders from a woman.

"One of you stay with Robin. Two others—Dominic and Heath—go and retrieve the bear from the other side of the river," Wolf commanded. "It lies near a small knoll in a thicket of oak and ferns. The rest of you have work, do you not?"

With a few glances cast among them, the men took their leave, and she was alone with him again, aside for the still-unconscious Robin. She cleaned his shoulders, abdomen, and back, washing each cut and scrape, sewing only a few stitches in the largest of the claw marks, trying not to notice the ripple of his muscles when he moved or the dark hair spanning his chest and arrowing down to the band of his breeches. Beneath her fingers, his skin was warm, his muscles hard as stone, and his eyes, smoky blue, watched her beneath half-lowered lids. "'Tis true, you know," he said when she'd bitten off a length of thread.

"What?"

"Half the men are in love with you."

"They just haven't had a woman in their midst," she said, feeling her cheeks turn a hot scarlet hue.

"They want me not to ransom you."

"And you, Wolf, what do you want?" she asked, her voice breathless.

He stared at the floor, then studied his hands for a second. When his eyes found hers again, there was regret in his gaze. "I have no choice in this, Megan," he said. "'Tis out of my hands." His lips were blade-thin. "You are wed to Holt."

She choked back a cry of desperation, for she realized then that she was beginning to care for this rogue with his tortured soul and seductive gaze. She'd known from the first time she'd seen him and he danced with her that he could be dangerous to her heart, and later admitted to herself that she was attracted to the demon, but now her feelings had deepened. "As I said, I—I love him not . . ."

"Then you should not have spoken the vows."

"And had I not, I would never have met you." Proudly she lifted her jaw and tossed her hair off her shoulder.

A sad smile touched his lips. "'Twould have been better for all."

From his pallet, the wounded boy moaned, and Megan hurried to his side. "Robin? Can you hear me, lad?"

Groaning, he blinked his eyes and a smile lighted his face. "Is this heaven?" he asked in a rough whisper.

"Nay, just an old chapel." Tenderly, she brushed his hair from his forehead.

"Be ye not an angel?"

Megan felt tears gather in her throat. "I think not, lad."

"Ahh, but ye're prettier than any in heaven," he said before his eyes closed again, and his breathing was once more slow and steady. Adjusting the furs over his body, she glanced over her shoulder at Wolf, but instead of appearing relieved that the boy was coming around, he only glowered through the window at the snow falling to the frozen ground.

"He's right," Wolf finally said, turning to face her again. "You are an angel of mercy to most of these men." He didn't bother smiling. "And I, methinks, am the Devil."

Before she could answer, there was a commotion on the

other side of the rubble that was one of the standing walls. Wolf, pulling on his tunic and mantle, walked through the door with Megan at his heels.

Dominic and Heath had returned. They were leading Robin's gray rounsey, across whose swayed back was the gutted carcass of a great bear. Thick black hair covered the beast and blood was crusted over its nostrils. Its eyes were glazed and dead, its hideous claws sharp as steel.

"Ye gods, what was the boy thinkin'?" Odell muttered as the crowd around the riders grew. Dominic dismounted swiftly, and with the help of Peter and Jagger, pulled the dead bear to the ground. "We'll be havin's a new warm rug, now, won't we?"

Wolf dug his fingers into the dead beast's fur. "Robin will. 'Tis his kill."

Swinging a bloody sword, Heath laughed as he hopped to the ground. "Then why was it your blade we retrieved from the animal's heart?" He tossed the weapon to Wolf, who caught it deftly.

"I would not have slain it, were it not that Robin was in trouble."

"Good thing you were nearby," Odell muttered, sizing up the dead bear. "Or the boy would be dead now, instead of the beast."

Megan's blood chilled at the thought. 'Twas true enough that Wolf, demon though he professed to be, had risked his life to save the boy. Not only were his scratches proof enough, but the fact that the great beast was felled with a sword at close hand rather than an arrow from a distance, only proved to her that Wolf was far more virtuous than he would let anyone, even his most trusted men, believe.

Holt drew back his arrow until his bowstring was tight, then let go. The slim missile sizzled through the air, hitting the target with a snap. The arrow pierced through the tarp, which was painted in the shape of a boar and covered a haystack.

"Good shot," Sir Oswald said. "Right in the bugger's heart!"

Holt snorted at the praise, for Oswald, the ugliest of all the knights, was known to lick the lord's boots for favors.

"Has the sorcerer spoken?" Holt asked, withdrawing another arrow from his quiver and wishing that the painted pig was really Wolf, his tormentor. His eyes narrowed as he focused on the target.

"Nay, well . . . aye, he's spoken, but to the walls, and through the bars to no one. The man is daft, I say."

"Or pretends to be."

"If he were a true magician, why does he not save his skin and disappear from the dungeon, eh? Or why does he limp?"

"Mayhap 'tis all for show," Holt suggested, though the same thoughts had run through his own mind.

Oswald rubbed his flat chin thoughtfully. "Nay, methinks the man's a fraud."

"He has but one more day and then, if he doesn't speak of his own accord, I'll force his tongue."

The toad's eyes gleamed. "Flog 'im, will ye?"

"At the very least." Holt shot again, and his arrow was true once more, piercing deep into the heart of the painted beast. "Or I'll turn loose the peasants who believe he is the reason they lost loved ones to illness or injury." That thought brought a smile to his face. Many would thank him for the chance to seek a bit of personal vengeance for the curse. "Now, Oswald, deliver my message and remind him that I'm not known for my kindness."

The ugly knight, eager to become Holt's pet, lumbered off past the fish pond and toward the dungeons. Holt only hoped he could convey the proper fear to the man whom most believed to be the sorcerer who had cursed the keep.

For two days the prophet had held his tongue, though he'd been given no fresh water or food and had been chained to the wall, where he'd sat in the dirty straw of his cell, his only companions being rats and fleas. But no prodding would make him speak of Megan again. Holt had reasoned with the man, threatened him, and even tried to bribe him, but received no satisfaction. 'Twas as if his newest prisoner had no idea that he was being held against his will, that he was being starved, that he was being punished.

'Twas enough to drive a sane man mad.

Worse yet, the old man wouldn't die. Though he was

being given poison in his wine, Ewan lingered on, floating in and out of consciousness, asking about Megan and conversing with his dead wife as if she were lying in the bed with him instead of rotting in her grave as she had been for nearly two years. Holt had tried to visit Ewan, hoping to aid his ill health along, but each time he'd stopped at the lord's chambers, there were other guests, either the priest or the old hag Rue or sweet, young Cayley. 'Twas as if the old man had guardian angels posted and their vigilance was keeping him alive. Even the damned doctor had made it his practice to visit Ewan each day, checking his urine and telling all that the baron was not improving.

For that, Holt was thankful. Ye gods, if the man didn't die soon, Holt would begin believing in miracles. He thought of visiting old Jovan again, but seeing the apothecary was dangerous. There were too many suspicious eyes in the castle, including those of Cayley, who had once seen him with the old man. He sighed. The baron's second daughter had once trusted him, but now avoided crossing his path. Aye, if he hadn't had other plans for her, he'd bed Cayley himself.

Women, they were difficult to understand, though he tried not. Long ago he'd decided they were put on this earth for only one purpose: to pleasure him.

Wolf drew in an unsteady breath as Megan smoothed the salve over his injured muscles. Outside, the wind howled around the old chapel, but within the decrepit building, it was warm. They sat by the fire, watching the flames throw golden shadows on the stone walls and listening to Robin's even breathing. The boy had awakened but once today, eating only a few mouthfuls, moistening his lips, then drifting away again.

Megan's fingers slid across Wolf's back and over his shoulder. His body stiffened, though not from pain, but the sweet, gentle pressure of her hands. The ointment eased the burning of his wounds, but her hands created another heat, one rising up from the center of him; and he shifted as his manhood swelled against the ties of his breeches. Such sweet, sweet torment.

Grinding his back teeth together, he ignored the desire

throbbing through his veins and prayed noiselessly that it would soon end.

"Tell me of Holt, why you hate him so," she said. "'Tis only right that I should know of him, since you're planning to return me to him."

Wolf's jaw ached from clenching.

Her fingers were more persuasive. "Should I not know the man to whom I'm married?"

"You're married not to a man, but a beast from hell," Wolf said, and whether it was right or wrong, he told her all that he knew of Holt, of how Holt had ridden with Tadd of Prydd and how, while Wolf struggled with consciousness, he had held Mary down so that Tadd could rape her.

The fingers on his back stopped their fluid movements. "Why should I believe you?" she asked. "You are a criminal."

"I only say what I know."

"I believe you not." But there was doubt in her voice.

Wolf whirled around and grabbed her hand before she could touch him any longer. "Believe what you want, woman. You asked and I told. 'Tis simple." Angry with himself, with her, with the world in general, he snatched up his tunic and tossed it over his head. When he looked down at her, he saw the fear in her eyes, knew that he'd been its source, and silently damned himself. She was the root of all his confusion and malcontent, she was the reason he wasn't thinking, she was the reason he felt the need to stay within the confines of the camp rather than to go out riding, and she was the reason he wasn't following his plan and sending her back to Dwyrain where she belonged.

With her husband! He strode outside without his mantle. The breath of winter swept over the land, causing pieces of ice to gather in the stones by the river and dusting the forest floor with snow. He should have been freezing, but his skin was still warm from her touch. Christ Jesus, he'd been such a fool to let her into his heart, for, though he denied it to himself over and over again, she'd gained purchase deep in that locked chamber of his soul. A string of curses rolled off his lips as he crossed the campsite. Some of the men warmed their hands near the fire; others worked in their tents. The bear's hide was stretched on poles, the meat cut away, the claws and teeth saved for Robin when he awakened.

What was he going to do with the woman? What? He had no choice but to send her back to Holt, but his guts ached and his mind burned with foreboding at the thought. Angrily, he spit into the ferns growing near the river. He would have to kill Holt, he decided again, and make Megan a widow. Though she professed not to love her husband and Wolf believed her, killing him would be cold-blooded murder. Despite the fact that Holt had been a part of Mary's rape, he was not wanted by the law; in fact, according to his spies, Holt might very well become the baron if Ewan were to die.

Which was another source of his irritation. Plucking his knife from its sheath, which was strapped to his waist, he squatted by the river and stared into its swiftly moving depths. The plan in which he'd found so much delight was now causing him only pain. Cleaning his fingernails with the tip of the blade, he argued with himself, but could find no solid reason, other than his own selfish lust, to keep her any longer. Her father was dying and he would not hold her prisoner when she might not see the old man again. Mayhap she could get her marriage annulled if she pleaded with Ewan of Dwyrain.

Ah, she was trouble. Sweet, tempting trouble. As Mary had, as Morgana had long ago, Megan touched his black soul.

Would he never learn? Years before, when he was known as Ware of Abergwynn, he was half in love with the woman who would become his brother's wife and lady of the keep. That alone was a curse, but later, he'd lost Garrick's castle to his enemy while left in charge.

Wolf slammed his knife into its sheath and kicked at the icy stones of the bank. He'd never forgiven himself for that mistake, and it wasn't his last, oh, no. Then there was Mary . . . sweet, trusting Mary, turned into a pitiful, withdrawn half-brained woman after Tadd of Prydd had raped her. Closing his eyes, Wolf tried to block out the memory of a panting Tadd rutting on Mary while Holt helped hold the girl down. Her screams reverberated through his brain, haunting him. Once again, he'd been useless.

And now he found his sworn enemy's wife attractive. More than attractive. If he cared not for Megan, he'd love to bed Holt's bride and laugh about it, to send her back to her husband, defiled and dirty. He would never rape her, but he would seduce her. After she lost her heart and virginity to him, he'd toss her back to the man to whom she'd vowed everlasting love and fidelity.

But he couldn't. Because of Megan and that blasted thread of nobility that bound his soul. Try as he might, he was never able to unwind it.

"Hell," he muttered, damning himself again. He had no choice but to send her back.

Injustice gnawing on his guts, he spit again. 'Twas settled. Come morning, he'd send two messengers to ride to Dwyrain with ransom demands. This woman, like every other woman he'd been cursed to care for, would soon be out of his life forever.

Eight

"Oooh," Robin moaned, wincing as he levered himself onto an elbow. "Where—what—ooh!" He flopped down on the bed, and Megan felt tears of relief star her lashes. The boy was alive! He was going to live. She whispered a quick prayer of thanks before taking his rough hand in hers.

"Robin?"

"Go 'way."

"'Tis Megan."

Eyes closed, he moved, his tongue moving over his teeth. "The lady?" he murmured.

"Aye." She squeezed his hand and one of his eyes cracked open, only to close for a second.

"Oh, Lady Megan!" His eyes flew open again, this time clear and bright. "What happened . . . ? Oh, the bear."

"Aye, you and he had a bit of a disagreement, and he got the better of you."

Robin groaned and blushed. "But how did I live?" Trying to raise himself upright, he sucked in a swift breath.

"Careful—you didn't come out of this without a wound or two."

"I feel like dog dung. Did you find me in the forest?"

"Nay. 'Twas Wolf. He came upon you and ran the beast through."

Clarity sparked in the boy's eyes as if suddenly his

memory had returned. "'Tis true," he finally said, and his pale face colored. "I should not have gone after him."

"Not alone," she said, but decided he was punishing himself enough and did not need to be told that he'd been foolish. "If you're feeling well enough, Odell has cooked part of the beast, and 'twould be justice for you to eat a piece of him."

Robin laughed and the sound touched Megan's heart, even though he winced in pain.

"Where's Wolf?" Robin asked, glancing through the dark chambers.

A fine question, Megan thought, for she'd wondered that herself. He'd left the camp hours before with Bjorn and Cormick. Somberly, they'd saddled their mounts and ridden away without so much as a word to her or any of the men. They could be hunting, she decided, though with the bear, they had meat enough for nearly a week. They could be out robbing someone traveling on the road or searching for Holt's soldiers, or they might be in the nearest town, drinking ale, playing dice, and whoring.

She scowled at the turn of her thoughts, for jealousy invaded her blood whenever she thought of Wolf lying with another woman. 'Twas an image that burned in her thoughts each time he left the camp.

"Wolf and some of the men have been gone this afternoon, but when they return, he'll be pleased to see you awake."

Robin struggled to his feet and Megan wanted to restrain him, but didn't. The boy wasn't woozy, though he grimaced a bit as he walked outside and felt a blast of winter air rip through his thin body. She handed him a hooded cloak, which he donned, and Odell, stirring the coals beneath a boiling pot, cracked a smile at the boy. "So ye decided to stay with the livin', did ye? A fine choice, m'boy. Come and see the skin of the beast ye helped slay."

Cackling, Odell led the eager boy to the bearskin, and Megan rubbed her arms against the cold. Though she was this motley band's captive, she'd never felt more free. With no castle walls to surround her, no priest's silent scorn, no duties aside from those of surviving, she experienced a vigor she'd never enjoyed as daughter of the baron.

A sharp whistle and hoofbeats announced Wolf's return. Megan bit down hard on her lip and tried to stop the sudden clamoring of her heart. 'Twas foolish. He cared not for her. As he rode into the clearing, she couldn't keep an expectant smile from creeping over her lips. His gaze touched hers for a silent heartbeat, then landed full force on the lad. "There ye be, Robin," Wolf said, falling into the easy speech of his men. "And Odell, here, had given ye up fer dead."

"Nay, I never said—" Odell protested, but caught the twinkle of devilment in Wolf's eye. "And curse and rot yer soul, ye foul creature of the forest," he said with a grin as he realized he was being teased.

Wolf slid lightly to the ground and touched Robin gently on the shoulder. "If I had any brains, I would have your skin stretched like the bear's!"

Robin folded his lips in upon themselves and stared at the ground.

Wolf wasn't finished. "Goin' after that one"—he hitched his chin toward the glossy black hide drying beneath a tarp—"could've cost you your life."

Robin's gaze didn't falter, but his jaw jutted mutinously and the muscles in his shoulders bulged a bit.

"'E's alive, ain't 'e? Jest a mite clawed up, and we got meat enough fer the week and a fine new robe—"

"The skin is Robin's, Odell," Wolf reminded the older man quickly.

"I know, I know." Grumbling under his breath, Odell ambled back to the fire, and Wolf, locking eyes with Megan for an instant, called a meeting together.

Megan wasn't about to be treated as an outsider any longer. Despite Wolf's hard glare, she walked to the fire and sat on a stump, warming her hands, while the rest of the band gathered together. Meat sizzled over the fire, the flames danced wildly with a breath of wind, and afternoon faded into night.

"There be no women in our midst," Odell said, though not unkindly.

"I'm here. I'm a part of this group, even if only as a 'guest.'" Defiantly, she refused to budge.

"This concerns you not," Wolf said.

"Then why should I have to leave?" Crossing her ankles,

and tucking her arms under her breasts, she turned her face up saucily and smiled, silently begging him to continue.

"Megan, please," he said with a quiet calm that was more frightening than a furious rage. "'Tis man-talk."

"Have I not cooked for you?"

The men exchanged glances, but no one argued.

"Have I not helped mend your torn breeches? And you, Peter, did I not find some softer fabric for your eye patch?"

"Aye," he agreed, though he wouldn't meet her stare.

"And Dominic, when you needed help cleaning the weaponry, did I not offer assistance?" Before he could answer, her gaze swept to Heath. "I've helped you tan hides, and Lord knows I've done my share with Odell."

Several men laughed and nodded their heads.

There was a quiet muttering in the background as Heath whispered something to Peter.

"Have I not cleaned, hunted, and helped make camp?"

"Can't argue there," Robin said, his eyes shining in awe as he looked at her.

She stood slowly, inching up her chin, standing toe to toe with the lord and master of the outlaws, the man called Wolf, the renegade to whom she'd unwillingly given her heart. "And have I not, when you were injured, stitched you together and balmed your wounds?"

A muscle in the side of his jaw tightened.

"Why then, just because I am not a man—nay, because I am your guest—would I not be allowed to listen and speak my mind? Have I not done everything I could to help you?"

"But you tried to escape."

"And failed."

"Why not let her listen in?" Dominic rolled his hands toward the darkening sky.

"Aye, but she's got no say." Jagger, sitting on a rock, hung his hands between his legs and shook his head. "The rule is 'no women—'"

"So be it!" Wolf declared. "Sit, Megan; hear what we have to say, because I lied when I told you the talk is none of your concern." He glanced around the fire to each of his men, their hooded cloaks dusted with snow and their faces illuminated by the golden flames. Megan eased back onto her stump but heard the knell of doom thundering in her ears. "Bjorn and Cormick have already been sent to Dwyrain. In Bjorn's pouch, he carries a letter from me that states that I have Holt's wife and am willing to return her in exchange for gold."

Megan felt as if the world had begun to spin.

"Just like that?" Odell wondered aloud.

"It should have been done a week ago."

"By the gods," Odell whispered.

Megan's heart pounded painfully in her chest. *No! No! No!* she inwardly cried. She could not think of leaving. Not now. Not ever! "You are sending me away?" she asked, her voice catching. Somewhere nearby, an owl hooted mournfully.

"Aye. Your father is ill, Megan," he said gently. "The day I took you from the castle, he fell and had to be carried to his bed, where he has remained."

"Nay!" she cried. She knew, of course, that her father was no longer the strong leader that he'd once been, that ofttimes he'd been confused, that he'd even thought that he talked with her dead mother and Baby Roz, but Megan refused to think Ewan would die soon and refused to believe the painful words. "'Tis but a trick to lure me back there."

"No trick," Wolf said gently, then cast a tormented glance to the stars just starting to appear in the vast, dark sky. "Asides, you needs be with your husband."

"After what you told me of him, you would send me back?"

"'Twas not I who married him," he reminded her. "And in my letter, I've demanded that as part of your ransom, no injury befall you. Should I hear that you are being mistreated, I've vowed to storm the castle, sneak into his bedchamber, and cut out his heart."

"You think a threat will change him?" she mocked.

"Would you rather stay here?" A challenge flamed in his eyes.

"Never!" she lied, feeling torn between two homes, the castle, with its secure walls and comforts, and the forest, where she felt free even though she was held captive.

"So be it." He searched the faces of his men as Megan's heart turned to ice. "We'll wait here for Cormick and

Bjorn's return, then send Lady Megan home, break camp, and move on."

"Bring in the new log," Holt ordered, his face flushed from wine, as peasants and knights guided a huge horse into the hall and rolled the log onto the iron dogs in the fireplace, sending ash and embers flying. Sparks and laughter erupted as Holt lit the new log and watched the dry wood catch fire.

Shouts of "wassail" and "drinkhaile!" floated over the songs being played by the musicians in the gallery, an alcove cut high into the wall facing the lord's table, where Holt sat near a comely seamstress.

The Christmas revels were upon them, the great hall decorated with ivy, holly, and mistletoe, and peasants, knights, servants, and lords all rejoicing. Holt had decreed that there would be merriment in the halls of Dwyrain despite the fact that his wife was missing and the tired old baron was hovering near death.

"If only Lord Ewan could see this," Rue whispered to Cayley as she wiped her hands on her skirt and tapped her foot in time with the drummer. They stood near the stairs, where pages and servants hurried to and from the kitchen. "'Tis a pity he can't join us." Sadness stole through her old eyes.

"Aye, I think I'll take something up to him. Cook's saved him a joint of venison and some pheasant, along with his soup."

"A good daughter ye are, Cayley girl," Rue said, slipping back to the name she'd called Cayley when she was but a child.

Not as good as you think, Cayley thought as she hurried to the kitchen and carried a tray to her father's room. But the baron didn't move when she entered. The tempo of his breathing never wavered, and even though she spoke to him, he remained blissfully asleep, unaware that there was treachery within the castle walls, that Megan had not been found, that the outlaw roamed free. Nay, her father was probably dreaming of happier times when the family was together and his wife and all his children were alive.

"Sleep well," Cayley said, pressing a kiss to his temple and adding more heavy logs to the fire in his room. She tore off big hunks of the meat, wrapped the greasy chunks in a towel, poured wine into his cup, and took the bottle. Her heart thudding in fear at her plan, she left his tray at his bedside and knew that he would eat no more than a few spoonfuls of broth and drink even less wine. Once a robust man, he had wasted to nearly nothing. Something had to be done, and Cayley, though she cringed at the thought, was the only one to do it. Whereas Megan had always leaped at adventure, had ridden as well as Bevan and shot an arrow straight and true, Cayley had been content to be considered silly and pampered, enjoying the attention of men and pretending that she was helpless.

Ofttimes her mother had reprimanded her, telling her that she was lazy and needed to work some around the castle. Lady Violet had insisted that her daughter learn how to embroider, keep the books, and care for the poor by passing out alms—money and any uneaten food in the castle. Violet had even dragged Cayley with her to the nunnery, hoping her second daughter would take an interest in some charity, but Cayley, at that time in her life, had been interested only in herself. She'd seen no reason to do for herself when others, be they friends, relatives, or servants, were willing to do for her.

"Stupid girl," she told herself now, for she had no skills on which to rely and few friends to help her. Oh, if only Gwayne were here, but that thought was not as comforting as it had once been. She'd heard nothing more of his betrothal, but she saw him in a different light and what she had once considered clever, now she thought mean. He was vain and pompous. In all the while he'd courted her, he'd never once spoken of love or marriage.

Well, she had not the time to be thinking of him. She had much to do. Gritting her teeth and wishing she'd taken the time to learn how, if nothing else, to handle a weapon, she set her plan into motion. She'd have to rely upon her wits rather than swords, axes, and arrows. She stopped at her chamber to don her hooded cloak, ducked through the corridor, and was relieved to find no guards at their posts.

Darting down the stairs, her cloak billowing behind her, she slipped through the kitchen and out the door.

The sound of music from lutes and pipes followed Cayley

as she held her skirt high and ran. Her boots sank in the mud and mire as she crossed the inner bailey to the north tower, under which were the dungeons.

"Be with me," she prayed, her voice the barest of whispers as she opened the door to the guardhouse. Curved stairs led ever downward. In the darkness, rats scurried from her path. She carried only a solitary candle, its flickering light reflecting on the cold stone walls, which always appeared wet. The smells of rotting straw, mildew, and urine rose from the dungeon, nearly choking her. The guards, too, were in the keep, their sorry charges left alone in the dank cavern, which held the enemies of Dwyrain.

Shuddering, Cayley made her way down slippery steps and past cells, where eyes gleamed at her from within the gloom.

"Who goes there?" one raspy voice asked.

"'Tis the lady." Another, deeper, voice.

"What lady? Violet?"

"Nay, she's been dead two or three years. 'Tis her daughter."

"A comely wench, say what?"

"Sorcerer?" Cayley said, her voice thinner than usual, a tremor running through it. "Are you here?"

"So you've come." His voice was smooth as the ice that sometimes covered the lake in coldest winter.

"Aye."

She walked on, holding her candle aloft, trying to keep her wits about her when she imagined all sorts of vile creatures swooping out of the darkness at her.

"Good. I have much to say."

She followed the sound of his voice to the lowest cell, where water dripped from the ceiling and the straw on the floor was moist and fetid. The stench was unbearable, the rooms cold as death.

"I have no key," she said, shivering, "but I overheard Holt say that you've been given no food."

"'Tis true."

"Nor water."

"I've survived."

"I don't know how." She held her candle aloft and found him chained to the far wall. "My God," she whispered, crossing herself as before her very eyes he slipped out of his shackles and limped, unbound, across the cell. "How did you—?"

"'Tis not magic, child," he said in his soothing voice. "I found a nail in the old straw and was able to pick the locks. The guards, they know not."

"You're not afraid I will warn them?"

"I think not, though you do not trust me."

"I hated you."

His smile was cautious. "I know." Through the bars he asked, "And now?"

"Now there is trouble dark and deep within Dwyrain, but I think you are not the cause. I—I cursed you, said I wanted you to roast in hell and—"

"'Tis forgiven. Asides, anyone who would steal venison from the lord's table and wine from his mazer would not endanger their only friend."

"You—you are my friend?" she asked as she handed him the bundle of meat and bottle. He ate hungrily and started to drink from the bottle, only to stop and spit the wine on the floor.

"What?"

"'Tis poison you bring!" he said, coughing and gasping.

"No—"

In the candlelight, his eyes turned harsh. "'Tis only a little, but enough, if given over time . . ."

"Dear God, no," she cried, stepping away and nearly dropping her candle. Wax slipped down the metal holder and burned her hand. "'Twas meant for my father. No one else would dare touch wine from his cellar. I brought it to you only so no one would notice." Her throat turned as dry as milled flour and ugly thoughts began to fill her mind.

He eyed her in the darkness, then spit again. "Your father is being poisoned."

"No, I'll not believe . . ."

"'Tis true, Cayley. Whoever is giving him wine each day is making sure that he will die."

She leaned against the wall. "Holt," she muttered, finally understanding why her sister did not trust the knight who would now inherit Dwyrain. "Holt allows no one to take my father the wine except one of his most trusted knights—or Nell. Because of the revels, 'twas forgotten . . ."

"Listen to me, Cayley," the sorcerer said, his voice low and deadly. "You must trust me."

She bit her tongue. Though she wished him no ill will, she could not forget the pain and suffering that had been with Dwyrain these two years past. "Trust you?" she repeated. "Even though you cursed the castle and—"

"I thought you understood, girl!" he said, losing the calm that had been with him each time she'd seen him. His fingers curled over the rusted bars of the cage in which he was kept. "I told Megan only what I saw. It came to pass through no fault of mine, but if you do not listen to me and help me, your father will die, Megan will return to Dwyrain only for Holt to shame her and use her to gain possession of this keep, and you and everyone you hold dear will live as his prisoners."

Wolf stayed out much of the night, but Megan sensed his presence the instant he walked through the door of their chamber in the decrepit old chapel. She'd lain for hours, not sleeping a wink, jumping at every sound.

A few embers glowed red in the fire and he paused to add another log. Lying on the pallet, Megan feigned sleep, while plotting how she would elude him. She would not let him haul her back to Dwyrain like a prisoner. Nay, if she intended to return to Dwyrain, 'twould be her own way. She wouldn't be traded for a few coins, like a sack of flour or prized horse! If this taste of freedom had proved anything to her, 'twas that she was her own woman and she needed no man to tell her what to do.

Soft snoring rippled down the roofless corridor from the chamber where Robin and Odell were sleeping near their fire, but Megan found no comfort knowing they were close by. Whenever she was alone with Wolf, 'twas as if they were the only two souls in the world and she thought of nothing save him.

For the past few nights, Wolf had taken up his vigil at the doorway, watching over her but not lying beside her beneath the furs. 'Twas better, she supposed, as when he was near her, his body molded around hers, her thoughts turned wanton and through the hours of the night, she fought the urge to turn in his arms and kiss him, to kindle the sinful flames of passion that perpetually ignited whenever his skin touched hers.

She heard his boots scrape against the floor. "I know you sleep not," he said and sighed wearily as he slid to a sitting position near enough to the fire that golden shadows were cast upon his face. "I brought you something."

She didn't move, but through slitted eyes watched as he opened his bag and removed a tunic—shimmering green silk trimmed with gold velvet.

"Something to replace the tunic you tore up to bind Robin's wounds."

Unable to ignore his kind gesture, she pushed herself to her elbow and shoved a handful of hair from her face. "Is this what you want me to wear when you return me to Holt?" she asked, unable to keep the sting from her words.

His lips flattened.

"So that he will want me? So that he will take me as his bride?" She couldn't help the hurtful words, and they tumbled out of her mouth in rapid succession, one after the other, meant to wound as she'd been injured.

Tossing the tunic to the floor, Wolf leaped to his feet, strode to the pallet, and yanked her from the covers. His fingers held her fiercely, digging through her chemise to her upper arms and dragging her to her feet. "Understand this, woman," he said in a voice that was nearly a growl. "I want you not to return to Holt, and if there was a way to keep you from him, I would. But there is none. In the eyes of the land and the church you are his wife; you pledged yourself to him and there is nothing I can do about it."

She hoisted her chin upward and narrowed her eyes at him. "Then let me go," she demanded, knowing that deep in her heart it would kill her to walk away from him. "Leave me to my freedom."

"Is that what you want?"

"Aye," she said without hesitation, though deep in the darkest recess of her heart, she knew that what she truly wanted was to stay with him, to be his wife, to become an outlaw's woman. Shame burned up her spine, but she could not lie to herself. This man touched her as no man ever had and none ever would again. She was as certain of that single damning fact as she was of her own name.

"You vex me."

"As you do me."

"You test my will."

"You try mine."

"I cannot have you here with me."

"I know. Oh, dear God in heaven, I know," she said, and her skin, beneath the tense fingers holding her in a death grip, tingled. Her flesh, where his breath brushed over it, heated; her heart, trapped deep in her ribs, hammered anxiously.

His eyes were as tortured as her own condemned soul. "God have mercy on me," he muttered roughly as his lips crashed down on hers, hard and hot, unforgiving and filled with want. Desire trumpeting through her body, Megan sighed, opening her mouth to him, feeling her bones turn to jelly as together they fell upon his pallet.

Passion turned her thoughts around. She would not listen to the doubts swiftly slipping from her mind. Though he was a murdering outlaw, she wanted him. Despite the fact that he could cause her to act like a shameless kitchen wench, she hungered for him. Even though she would be banished for the rest of her life, constantly reminded that she was a wanton harlot, she could not resist him. That she was married was of no consequence; this man, this Wolf, was her one true love.

His kiss was deep and anxious, his moan as fierce as the tide at midnight. Sliding the neckline of her chemise over her shoulder, he pressed warm lips to her bare skin. With a gasp, she quivered inside. In the firelight, his face was composed of deep angles and grooves, dark shadows and golden slopes, and he was anxious as he kicked off his boots.

"I want you," he admitted, his countenance fierce, as if in the saying of the betraying act he would have to fight. He untied the ribbon of her chemise, letting the soft fabric fall open so that he could view her breasts in the firelight. "But you are Holt's wife." He traced the rim of her nipple, that dark ready circle, with the tip of his finger.

"It matters not," she gasped when he found the hard button and rolled it between his finger and thumb.

"Yes . . . yes, it matters." But he pulled her close and clamped his mouth to her breast, kissing, teasing, tasting, laving while she writhed against him. Heat boiled through her blood, and deep in the very depths of her, where she was untouched, she felt a new tingling and warmth, a dark yearning that only he could fill.

She didn't protest when he yanked down her chemise, baring her torso to the shadowy light, looking down at her with the savage possession of one who was used to taking rather than asking.

"You are sure, m'lady?" he asked, his voice ragged as he skimmed the hated flimsy garment down her legs. She lay naked before him, her skin flushed with desire, the nest of curls at her legs dewy with a craving she'd never before felt. She nodded.

"You want me, little one."

"As you want me."

"Aye," he admitted, taking her hand and placing it on the front of his breeches. Through the fabric, she felt his manhood, stiff and upright.

Her throat went dry and she leaned upward, kissing him and sliding his tunic over his wounded shoulders. "Show me."

His lips locked over hers and he rolled her onto her back. Pressed into the rugs, she welcomed his weight as he rubbed against her, his breeches rough upon her skin, the dark hairs that swirled over his chest tickling her breasts. Her skin was afire, her senses alive, and he dragged his mouth from her lips, past her chin, along her neck, and lower, pausing at the circle of bones at the base of her throat.

She bucked as he kissed her breasts again and slid ever lower, his tongue rimming her navel as her fingers clenched in his thick hair. She could scarcely breathe, and her heart was pounding in a wild, uneven cadence as he slid his hands down her legs, slowly and lazily, drawing them up as her mind swam in the warm whirlpool of his love. Writhing against the pallet, she caught her breath when his fingers first touched her in that most private of places and then gently probed, moving slowly at first and then faster as the heat within her grew. She cried out in lust and fear, moving with him, letting him take her on a ride she'd never felt before.

"That's it, little one, give yourself up," he said against her inner thigh, and something inside of her broke, a dam that was holding the heat at bay. Faster and faster he stroked her, sending her hips into wanton thrusting. With a cry, she lifted up, only to fall back to the fur, her skin drenched, her mind spinning. She had trouble finding her breath and her heart would not be quiet, but he was not done.

As if there was more loving to have, as if the earth hadn't splintered before her very eyes, he slid beneath her legs, lifted her rump with his hands, and kissed her more intimately than she'd ever expected.

She convulsed, but he held her tight, whispering into her that 'twould be all right, that she would fly like a falcon again, and before she could protest, he was close to her, his breath hot, his mouth wet, his tongue seeking new areas to plunder. Shuddering, she closed her eyes and bucked upward, wanting more, so much more, until it came, that wonderful hot spasm of release, and the world spun again.

As she cried out, he slid up her body, holding her to his rock-hard muscles, cradling her as the first tears—of joy or sadness, she knew not which—slid down her cheeks. She sobbed brokenly and realized that she cared for him far more than she'd ever dared admit to herself, that she was a soul lost and he was her anchor—that, curse and rot his stubborn hide, she loved him.

❈ *Nine* ❈

"'E just took off. I don't know when, but I woke up needin' to relieve myself and noticed 'e was gone," Odell said, shaking his head and staring at the ground as if he expected Wolf to flog him for letting Robin slip away. A few men had awakened and gathered around though dawn had yet to send her gray light through the valley.

Megan had awakened from a particularly wanton dream when Wolf, his arms surrounding her, had started. "Something's amiss," he'd whispered into her ear, and she knew he was right, for Odell was cursing loudly and angrily. They'd hurried down the crumbling hallway and outside to find him muttering, grumbling, and swearing by the remains of last night's fire. Odell had admitted then that Robin was missing.

"Why?" Wolf asked as he rubbed his jaw and glared at the older man. "He was injured, for God's sake."

"'Twas that he felt like a fool. Embarrassed he was about nearly being killed by the bear. He'd hoped to bag that beast and bring it to the camp so that he would look like a man rather than the boy we take him for."

"He is a boy," Wolf said.

Odell dug at the coals with a stick as Peter carried over more firewood. "Aye, but he wants to be thought of as a man." He looked over his shoulder at Megan. "Especially since the lady arrived."

So 'twas her fault the lad was missing, she thought and

read the silent suspicions on the men's faces. "Where would he go?" she asked, knowing that he had no home.

"After Cormick and Bjorn." Wolf's voice was filled with conviction and he stared at the surrounding woods as if he was envisioning Robin's flight. "He asked to be sent to Dwyrain as a messenger."

"Aye," Odell said, as a pitchy log caught fire and flames popped and crackled, lighting the ground surrounding the fire pit.

Wolf, who'd been calm, kicked angrily at a stone near the bear's hide and flung Megan a dark look.

He blames me. Everyone blames me!

"I'll go after him. Jagger, come with me; Heath, go to the village, see if there's word of him. Dominic, you're in charge, and no one," he said, eyeing each and every man until his gaze landed with deadly aim upon Megan, "is to leave. As soon as Bjorn and Cormick return, we'll break camp and move, but until then, we stay here."

No one dared argue, and as the first light of morning crept across the land, he and Jagger climbed upon their horses and rode through the trees. Megan watched horses and riders disappear through the trees and she shivered, not from the frosty wind that chased down the river and knifed through her bones, but from the horrid thought that she might never see Wolf again.

They caught up with the boy in early afternoon, when they spied the gray hack he'd taken with him tied to the bare branch of an apple tree. Robin, wrapped in his mantle, was lying on the ground and didn't start when Wolf and Jagger approached, nor did he open his eyes when his name was called. Only when Wolf touched the lad's shoulder did he awaken, blinking hard as his eyebrows slammed together in confusion.

A second later his situation must've dawned upon him and he started. "Wolf! J-Jagger."

"Aye, lad," Wolf said, squatting next to the boy and rolling back onto the worn heels of his boots. "'Tis time you came home."

Robin closed his eyes for a second. "I didn't do a very good job of runnin' away."

"Is that what you want? To be rid of the band?"

Robin looked down at his hands, as if fascinated by the dirt beneath his fingernails. "Nay, I—" He struggled to a sitting position. "I just wanted to be a part of the group, not treated like a lad." His jaw, unblemished by a beard, jutted in silent rage and Wolf remembered himself as a youth, straining to be a man, defying his older brother, thinking battles and killing for a cause were noble and glorious pursuits. How many times had Garrick said the words that echoed through his mind?

"Be patient, Ware," Garrick had advised. "Study hard, learn your skills, do not hasten off to war." Every bit of his counsel had fallen on deaf ears, for Ware of Abergwynn had been prideful, mulish, and eager to prove himself a man.

"You will come with me when I meet with Holt," Wolf said now as he clapped the boy on the back. "He will have men with him and want to kill me. You will guard me against them."

The boy's eyes widened expectantly and Jagger coughed, trying to catch Wolf's eye. "Truly?" Robin asked.

"Truly."

Again Jagger coughed, and this time he said, "Do you think it's wise, with one so young—"

"'Twill be fine. There will be others as well, but Robin will ride with me."

A smile split Robin's stubborn jaw. "When?" he asked. "When do we ride?"

"Upon the return of Bjorn and Cormick," he said, then repeated Garrick's oft-spoken but never heard advice, "Be patient, lad; there are many years yet for battle."

With Wolf in the lead, they made their way to the camp, avoiding any of Holt's soldiers and seeing only a few carts and travelers upon the road. It was dark by the time they returned, but Megan was waiting, her beautiful face expectant when Wolf rode into the circle of light cast by the fire.

"So you're safe," she said to the boy as Robin dismounted.

"Aye."

"Well, come along. Odell's made a fine stew with some of the bear meat . . ." Wolf watched as she helped the boy to a trencher of the thick, greasy soup. Robin's eyes glowed and he couldn't keep a grin from his face as she fussed about him. Aye, he was smitten, as were several of the men. Peter's one-eyed gaze followed her about when he thought no one was watching, and even gruff Jagger managed a grin when she was near. 'Twas a problem. Wasn't he, too, enchanted by the lilt of her voice or the sparkle in her golden eyes? Didn't he think much too long about the slope of her shoulders, the sway of her rump as she walked, or the bounce of her breasts? 'Twas enough to distract a man, to cause his member to spring to attention at the most awkward of times. Already, the men, though they knew it not, were vying for her attention.

'Twould be good to be rid of her, or so he tried to convince himself, though he could not shake the memory of their lovemaking.

Cupping her hand near her mouth, she said something into Robin's ear and he threw back his head and laughed uproariously, as if she were the most clever woman on earth. Jealousy, his old enemy, slithered into Wolf's veins and caused his jaw to clench so hard it ached.

He could not let himself become too attached to her because she was the cur Holt's wife and could never be his. That painful thought brought him up short. He'd not considered marriage since Mary's death, had vowed that he'd never allow a woman close enough for him to ponder wedding her, but with Megan, he'd let his mind run wild.

"Bloody fool," he muttered low and under his breath. Somehow she'd gotten to him, and if he didn't keep some distance between them, he'd try to bed her. Hadn't he nearly done the deed just this past night?

Though he'd love to humiliate Holt further by stealing his wife's virginity, he could not dishonor her or shame her by claiming her as his own when he had nothing to offer her— no castle, nay, not even a house, no money, and no life except to run from the law.

He had to return her to her husband, or, as he'd decided more often with each passing day, kill the bastard and make her a widow.

* * *

Megan slipped from beneath the furs. Holding her breath, she pulled on her clothes and silently prayed that Wolf, wherever he was, wouldn't return before she'd escaped. He'd stood at the door of the chamber, not crossing the threshold, not allowing himself near the pallet early in the night. Once he appeared convinced that she was asleep, he waited a few more minutes, then left his post. Now was the time to escape.

Heart thudding, she walked to the sack he kept near the door and reached inside. Her fingers scraped a hatchet and a mason's tool of some kind before brushing against a small dagger with a curved blade. Her fingers curled around the smooth bone handle. Slowly she extracted the wicked knife, then searched further until she came to a length of rope, the same rope he'd used to restrain her. It was fitting somehow that she'd make good her escape with some of the very tools he'd used for her capture.

She had no choice but to leave. Knowing the depth of her feelings for Wolf and that he planned to ransom her to a cruel husband she should never have married, she wasn't about to stay here and wait like a lamb for the slaughter. Nay, she had to find a way to wrest herself free of the shackles of her marriage. Since nearly making love to Wolf, she'd known she had to come up with a plan to liberate herself.

The first step was to sneak away from the camp. Biting her lip, she crept to the window and, as she had once before, hoisted herself to the ledge and slipped through the opening. She landed without a sound on the frosty ground and silently cursed when she realized her footsteps were visible in the snow. A hunter such as Wolf would track her without much trouble, but there was naught she could do.

Then she saw him. Sitting near the fire, staring into the flames, his expression hard and faraway, as if he, too, were laying plans. Golden shadows played upon his face and a thick black cloak kept him warm. Her heart nearly broke when she realized she was leaving him forever, that this would be her last vision of him, a lonely man staring into the flames.

Just leave! Now! While he's let down his guard!

Silently she sneaked around a crumbled corner of the

chapel, and praying she wouldn't snap a twig, slunk past the tethered horses. One, a bay mare, nickered before Peter, from his guard's position near the rear of one of the tents, hushed the horse with his gentle voice.

Megan nearly jumped from her skin. Quick as lightning, she ducked into the woods and watched while Peter stood with his backside to her. Leaning against a tree, he stared with his solitary eye across the river. Eventually, he took a short walk around the animals before striding to the fire. Megan didn't wait. This was her chance.

Certain he would turn and spy her in the withering moonlight, she untied a small brown horse that wouldn't easily be missed. She would have loved to steal Wolf's destrier, but he was a tall horse, a restless animal, and Peter was certain to notice he was gone.

The brown, a swift little jennet, was a calm enough beast, and Megan worked nervously, untying the tether, praying the horses wouldn't make any noise. Once the tether was unbound, she led the mare into the woods near the river. They walked close to the rushing water so their footsteps were muffled by the noise. Only when they were far enough from camp that the fire no longer glowed through the trees did Megan loop the rope around the jennet's nose and ears, then climb upon her slick back. The horse snorted and sidestepped, but 'twas no matter. No one would hear.

"Let's go, girl," Megan said, planning to reach the road, where the mare's hoofprints would blend with those of the others that had passed during the day. The snow had fallen much earlier and though a few solitary flakes drifted to the ground, most of the white powder had lain in patches since the afternoon.

As she rode, she trained her ears backward, listening for the barest of whispers or the clop of horses' hooves, half expecting a band of men to leap from the shadows at any second. Nerves strung tight, hands sweating in her gloves, she felt as if the mare were moving much too slowly, that she had to put distance between her and the camp. But Wolf was not the only enemy she feared, for, if Wolf's spies were correct, Holt's soldiers were scouring the hills and woods, searching for her.

"Come on, come on," she encouraged, though they were

traveling as fast as possible through the forest and the overgrown deer trail that curved away from the river and—

"Well, well, well." Wolf's voice rang through the forest and her heart flew to her throat. Where was he? "Taking a midnight ride, m'lady?" The sound ricocheted around her and she squinted into the gloom.

"Aye, I'm leaving," she said boldly. Damn, if only she could see him! "I'll not let you sell me, Wolf." He'd have to chase her down if he wanted to catch her. She pulled on the reins, hoping to turn away from the sound. "Hiya!" she yelled at her mare, but as she started to urge the fleet horse forward, he appeared from the shadows, dark, looming, and furious atop his destrier.

"We need to talk," he said, grabbing the reins and stripping them from her fingers. Hopping from his horse to the ground, he reached upward, caught her hand, and caused her to tumble into the strength of his arms.

"Unhand me," she commanded, but he only held her tighter. She slapped at his face, tried to kick, but he laughed at her foolish attempts. "I'll not let you send me to Holt!"

"You were told not to leave camp."

"By the leader of an outlaw band! A criminal!"

"Is that what you think of me?" he asked, and in the moonlight she saw that his eyes were hooded, his jaw clenched, his lips white and thin as the blade of a new sword. Menacing and seductive he was, and her heart thudded, not with fear, but with a new, restless longing. Her mind burned with images of lying with him on the pallet, how she'd writhed and begged like a common wench. Her throat turned to sand and her pulse throbbed at the feel of him.

"You should have thought of that afore you decided to marry him."

"Just let me go. What matters it to you? You'll get your ransom, for my father will pay it, and I'll not have to be returned to a husband I detest."

"A husband who will hunt me and my men like foxes in the field for the rest of my days," he reminded her, his voice edged in anger.

"Would you not enjoy it? Giving chase, eluding your enemy, vexing him?"

He searched her face for a heart-stopping instant. "Aye, 'tis true. I'd like nothing better than to cause Holt anguish and laugh at him, but there comes a time when a man must stop running."

As his gaze touched hers, she was suddenly lost, her anger drained away, and the cold, brittle night closed around them. A rush of wind rattled the dry leaves, sending them skittering across the snow-dusted ground. "What are you running from?"

His smile gleamed white and wicked in the darkness. "I know not," he said, shaking his head. "Myself, mayhap, or the mistakes of my youth."

"You will make another if you force me to return to Holt."

"Do you not want to see Dwyrain again?"

"Yes, but—"

"And your father?"

"Aye. I miss him."

"Then you have to go to Dwyrain as Holt's bride," he said, but his lips barely moved. When she stared at them, that newly awakened beast of desire lying deep within her stretched its legs and unleashed its sharp claws. She could not trust this man, didn't dare give him her heart, but the deed was already done; nothing remained but the physical act of loving him. What would be the consequences of that one, dark, unforgivable act?

She would be condemned. For the love of Jesus, she could not, as a married woman, even consider adultery, but the strength of his arms holding her close to his chest, the thunder of his heart beating a hard cadence not unlike her own, and his eyes, hidden when a gust of wind blew his black hair before them, worked to change her mind. What would be the harm of it?

Were she to give herself to Wolf, her marriage would certainly be annulled and she would not be forced to stay with Holt. However, her father would never forgive her for bringing shame to the house of Dwyrain. Ewan would surely disown her and mayhap banish her. Then she would lose everything.

"Come," he said, carrying her to his horse.

"No!" Desperate to free herself, she pushed hard against the wall of his chest. "Let me go."

"I cannot."

"Then 'tis about money—pieces of gold and silver—nothing more!" she accused, and she felt him stiffen.

The skin over his face tightened but he didn't answer. As he reached for his mount's reins, she felt his grip lessen. Using every ounce of her might, she twisted hard and kicked at the horse. With a surprised snort, the animal backed away. Muttering under his breath, Wolf tried to restrain the beast, but the destrier tossed his great head, let out a frightened neigh, and began to rear. Heavy hooves flailed, striking the air, causing Wolf to step away.

"By the gods—"

Megan writhed and yanked herself free, her feet touching ground as Wolf tried to soothe his horse. The mare shied and Megan took off running, heading through the bracken, her boots slipping on the snow, her face being attacked by branches and vines.

"Megan! Holy Christ, where do you think you'll go that I'll not find you?" he said, and then there was silence. Her throat tightened and she knew he was stalking her through the thin, leafless trees. She ran faster and faster, intent on getting away, not because she feared him, but because she couldn't trust herself alone with him, and if she was forced to return to the camp with him, her plan to extricate herself from her marriage would be thwarted.

Her breath was coming in short, shallow gasps, her legs beginning to ache, her mind spinning ahead when he caught her. "Little one, stop," he ordered and then, as if from the very soul of the forest, a hand reached forward and clamped over her arm.

"No!" she cried, but he tugged, spinning her against him, enfolding her in his arms.

"Shh!"

"Leave me be, you bastard!" she half screamed, her fists raining blows on his neck and shoulders.

"Ahh, my lady," he said as he held her and stared into her furious eyes. "If only I could."

She tried to step away, but could not, and when his lips, cold with the night, found hers, she gasped. Her skin was instantly alive, her heart, already drumming, beginning to beat an erratic, wild tempo. She could not trust herself to kiss him, to touch him, to feel his body against hers, but neither could she stop.

Inside, her bones melted as surely as a candle left too close to a flame, and a wild storm of yearning began to rage deep in her heart. As his tongue parted her lips, she opened to him, unable to resist, hot blood flowing through her veins. A primal throbbing started deep within, yearning and moist, and his mouth was savage, his tongue merciless in its assault.

The wind swirled around them, billowing his cloak, stirring the dry leaves clinging to the branches. Moaning, desire pulsing through her body, she closed her eyes, lost in the scents of smoke, leather, and that musky odor that was only his.

His mouth was insistent, his tongue bold, his hands possessive as the kiss deepened. Denial formed in her mind, only to skitter away like the stars fleeing the dawn. Her arms, as if they had a mind of their own, wound around his neck, and the world began to spin. She didn't protest when he lifted her from her feet and carried her to the base of a strong fir tree with its soft carpet of needles.

"Say no," he begged in a deep rasp as he untied her mantle, but no words formed in her throat. "By the gods, Megan," he insisted, his face tense, his eyes filled with a savage fire. "Stop me."

"I—I cannot."

Before the words were out, he kissed her again, his mouth warm and wet as it touched her eyes, her cheeks, her throat. He yanked the mantle over her head, and soon, her tunic as well. Her breasts, straining upward, proud nipples erect, beckoned him, and with a tortured groan of surrender, he dropped his mouth over one proud point and began to suckle.

Megan jolted, her body arching upward, her spine bowing as she held his head close. He captured her buttock with one big hand and held her close to him, letting her feel, through the rough fabric of his breeches, his hot, swollen member. He kissed and suckled, teased and tormented, until the silk fabric was wet and cool where the wind caressed it.

"This is wrong," he said with a fatalistic groan. He lifted the garment over her shoulders as if it were a bridal veil.

"Nay, 'tis right."

The breath of winter skimmed over her naked flesh, and Wolf stared down at her an instant, before reaching for the ties of his breeches. Slowly, he undid the knots, and Megan, watching him, lost her breath.

Discarding cloak, mantle, and tunic, he kicked off his boots, then, with his breeches open, he guided her hand to his crotch. "This is how much I want you," he said when she felt his hard, hot flesh. "I ache and yearn for you, and I would do anything if I could end this torment another way."

Leaning forward, he kissed her lips. "I planned this not," he said, in a voice filled with conviction, as his weight carried them to the tangle of clothes that was their bed. "I wanted to hate you."

"Aye." Reaching up, she touched the side of his face, feeling the stubble on his cheek against her palm. "And I wanted to detest and thwart you."

"Do you still?"

She couldn't hide the mischievous smile that played upon her lips. "Aye," she agreed, wrapping her fingers around his neck and drawing her face close to his. "Can you not tell how much I despise you?" Laughing, she kissed him, and he groaned.

"'Tis serious, I am."

"Then prove it, outlaw." She held his gaze, and as he cast off his breeches, she felt only a tremor of fear. She loved this man with all her heart. 'Twould always be so. 'Twas right that they joined, as natural as the turn of the seasons.

His lips crashed down on hers again and he covered her body with his, keeping her warm as his knees pushed her legs open, and he touched her breasts with hard, eager fingers.

"You are a virgin?" he asked, his breath a warm balm against her skin.

"Aye."

"Then I will be gentle."

"Nay," she said, looking up at him, feeling wild and reckless, her skin on fire, her pulse pounding. "Take me as you would to pleasure yourself, Wolf. Let me feel what it is you want."

With only a second's hesitation, he wrapped his arms around her middle and splayed his fingers over the curve of her spine and the cleft of her buttocks. "We will pleasure each other, woman," he said slowly and lifted her hips to kiss her abdomen and the thatch of curls between her legs. His fingers and tongue were magic. The world swam again and Megan let go, losing herself in the uncharted waters of desire. He touched and kissed her in the most intimate of places, teasing her, heating her blood, bringing her to the brink so that she bucked up against him, demanding more as she cried out in sweet, sweet torment.

"In time, little one," he promised against her thigh, and she arched upward again and again, straining for a release only he could give.

"Please," she begged under the gentle, relentless assault of his tongue and fingers.

He was sweating despite the frigid air, and she saw his face, tight with restraint, as he climbed upward, spreading her legs wide. Without kissing her, he took her in one, strong swift thrust that caused her to let out a cry as raw as the night itself. A bright burst of pain knifed through her, but he held her fast, withdrawing slowly only to enter again. "'Twill be all right," he assured her, and his lips found hers again.

Desire pounded through her brain as he began to move more swiftly. His muscles strained and her fingers dug deep into his skin as he loved her, faster and faster, easing that first tiny bit of pain until she felt nothing but that same dark, dusky yearning that she experienced when he kissed her. In that sublime second, she was swept away, and the stars flashed a brilliant hue as he convulsed against her. "Megan!" he cried fiercely. "Oh, love!"

With a triumphant yell, he fell against her, crushing her breasts, his sweat-soaked body joined with hers as she floated away on a cloud of contentment, not thinking of the morrow, not worrying about her freedom, not concerned with anything other than this one glorious man.

"Are you hurt?" he asked, when his heart had quit beating so wildly he thought it might burst.

"Nay." Her breath was feather-light upon his skin, and he wrapped them both in his cloak, holding her close to him, trying to protect her from the cold winter air. Tenderly, he kissed her forehead and wondered why this woman touched him so deeply. What was it about her that had crept so easily past the barrier he'd worked years to construct, the wall that kept him from caring too deeply for anyone?

Cayley hoped to visit the cripple again. The man, whom she'd sworn to detest, held a fascination for her. She sneaked out of her room and was halfway down the hall when she heard the laughter—a woman's laughter, soft but distinctive—chasing down the corridors. The bolt on Holt's door clicked loudly.

Cayley ducked into the shadows.

"If ye be needin' any more favors, m'lord," Nell, the freckled seamstress, said as she tossed her hair from her face, "let me know."

Holt's voice was low. "Mayhap next time you can bring your friend, Dilys, with you?"

The seamstress pouted. "Dilys? She's scrawny."

"Ah, but she has some fine qualities. I think she could learn to pleasure a man."

"She's but a lass, barely ten." Nell shook her head. "Nay, I think not—"

"Bring her with you tomorrow," Holt ordered, grabbing Nell by the neck of her tunic and running his hands familiarly over her breasts. She arched her spine and purred like a cat. "You need not Dilys, m'lord," she said, lolling her head and exposing her throat and a breast that Holt chose to bare. His fingers ran distractedly over her nipple. "I will do whatever you want."

"You're but one woman, Nell, and an amply endowed one at that. But sometimes one mouth is not enough. Bring Dilys to me tomorrow." His voice turned hard and he pinched her nipple, causing her to cry out. "And tell her not what I intend to do with her. 'Tis better when there's a bit of surprise—aye, even fear—involved."

"You intend to frighten her?" Nell asked, trying to step away, but Holt wouldn't let go.

"Just a wee bit. 'Twill be fun. Come, Nell, be a good lass."

And with that, he covered her breast and shut the door. Nell slipped down the stairs and Cayley cringed, the contents of her stomach turning sour.

Wolf's gentle snoring was soft against her nape and Megan, too, wanted nothing more than to sleep with him in the waning moonlight, to cling to him and hold him forever.

But she could not.

They'd coupled thrice already and she tingled at the memory of each savage union, when they'd used the soft fir needles and their clothes for their bed. Finally, sated and spent, he'd fallen asleep, and now Megan had to make good her escape. Though she longed to stay with him, this was her last chance to leave. She planned to ride to Castle Erbyn and speak to Lady Sorcha. If Wolf spoke the truth about Holt, then her husband was a traitor to Dwyrain. However, Ewan would not take the word of an outlaw against that of his most trusted knight. Therefore, she must uncover the truth herself by speaking with Lady Sorcha, who was Tadd of Prydd's sister.

Surely Sorcha would know of Holt, had he been in Tadd's army, thus proving Wolf to be honest or a liar of the highest order. Gently, she lifted Wolf's arm away from her waist and slid out from under his cloak, which they'd used as a coverlet. The air was chill upon her skin as she silently pulled on breeches and tunic while forgoing her mantle, which was crumpled beneath his body. Hardly daring to breathe, she edged to the horses, tethered together in a thicket of oak. Untying the reins and rope with fumbling fingers, she sent up prayer after prayer that Wolf would sleep.

Once the knots were free, she led both beasts away from the fir tree and deeper into the woods. She couldn't take a chance that he might catch up with her, for if he did, everything she'd planned would be ruined—the execution of her plan was certainly the salvation for them, each and every one.

Nervous sweat collected on her skin as she slid a bridle over Wolf's stallion's head. She didn't bother with a saddle, and shivering, she climbed onto the destrier's broad back and held on to the reins of the smaller horse's bridle. Guilt clung close to her as a shadow as she clucked her tongue and followed the lowering moon. He would awaken alone, without even a horse to carry him to camp. She found no satisfaction in the thought, but urged the horses forward and wondered why she didn't feel relieved that she'd outtricked him.

Tears filled her eyes and she told herself their sting was from the fierce wind tearing through the hollow and had nothing to do with leaving her heart in the forest. Somewhere overhead an owl hooted, as if mocking her for her foolishness, but she stiffened her spine and refused to glance over her shoulder, didn't notice that she was being watched, that standing deep in the shadows of the forest, the outlaw called Wolf watched her leave him, making not one single sound of protest.

'Twas his punishment for bedding her. Despite the demons that had screamed in his head, despite each of his promises to himself, despite the fact that she was his enemy's wife, he'd made love to her with a passion he'd never before felt.

Never had the earth shifted beneath him, never had he joined with such a willing, loving virgin. Never had he felt such a total release of his soul.

His fists clenched as he hid in the night-shrouded forest and he sent up a prayer—the first in years—for her safety. The urge to chase her was strong, and he had to force himself to let her go. 'Twas what she wanted.

❧ Ten ❧

"**Y**e *lost* 'er?" Odell repeated, eyeing Wolf as if he'd finally and truly gone daft. He pushed off his hood, though the wind was bitter cold as it raced and screamed through the surrounding trees. "Two 'orses gone, too, includin' yer favorite?"

"That's what I said," Wolf grumbled, meeting the gaze of each of his men with his own brutal stare. Amusement flickered in more than one pair of eyes and smiles were held in check by quivering muscles near the corners of their mouths. Apparently, they thought it great sport that their leader had finally met his comeuppance, and by a woman, no less.

Let them think what they would. Bone-tired from a night of lovemaking and then hiking back to the camp, he wanted none of their nonsense, but understood that he would be the butt of jokes for days to come. 'Twas part and parcel to her release. At the thought of her leaving, he felt a deep emptiness, as if she'd cut a hole in his heart.

"Christ a'mighty, what about Bjorn and Cormick? They're going to look like bloody fools demandin' ransom for a woman who comes dancin' through the gatehouse with two of the finest 'orses in the land!" Odell spit disgustedly into the fire and the flames crackled and hissed. "By thunder, Wolf, sometimes I donna know what goes through that stubborn 'ead of yers!"

"Bjorn and Cormick will return before Megan reaches Dwyrain."

"You 'ope; elsewise, they might be in for the fight of their lives!" Odell made a sound of disgust deep in his throat.

"He's right about that," Peter agreed, his one good eye clouding with concern.

"'Olt'll torture 'em, sure as I'm an honest man." He threw his hood over his head again.

Jagger snorted. "We know how honest ye be, Odell."

The older man spit again. "'Olt, 'e'll use the rack or worse. Pokers, heated in a fire, or the press, or 'eaven only knows what else. Whatever it is, 'twill be wicked." His eyes glowed as hot as the coals in the campfire. "I've heard stories about 'im cuttin' out men's tongues or slicin' off their cocks and—"

"Enough!" Wolf commanded. He'd take a bit of ribbing—that was to be expected—but no one could accuse him of putting his men's lives in jeopardy. Striding to the fire, he warmed his hands and feet. His toes were numb, near frozen from wading across icy streams. "We ride at dawn, Jagger and me. The rest of you will stay here and guard the camp in case Cormick and Bjorn return and somehow we miss them. If no one returns in three days, move the camp to the hills behind Prydd. I'll find you."

"Nay, I'll not be left behind—"

Wolf's harsh glare stopped Odell's quick tongue. With a sheepish glance, he lifted his cowl and scratched his balding head.

Robin's chin jutted forward. "Ye said I could ride with ye," he reminded Wolf.

"When it came time to deal with Holt."

"Be ye a liar?" the boy insisted.

"Nay, but—"

"Ye promised," Robin said stubbornly.

"That ye did," Peter reminded him, and Wolf's fists clenched.

"Is yer word not good?" Robin asked, and again the men stared at him.

Knowing he was making a mistake, Wolf nodded. "Aye, you ride as well . . . but no one else," he added when he saw an eager light appear in more than one man's eyes. It had been long since they'd battled; many were thirsty for the excitement of waging war. "We'll ride straight to Dwyrain. Once there, we'll help Cormick and Bjorn if they need it."

"What of the lady?" Robin asked boldly, and the men who had been restless suddenly quieted, only the wind rushing through the leafless branches and stirring up the flames of the campfire making any sound.

"What of her?"

"Will ye not bring her with you when ye return?"

Two dozen eyes bored into him and Wolf realized then that she'd touched each of the men in special ways. Damn her. "Nay," he said gruffly as he read bitter disappointment on the boy's young face.

"But—"

"She wants not to be with us, lad."

Squatting near the fire, Wolf stared into the flames, and that hopeless idea settled as surely as lead in his heart. Why had he been so foolish, thinking she could care for a rogue like him? When had he lost his heart to the saucy tart with a tongue that could sting like a whip? 'Twas a silly notion to think that she could really care for him, and Wolf didn't appreciate being considered a fool.

Nor could he explain why he'd let her go, how he'd felt as if he were a self-serving king holding a rare, unhappy bird in a cage. She was a noblewoman by birth and could not be expected to give up everything that she had at Dwyrain— wealth, family, servants, even a husband—because an outlaw fancied her. It had taken every bit of his willpower to let her leave after making love to her, but his instincts told him he had no choice.

If she escaped and returned to Holt, the bastard might not harm her, though the fact that she wasn't a virgin would be difficult to disguise and would enrage Holt even more. Wolf's jaw tightened when he imagined his old enemy taking out his vexation, vengeance, and anger on Megan.

Holt had better not be so foolish, for if the bastard ever laid one hand on her, Wolf would gladly slit his throat. And then again, if Holt truly became Megan's husband, joining feverishly with her . . . getting her with child . . . By the gods, what a mess. Already, Megan could be carrying the first beginnings of their own babe. His throat turned as dry as seeds in the wind. What if even now there was a child growing in her womb? Would Holt claim the infant child as his own issue?

His fury became dark, his eyes narrowing with a new-found reason to hate his old enemy. Rage burned bright in his blood and his fingers curled anxiously around the hilt of his sword as he thought of it, the mating of Holt and Megan. 'Twould be a pain he would never be able to expunge, one he would bear as his own personal cross, one he would carry with him to the grave.

He felt the men's stares and scowled to himself. Life as an outlaw in the woods had lost much of the appeal that had once been strong within him. There were several men in the band who were capable of leading the others. Bjorn was strong and fierce, a levelheaded man capable of extreme savagery if 'twas necessary. Jagger, too, was strong, though somewhat dim-witted, and then there was Odell, with his mercenary heart. Nay, he'd be a bad choice.

"Make ready," he said as he turned on his heel and returned to the pallet in the empty chamber he and Megan had shared. The ashes were cold where the fire had been, a chill wind blew through the window, and the room was as dark and cold as the bottom of the sea. Gritting his teeth, he flung himself down and drew up the hides and furs, trying to ignore the scent of her, which lingered on the bed. "Damn it to hell," he growled and attempted to push aside the vivid images of making love to her, how her supple legs surrounded his waist, how she smiled up at him in the moonlight, how her skin, so white, was smooth as marble, how her blood would fire so easily.

I love Holt not, she'd said over and over again, but she'd been eager to leave. Why? Had she lied to him, and did she truly care for the man she'd pledged to love before God and country? Or was it, as she'd insisted, a marriage she couldn't avoid? Then why return to the scoundrel?

Because she thought you were going to sell her to Holt! Why would she want to stay? What choice had he given her? Tossing off the damned coverlets, he rolled to his feet and decided he had to hunt her down. Before she reached Dwyrain, he had to find her and speak with her and . . . and what? Offer her the life of an outlaw? A future running from the law? No home? No warm hearth? No servants? No real bed? What of children?

"Bloody Christ," he growled, stalking out of the room and striding to Jagger's tent, where the big man was already snoring. He placed the toe of his boot against Jagger's ribs and the man snorted, cried out, and was on his feet in an instant, a blade ready in his hand.

"For the love of Jesus, Wolf, ye scared the piss right outta me!"

Wolf had no time for explanations. "I ride tonight."

"But ye just got in."

"It matters not."

Muttering under his breath, Jagger found his mantle. "I'm beginnin' to think that Odell's right about ye, Wolf," he said, shaking his head and adjusting his hood as he stepped out of the tent and frowned at the snow beginning to drift from the dark heavens. "Ever since ye kidnapped the lady, ye've been actin' strange, like ye're not right in the head."

"I'm not," Wolf admitted. "Now, will ye ride with me or not?"

"Aye, I'm with ye, but what about the boy? He'll only slow us down."

"He comes," Wolf said, hoping that he wasn't sending Robin to an early grave.

Cayley couldn't help herself. 'Twas as if the magician had cast a spell upon her. She stealthily crossed the bailey, sending a goose squawking and nearly bumping into one of the stableboys, who was leading a gray jennet from the farrier's hut. 'Twas nearly dark, the air cool as it pressed hard against her cloak as she approached the north tower. She carried with her a bucket of Cook's bean and brawn soup and a dark loaf of bread. The smell of the soup caught the attention of some of the baron's dogs, who were being walked near the dovecote. They turned their noses upwind, let out hungry whimpers, and were reprimanded by the page whose duty it was to care for them.

Cayley clutched her cloak around her and stepped around the piles of horse dung that had not been cleaned away by the gong farmer.

The stairs leading downward were as dark as pitch. She snagged a rush light from its sconce, mounted near the door, and used the flickering light to guide her down the gritty steps. As she hurried by some of the cells, she heard hoots and whistles, but she ignored them and hurried onward.

In the dungeon, the sentries had changed, and one of the men she trusted, Sir Stephen, a gangly young knight with pockmarked skin and hair as straight and unruly as straw, was guarding the prisoners.

"Who goes there?" Stephen called out.

"'Tis only me," Cayley replied, feeling suddenly as if she needed fresh air. How could the men stand to be held in such decay and filth? "I brought fresh food for the prisoner and for you, Sir Stephen."

"Say what? Did Holt send ye?"

"Nay, 'twas mine own idea," she said as she approached his stool and small table. "I thought some good food might jolly our prisoner into telling me more about my sister."

Stephen snorted and shook his head. "Ye're wastin' yer time, m'lady. Kind as ye be, the man's daft. Completely out of his mind." Stephen pointed a finger at his head and rotated his hand. "You'll not get a straight answer from that one."

"At least let me try. Now, about the soup." Stephen, ever hungry, tore off a thick hunk of bread, dipped heartily in the broth, and motioned for her to do the same. "Has the prisoner given us his name?"

"Naw, but I 'aven't asked. Don't care what 'e's called." He ate hungrily, chewing with a great amount of noise, grinding teeth and making contented grunts as she tore off a piece of bread and dunked it in Cook's stew.

"I'll give this to him, if you let me into his cell."

"Say wha—?" He lifted his head and greasy soup dripped into his scraggly beard. "You want inside?" he asked, hitching a thumb toward the barred alcove the sorcerer now called home.

"Yes."

"Nay, m'lady, I cannot trust 'im."

"But he's bound, is he not?"

"Aye, but 'e's supposed to be some kind of magician, say what. 'e might jest disappear if I lets ye into the cell."

"If he truly was a sorcerer, why would he not escape with the door locked? Why would the restraints hold him?"

Stephen considered as he chewed, then wiped his mouth with a grubby sleeve. "I guess they wouldn't."

"Right. So there's no reason I can't speak with him and find out what more he knows, is there?"

Stephen frowned. Even in the poor light, she saw great lines furrowing deep in the skin between his eyebrows. "I don't think that—"

"And as the baron's daughter and lady of the castle, I'm not asking you to open the cell to me, I'm ordering you to do it."

"Well, that's it, then, ain't it?" Shoving away from the table, he rattled his keys and opened the metal door, which screeched on its rusting hinges.

Cayley slipped through the opening and found the magician seated in a dark corner of his cell. Above him, there was a small hole bored into the wall to let in a bit of fresh air. The breeze was faint, but enough to make it easier to breathe. "You want to know more of your sister," he said in that calming voice of his.

"Aye." She handed him the bread, and he took it gratefully. Then in a voice so low she could barely hear him, he said, "Two men are riding to Dwyrain. They come with news of Megan and will be treated as enemies, for they are outlaws."

"Criminals?" she gasped, her heart pounding in dread. "They know of Megan?"

"Aye, but they will not speak, for they are loyal to their leader, a man who hates Holt."

"How do you know this?" she demanded.

"I know." Again, the calm, reassuring tone that frightened her.

"Who be they?" she asked, glancing over her shoulder to the guard, but Stephen paid no attention to them as he dipped into the soup again.

"They be friends, though they will be brought to this prison and flogged. One will die. The other will help you find your sister and save the castle."

"Die?" she repeated, her throat turning to dust. "Die?"

"Aye, there is naught either of us can do."

"You speak with a devil's tongue," she hissed, frightened. "How can I trust you?"

"How can you not?"

She wanted to run, to hide, to wake up from this foul nightmare she'd been living, the one that had started when Megan had been kidnapped and her father had collapsed, leaving Holt to rule Dwyrain. If only Megan had fought her attacker, if only she'd escaped, then maybe Cayley herself wouldn't have to fight, wouldn't be forced to meet with prisoners in the dungeon or make plans to save her father and the castle. Her shoulders were just too small to carry so big a burden.

"You are stronger than you think," he said, as if reading her thoughts. "You doubt me still, but all that I have said, 'twill come to pass."

"Where is Megan?" she demanded.

"That I don't know," he admitted, his voice more ruffled than before, as if he were irritated at the limits of his powers, "but you will need these men and must befriend them as you've befriended me."

"But they are criminals."

"Friends," he said as Stephen rattled his keys again, indicating that it was time for her to leave. Obviously, the soup was gone.

Megan's stomach grumbled loudly as she rode onward. She paused only to eat once a day, and that was usually a scant meal, as she had no money and her only weapon was a small knife. She'd fashioned a basket with willow branches and had caught fish from each creek she'd crossed, plucked winter apples from a tree she'd discovered on the first day of her journey, and stolen eggs twice from a farmer's untended chicken's nests.

Four days had passed since she'd left Wolf, and as she rode through the snow and sleet, past villages and through dank woods, her thoughts continually strayed to him and she tried to imagine what he'd done when he'd found her missing. Had he been furious and enraged, or relieved to be rid of her? Had he ranted and raged, damning her to hell, or had he smiled inwardly that she was no longer his burden? Had he returned safely to his camp, only to be the laughing-stock of his men? She smiled faintly at that thought. Had he then climbed aboard another swift steed and set off after her? Would he appear at the next bend in the road? Her heart raced impatiently with that thin hope. Or would he meet with Holt and try to explain the fact that he had no wife to return for his blood money?

Not that she cared. Wolf could suffer these and every other kind of indignity for his plans to ransom her to an enemy he detested.

But she couldn't stop her heart from taking flight every time she approached another traveler, a man who sat tall upon his mount, a man with black hair and broad shoul-ders. Her pulse always pounded wildly for a second, only to return to its regular, even cadence when she drew close and she saw that the rider was not Wolf and bore not much resemblance to him. Oh, wayward, willful heart!

How willingly she'd given herself to him! The shame that should have been her companion, the disgrace of having lain with him, did not chase after her. Truth was, she had no regrets. If she could spend another night with him, she would gladly share his bed and suffer the consequences, for she was not married in her heart, nor had she slept with her husband.

Her plan—pray that it worked!—was to prove Holt to be the traitor she knew him to be. She'd find that proof in Erbyn, which was still several days' ride away. *God help me,* she silently prayed as the snow fell in flurries that obscured her view and chilled her deep into her bones, *and please, please be with Wolf. Give him peace and keep him safe.*

Absently, she rubbed her abdomen, heard her stomach growl again, and wrapped her shawl more tightly around her neck. She only hoped that Sorcha of Erbyn could help her.

Holt eyed his new prisoners with disgust. How easily tricked they'd been, how angry they were that when they'd shouted that they came in peace, they were set upon by half his army. Now they knelt before him, their hands and feet bound, ropes around their necks like common beasts of the field, their noses nearly pressed into the frozen mud and manure behind the stables. Sipping from a mazer of wine, he walked in front of them and felt a grain of satisfaction. Things were finally turning around. These poor, idiotic brutes, sent by Wolf the outlaw, were under his power.

"Did you think I would barter for my wife?" he asked, his long surcoat twirling behind him.

"I only bring the letter." The big blond one had the nerve to glance upward, but at a lift of his eyebrow, Holt signaled for his soldier to pull on the noose. Oswald was only too happy to wrap the heavy rope one more time around his fist, causing the kneeling cur to cough.

"Aye, you bring a letter from the Wolf." Holt read the perfect scrawl again. 'Twas true the outlaw was no common man, but educated and, no doubt, from a noble house. "But *friend*, 'tis not only a gentle missive, but a demand for ransom."

This time the yellow-haired giant didn't say a word.

"Fancy that." Holt clucked his tongue, then took a long swallow from his cup. "Nay, I think not. Instead I think you and your companion here will join my other guests in the dungeon."

"Wait!"

Holt's temper snapped as he spied Cayley striding across the outer bailey. Without being restrained by a wimple, her blond hair flew behind her like a golden banner. Her small face was set with anger, her jaw stretched forward defiantly. He'd taken her for a brainless twit, interested only in herself, but lately, since her father had fallen ill and Megan had been kidnapped, Cayley made herself a much stronger presence than she had been. 'Twas no wonder why Connor wanted to bed her, though Holt had no intention of honoring his bargain with the surly knight. Nay, he had other plans for his feisty sister-in-law. 'Twas almost as if she'd risen to new heights in the face of adversity, and it bored Holt. Now, she was bearing down on the men as if she were driven by an inner fire, her boots clicking on the hard, frozen ground.

"Who are these men?"

"Criminals," Holt replied, and she wasn't surprised or even repelled. "'Tis no concern of yours."

"Why not? Am I not the baron's daughter, his only issue here at the castle?"

"Cayley, dear, this"—he waved toward the men groveling at his feet as if they were insignificant flies swarming over horse dung—"is to be handled by men."

"I see not why. If they are here to ransom Megan, then give them the money or whatever 'tis they demand."

So she knew about the ransom. Either she'd been hiding nearby listening to the conversation or she had a spy within his ranks of soldiers—a spy who had run to her with the news. "Nay," he said with forced patience. "I'll not pay. 'Tis what the criminals want. They won't be satisfied with the first demand, but will ask for more, again and again. 'Tis impossible to barter with them. They have no sense of honor."

"Such as yours?" Something flickered in her gaze, a hint of distrust that he hadn't seen before.

"Aye, such as mine." Holt ignored her and glanced at Oswald. "Take them both to the north tower and leave them there until I call for them."

"Nay. They are our guests. If they can tell us that Megan is well and safe—"

"She is," the blond one said.

Oh, he was a bold, rebellious one, and Holt could almost feel the snap of his whip as he cracked it over the outlaw's broad back.

"Where is she being held?"

"That I cannot say."

"Cannot or will not?"

"She is safe. Unhurt. She will be returned when the demands of the letter are—aahh!" Holt kicked the lying cur in the ribs, the toe of his shoe digging deep in the hard-muscled flesh.

"Where?"

The big man had the insolence to lift his head and glare at Holt with unyielding eyes. Though there was already a bruise forming on his skin, he didn't flinch when Holt rounded and kicked him again.

"Stop!" Cayley cried. "Do not—"

"Take her away!" Holt ordered to another guard standing near the inner gate.

The soldier hesitated. "But she's the lord's daughter—"

"Take her!" Holt was sick of excuses and whining and pathetic attempts by the men to weasel out of their assigned tasks. "Do it now. Lock her in her room."

"Nay, Holt, you cannot!" Cayley cried, frantic. "You must keep these men safe!"

"I can do anything I wish, and I will," he said, his hands curling around the stem of his mazer just as Father Timothy hurried out of the chapel. The clumsy priest nearly stumbled over the hem of his robe at the sight that met his eyes, and for a second Holt thought the priest had drunk too much of the holy wine again. Lately, Timothy had been having second thoughts about his allegiance to Holt and he, as a minion of the Almighty, was becoming a royal pain in the arse.

"You are not yet baron!" Cayley cried.

Holt turned to the immediate problem of Cayley's newfound sense of injustice. "'Tis only a matter of time, m'lady, before the baron leaves this earth."

She gasped. "Nay!"

He couldn't help but smile. He crooked his neck, hitching his head in the direction of the keep as he ordered the nearest soldier, "Post a sentry at her door."

"I'll not be treated as a prisoner!"

Holt rolled his eyes. "Of course you will, m'lady," he drawled, "unless you do as you're told, which seems to be harder for you each day. Now, guard, take her."

He watched as a knight, a silly fool of a lad named Foster, grabbed Cayley's arm and led her toward the keep. The girl fought and argued, yanking hard against the hard manacle of the lad's grip, but Foster forced her across the snow-dusted grass of the bailey.

One of Holt's first duties as new lord would be to marry her off, and not to Connor, who wanted her so badly. Nay, Cayley, the beautiful, mule-headed daughter of Ewan of Dwyrain, would be worth much to some of the older barons whose wives had died. He would have to pay no dowry, because there was one man, Baron Rolf of Castle Henning, a tired old soldier, who was rumored to like to watch his young wives play and mate with his soldiers or servant boys while he watched. 'Twas said that Rolf had an entire chamber filled with peepholes where he could witness his wife's seduction and betrayal, then find her unfit as the lady of his castle. Four of his wives had died and two had disappeared, run away, it seemed. Yea, Rolf would be a good choice to tame Cayley.

As soon as he was baron, Holt would force her to marry. Today, however, 'twas his mission to deal with the two traitors who dared try and sell him his wife. "Take them away," he ordered the soldiers who held the ropes surrounding their necks. He finished his wine. "I'll flog them later."

Father Timothy made the sign of the cross over his chest as he watched Cayley being dragged into the keep against her will. "In the name of our God, Holt," he said in a low, desperate voice as his gaze shifted over the few meager troops still holding the prisoners, "what are you thinking?"

"I'll have no disrespect," Holt said, tired of arguing with everyone. Cayley was supposed to be her submissive self and the priest had promised to be his ally. Now . . . since the time the sorcerer had been dragged into the dungeon, loyalty to him had begun to waver, Cayley appeared to have grown a backbone, and the priest was suddenly God-fearing.

Father Timothy eyed the two new captives, then his gaze wandered after Cayley again. She was struggling like a beast from hell against the soldier's grasp as he hauled her up the steps of the keep. From the corner of his mouth, Timothy said, "Lady Cayley cannot be treated like a common wench, and these men," he motioned to the new prisoners, "if they bring word of Lady Megan, should be taken in as guests of the baron."

"Even if they bring a note of ransom from the outlaw Wolf?" Holt asked, arching one eyebrow disdainfully. "I think not."

"'Twould be the Christian gesture to offer them—"

"Food and shelter?" Holt cut in sarcastically as he sneered at the two captives. "Or, mayhap a cup of wine and a trencher of brawn? Or . . . wait, they might prefer a night in bed with a wench from the kitchen!"

"Nay, Holt, do not mock me. 'Tis only that if you are to become baron, you must look like a fair and even-tempered leader."

"'Tis not a matter of 'if,' but 'when' I become baron, Timothy," Holt said, his eyes narrowing on the soldiers and prisoners. "'Twould be a good idea to remember where your allegiance lies, for I know much about you."

The priest's face sobered and turned a sick shade of gray. 'Twas so easy to humble a prideful man whose guilt and piety constantly battled with each other. "Aye, 'tis right you are," Timothy said and crossed himself hurriedly.

Holt chuckled. "Amen." He motioned to his beaten prisoners. "Take their sorry arses into the dungeon and put them in the lowest cells, next to the sorcerer. Mayhap we'll get lucky and he'll place a curse on them so that they'll talk."

The blond one sneered and the other glared with eyes filled with hate. Well, let them rot. There would be no bartering with him about his wife, and if he ever found the outlaw rogue who had stolen her away, he'd personally see the man drawn and quartered.

Cayley paced from one end of her chamber to the other. Who would save her father now that she'd been foolish enough to get herself trapped in her room? For the past few days, ever since the sorcerer had convinced her that Ewan's wine had been poisoned, she'd poured out his mazer and filled it herself. She had no idea who was fouling his drink, though she'd tried to watch as Cook prepared Ewan's dinner. Nell sometimes carried Ewan's tray to him, as had she. There were others as well, pages and serving girls, none of whom Cayley thought would try to kill the baron. No, the poison had to have come from Holt, who was rarely in the kitchens . . . but he visited her father daily to report to Ewan about what was happening within and without the thick walls of Dwyrain, and though Ewan hardly responded, Holt considered it his responsibility to tell the old baron everything.

And doctor his drink?

Cayley's heart sank. It didn't matter that she had poured

Ewan wine from a new jug before his tray was taken to him. The dark deed was done later.

How could she have been so blind? "Father, I'm sorry," she said softly, wishing there was a means of escape from her chamber and knowing there was none.

She should have confided in someone, but she'd been frightened and wasn't sure whom to trust anymore. The castle had once been a happy place where she'd grown up in the glow of her parents' love, with siblings around her. 'Twas no longer. In the past two years, Dwyrain had become dark and sinister, not the same safe haven she'd lived in all her life.

She no longer walked freely through the gardens of marigolds and fragrant roses, nor did she linger at the dovecote, watching the birds fly in and out, nor did she ever take long walks through fields strewn in wildflowers. This year, she found no joy in her favorite season—the Christmas revels, with their merriment, dancing, feasting, and general feeling of goodwill.

A soft knock sounded on the door, and the sentry opened it to allow Rue, the old nursemaid, into her room. With a cry of delight, Cayley ran across the chamber and flung herself into the old lady's arms.

With a cluck of her tongue, Rue asked, "Now what did ye do, Cayley girl, to get yourself locked away?"

"I asked that Holt hurt not the new prisoners—the messengers from Wolf."

"And he disagreed?" Rue lifted a graying eyebrow. "Ah, child, will ye never learn? As stubborn as yer sister, ye are. Well, we'll just have to find a way to get Holt to set ye free, now, won't we?"

"Aye, but first we must take care of Father." Cayley swallowed hard, hoping she could trust the nurse and knowing she had no choice. Many people, servants, knights, and freemen, had, because of the sickness and curse, been unhappy with Ewan's rule and were embracing Holt as their new leader. They apparently thought Holt could assure them of more prosperous and healthier times. Some of the baron's most trusted men had turned away from him and become followers of Holt. She only hoped Rue, who had lost her own daughter to the sickness, had not turned her allegiance away from Ewan. "You must help me, Rue," Cayley said, desperately clinging to the older woman's sleeve. "You must help me thwart Holt's plan to murder Father!"

"Worry not," the strange one in the next cell said as the rush lights burned low in the dungeons of Dwyrain.

Bjorn turned toward the sound and thought he heard the rustle of wings, as if a bat or bird was with the cripple who dared speak to him. Bjorn was not a man easily frightened. Ofttimes he was told he was much too bold and reckless, that he cared not for his own life.

'Twas true, he thought, for though he loved the freedom of living the life of an outlaw and spat upon the rules and laws of the land, there was a part of him that wanted always to defy death, to test his courage, to kill that sorrow that was buried deep within him. He longed for a chance to find out the truth of his birth. Was he, as Tadd of Prydd had insisted, just the bastard son of a whore or was he, as his mother had assured him, a prince among men, the son of German royalty? He wondered now, as he stood in a wet cell that was cold as a corpse, who his father was and he thought again of Leah, poor, tormented Leah of Prydd, a woman who had touched his heart, a woman who, beaten, raped, and nearly killed by Darton of Erbyn, had entered a nunnery where she would be safe from the evils of all men and would devote herself to God.

Bjorn believed not in the Father. Especially not in this wretched cell that smelled of urine, dung, and human fear.

"Who are you?" he asked the calm voice.

"A friend."

Bjorn snorted. "I have no friends at Dwyrain."

"Nor I," Cormick agreed from the next cell.

A cat slunk through the shadows, its eyes reflected in the fading light from the torches mounted on the wall. Silently, the rail-thin cat stalked rats and mice that crawled noisily through the straw and damp rushes strewn in a bare layer upon the floor.

"Wolf comes to free you," the smooth voice said in a tone that only Bjorn could hear. "You must be ready."

"How know you this?"

A pause. "I see it as clearly as I do you."

Cormick coughed. "Well, I see nothing in this damned place! 'Tis darker than pitch at midnight."

"'Tis not with my eyes that I see," the strange one protested.

"Then ye're addled," Cormick decided with a grunt, but Bjorn had experienced many unexplained things in his life. Had not Sorcha of Prydd brought him back to life from the very brink of death? Had she not done the same for her sister, Leah? Aye, he trusted her witchcraft more than he trusted any faith in God.

"Believe me," the odd one insisted. "He comes."

"I'll be ready," Bjorn promised, eager to have a chance to kill Holt with his bare hands. It mattered not whether he lived or died, only that he fought bravely. He only hoped the half-brained sorcerer was not a fraud, for this time, he was certain, he would fight to the death.

Holt fingered his whip lovingly. The leather pommel fit his grip perfectly, and the resounding crack when he flipped his wrist could cause a faithless man to suddenly fall on his knees and pray for God's forgiveness. Aye, the whip was a weapon of power and fear, one that took long to kill a man, but gave the owner time to savor the killing.

Connor and Kelvin were with him as he entered the dungeon, and their footsteps no doubt caused dread in the hearts of the wretches chained within the prison. A thrill of power, not unlike the excitement he felt each time Dilys, the milkmaid, was hauled into his room, scorched through his blood. She was a tiny thing, with only the smallest of breasts budding, and Holt had not bedded her; in truth he thought her not ready, but he bared those tiny breasts of hers and made her play with them, her eyes downcast, as he fondled Nell in her presence. She was too young to be a decent whore, but in time she would learn to pleasure him and his men, for soldiers, if not given a bit of feminine pleasure, were a surly lot. Holt had picked out the girls he planned to use to service them—Dilys was the youngest—but in time, two years or less, he planned to deflower her and show her what it was to pleasure a man. She was already learning from Nell, whose ripe, full breasts and fat, round rump were a willing source of pleasure.

Though she was not Megan. His guts tightened again, for 'twas Megan with whom he wanted to lie and with whom he wanted to beget children. More than anything, he wanted her submission, he wanted to thrust his body into hers and see the surrender in her eyes. He could not think of her now without his damned cock bulging in his breeches.

Holt planned to be a strong ruler. His men, allowed to wager on dice, cockfights, and the baiting of bears, would also enjoy the women he provided and the wages he paid. In return, he would demand and receive their undying loyalty.

At the final bend in the stairwell, he held his rush light higher and made his way through the stench to the farthest cells, where the jailer sat on a stool, his mouth open as he snored, drool gleaming in his gray-flecked beard.

"Wake up, you dolt!" Holt kicked at the man, who started and blinked.

"Eh—wha—oh, Sir Holt, er, m'lord, 'tis sorry I am ye caught me nappin'. I was jest restin' me eyes and—"

"Don't bother with excuses, man," Holt said, his skin crawling. He hated dark places, and being on the right side of the cell door didn't keep him from feeling as if he couldn't breathe. Biting back the urge to flee, he stared at his three most recent captives. "Have you anything to say of my wife? Where is Lady Megan being held?" He waited, then, his fingers curving over the handle of his whip. The men in chains stared at him but held their tongues.

"You have but twelve hours to change your minds," Holt said. "Tomorrow, before noon, I'll haul your sorry hides to the bailey, where you'll be tied and your shirts removed. I'll flog you within an inch of your miserable lives and then you'll tell me what you know!" He waited, half expecting one of the men to break down, beg his forgiveness, and cleanse his soul by spilling the truth, but he heard nothing but the steady drip from the cistern and the rustle of the grimy rushes on the floor. "So be it," he finally said, rage firing his blood as he cracked the whip, and the sound reverberated against the stone walls. "But think not I'll have pity on anyone who helped the outlaw bastard steal my wife!"

Megan's teeth chattered and her fingers and feet were numb with the cold. She'd been riding over a week and had fought the urge to pull on the reins and turn around. Unable to feed herself or the animals, she sold the smaller horse and had enough money in her pocket for several nights' lodging and warm meals, but she didn't dare stop, not until she reached her destination, not until . . . dizziness swept over her, the same sensation she'd had for two days. Oh, what she wouldn't give for a cup of hot cider or some of Cook's venison broth . . .

Swaying in the saddle, she clung to the reins and tried to keep her wits about her. Snow fell from the sky, collecting and freezing on her mount's mane. Though she wore gloves, her hands were clenched over the reins and couldn't feel. She could barely move her fingers. Undaunted, she kept on, certain she was nearly to Erbyn. If only she could talk to Lady Sorcha, find out the truth about Holt, and return to Wolf . . .

Wolf! Her heart cried for him and she bit her lip. Where was he now? Did he think she had betrayed him? Would she ever see him again? She had to! She was a woman with a mission, a woman who was determined to choose her own fate, a woman who—

The blackness threatened to overtake her again. Moving from the outward corners of her vision, slowly encroaching, it advanced. Squeezing her eyes shut, she tried to clear her head and clung to the saddle pommel, but no matter what she did, the dizzy sensation continued to overtake her and she could no longer tell which was up and which down. The earth tilted.

"God help me." Reining in her horse, she attempted to dismount. The blackness threatened again. She was halfway off the horse, her foot searching for ground that wasn't there. With a cry, she fell, toppling to the ground in a heap. The last thing she saw was the clouds swirling wildly as her head banged against the hard, icy road.

Then there was nothing.

❈ Eleven ❈

Crack!

The whip buckled, then hissed forward. Like a snake, the tip bit into his flesh, stinging. Bjorn's body jerked. Pain exploded in his muscles.

"What know you of Megan?" Holt demanded, standing behind him and ready to flail again. "Speak, outlaw!"

Bjorn bit hard on his tongue and closed his eyes, bracing himself for the next blow. His body was on fire, his legs weak, his wrists raw and bleeding where they were bound by leather cuffs and ropes. The outer bailey of Dwyrain swam before his eyes. Dark clouds, swollen with rain, rolled across the sky, and the wind was chill and harsh, cutting through his soul as easily as the whip sliced through his flesh.

"So be it, criminal. Just remember, you chose your own fate!" *Snap!* The thin rope of leather slapped hard again. Bjorn convulsed, pulling at the straps that held his hands. Numbing blackness threatened to swallow him and he prayed it would be so. Around him, peasants, servants, and soldiers stared at him, some with faint smiles, others holding hands over their mouths as if they were about to be sick, still others with lifeless eyes, as if they cared not. Work had stopped in the castle and he and Cormick had become the main attraction.

"Speak, damn you!" Holt thundered, and Bjorn felt a

small measure of satisfaction at the vexation in his tormentor's voice. "For the love of Christ, tell me!" Another flick of Holt's cruel wrist. The whip cracked, then sizzled as it flayed another strip of skin off Bjorn's shoulders. With all his strength, he held his tongue and didn't look to his side, where Cormick was already sagging against his restraints, blood oozing from his mouth, eyes closed, his skin split open from more than a dozen brutal bites of the whip.

"Stop!" a woman's voice—the blond girl Cayley—yelled from a window high in the keep. Bjorn could barely see her. "For the love of God, Holt, stop this!"

"Bloody Christ," Holt muttered, then turned to face the keep. "If what I do offends you, m'lady, do not watch. I only make an example of those who are disloyal to Dwyrain!"

"By beating them until they die? This man was only a messenger, who wanted to help you find Megan—"

"I barter not with the demon outlaw!" Holt said, his temper snapping. In a softer voice, one she would not be able to hear, he growled to one of his men, "Go up to her chamber and keep her away from the window until I'm finished."

The fat-necked soldier was quick to run to the keep, but not before Cayley yelled again.

"Stop this torture now! The baron would not approve. This is still his castle, his soldiers, his prisoners, and—"

"I spoke with your father this morning, m'lady. 'Twas his idea to flog the truth from these men in an effort to find Megan. 'Twas he who insisted the traitors not go unpunished."

"Nay, my father would not . . . Who are you? Stay away! Nay! Leave me be! Unhand me, you brute!" she cried, and then there was silence in the bailey once again.

Holt, grumbling about hardheaded women, advanced to the brace where Bjorn was bound. With the handle of his whip, Holt bashed the side of Bjorn's face, rattling his teeth. Pain, in a blinding flash, ripped through Bjorn's jaw. "I'll find out the truth, you know. One way or t'other. You'd better talk while you can, you dirty, lying dog."

Bjorn spit blood and hit Holt square in the face.

"You stupid bastard." Again, the whip handle crashed against his face. With a sickening pop, his nose broke. Blood spurted. Pain screamed through Bjorn's brain, but he managed to look Holt square in the eye.

Through rattling teeth, he muttered, "Go to hell, you son of the Devil!"

Several peasants laughed and Holt's face turned red in rage. White lines edged the corner of his mouth. "You first," he growled and struck another blow. A flash of blinding agony flared behind Bjorn's eyes and the blackness that he welcomed came at last to claim him.

Cayley shoved her trencher aside. Ever since Holt had banished her to her chamber, she'd seethed. Treated like a wayward child! Not trusted even to take meals in the great hall! Restrained by a big, burly, stinking knight while the outlaws were being flogged! She glanced at Megan's bed and felt a deep pang of sorrow for the sister she'd tormented and teased.

Climbing into the window, she stared down at the bailey and felt sorry for herself. Even the girls plucking eggs from nests, milking cows, or herding the geese had more freedom than she.

From her position, she heard the pounding of the carpenter's hammer and the clank of steel as the armorer forged new weapons. Smoke drifted to the sky and a thin, cool mist shrouded the forest far beyond the castle. The chapel bells rang and she watched Father Timothy and Holt, heads bent against the wind, hurry down the steps and into the bailey. They were arguing, Holt's face stern, the priest's worried.

She shivered and felt as if death were near. If only Megan were here or her father were well or her brother hadn't died. But idle wishes helped no one. For the first time in her life, she had no one to turn to, no one to take care of her. "Please, please help me," she murmured, hoping God was listening.

Wringing her hands, Cayley tried to think of a way to see the crippled sorcerer again. Though she'd once hated him, she now believed that he was good, that his interests in Dwyrain were pure, that he, if anyone, could help break

Holt's horrid death grip that was clamped firmly over the throat of the keep.

The door opened and a soldier allowed Rue, wearing an apron and carrying a basket of herbs and eggs, into the room. The door closed with a thud. Rue crossed the chamber in surprisingly swift strides. Sighing loudly, she took Cayley's fingers in her own bony hands.

"Something's wrong," Cayley said.

Rue slid a glance at the door. "Aye," she admitted in a soft whisper.

"Father!"

Rue gripped tighter. "He is not long with us, aye, but he no longer drinks fouled wine. 'Tis you I fear for," she said. "Holt has sent a messenger to Rolf at Castle Henning, offering you to be the old baron's bride."

"What—?" Cayley could hardly breathe and her legs threatened to turn to mush. Rolf was an old man—an enemy of her father—one who had been married many times and whose wives either died or disappeared. "Nay—"

"Aye, 'tis true," Rue said, finally releasing Cayley's grip and rubbing her arms as if she were cold from the inside out. Cayley's strength gave way and she fell against the bed. Marriage to Baron Rolf? Her stomach turned over and she had to fight the urge not to retch.

"It could be worse," Rue said, avoiding her eyes.

"How?"

"Holt—he's already promised you to Sir Connor, but he wants not to marry you, because . . . well . . . you know . . ." She fluttered her fingers in the air. "But Holt wants to marry you off and not to Gwayne of Cysgod, though I know you wanted to be his wife."

"Gwayne is of no matter," Cayley said quickly, her head spinning. Her love for Gwayne was not deep, she now knew, just a childhood attraction, but Gwayne would be a much better mate than either Rolf or Connor. Her skin pimpled in goose bumps from fear of the dead-eyed knight and the sick old man. "I have to get out of here," she said. "I—I have to find Megan, to get help from a baron who is friendly to my father . . . or a priest of—"

"Slow down, child. You be rattled and—"

"But there is no time!" she said, feeling as if a cold, hard hand was slowly squeezing the life from her. "You must help me."

"Aye," Rue said, nodding. "I know. I asked Holt to set you free and he laughed at me. Told me 'twas not my place to even make such a suggestion." Her jaw tightened so hard that the bone showed white against her chin. "He's loathsome, Cayley, and cannot be allowed to rule Dwyrain." Then, as if feeling the need to explain herself, Rue glanced down at her hands. "He's taken a fancy to Dilys," she said and shook her head. "Poor girl. My only granddaughter. A comely, sweet lass, but sometimes slow." She swallowed hard and her eyes narrowed with injustice. "'Tis difficult for me not to pour the poisoned wine I steal from your father's chamber into Holt's mazer. 'Twould please me to see him sputtering and gasping for his life."

"Aye, and I would slit his throat if I could," Cayley agreed, surprising herself, for she'd never been a savage woman, had never felt the need for revenge, never wished a man dead except for the sorcerer before she'd met him. When she'd blamed him for the deceit, sickness, and pain at the castle, she'd thought she'd like to see him dead, but now, she knew differently. He was a kind and good man—a strange one with near-magical powers. But not so Holt. He was the very Devil incarnate.

Rue reached into her basket, beneath the eggs and a soft cloth, to the small dagger she'd hidden there. "For your protection and escape," she said, handing the knife to Cayley. Its handle was carved from wood, its fat, short blade straight and deadly.

"Escape?" she repeated, gnawing on the inside of her lip as she twirled the tiny weapon in her fingers. "There is no way I can escape."

"I will help you," Rue vowed. "Now, I must leave or the guard will become suspicious. We will both think, and when I return, we will have a plan for you to escape Dwyrain, find Megan, and warn her of the horrid beast her husband is."

"And what then?"

"I know not," Rue admitted. "Pray your father does not fail." Adjusting the eggs and herbs over the towel in her basket, she left the room quickly and Cayley heard the bolt being slammed over the door. She could not break down the thick planks with her bit of a knife, nor could she carve her way through the stones of the floor. Her only means of escape was through the hole in the roof for the fire or the window, which was far above the frozen loam of the bailey. Oh, would she were a sorcerer, then she could find a way to escape. At that thought, she rounded her bed and walked to the window, where she could see the north tower. 'Twas there, deep below, where the sorcerer was held. She had only to set him free and he would help her escape and find Megan.

Oh, cursed fates, what could she do against an army the size of Holt's?

'Tis not the number of men who fight for a cause, but the convictions of those who do, lass. Her father's words swam in her mind and she knew that there had to be a way to leave these castle walls behind and find Megan.

"Ahh . . . she awakens . . ." a gentle female voice, one Megan had heard in her dreams, whispered.

"Praise God," another, deeper, voice intoned.

"Maybe now we'll find out who she is." Another woman, one with a slight lisp.

Those soft, soothing voices surrounded her and Megan blinked several times against the light of a candle being held near her face. "Where am I?" she asked dazedly as the women, several of them, exchanged glances. Only then, when her eyes adjusted to the yellow candlelight, did she realize that they were nuns, dressed in their somber habits and wimples, staring at her as if she were some oddity—a freak of nature. The room was a dark chamber with a single window and cavernous ceiling.

"'Tis the Sacred Heart Nunnery where ye be," one of the women said. She laid a smooth hand to Megan's forehead. "I'm Sister Leah, and you . . . ?"

"Megan of Dwyrain," she said without thinking, and then gave herself a swift mental kick. Kind as these women were, they believed in God and truth and all that was holy. They wouldn't look kindly on a bride who had been kidnapped from her husband, then refused to return to him after lying with another man. A cold blush stole up her face and she tried to lever herself up from the hard pallet on which she rested. "I . . . I must not tarry."

"You're ill," one of the sisters said. "A farmer found you on the road not far from here two days ago and you have not once opened your eyes or taken any nourishment."

"Aye," she said, her voice scratchy, her throat dry as flour, her mouth tasting foul. Foolishly, she ran her tongue around her teeth and nearly retched.

"Be quiet," Sister Leah suggested with a patient smile. "We will bring you food and fresh water and you'll feel better. Then you can tell us why you were traveling alone."

"My horse?" Megan asked.

"Horse?" The nuns exchanged knowing glances, which Megan read much too easily. They thought she was not fully awake—that her mind was playing tricks on her.

"My destrier." *Wolf's* horse. "A black stallion with three white stockings and a small white patch on his forehead."

Three heads slowly wagged side to side. "The farmer brought you in his cart, and 'twas pulled only by a brown workhorse with a back that looked near broken."

"This is a warhorse, a steed that . . ." She let her voice drift into silence, for what could she say? That she'd stolen the horse off an outlaw who had kidnapped her and then eventually loved her, as a man loved a woman? That the horse was probably stolen from some nobleman the outlaw had robbed? Swallowing any more arguments, she said instead, "I am on my way to Erbyn."

"Erbyn?" The first nun, Sister Leah, stared at her with puzzled eyes. "Why?"

"'Tis the Lady Sorcha I must see." Her voice was weak and she could hardly remain half sitting. With a sigh, she fell back on the small bed and the chamber spun before her eyes.

"I'm Sorcha's sister," Leah said. "Erbyn is close by."

With what small amount of strength she had, Megan struggled to sit up again. "Then I must go there. I have to find her and talk to her . . ."

"Shh. 'Twill all come to pass. First, Megan of Dwyrain, you must get your strength back so you're able to travel."

* * *

Ice surrounded the edges of Hag's End Lake, a smooth
body of water rumored to be haunted by the ghosts of dead
Welsh warriors. Wolf drew up on the reins, motioning for
Jagger and Robin to remain silent and invisible in the
shadowy forest surrounding the banks. Closing his eyes,
Wolf tilted his head. From his mouth came the harsh shriek
of a hawk's cry. The scream split the cold forest air. Jagger
blew on his hands. Robin bit on his lower lip.

Wolf waited.

Stillness whispered through the dry leaves and steam
seeped from the horses' nostrils as they breathed hard and
stamped impatiently.

"'Tis no use," Jagger finally said.

"Shh!"

They were close to Dwyrain, less than a day's ride away,
and Wolf wasn't turning back. 'Twas time to face his old
enemy and end the burn for revenge that fired in his gut.
And time to find Megan, his mind tormented him again.
There had been but a few minutes when he'd not thought of
her and, in truth, it wasn't revenge that spurred him on so
much as the need to see her again. *What if you do see her
again? What then? Will you steal her away once more? Bed
her ruthlessly? Try to hold her close when she wants nothing
to do with you?*

Bittersweet agony ripped through his soul. How foolish
he'd been to let himself care for her, to let his emotions
become entangled with her when he'd vowed years ago
never to let a woman close to his heart.

Now he had no choice but to follow his convictions. He
could offer her nothing, but he could save her from a
marriage that was certain to kill her spirit and dull her
bright mind.

So now you're a god—or a priest? his mind taunted, and
Wolf ground his teeth together in frustration. Though she
had stood before the altar and pledged her troth to Holt,
Wolf believed in his heart that she didn't love the cur and
never would.

Since when do you believe in love?

Ignoring the demons in his head, Wolf lifted his hands to
his mouth once more, raised his chin to the sky, and gave
the hawk's mournful cry.

Again, nothing.

"Why not howl like a wolf?" Jagger said and was rewarded with a hard glance.

"And announce to everyone within earshot that I be here?"

Jagger chuckled at his joke or Wolf's consternation, Wolf knew not which. Robin, swallowing a smile, stared at the ground. Around his neck he wore a strand of bear claws from the beast that had nearly taken his life.

An answering cry split through the forest, so loud it nearly parted the shroud of fog that clung low to the hills.

"I'll be damned!"

"No doubt, Jagger. Come." Wolf leaned forward in the saddle and urged his mount to the edge of the lake where another rider appeared through the icy mist. "Jack."

"Aye, and how d'ye be, Wolf?" the hunter asked, his eyes dark and worried.

"I've been better."

"Haven't we all? Haven't we all?" Jack said. "And the lady? Is she safe?"

"Megan?" Wolf asked, alarm causing the hairs on the back of his neck to rise. "Is she not at the castle?"

"Nay, the messengers came in peace, bringing your letter of ransom, but Holt turned on them." Quickly, Jack explained about the capture of Bjorn and Jagger, as well as the return and imprisoning of the sorcerer. According to the hunter, Holt had control of the castle and sent search parties out patrolling for his wife, but his two most diligent men, Sir Connor and Kelvin of Hawarth, had become disinterested.

Holt had reprimanded them and they'd laughed in his face. Furious, he wouldn't give the men any more chance to snigger at his foolishness. He planned not to pay ransom for his wife and had declared it a sign of weakness to give in to the demands of criminals. His answer was that he intended to flog the truth from Bjorn and Jagger and any other poor soul who might have some knowledge of Megan's whereabouts and happened to wander through the gates of Dwyrain.

"But Lady Megan, no one has seen her?" Wolf asked again, fear congealing his blood.

Jack scratched the whiskers on one cheek and shook his head. "Yer men claim she is with you."

"She escaped," Jagger said with a wide grin. "Think on it, a tiny woman like that, slippin' away from Wolf."

Robin's smile was smug, as if he thought it a great joke that the bit of a woman he adored had tricked Wolf.

"She's not returned to Dwyrain," Jack said.

Desperation took a stranglehold on Wolf's throat. 'Twas possible she was safe with friends somewhere, that she had decided not to return to her father's castle and her husband's ire, but 'twas unlikely. She could have been captured by another band of outlaws—there were many in the surrounding woods—but Megan was smart, an accomplished horsewoman, and was riding the best steed in the land. Also, he was certain that she would be more careful than she'd been on her wedding day, when Wolf had abducted her.

"So there has been no sign of the lady, but my men and a strange sorcerer are being held captive?"

"Aye." Jack studied the rocks and ferns on the ground. "Not only being held, but beaten as well. Two days past, they were flogged within an inch of their lives and when I left the castle on this hunt, one, the dark-haired one—"

"—Cormick."

"Aye, he be the one. He . . . well, he was lingering near death. The priest had already been called to his cell."

"Nay!"

Jack lifted his eyes. "Aye, Wolf. 'Tis the truth I speak."

Robin's grin disappeared and he swallowed as if with difficulty.

Guilt galloped through Wolf on sharp, steel-shod hooves that ripped at his heart and soul. He should have expected this, he decided, fingers clenching around the reins, but there was an unwritten law—a code of honor that outlaws and noblemen alike respected—that messengers were not to be handled as prisoners, though he knew some of his men had at times attacked the bearer of bad news rather than the source.

Torn, he glanced behind him, as if in studying the undergrowth he could determine what had happened to Megan. Surely she was safe and, after hearing of Holt's reign

of terror, he was grateful she hadn't returned to Dwyrain
. . . but where was she?

"We needs save Bjorn and Cormick," Jagger reminded
him, as if reading his pained thoughts. This was his fault—
everything that had gone wrong could be laid at his own
feet—but he could undo nothing, and if he followed his
heart, he would chase down Megan wherever she was and
demand that she become his wife—the bride of an outlaw
of the forest. The thought was like salt water on a wound,
for he physically jerked when he imagined giving up his
freedom for a woman. But not any woman, he reminded
himself bitterly—Holt's wife.

Jagger cleared his throat and glared at Wolf as if he
suspected him of some deep treason. "Aye," Wolf agreed
reluctantly, "we must save the men and then we will find
Lady Megan. Dwyrain is but a day's journey from here."
That thought, too, was worrisome. Mayhap Megan was
indeed still trying to return to Dwyrain. Mayhap her horse
was stolen or lame and she was on the road. If 'twere so, she
had to be stopped afore she walked innocently through the
gates of the keep, like a calf to the slaughter.

The knock on the door was firm. "Cayley, child," Father
Timothy greeted her as he let himself through the door.
"I've come to pray with you." He closed the door behind
him and Cayley shivered at the thought of being alone with
him. She was also expecting Rue soon; the nursemaid had
promised to help her with plans for her escape. Time was
passing much too quickly and if Cayley were to help her
father, she had to ride for help soon—tonight, for the moon
was full and bright in a cloudless sky. Drat and spit that this
was the night the good father chose to come to help cleanse
her soul.

"Kneel beside me," he ordered, and Cayley lowered
herself onto the rushes, where the priest was already positioned so that he could face the door. "Aye, that's good," he
said when she was beside him. Clearing his throat, he held
his breath for an instant, then said so softly she barely heard
him, "I have a confession to make."

"You?" she replied, sensing a trap.

"Aye. I've not always been faithful to my vows." He

clasped his hands in front of him as if he were praying. "I—I have strayed, been lured by the temptations of the flesh rather than traveling down the path that leads to the purification of the soul."

She bit on her lip, refusing to be drawn into this unlikely confession. Father Timothy was a shrewd and not particularly pious man; she believed he had broken his vows a hundred times over, but she didn't trust him enough to admit as much. He could be a spy sent by Holt to trap her into saying something incriminating. "Mayhap you should pray for God's forgiveness," she said.

"I have, child. Many times, but I feel that God is asking more of me than a simple confession. I think he wants me to prove myself, to show Him that I will not fall prey to the lust and greed that sometimes afflict me." He was looking at her no longer, instead staring at the door over the fingertips of his tented hands, as if he expected someone to burst through at any second.

"Why are you confiding in me?"

"Because your heart is pure." He swallowed hard, his Adam's apple bobbing nervously in his throat. "'Tis true I've harbored a feeling akin to love for you . . . and not the love of a priest for one of his flock, Lady Cayley," he said hesitantly, his eyes sliding her way for just a second. "Nay, I've wanted you as a man does a woman."

She recoiled at the thought. "No, Father Timothy, do not say any more, please."

But her words fell on deaf ears, for his words tumbled freely and more quickly from his mouth, like a stone gathering speed as it rolled downhill.

"'Twas vexed I was that I had pledged myself to God and the rules of the priesthood; aye, the vow of chastity became a burden, and I . . . I was jealous of those who did not have to abide by its rigid rules."

"You need not tell me this—" she said, trying to scoot away, but he grabbed her hand and his eyes flared with a newfound conviction.

"Oh yes, I do, but 'tis not all that I must suffer," he said as if humiliated beyond words. "I must offer myself up as a sacrifice to cleanse my soul."

"Nay," she said, trying to draw away, but his grip was

strong and the fire in his gaze convinced her that he would not be denied. Whatever sacrificial torture he'd planned for himself, it somehow involved her. "You needs seek counsel. Mayhap the abbot—"

"I know the way to my salvation," he said and reached beneath his vestments. Cayley nearly swooned. Was this man of God going to disrobe before her?

She yanked back her hand just as he pulled a long length of rope from beneath the folds of his robe. "What?"

"'Tis for your escape," he said, and her heart turned to stone. If the priest knew of her plan, thin though it was, who else had guessed that she had plotted to break free of the castle walls? Fear pounded in her heart. She had no idea how she was to escape, only that she would swallow her pride and ride like the wind to Cysgod and beg Gwayne and his father, Nevin, for their help in overthrowing Holt and saving her father. Once that was accomplished, she would search for Megan. If, God forbid, she was refused help at Cysgod, she would ride to . . . where? Erbyn? Abergwynn? Ah, but 'twas nearly a week's journey to Abergwynn. Pennick was closer . . . oh, 'twas too much to think of.

The priest, eyes fixed on the door, continued. "'Tis to Rue I spoke, and she told me of your plan." He rubbed his chin with the tips of his fingers. "'Tis a prideful, blind, and ambitious man I've been, Cayley. Now I must atone."

"By helping me?" she asked, not daring believe that she could trust him.

"Aye, 'tis one of my penances." He reached deep into a pocket in his vestment and withdrew a small leather pouch. "'Tis money. Take it."

"Money?"

"From the chapel." He blushed. "Do not ask how I acquired it; 'tis yours now."

"Another of your penances?"

"Aye." He slapped the bag into her hand and she dropped it as if her flesh had been seared. The coins clinked loudly and Father Timothy shot a glance to the door. "Do not warn the guards," he ordered.

She didn't dare ask him if he had more penances. He could be either addled or trying to make her prove her disloyalty to Holt. He swept up the bag of coins and forced it into her hand, folding her fingers over the soft, worn leather. What if this was only a ruse? What if he hoped only to gain her confidence, then expose her to Holt? Nay, she could not trust him.

"I've made poor allegiances here in Dwyrain," he admitted. "Today, when the men were beaten, I realized how badly I've chosen my friends, the men in whom I've trusted. I . . . God in heaven, forgive me. I've witnessed human suffering and felt that it was right, that I, as a priest, could mete out pain in the name of the Lord, that I had the right to be the judge of men whose only sin was they were as weak as I was. I was wrong."

He sounded sincere, in his own guilty hell, but he could be a fine actor, playing his part well. His eyes didn't meet hers and he was shaking, but she remembered too many times when he'd enjoyed the belittlement of a sinner, the superiority he wore like a halo bestowed by God.

Swallowing hard, she shook her head. "I plan not to leave the castle," she said, resting on her knees and beginning to sweat anxiously. Moisture collected beneath her hair and on her spine.

"Do not lie, child. Rue said—"

"Rue is kind, aye, but old and sometimes her mind strays. If you want to pray, Father, I'll pray, but believe me, I plan not to go against Holt's wishes. My father named him as the next baron and I would not go against his word."

Timothy's lips pursed. "One of the prisoners is near death," he said.

Just as the sorcerer predicted! "Nay."

"You might pray for his wretched soul." He wiped his hands on his robes and sighed loudly. "For that of your sister, too, for if she returns to Dwyrain and has not been faithful to Holt, he will kill her."

"No, please—"

The priest's face was somber. "Say what you will, child, but mind, if you need my help, I'm at your service." Climbing to his feet, he left the rope in the middle of the floor. "'Tis not that far to the bailey from here, and one of the stable boys left a hay cart filled with straw beneath your window. 'Twill be there until morning. Rue will be in to see you before you sleep, and, should you find a way out the window, she'll untie the rope and drop it into the cart."

"I told you I plan not to—"

Holding up a hand to silence her, he said, "I blame you not for how ye feel, Cayley. My thoughts of you haven't always been pure, I've enjoyed too much the Lord's wine, and I've been a prideful man worried about earthly things. I've . . . I've forgotten my purpose. But no longer. I pledge you this, my lady, I am your humble servant, as I am the servant of God." He laid a cool hand on her shoulder, muttered a short prayer, and then hurried out of the room, leaving the length of rope and small sack of coins behind. She tucked the coils beneath her bed, hid the pouch in the thick fur coverlets piled over the mattress, then walked to the window and peered down the sheer rock walls of the keep.

As Father Timothy had promised, a farmer's cart filled with hay was positioned beneath the window of her room. If she were brave and if she could trust the priest, she could secure the rope on one end to the foot or post of the bed, throw the coil through the window, slide down the thick hemp snake, and sneak to the stables.

Before fleeing, however, she would have to try to free the outlaws, and the sorcerer, to aid her. If Holt found her, he'd kill her or flog her as well. She cringed inside and wished that someone, anyone, would come to her rescue. She wasn't cut out for danger and would rather be weaving or embroidering than doing anything so rebellious as plotting this escape.

But she had to work fast, before the prisoner died. Whether she wanted to or not, she was forced to trust the priest.

"'E's dead, fer sure," the jailer said. "Barely alive when we brought him in."

Holt scowled down at the body. The stench and squalor of the dungeon turned his stomach and the glassy-eyed body, battered from the flogging, lay curled in a ball in the corner. Holt hadn't intended to kill the man, not so soon, not until his tongue had been loosened, but the shorter, dark-haired outlaw had given up the ghost and died before uttering a word, not even his name.

"You'll pay," a deep, rolling voice warned.

Holt's head snapped up at the ominous words coming from the next cell. The blond outlaw sat cross-legged in a corner, his eyes burning feverishly bright as they bored into Holt.

"Upon my mother's grave, I vow, Holt of Dwyrain, I'll kill you with my bare hands."

"You're in no position to start handing out death sentences." Then why did his insides turn as weak as jelly? The man was locked and shackled, he could do nothing but talk, but Holt felt a tremor of trepidation slide down his backbone in this dark part of hell. "You're the prisoner, not I."

"All in good time."

Through soggy rushes, Holt advanced upon the barred wall separating the cells. "But your time isn't good now, is it?" he said with a nasty sense of satisfaction. "Your time is spent healing in this rat-infested hellhole. You're in no position to bargain or threaten me."

"As long as you live, I will be your enemy."

"Nay," Holt said, his temper snapping, "as long as *you* live, which, judging from your friend's length of time on this earth, won't be long. If I were you, my *friend,* I'd be less inclined to wag a tongue that could easily be cut off and be more interested in telling the truth so that I would be set free."

The blond one had the audacity to laugh, sending Holt's anger screaming through his blood. He was tired of being laughed at, furious that men—even this lowly prisoner— had the audacity to snicker at him. "You have one day to change your mind, and then, piece by piece, I will cut you apart. First, a finger or a toe, then part of your ear—even your balls—until you loosen your tongue."

Furious because the man was not intimidated, he motioned to the body. "Burn or bury this and tell me when our prisoner changes his mind!"

The blond prisoner's silent rage followed him up the steps like a shadow and Holt felt an unlikely tremor of fear. Outside, the night air was cold but fresh, and he shook off the dark images of the cells.

He had to do something. Things were not happening rapidly enough. Though there were men searching for the outlaw and Megan, it had been weeks since her capture. Wolf and his band had quite successfully eluded them. Since the day when they'd come upon the old camp by the creek where Connor had discovered Megan's wedding ring, there had been no sign of the outlaw.

Until now when Wolf's two messengers had appeared. Now, because of Holt's harsh need for justice, one of the two men who knew where Megan was hidden was dead. The other—that big blond brute—had to be kept alive no matter what.

There was too much disloyalty in the castle as it was. Many of the men were beginning to doubt him. Oh, they'd been only too happy to swear their allegiance to him when they realized that Ewan of Dwyrain was failing, that his mind was no longer sharp, that he was not the dauntless and feared leader he'd once been, but now, ever since Megan had been captured and the men had been tested, their loyalty questioned, Holt had felt that the tides of allegiance had shifted from him and to the dying baron. Curse the old apothecary; had Jovan been right in his dosage, the old man would have died weeks ago, but instead Ewan of Dwyrain lived on, lingering in his bed, muttering his thoughts to a wife who was already in her grave.

Well, Holt was tired of waiting. Everyone expected news of the baron's death and now they would get it. 'Twas only a matter of laying a thick robe over the elderly man's face. He was too weak to struggle and he'd die quietly. Then Holt would summon the guard and the castle would learn the news that the old baron had left this earth to join his wife. Holt would become the new ruler.

Swiftly, he mounted the stairs, and with a nod to the guard, entered the baron's room. He closed the door firmly behind him and saw in the quiet light the face of a once-strong man. He hesitated only a second, calling softly to the baron. Ewan's blind eyes turned in his direction and he managed a weak smile.

"M'lord," Holt said. "I've come to help you."

"There's news . . . of my daughter?" Hope brought a smile to his weathered face.

"Soon."

"Ahh. 'Tis a pity."

"That it is, m'lord. That it is." Without another word, Holt snatched a fur coverlet, and using every ounce of his strength, held the once-comforting blanket tight over Ewan of Dwyrain's face.

❋ *Twelve* ❋

"Come," the calm voice ordered.

Bjorn, seething with injustice, spit on the floor of his cell. His muscles were on fire, his face throbbing, his jaw swollen, perhaps broken.

"Come." Again, the soft-spoken command.

"Go to hell," Bjorn growled.

"Am I not already there?"

Bjorn's jaw tightened and made a horrid cracking noise, but he didn't budge. The prisoner in the next cell was certainly half crazed. Though everyone here thought him some kind of magician, what lord of darkness would allow himself to be caged like a pathetic animal? Nay, he was just a half-wit who spoke in a kind turn of phrase.

"Do not let your friend die for naught."

"My *friend* will be avenged," Bjorn vowed, his lips pulling tight against his teeth. Fury and injustice beat fiercely through him and he blamed himself for Cormick's death. Had he been more cautious, been ready for the men they approached to turn on them, they would not have been captured and beaten and Cormick would not have been killed. He should have known there was no honor in Holt of Dwyrain and both he and Wolf had been foolish to think that Ewan's good word would still be law.

"Aye, but Cormick will not be avenged by a beaten, savage man who wants only fast justice. Nay, the way to win this battle is to destroy Holt by more than fists and swords."

"Ah, ye speak as if ye've got only half a brain."

"Shuddup in there," the jailer shouted. A rotund man who sat half the time at his post and walked the halls and stairs the rest of his shift, he glowered at the prisoners as he polished the blade of his sword. "There'll be no talkin'."

I can soothe your wounds. The words came to him, though he wasn't certain the sorcerer had spoken. Bjorn glanced to the jailer, who hadn't looked up and was busying himself with cleaning his weapon.

Through the flickering, smoky light, Bjorn stared into the next cage and was certain that he could see the sorcerer's kind face. There was not a trace of malice, no evil, but his eyes glowed a deep summer blue. *Come!*

Bjorn jumped. This time he was certain the man had not spoken. His lips hadn't moved and the noise that rattled through his brain sounded as if it had traveled a long distance, even through a long tunnel.

Do not be afraid.

"I fear nothing!" Bjorn stated fiercely.

"Yeah, and bully fer you," the jailer said. "Now, hush! Jesus God, do ye want another beatin'? That's what ye're askin' fer."

The lady Cayley comes and will save you, but you must be strong to help her; a weak man will only slow her on her quest to find her sister.

"By the gods!" Bjorn thundered, standing and stepping to the other side of the cell, tripping on his shackles and falling against the screaming muscles of his back.

"Enough from ye!" The jailer jumped from his stool, forced his sword into its sheath, and strode to the door. "Sir 'Olt, 'e's got no love fer ye. If ye were to 'ave a mite of an accident, 'e wouldn't be cryin' a river of tears over yer body, let me tell ye."

"Untrue." This time the strange one spoke. "Holt needs this man to take him to the outlaw who stole his wife, and if he is harmed, Holt will surely punish whoever it was who let the 'mite of an accident'—I think you called it—happen. Think you twice afore you hurt the one man who can help Holt find his wife."

"I'll never—" Bjorn started, but that faraway voice stopped him.

Hush. The guard will leave us be.

"Bloody Christ," the jailer muttered, but returned to his seat and removed his sword from his sheath again. With one eye on the cells, he snagged his rag and began to rub the blade with renewed fervor. Soon, with only the drip of water and sound of mice scurrying through the crevices in the walls for noise, the guard was caught up in his work.

Bjorn turned to the cripple.

Come to the cell wall. I will help you. Do not be afraid.

"I fear nothing," Bjorn whispered, but, in truth, his heart was thundering loudly, his face and back throbbing in pain, and it took most of his courage to walk the few steps to the rusted bars separating his quarters from the sorcerer. Not long ago, he'd been nearly killed by a rampaging horse and Sorcha of Prydd had used some of the spells from the old ones to heal him. He'd been brought back to life from the brink of death. But this man—this cripple who could not heal himself—was different. Oddly reassuring and yet . . . By the gods, what did he have to lose? He was in prison, sure to be tortured again, probably killed. He had no choice but to place his trust and his life in the strange fellow's hands. Squaring his inflamed shoulders, he shot his hands through the bars, and the sorcerer, who appeared to move without sound, placed his soothing fingers on Bjorn's torn flesh.

"So, Lady Megan, you've traveled a great distance to see me," Sorcha of Erbyn said as Megan slid to the muddy ground within the gates of the largest castle she'd ever seen. Thrice the size of Dwyrain, Erbyn rose like a great yellow-gray dragon from the very cliffs on which it stood. The battlements were high and wide, the towers strong, the keep massive. Servants, pages, and peasants scurried through the bailey; carts pulled by old workhorses and travelers on swifter palfreys and jennets passed through the gatehouse. Chickens clucked and squawked, cattle bawled, and children ran through the few flakes of snow that fell from thick, slate-colored clouds.

Sorcha held a forest-green cloak around her. The hood was trimmed in rabbit fur and the hem flapped loudly in the wind. "Come into the keep and have a cup of wine by the fire. You, too, sister. 'Tis much too cold a day for travel."

Leah slid down from her spotted mare and embraced her sister. "So good to see you."

"Aye, and you." Sorcha held her sister at arm's length and studied her face, as if searching for traces of unhappiness.

"How is my niece?" Leah asked.

Sorcha laughed, the sound ringing over the pounding of a carpenter's hammer, the creak of the windmill's sails, and the cursing of the master mason who was unhappy with one of the freemasons' cuts of stone. "Bryanna is as beautiful as her aunt and mean-tempered as her father."

"I heard that!" A big man with sharp eyes the color of ale, thick brows, and a vexed expression approached. By his dress and manner—that of pride and arrogance—Megan guessed him to be the baron, Lord Hagan of Erbyn. "You're ever a witch, Sorcha."

"And you'd not have it any other way," she teased, clasping his hand. "Lady Megan of Dwyrain, please meet my husband, the ogre."

Laughing, he placed an arm possessively around Sorcha's small waist. "Forgive my wife; she sometimes forgets her manners." He caught a page's eye. "Have rooms prepared and tell the cook we have guests!"

The lad with straw-blond hair and crooked teeth nodded heartily, anxious to please. "Aye, m'lord." He turned and ran toward the keep, while another boy of eight or nine appeared and, without a word, took the reins of their mounts and led the tired horses toward the stables.

The big man with tawny eyes smiled. "Now, Leah . . . so good to see you again."

"And you, Lord Hagan."

A pang of loneliness tore through Megan when she thought of her own family, so small now, but so close. Her father near death, or so she'd been led to believe, and her sister, fair and giddy, never thinking about the morrow— how did they fare? It had been weeks since she'd seen them and though she'd often fought with Cayley, now she wished to be able to sit down and talk to her, to confide in her.

Great snowflakes fell from the sky in earnest. Scowling at the dark clouds, Hagan shepherded them into the great hall. Once seated near the fire and drinking wine, pleasantries aside, Megan explained her reasons for riding to Erbyn. She told of marrying Holt and being kidnapped by an outlaw who, he claimed, was Ware of Abergwynn.

With the three sets of eyes steadily upon her, Megan barely touched her wine as she spoke. ". . . I am worried that my father and I have been deceived by the man I married, a man I do not love. If it be true that he rode with your brother, Lady Sorcha, if he lied to my father, if, indeed, he committed the horrid crimes that Wolf claims, then Dwyrain is in jeopardy and . . . and I would want my marriage annulled. I need to know the truth and return to Dwyrain." *And to Wolf,* she thought miserably, knowing that he would never again touch her, never speak to her, as she'd deceived him by lying with him, feigning sleep, then stealing his horses and leaving him stranded. That thought brought with it a deep ache in her heart, and her hands shook slightly as she took a long sip of wine.

"Everything Ware has told you is true," Sorcha assured her with a thoughtful frown. "Leah knows." The sisters' gazes touched and they shared a silent painful moment before Sorcha looked at Megan again. "My brother was a cruel man with no thought but of his own wants. He cared not for Prydd, nor his family, nor the servants or peasants who lived within the castle walls." She swallowed and stared at her hands before squaring her shoulders and tossing a mane of wild black hair over her shoulders. "Aye, Tadd raped Mary, the fisherman's daughter. She was not his first, nor his last. On that day, there were several soldiers with him. Holt was there."

"You remember him?"

"A bit." Sorcha shivered. "'Twas a bad time in our lives." She glanced at her sister.

"Aye. Our darkest hour." Leah made a swift sign of the cross over her chest and blinked for a few seconds.

Relief that Wolf hadn't lied came to her but the truth was damning, for she was married to this monster of a man.

Leah said, "Megan has traveled a long distance and was ill when she was found by a local farmer who brought her to us. Now that she knows the truth, I think she should rest."

"Nay, I must return to Dwyrain. My father—"

"Would want you to be well. Let us eat and rest. Tomorrow we can talk of traveling to Dwyrain," Hagan interjected, his face a mask of hard determination.

But each day so far from home—away from Wolf—was an eternity to Megan. Since she knew the truth, she was eager to return, to face the man who had lied to become her husband.

"When you are strong enough to leave Erbyn, my best men will ride with you," Hagan decided aloud. Though he stared at the fire, his eyes were trained on a far distance only he could see. "I have waited long to purge the land of anyone who rode with Tadd or my brother Darton. I, too, will ride to Dwyrain." A cold smile crossed his square jaw. "'Twill be a pleasure."

A piercing cry rang from the rafters. Megan jumped.

"Ah," Sorcha said with a smile. "The lady Bryanna is hungry. If you'll excuse me."

An ancient woman with gray hair descended the steps. Smiling and wizened, lines of age etching her skin, she was carrying a small, howling bundle. "I've never seen a babe with such lungs in her."

"'Tis a sign for strength of character, Isolde," Sorcha said as she took the crying infant from the old crone's arms, and the nursemaid cackled affectionately. One little fist had escaped from the blankets and a head of black curls was visible as the babe let out another lusty cry. "Come, little one," Sorcha cooed, kissing the child's soft crown. "'Twill be only a minute. I know . . . I know."

Hagan watched his wife ascend the steps and a kind, nearly reverent expression changed the hard contours of his face as his gaze followed her. The love in his eyes touched Megan. Here was a man who would lay down his life for his lady and child, a man devoted to her, a man, upright and law-abiding, who wanted only to provide for and protect his family and castle.

Unlike the renegade outlaw to whom she'd given her heart.

"Did Wolf kill Tadd?" she asked once Hagan had turned to her again.

"Aye. After Tadd nearly killed me." He finished his wine and set his mazer on the hearth. Then he told her the story of Sorcha of Prydd, his wife, born with the birthmark of the kiss of the moon, an ancient prophecy stating that whosoever was born with the mark would become the savior of Prydd. Many had scoffed at the thought of a woman becoming a leader, mostly Tadd, Sorcha's older brother, but in the end, she proved herself to be uncommonly brave and determined.

Megan withered inside. Sorcha had done so much for those who depended upon her, while Megan had brought only fear, distrust, and now, by marriage, the reign of a cruel baron. Unwittingly, she'd become the curse of Dwyrain. And now she was in love with a wild man, an outlaw of the forest, who used her only for revenge against a sworn enemy.

As if reading her thoughts, Hagan said, "Wolf breaks the law without a thought, he takes refuge in the forest and disdains life within a castle, he makes his own rules and lives by them, but he is a good man, Lady Megan; his heart is pure."

"I—I believe you."

"Good. Then eat the food that Cook has prepared and rest. We'll talk of riding to Dwyrain tomorrow."

Megan didn't argue as a page brought in a trencher filled with eggs and eels, a round of cheese, and a few tart winter apples. The cold seeped from her bones and she realized how badly she missed a part of her life at Dwyrain. The adventure of living in the forest was appealing, though, and she thought of the outlaw band—grizzled Odell, innocent Robin, even-tempered Peter with his one eye—but she knew that the source of her fascination with the life of the thieves was their leader. Where was he now? Was he following her? Would he even now burst through the gates of Erbyn? If he asked, she would eagerly give up the comforts of the keep to be with him.

Silly girl. Foolish heart. He was probably glad to be rid of her and the problem of returning her to her husband.

Holt.

Her blood curdled at the thought that she was, in the eyes of the church and in accordance with the laws, bound to him for the rest of her life.

She'd finished eating when Sorcha, carrying the tiny babe,

swept down the stairs. No longer wailing, the infant's face had lost its scarlet hue and was as smooth and white as her mother's. "She'll not be an easy lass," Sorcha said proudly. "Headstrong."

"Like her mother." Leah swallowed a last bite of eel and sighed contentedly. Fluttering her fingers, she indicated that she wanted to hold her tiny niece, and Sorcha reluctantly gave the swaddled babe to her sister.

"I know of Ware of Abergwynn," Sorcha said. "I knew him first as Wolf, the outlaw. But he is Baron Garrick's younger brother who, in his youth, was overly confident and eager to prove himself a man. Unfortunately, when his brother trusted him to rule the keep, he was overthrown by a traitor, his own cousin, Strahan." She crossed her legs and laced her fingers over a velvet-draped knee. "Ever since that time, Wolf has been a man haunted by his past, an outlaw who is forever chased by the demon guilt. Though Garrick blamed him not for losing Abergwynn years ago, I think that Wolf has never been able to redeem himself in his own eyes.

"At the time he and Lady Morgana's—she is now married to Garrick—anyway, her brother, Cadell, escaped from Strahan only to be forced over the cliffs at Abergwynn and into the sea far below. Their bodies were never found. They were both thought dead for years until the outlaw Wolf turned out to be Ware of Abergwynn."

"What happened to Morgana's brother?" Megan asked.

"Never heard from since. 'Tis presumed that he died in the fall off the cliffs or drowned in the sea."

"And Ware blames himself for this as well?"

Sorcha lifted a shoulder. "I say only what I've been told by those who were there. 'Twas a long time ago. Over ten years." She cleared her throat, dispelling the dark mood that clouded her eyes. "'Tis late and you need your rest, Lady Megan."

"Nay, now that I know the truth, I must return."

"Tomorrow," Sorcha said. "With Hagan and his army."

"Curse your bones, Megan," Cayley growled under her breath as her fingers curled more tightly over the rope. Fighting a fearsome dizziness, she climbed out the window, swallowed back her qualms, and began to lower herself slowly into the waiting cart filled with straw. If only her sister hadn't gotten herself into such a mess, then she wouldn't have to go through this torture. Her arms and shoulders ached from holding up her weight, her shoes slipped on the stones of the castle wall, and the rope felt as if it were shredding the skin off her hands even though she was wearing gloves.

Finally, she was close enough to the cart to jump. Silently counting to three, she let go and fell, landing in the piled straw with a soft thud. The night air was crisp and cold, her breath fogging, the moon shining bright and nearly full to give some light. Rolling off the cart, she alighted on the hard ground and twisted her ankle. Holy Mother, she wasn't any good at this!

Biting the urge to cry out, she hurried onward. Fear crawled up her spine, and she was constantly looking over her shoulder, certain she was being followed. As she passed the fish pond, she heard a splash in the water and nearly screamed. Her hasty footsteps echoed down the path near the beehives and through the bedraggled gardens.

Beneath her black-hooded mantle, deep in a pouch strapped around her waist, was the small knife Rue had given her, and she prayed that she didn't have to wrestle with the guard and his huge sword. Dear God in heaven, what was she doing?

Tamping down the dread that stole the spit from her mouth, she opened the door of the north tower and tiptoed quietly down the steps. A few rush lights still burned, fouling the air with their oily smoke and causing shadows to shift in the narrow, dark halls. This was no mission for a lady—no mission for a sane person—but she continued downward, half expecting some burly guard or ghost of a dead prisoner to jump out at her. *God be with me,* she silently prayed as she rounded the final corner.

She comes. Be ready! The unspoken words charged at Bjorn from the next cell, and he saw the stranger arise. Using some small piece of metal, the sorcerer silently unfastened the manacles over his wrists, then did the same with the shackles at his feet. *Come closer.* As Bjorn edged closer to the barred wall, a hand shot through the metal slats and a nail was dropped into his palm. Sweating nervously, Bjorn glanced up at the guard and worked at his own bindings.

The man was so strange, he frightened Bjorn, but Bjorn was thankful that the fire in his back had faded to a dull ache, and his face, swollen and no doubt bruised, was stiff and sore but no longer throbbed in agony. Whatever magic this man possessed, 'twas powerful.

Now, lure the guard into your cell and we will steal his keys. You are stronger than I if he resists.

Bjorn no longer questioned the sorcerer's commands. As if he were a knight who had pledged fealty to this peculiar baron, he climbed to his feet and felt a new freedom in his ankles and wrists. Revenge tainted his blood and he wanted nothing more than to seek out Holt and slit his traitorous throat.

Later.

He had to appear weak, he had to appear as if he needed assistance, he had to worry the simpleton sentry. Grabbing a handful of the foul rushes on the floor, he shoved them into his mouth. Straw and hair, dirt and all manner of grime and refuse clogged his throat, and as he coughed it up, he began to retch violently, his body racking against the putrid matter.

"Hey—what?" The guard glanced up.

Bjorn kept coughing, spitting, and vomiting.

"Oh, ye gods, what's 'appened to ye?" Disgust and worry edged the jailer's words. He climbed off his fat rump and grabbed his keys, as well as a candle for light. "Don't ye be dyin' on me, ye hear? Sir 'olt, 'e wouldn't like it if ye did somethin' as infernally stupid as leavin' this life." Keys jangling, he opened the cell door and slipped through, slamming the heavy bars into place behind him. "'Ere now, what's got into ye?"

Bjorn waited until the man was near, then he grabbed with both hands the manacles that had bound him, and with a quick lunge, forced the sentry backward. The candle dropped, hot wax sprayed on Bjorn's legs, and the soggy rushes on the floor caught flame, only to sputter out.

"Hey! Wha—?" the startled jailer yelled as links of chain

wrapped around his thick throat. Using his weight, Bjorn jammed his heavy body against the wall of bars that separated his cell from that of the stranger.

Coughing, choking, swearing, and stumbling backward, the guard kicked forward, attempting to wound Bjorn between his legs, but Bjorn, finding some sort of sweet justice, only tightened the noose. The guard wound his meaty fingers around the steel coil cutting off his wind, but Bjorn pressed harder until the man was backed against the bars, and the stranger wrapped his own manacles around one of the jailer's legs, looping the chain through the bars and clamping on the other cuff to his free leg.

"Hold him," he ordered. With deft fingers, he tore a strip of cloth from his tunic and forced it into the guard's gaping mouth. Only when the man sagged against the bars, his legs wobbling, did Bjorn release him and snap his manacles over the man's thick wrists. The jailer-turned-prisoner struggled, shaking his head and throwing himself against his bonds, but to no avail. Bjorn grabbed his keys, sword, and dagger, then hurried through the door, unlocked the stranger's cell, and ran toward the stairs, nearly knocking over Lady Cayley, who was hastening soundlessly down the steps.

"You're free?" she cried, stepping backward, surprised.

"Aye. Let's go."

"But how—?" she asked as she squinted into the darkness.

"Later, woman!" Bjorn insisted. "Now hush."

"He's right. Come quietly," the sorcerer agreed.

Bjorn grumbled, "I don't know why we need her!"

"Trust me. She is on our side."

He felt, rather than saw, the woman's back stiffen. "You doubt my integrity?"

"Nay, lady, only your ability." Bjorn had no time for a woman—a rich, pampered daughter of the baron—getting in his way.

"Even though I risked my life to come down to the dungeon to save you, even though you are a common outlaw, you doubt me?" she said, her voice filled with indignation.

A woman would only slow him down, but Bjorn would not question the sorcerer, not when the man had healed his wounds and shown him how to gain his freedom. Now, if only he could sneak into Holt's room and—

Enough! We must flee the castle before we're discovered! Trust this woman; she needs us as much as we need her.

The cripple, even with his limp, was swift enough, and Cayley led the way to the stables, where no guard lingered. Inside, the horses snorted and rustled when they sensed the intruders. But each animal quieted as the magician touched its coarse winter coat. 'Twas too dark to see much, but Bjorn found his stallion and Cormick's fleet mare for the woman while the sorcerer untied a quick horse to claim as his own. No bridles were in evidence, but Bjorn cut lengths of rope with the jailer's knife. He fashioned the twine into halters with reins, and soon they were leading their steeds out of the stables and into the moonlight.

Don't worry about the guards, the strange one intoned without words. *I shall handle them.*

The horses' hooves rang through the bailey as they approached the main gate. Bjorn thought 'twould be easy enough to lure the guards from their posts and pounce on them, but he sensed that the magician had another plan.

Be ready!

The sorcerer rode his horse into the middle of the bailey and threw his head back to howl like a dog at the moon.

"Wait!" Bjorn commanded. "Do not—"

But the deed was already accomplished, and men were beginning to awaken and shout.

"What's he doing?" the lady asked, horrified.

"I know not! Shh!" Bjorn kept his horse in the shadows of a hayrick. The main gate was open, the portcullis not yet dropped for the night.

"Halt! You in the bailey! Who be ye?" one guard asked.

"Know ye not?" the magician asked.

"Speak up, man!"

"I be the voice of the Devil. Lucifer's my name."

"Holy Mother," Cayley whispered, swiftly making the sign of the cross over her ample bosom.

"For the love of Christ, he's either drunk or as mad as a dog!" the guard growled. "He'll wake up the whole damned castle."

"Who is it?" another sentry asked, and he, too, was lured

into the inner bailey, where the magician, arms spread wide, began to bay soulfully again. In a rustle of feathers, a great owl hooted and landed squarely on the man's out-stretched arm. Bjorn watched in fascination as the wizard didn't flinch when the curved talons bit into his skin.

"Come," Bjorn ordered and kneed his mount. The horse took off like a thunderbolt, leaping forward, in its anxiety running toward the gatehouse. Cayley's horse gave chase.

"Stop! For the love of God, what's that?" one of the guards yelled.

"Who goes there?" another demanded as Bjorn's steed raced under the portcullis, steel hooves clattering over the drawbridge.

"'Tis the prisoner! 'E's escaping!"

"Nay, it couldn't . . . God's blood, there'll be 'ell to pay now!"

Bjorn heard no more. Over the ringing of hooves, shouts of alarm, and that horrid, soul-scraping, keening wail, he heard only the sound of his own heart beating a wild tattoo in his chest. "Run, you bastard, run!" he yelled at the horse, who was already nearly taking flight.

Down the road they sped with only a ribbon of moonlight as their guide. He glanced over his shoulder and saw that Cayley was tucked low, her black mantle billowing like a dark sail behind her as Cormick's game mare swept across the night-darkened countryside. The wind whipped past them, bringing tears to his eyes, and Bjorn's heart beat stronger, for this was the first taste of freedom he'd had in days, and oh, 'twas sweet.

The road forked, and they turned south, toward the nearest woods.

Zing!

An arrow hissed past his ear.

Thwack! Another landed in a tree to his right, and he heard the shouts of men on horses, already giving chase. A hasty look over his shoulder confirmed his worries; whatever advantage they had was surely fading.

"Bloody hell," he grumbled. Without another thought, he turned off the road and into the blackness of the woods. Cayley's horse didn't break stride, and together they slowed, moving silently and doubling back, delving deeper into the woods as they crossed a stream and peered through the leafless branches to the starry sky. In a thick copse of pine, he stopped and grabbed hold of the reins of Cayley's mount. Silently, he pressed a finger to her lips and felt her hot breath on his skin. The forest shivered with the rapid thuds of hoofbeats pounding over the frozen road. The soldiers passed not 20 feet from them, their horses galloping swiftly to the south, their torches held aloft, blinking like evil red-gold eyes before disappearing in the distance.

Once they could no longer be heard or seen, Bjorn pulled on the reins of his mount and headed north, to the camp near the old chapel where Wolf had said they'd meet.

"Oh, dear God in heaven," Cayley murmured, her voice trembling. "They'll find us."

"Not if we shut up and hurry."

"But they'll send dogs and—"

"Just ride, woman. Do not cry, do not beg, and do not whimper, or I'll leave you."

"You wouldn't!" she said, and he sensed her bristle. At the very least, she had some backbone.

"Not if ye behave yerself. Now, hush!" He felt her need to sputter and hiss at him, but she didn't utter another word. "We'll find Wolf."

Wolf. The man he'd trusted with his life. The man whom he'd revered. The man who'd nearly sent him to his death. The man whom Cormick had considered his family.

Angry with himself, with Wolf, with the damned martyr of a magician, he glanced at the woman huddled on her steed. She trembled from the cold, and when she glanced his way, there was pain and anger in her gaze. "We should have left him not," she finally said.

"Who? The wizard?"

"Aye. He gave up his life for us." Her gaze, filled with blame, cut him to his bones.

"'Twas what he wanted," Bjorn muttered, but couldn't stop the blade of guilt that twisted in his heart. What the lady was saying had already crossed his mind. "Shh. Be still. As you said, Holt's men could have dogs with them and find us." He clucked to his horse, urging the stallion through the undergrowth, but his thoughts were at Dwyrain with the sorcerer.

God be with you.

* * *

As if he'd heard a scream from the dead, Holt awakened with a start. But the blood-chilling wail didn't stop with his nightmare; no, it echoed through the castle, tumbling off the stone walls.

'Twas Ewan's ghost returned to haunt him!

Guards shouted, footsteps thundered through the hallways, someone began pounding on his door.

"Sir Holt!" Red shouted. "The prisoners have escaped!"

"What?" Anger tore through him. "But how?" He threw on his breeches and tunic, then opened the door to find the rotund knight breathing hard and sweating despite the cool temperature of the castle at night.

"'Tis true. We were tricked, we were. By the magician!"

Another keening wail raced through the corridors of the castle. Holt's heart nearly stopped, for it sounded to him as if the very beast from hell had been unleashed in the bailey.

"What in the name of Jesus is that noise?"

"The sorcerer, Sir Holt. He's . . . he's possessed! Call the priest."

"The man's a fraud. As you said, he's used his magic to confuse you," Holt sneered, hiding his own fear. Was he the only man in the castle with any brains? Strapping on his belt, sword, and dagger, he strode out of the room. Whatever trick the cripple had played, 'twould be his last!

Guards and servants were scrambling through the hallways, muttering oaths, whispering prayers, causing the rush lights to flicker as they passed. Outside, the noise was louder, a piercing, haunting scream that turned Holt's insides to water. The sorcerer sat on his horse, his arms thrown wide, a huge ruffle-feathered owl sitting on his shoulder.

"Stop!" he commanded, but the man continued his screaming as if he heard nothing other than the demons in his head. "Do you hear me, man? Stop this infernal—"

"Hey! Halt! Stop!" Out of the shadows, two horsemen spurred their mounts through the untended gates. "Oh, for the love of Jesus. 'Tis the prisoner! He's escaped!"

"What?" Holt's eyes narrowed on the fleeing horsemen.

Not one, but two of them. "The prisoner—?" His mind spun backward to the flogging. No man he'd beaten so hard would be able to ride, and who was the other one—the smaller rider? Certainly not the dead man, returned to life like Lazarus. Nay, that criminal had been buried in the woods outside the castle—the maggots were feasting on his flesh already. A cloud crossed the moon, casting a shadow on the land, and Holt felt as if the cold hand of death had grabbed his heart and squeezed so hard he couldn't catch his breath.

"Stop them," he yelled, but his men stood transfixed, staring as the sorcerer howled at the damned moon like a wolf from the depths of hell. *Like a wolf—sweet Jesus, the man is mocking me.* "Red, Oswald! Get some men together and stop those two!"

"Oh . . . aye." Red snapped out of the spell that had disabled him.

"After them!" Holt ordered. "After them!"

Red's gaze swept the gatehouse. "Damn it." Drawing his sword, he sprinted toward the stables, hitting men on the shoulders and hurling orders. Several men managed to break the spell and took off after him, their boots thudding on the frozen mud of the bailey.

Father Timothy, rumpled and cross, strode out of the chapel. Befuddled by the wailing and the crowd, he demanded, "What's the meaning of this?"

"Prisoners have escaped!" someone in the crowd yelled.

"The sorcerer is possessed!" Nell proclaimed.

Timothy's steps faltered. "I think not."

"Listen to him, Father," the candlemaker insisted. "'Tis what he said, that the Devil had control of his tongue!"

"Nay, this I do not believe." But the priest was more ashen-faced than before and trepidation contorted his fleshy features. His fingers anxiously rubbed the beads of the rosary hanging from his pocket.

Holt drew his sword and made his way through the crowd that had gathered, forming a crescent of onlookers near the center of the spectacle.

"You there, hush!" Holt commanded as he approached.

The shrieking didn't stop; 'twas almost as if the man took

no breaths. Children were crying, women on their knees, men staring at the sorcerer as if he were the Christ arisen again.

"Stop now, or I'll kill you."

"Nay!" one woman, the baker's pregnant wife, cried. "Sir Holt, you cannot. He's but a half-wit or . . ."

"Pull him down!" Holt ordered his soldiers.

"Oh, please, no. He means no harm."

"Do you not remember that he cursed Dwyrain?"

"That's right," the miller said, his frown deep. "We all suffered much. I lost a son."

"And I a sister," a woman said, but there was no conviction in her voice.

"My boy lost his leg," another woman said with a catch in her voice. They stared at the man as if he were a saint rather than the hellmonger he was.

"Show some mercy," Father Timothy pleaded, and Holt saw that his misgivings about the priest had proven true. Holt had always doubted the man's allegiance to him. Timothy was weak in his faith and in his convictions. Holt had no use for him.

"The sorcerer is not a man of God, but practices pagan magic," he reminded Timothy.

"He's misguided."

"As well as being a traitor to Dwyrain. This man helped the prisoner escape," Holt said. How had the magician managed that? Who was the second rider? Several men appeared at his side, and while the man screamed, he was dragged from his horse, and the owl, startled, flew away with a great flapping of his wings. Feathers fluttered to the ground. Two huge, burly soldiers held the prisoner fast, and the sight was pitiful, for he was a thin cripple who struggled not and would become a martyr if Holt wasn't careful.

"Who are you?" Holt threw at him, asking a question that had never before been answered. "Why are you here?"

The screaming suddenly stopped and the man's fevered, mindless eyes once again were eerily intelligent, more frightening than when he appeared riotously insane. "I, Sir Holt, am your conscience, that nasty prick of worry that you've hidden deep but sometimes keeps you awake at night."

The moon appeared from behind a cloud, bathing the

sorcerer's face in a silvery, nearly angelic glow. Holt shivered in his boots.

"What say you?" Holt asked again. The man was truly addled, but a drip of fear slid down Holt's spine.

"I'm your conscience, for I know what you've done."

There was no reason to listen to this. "Take him away!" Holt roared, trying to stem the dread that was slowly scraping at his soul.

"Is not the baron dead?" the cripple demanded.

Holt rounded and crashed his fist into the madman's face. Several women gasped and fell to their knees, praying loudly. The wind picked up, scattering dry leaves and playing with hems of surcoats and mantles.

"Ask him," the prisoner said to the crowd. "Ask him if he hasn't been poisoning Baron Ewan each day, and when the old man didn't die quickly—"

"Enough! Take him to the dungeon. He'll be hung at dawn!"

The magician had the audacity, the sheer, stupid insolence, to laugh. "Is that what you do to your adversaries, Holt? Kill them? Sneak into their chambers and place the skin of a bear over their faces until they can no longer draw a breath, as you did with the baron? Or do you marry them off, as you plan to do with Lady Cayley? Are you not planning to have her wed an old, cruel man who will kill her?"

"Take him away!" Holt swallowed hard. How had this . . . this addled half-wit known what he'd done? If anyone found out about the death of Ewan or if Connor discovered that Holt planned to betray him . . . He felt a tremor of fear, for Connor was a coldhearted bastard.

The guards pushed their captive roughly toward the north tower, but the sorcerer laughed again, the sound hideous to Holt's ears. "Enjoy your short rule as baron, Holt of Prydd," the sorcerer said with a patient, knowing smile. "'Twill soon be over!"

Holt's temper exploded and he caught up with his captive. "You fool," he uttered as he smashed a fist into the cripple's gut, causing the man to double over. If not for the guards holding him upright, he would have fallen to the ground.

"Did you see that?" a man's voice, one he didn't recognize, yelled loudly.

"A brute, he is," a woman murmured. "Lady Megan is lucky that she escaped becoming his bride."

"Thank God Baron Ewan is alive."

If you only knew, Holt thought, but he held his tongue. 'Twould look suspicious if he alone knew that Ewan had already left this world and joined his dead wife and children. That thought warmed him. Soon enough, come the morning, no one would any longer question his authority and refer to Ewan as the rightful baron of Dwyrain. 'Twas his now.

"Sir Holt!" Mallory yelled as he ran, ashen-faced, down the keep steps. "'Tis the baron."

"Did he call for me?"

"Nay," Mallory replied as he crossed the mashed grass of the inner bailey. "'Tis Lord Ewan. I'm afraid . . . 'tis dead he is."

"No!"

Gasps and wails met the soldier's announcement.

"'Tis true . . ." Mallory searched the crowd. "Father Timothy, please—"

"Did not the magician say—?" a woman asked.

"Shh!" her husband commanded.

"Say no more." Timothy held the skirt of his robes high and marched soberly to the keep.

"The baron? Are you sure?" Holt asked. He started toward the keep.

Mallory placed a hand on Holt's arm, restraining him. "There's more," he admitted, staring at the ground and tugging on the end of his moustache. "'Tis Lady Cayley."

"Yes, yes, what about her?" Holt shoved the man's hand off him and strode toward the great hall.

"She's missing, m'lord."

Holt whirled so swiftly he nearly fell over. "Missing?"

"Aye." Mallory paled and his Adam's apple wiggled nervously. "She escaped down a rope from her window."

"For the love of God," Holt growled, looking at the gate where the *two* horsemen had escaped. The tall blond outlaw and *Cayley?* Ewan's weak, whimpering, and flirtatious second daughter? His blood boiled. Not only had his own wife eluded him, but her simpering younger sister as well. Every muscle in his body grew taut as a bowstring and his eyes narrowed on his pathetic troop of soldiers. "Can't we hold anyone in this keep? Now, if you don't want to be flogged, beaten, or hanged, I suggest you take off after the prisoner and return him dead or alive. I care not which." Though a few troops had left, too many stood idle. "Go!"

"And . . . and the lady?"

His jaw clenched so tight it ached. Both Cayley and the prisoner were worth more to him alive than dead, but he cared not. "Kill her if she won't return peacefully."

"But she's the baron's daughter!" the cook proclaimed, unable to hold his tongue.

"Nay," Holt snarled to the pathetic people clustered around him. "If what Sir Mallory says is true and Ewan has given up his life, then I'm baron of Dwyrain!"

Megan stirred and reached for Wolf, but her hand found only an empty place on cold linen sheets. Opening her eyes, she blinked in the darkness and wondered where he was, what he would be thinking. Her dream of holding him close, of feeling his warm body and demanding lips, had been so real, so vivid, and she'd thought for just an instant that he was here with her.

"So ye're awake." The voice, that of the old crone, startled her and she scooted upward in the bed, holding a blanket over her chest.

"Aye," she said as the woman lit a candle from the dying embers of the fire.

"I know ye be worried about yer man, the outlaw Wolf."

"How would you know . . . ?"

"I see things, lass. 'Tis my curse." Rubbing the huge knots that were the joints of her fingers, the gnarled woman lowered herself onto the foot of the bed and gazed out the chamber's single window to the star-studded sky. "Something's amiss tonight," she said, as if to herself. "The gods are not happy."

"Gods—you mean God," Megan said.

"Aye, Him, too." Sighing, she placed a candle on a small

table near the bed and the flame flickered in the breath of wind stirring through the castle. "There's good and bad in the world, m'lady. Everyone has a share of each."

"What is it you're trying to tell me, Isolde?"

"There was a death tonight," the old one said, her eyes far away. "At Dwyrain."

"Nay—"

"Your father, lass."

"Nay! Nay! Nay! I believe you not!" Megan cried, though the lines of sadness around the old woman's eyes and etching over her forehead half convinced her.

"'Tis true. He was helped to his death by your husband."

The world jolted and spun. Megan's breath stopped dead in her lungs. "No," she cried, but sensed the woman would not have come here if she did not believe it.

"I sensed a tremor, child, a rending in the air. 'Twas Ewan giving up his life."

Megan's bones no longer supported her. She felt as if the world had stopped, as if life itself had withered. Her father, her wonderful father, now dead? Though she'd told herself that his death had been imminent, that there was a chance she wouldn't see him alive again, she could not believe that he was really gone. Tears gathered in her eyes, but she held them at bay, refusing to break down. "Leave me alone. I—I believe this not."

"There is more."

"I do not want to hear it."

Isolde reached forward and grabbed Megan's fingers, still clutching the coverlet. "Aye, this news is sweet," she said with a smile. "For every death, there is new life, and you, m'lady, carry new life in your womb."

Megan couldn't speak. Her words jumbled and clogged in her throat. *A baby?* Is that what the woman was saying? She was going to have a child? *Wolf's* issue? "How . . . how would you know?"

Isolde sighed. "'Tis a gift," she said.

"You practice the dark arts."

"Aye," she admitted. "Some say I be a witch, but 'tis not true. I'm a nursemaid. 'Twas I who helped Lady Sorcha come into this world."

Megan glanced down at her flat abdomen, now covered

with thick blankets. Could this be true? Could she believe this glorious gift had been given her and deny the woman's death sentence for her father?

"As for the babe growing within you, 'tis early yet, the child only just conceived."

Megan swallowed hard. *A baby!* Though she felt a deep grief at the loss of her father—if the old woman spoke the truth—the thought of bringing Wolf's child into the world brought with it a joy she'd never before known.

Isolde placed a warm, aged hand over the furs and blankets that covered Megan's abdomen. A small smile played at the edges of her thin lips. "I know not what it will be, 'tis much too soon. But ye must be careful, Megan. This babe was created by great love. You must take care of yourself and of it. Now"—she reached for her candle—"sleep well. Both of you."

Megan slid lower in the bed and placed a hand over the skin stretched between her hipbones. Could she believe this old woman? Was Ewan really dead? Did a child grow deep inside her?

Tears slid down her face and she knew not if they came from grief or happiness.

❧ *Thirteen* ❧

"Isolde told me you were with child," Sorcha said as her husband gathered together a small band of men to accompany Megan to Dwyrain. Leah had already left Erbyn with a sentry and was riding to her duties in the nunnery.

Now Sorcha and Megan stood on the steps of the keep, cowls pulled tight around their necks, hems caught in the stiff breeze. From the armorer's hut came the clank of a metal hammer repairing broken links of mail; from the outer bailey could be heard the slice of saws and chop of axes chewing through timbers for firewood and beams. In a lean-to near the farrier's hut a wheelwright pounded new spokes into a broken cart wheel.

Smoke filled the air and icy rain drizzled from the heavens.

Megan glanced away from the questions in the other woman's deep blue eyes. "Isolde is only guessing. 'Tis too early to tell."

"But 'tis possible."

"Aye." Megan nodded, biting her lip, mentally calculating and realizing that her time of the month should arrive soon, or mayhap was already a few days late.

"She is rarely wrong in these matters." Sorcha laid a hand on Megan's shoulder. "The babe. Is it not Holt's?"

Megan sighed, but didn't answer.

Sorcha persisted, "If you are with child and that babe is not your husband's, will he not know it?"

How could she possibly explain? Lord Hagan and his lady had a fine marriage where they teased often, touched intimately, and ruled together as one. Their love was deep and strong, their marriage as solid as the castle built high on this cliff. "I detest my husband and wanted to marry him not, but my father would not hear my protests. Then, on my wedding day, I was abducted . . ."

"By Wolf."

"Aye."

"And you fell in love with him," Sorcha said as if reading Megan's thoughts.

Pain clawed its way through Megan's tortured soul. "Aye."

"So you gave yourself to him."

Megan's spine stiffened and she lifted her head proudly, her hood falling away and her hair waving wildly around her face. "I would do it again if given the chance."

"Holt will not be pleased."

"Nay."

"He might want to harm the child," Sorcha said, her gaze clouding.

"He will never have the chance!" A fierce new fire grew within Megan and she knew she would do anything to save the life of her unborn infant. Should Holt try to harm her child, she would kill him.

"If, as Isolde says, your father has passed on, you must find a priest or abbot who will annul your marriage."

She thought of Father Timothy, a weak man with no convictions, a man who only wished people punished, and knew she could not speak with him. Nay, she needed someone with power, someone who understood her precarious position, someone who could strike down the marriage vows.

"Hagan will help you find the right abbot," she assured Megan. "Now, does Wolf know of the child?"

"Nay." She shook her head and bit her lip.

"Does he . . . does he love you, or was your seduction part of his plan to embarrass your husband?"

"I know not," she admitted, though she clung to the hope that he'd lain with her not because she was Holt's bride, but because he could not stop himself, that he, as she, was compelled to kiss and touch, to caress and bond.

"You must tell him."

'Twas not the first time the thought had crossed her mind. Wrapping her arms around her waist, as if to protect the fragile life growing inside her, she nodded. Should she meet Wolf again, what would she say? How could she tell him he'd unwittingly become a father of a bastard child? "I will, but not before I am free."

Instead of condemnation in Sorcha's gaze, there was silent praise. "God be with you, Megan of Dwyrain," she said, adjusting Megan's cowl again and kissing her lightly on the cheek, "and with your babe."

"'Tis time," Hagan said, astride a large gray destrier. He led a smaller horse, a bay with a notched ear. Climbing down from his mount, he handed Megan the bay's reins, then kissed his wife so passionately, Megan had to look away. "I'll be back," he promised.

"Ride safely," Sorcha said, kissing him lightly on the cheek and blinking against tears. A blistering howl rose from inside the castle. "'Tis your daughter, m'lord," Sorcha said with a smile. "Methinks she is hungry again." She shot Megan a glance that said, *See what you have to look forward to?*

"Take care of her and worry not about me!" With a final look at his wife, he signaled for his small army to move out. Megan climbed onto the bay mare and tugged on the horse's reins as Bryanna wailed again and Isolde, carrying the loud, tiny bundle, appeared in the doorway. Waving, Megan urged her mount forward and joined the soldiers in their march to Dwyrain. She silently chided herself for leaving the ragged outlaw band, with its well-meaning criminals and brooding rogue of a leader.

What would you do had you stayed with them? Tell Wolf that he will be a father? Hope that he would marry you? Even if you were not already wed to Holt?

Wolf, the outlaw, was not a man to marry.

Aye, she told herself, clucking to her mare, *but surely Ware of Abergwynn is.*

* * *

"Something's wrong," Jack said, eyeing the crenels of Dwyrain's north watchtower. "See there—one of the shutters is closed; the others are open." He, Jagger, Robin, and Wolf, astride their sweating mounts, were hidden in the forest and watching the castle through the wintry foliage that remained. The wind was biting, the clouds dark, sleet starting to fall. "The baron's standard is not flying . . ."

Wolf felt a stab of fear deep in his soul. His gaze moved to the flagpole. 'Twas true. The new colors waving vividly against the dawn sky were a deep blue field with a red chevron . . . the symbol Wolf had seen upon Holt's shield. A sickening dread stole over him. "Baron Ewan is dead. Sir Holt has proclaimed himself the new ruler of Dwyrain."

"So it appears." Jack spit on the ground. "'Tis cursed we are."

"Unless we defeat him," Wolf said, his eyes narrowing on his enemy's lair. His fingers clenched over the hilt of his sword. What pleasure he'd find in running the bastard through. Was Megan somewhere in the stone keep? A prisoner, mayhap, or Holt's willing wife? Had she returned to Dwyrain to her father, only to find that he'd died and she was forever married to the new baron? Had she shared a bed with the bastard? Given herself willingly to him? Been forced into submission? Had she suffered a beating at Holt's hands, and was she now his prisoner?

Guilt clawed at him. Had he not sealed her fate by stealing her from her husband? If Holt's wrath was aimed at Megan for her betrayal, was not Wolf responsible? Had he not incited Holt, humiliated and taunted the man in an effort to belittle him? Pray that he would not hurt her!

Rage stormed through his blood. Horrid, painful images of Megan being used by Holt brought a snarl to Wolf's lip. 'Twould be so easy to kill Holt and taste sweet, long-awaited vengeance. "Let's go!" he growled, eager to find Megan, to kidnap her if 'twas what it took to keep her safe.

"Be ye mad?" Jagger asked. "We can't ride through the gates, now can we?"

"Why not?" Robin, impatient for battle, demanded.

"I'll go ahead," Jack offered, "and I'll take with me the kills that I've got—" He motioned to the stag and boar he'd slain this morning and now were lashed to a sled built of poles. "I'll tell Cook that I'm taking a hunting party out this evening, and when we return, late, there may be three more men with me. No one will notice."

"And the men who leave the castle with you? Will they not wonder?"

"I'll choose my party well. 'Twill be made of those who detest Holt as much as we do," Jack said with a wicked smile. "There are men within the gates of Dwyrain who would follow you blindly on only my word."

"Good. While you're inside, learn what you can about Megan—if she's within the keep."

"I will," he promised. He rode through the underbrush to the road to join a small procession of carts and horsemen moving to and from the castle through a curtain of icy rain that washed away any lingering traces of snow and added to the chill that had already settled deep in Wolf's bones. 'Twas all he could do to remain where he was and not steal into the thick walls of Dwyrain to see for himself if Megan had returned.

'Twas simple enough to sneak into the castle with the hunting party. Once inside the walls, several of the men carried the kills of badger, pheasant, boar, and stag to the butcher and the tanner, while Jack and Tom, the carpenter's son who so often was in the north watchtower, led Wolf, Jagger, and Robin down a dark, winding staircase past the brewery, where the alewives stirred oaken vats of ale, and into a small chamber used for the hoarding of grain. With a few candles for light, the men rested on sacks of grain and watched shadows play on the rock walls.

Tom, about the age of Robin, peered over his shoulder as he spoke. "'Tis as if the beasts of hell have been let loose," he said, his green eyes wide in the shadowy room. "The baron drew his last breath last night and Holt proclaimed himself the new ruler of the keep." Tom's tongue rimmed his mouth nervously. "He sent men to chase after Bjorn, who escaped with Lady Cayley."

"What of Cormick?" Wolf asked, grateful that one of his men was free.

"Dead. Killed when he was flogged."

"Mother Mary," Jack said under his breath as he crossed himself hurriedly.

Wolf flinched and again guilt was his companion. Because of his own need of vengeance, he'd sent a trusting, faithful man to his death. Back teeth grinding together, he silently cursed the demons who drove him. If only he'd let things be, Cormick would be alive, Bjorn would not have been flogged, and Megan . . . oh, sweet spitfire of a woman . . . would be serving her time as Holt's wife. Nay, he could never accept that.

"Lady Megan has not returned?" he asked.

"Nay, neither Holt nor his men have found her."

Where was she? A dozen horrid thoughts crawled through his mind, but he pushed them aside. At least she was not suffering as Holt's wife.

"But when Bjorn and Cayley escaped, Holt was in a rage, and he plans to hang the sorcerer who was with them."

"Sorcerer?" Wolf said.

"Aye, the same man who is said to have cursed Dwyrain years ago, the cripple that Lady Megan met in the woods when her mare came up lame two years ago."

Wolf had heard the tale, of course. It had spread throughout the countryside like wildfire.

"'Twas as if he wanted to be captured again," Tom insisted as he anxiously picked at his teeth with the nail of his thumb. "He raced not to the gatehouse but stayed his horse, threw his hands wide as if to heaven, and screamed as loudly as if he were trying to wake the souls of the dead. An owl bigger than I've ever seen landed on his arm."

"He is being held prisoner here?"

"Aye, in the north tower dungeon."

"And is scheduled to hang?" Wolf asked uneasily.

Tom nodded. "My father was told to build a new gallows. Holt is said to want to make an example of the man and to prove that he is a strong baron even though his wife was stolen from him and neither he nor his best men have been able to find her."

Footsteps scraped upon the stairs. Wolf's hands curled over the hilt of his sword and Jagger flattened against the wall at the base of the steps, ready to jump the intruder.

Robin and Tom hid behind sacks of grain, their weapons unsheathed, while Jack waited in the shadows.

"'Tis only me," a woman called.

Tom grinned widely. "Rue. Thank the saints."

An old, thin woman appeared with a pitcher of ale, loaf of bread, and round of cheese. "'Tis not much, I know," she said, setting her fare on an upended cask. "But 'twas all the cook would give for fear the steward or one of Holt's spies might see him." She turned tired eyes on Wolf and offered him the pitcher. "The baron is dead, both his daughters are missing and, I fear, Dwyrain lost."

"Nay—" Tom argued, but Rue persisted, staring pointedly at Wolf.

"'Tis said you are Holt's sworn enemy."

Wolf took a long draft from the pitcher, wiped his lips with his sleeve, and nodded. "'Tis true."

"'Tis also thought that you are much to blame for the trouble here. If ye had not stolen Lady Megan, mayhap Holt would have been less angry and cruel."

Wolf passed the pitcher to Jagger, who took a long, healthy swallow. "What do you think, woman?" he asked.

"Holt is bad to his bones. I would waste no tears if Holt were found murdered," she said, as if she hoped to find the new baron with a sword run through his heart in the morning, "but I'm grateful that both Lady Megan and Lady Cayley are far from his grasp, even though this keep is theirs by rights." She sliced the cheese with a large knife and sawed off hunks of bread, which she passed to the men. "I think ye, Wolf," she said, wagging the tip of her blade at his nose as he sank his teeth into the crusty bread, "should see that both of the baron's daughters are safe so that someday they might reclaim Dwyrain. Ye started this, so I think ye should finish it."

"I intend to," he agreed, reaching for the ale pitcher again. "I'll start by freeing the magician this night. Mayhap he'll help me find Megan and Cayley, and then, I swear, once they're safe, I'll come for Holt."

"Will ye kill him?"

Wolf thought of Megan and how she might suffer at Holt's hands should he ever find out that Megan had given herself to his sworn enemy. Something deep in Wolf's heart stirred;

he couldn't bear to think of her with another man, especially not a cruel cur the likes of the man who had willingly held down a fair maid so that she could be brutally raped. The ale and bread suddenly tasted sour and stuck in his throat. When he lifted his eyes, he found Rue staring at him and he nodded. "Aye," he vowed, "if needs be, I'll send him to hell, where he belongs."

"We cannot stop!" Megan said, though every bone in her body ached, her head throbbed, and her legs were sore from three days of riding.

"The men are tired and you, m'lady, need to rest." Hagan's eyes searched the dusky countryside, looking for a spot near the road to make camp.

"Nay! We are too close." Though she dreaded facing Holt again, she'd felt drawn to Dwyrain, knew she had to return to her home. Hagan had sent word ahead to the abbot of St. Peter's in the hope of annulling her marriage, and Megan had been restless and eager to ride under the portcullis of Dwyrain. Despite her feeling of despair, she had been whispering prayers that Isolde had been wrong about Ewan, that he yet lived. Though Isolde had sworn that she'd seen him in his grave, the old woman could surely make a mistake now and again. Megan refused to believe that because the nursemaid had been correct about the baby growing in Megan's womb, this meant that she was never wrong.

"Here!" Hagan indicated a small field not far from the road. "We'll camp for the night."

She wanted to argue, to insist that they travel on, but she held her tongue. Hagan of Erbyn had been good to her and his men; she would not thwart him, but she couldn't shake the feeling—the dread—that something dire was happening within the stone walls of Dwyrain, that if only she were there, some kind of tragedy could be averted.

'Twas but a feeling, although 'twas so real. Goose bumps crawled up her arms and she refused to give in to the fear that gnawed at her insides, the fear that somehow Holt had caught up with Wolf and that even now, the outlaw might be dead, killed by her husband's hand. Shivering, she dismounted, and as the men started a fire and skinned the squirrels and rabbits they'd killed on the journey, she found the bucket tied to the saddle of her mare and walked to the stream. Dipping into the dark water, she was reminded of her stay with the sorry band of criminals she'd grown to love. She wondered about Robin. Had his wounds healed? Had Odell learned to cook any better? Was one-eyed Peter ever the quiet voice of reason whenever there was a fight? Did Wolf think of her as often as she did of him?

A knot tightened in her throat as an image of Wolf with his brooding dark looks, the pain of his past, the silent anger that drove him, crossed before her eyes. She lifted the pail, but in the ripples of the water she saw his face, handsome, arrogant, and proud, his smile as hard and cunning as the beast from which he'd taken his name. As she drew her bucket through the clear water, she heard the men behind her as they staked out the tents and told jokes. She absently rubbed her abdomen, trying to comfort the child growing deep within her womb. Would this tiny person ever meet his or her father? Would the outlaw Wolf ever learn that he was a father?

Rather than dwell upon the thoughts that were forever tormenting her, Megan squared her shoulders and sent up a prayer for his safety.

In a few days, they'd arrive at Dwyrain and then . . . then somehow she'd find a way to untie the dreadful knot of her marriage and become a free woman.

Why? To what end? So that Wolf will marry you? He's an outlaw, Megan, a criminal running from the law! Is that what you want your child to grow up with, knowing that his or her father is a common criminal?

Not common. Far from common. A nobleman turned outlaw.

She lugged the pail back to the fire and set it on the rocks surrounding the crackling kindling.

Aye! My baby will know the wonderful rogue who gave him or her life. By the gods, if it's the last thing I do, Wolf and his son or daughter will meet!

The moon was cloaked in clouds and no campfire guided them as they picked their way through the woods. Cayley was bone weary, her back sore, her spirits sinking with each plod of her mount's hooves. It felt as if it had been years since they'd seen civilization. The naked trees of the forest were gloomy and protected them little from the icy mist that drizzled from the sky. Wet branches slapped at her face and vines clawed at her cape.

Bjorn, the broad-shouldered outlaw brute, rode on and outwardly appeared not to notice the cold or feel the sleet, rain, or snow. Proudly, he sat astride his mount, moving onward, pausing only once or twice to hunt some small forest beast or rob an unsuspecting traveler. Since leaving Dwyrain, Bjorn had stolen two blankets, food for themselves and the horses, and several weapons. He never asked for gold, silver, or jewelry, didn't bother with anything more than they needed or could carry. Cayley had never actually seen him stalk his human prey; he'd done most of his thievery at night, and when she'd awakened, there had been a loaf of bread, a new thick blanket tossed over her, or a knife to keep in her boot. The horses had eaten well and Bjorn had refused to explain whom he'd had to threaten in order to survive.

'Twas thrilling, and had Cayley been a stronger woman, she would have insisted upon going with him on his nightly marauding. She thought he made camp close to his intended victims, for she knew that he would not leave her long alone in the woods with only a fire and her own small knives to protect her.

She'd imagined that she'd never sleep a wink, but each morning, 'twas Bjorn who placed a huge, callused hand on her shoulder and shook her awake. She'd slept without dreaming, her head resting on a root of a tree or a flat rock, her fingers curled over the hilt of her dagger.

"Holy Christ, Odell, what've ye done?" Bjorn muttered as the overgrown trail broke into a clearing near a river. The rushing sound of a waterfall greeted her ears; the grass and weeds of the small clearing had been trampled by horses, carts, and people.

From the tone of Bjorn's voice, she knew that something was wrong—very wrong. Cayley clucked to her mount, reaching Bjorn's side. "What?"

"They've moved."

"Who—what?"

"Wolf's band. The sorcerer told me that the band was ordered to stay here, but Odell, curse his flea-riddled hide, decided to move on." He slid from his mount, and still breathing fire and swearing, he kicked at a circle of stones that had once been the rim of a campfire.

Cayley, too, dismounted, and for a second, her tired legs were unable to hold her, but she steadied herself, stretched, and viewed the night-darkened landscape. Aside from the fire pit, there was evidence that people had recently been here, the broken grass, wheel ruts, and discarded bones from meals still visible. A huge skeleton of a building, half standing, half in rubble, loomed near the river.

"Used to be a chapel," Bjorn said tightly as if reading her mind. "We stayed here with your sister and Wolf told Odell not to move camp." He spat loudly. "That slimy little cur!"

"Where would he go?"

"Good question." He thought for a second. "Odell's a bit of a coward. He talks much, acts as if he's braver than the other men put together, but the truth of the matter is that he would do nothing to incite Wolf's wrath."

"So he was forced to move."

"Mayhap."

"What would cause him to leave?"

Bjorn rubbed the back of his neck. "Holt's army," he decided, and then, as if determining that they, too, might not be safe, said, "Come, lead your horse into the old chapel."

"A beast in the house of God?" she said, shaking her head at the blasphemy of it. "Nay, I don't think—"

"Hush, woman! 'Tis no longer a chapel and God will not care if one of his four-footed creatures stumbles upon the altar. Methinks all manner of beasts have already crept their way through the windows and open doors." His patience was nearly gone—that much was obvious—and the argument that simmered between them, which was her forever doubting or second-guessing his orders, flared again. He'd told her once that he thought her nothing more than a pampered, rich pain in the backside, and she'd let him know that he was an uneducated criminal brute. They were at a stalemate, stuck with each other until they could find Wolf and Megan.

From what Cayley had gleaned, and it wasn't much from this quiet, stubborn giant, Wolf and several of the men had fallen half in love with her sister.

"Come, m'lady," he said as she crossed herself with practiced fingers. "If ye want to save yer pretty skin, you'll do as I say and guide yer horse through the door!"

She had no choice and tugged on the reins, leading the animal through the icy mist to the shelter of the chapel. God forgive her, she had no choice but to depend upon this blond criminal to help her find Megan.

Tom and Robin's job was to open the gates, Jack's to guide Wolf to the dungeon where the sorcerer was held, and Jagger was to guard the door so that no one would surprise them as they made their quick escape. Wolf held his knife in his teeth and had one hand on his sword. The other trailed along the wall of the dank-smelling stairs that wound downward.

He had to fight his fear, for this was not the first time he'd been in a prison. Years before, he and his friend, Cadell, brother of Morgana of Wenlock, had been locked in the bowels of Abergwynn. 'Twas only through their quick wits and the guard's stupidity that they were able to flee the castle walls, only to be chased down by enemy men. Wolf— Ware at the time—had watched in horror as his friend had pitched over the cliffs to the black sea. Then, rather than be captured and imprisoned yet again, he had followed Cadell, throwing himself over the edge. . . . Wolf shivered inwardly. He *hated* dungeons, detested confinement. Tight places with locked doors made his skin itch and his head pound.

The guard was awake and held a knife in his hand as if he expected someone to try to help the prisoner escape. "Who goes there?" he demanded.

"'Tis only me. Jack, the huntsman."

"Oh, and what is it ye want, Jack?" the sentry, suddenly more at ease, wanted to know. While Wolf hung in the shadows, Jack, holding his candle high, approached the sentry.

"I'd like a word with ye. I saw yer son, Ian, in the forest the day before last. He was trackin' a stag on the baron's land without permission. Got off one good shot, but the deer sprinted away and the arrow missed its mark, landing in the trunk of an oak tree instead."

"For the love of Jesus." The guard made a hasty sign of the cross over his thick chest.

"I told Holt not."

"Thank ye for that much. I'm tellin' ye, Jack, that boy will be the death of me and his ma. Always gettin' into trouble, that one, not like his older brother—hey! What the—"

Jack sprang and Wolf lunged from his hiding place in the dark corner near the stairs. Together, they knocked the guard off his feet and wrested the knife from his hands. He fought, kicked, and swore as Jack lashed his hands behind his broad back. "I thought we might make a trade, Theodore," he said, holding his knife to the guard's thick neck. "I'll not tell Holt about yer boy and ye keep yer mouth shut about this."

"Nay, I cannot."

"Then ye'll die." Jack appeared about to slice his throat open, but Wolf stopped him.

"No more bloodshed."

"What?"

"Holt's blood is all that needs be spilled. This man has done nothing wrong."

"He'll sound the alarm."

"So be it."

Theodore listened to this exchange with bulging eyes. "No good'll come of this, Jack. What the hell d'ye think ye're doin'?"

"Saving the castle."

"By gettin' me killed? Holt'll have me hide when he finds out what ye're up to. Yer skin will be worthless, too!"

"Like as not."

Wolf reached for the guard's key ring. He saw the sorcerer in the corner of the cell, standing peacefully, though he was chained with thick links to the wall. "You're to be a free man," he assured the magician as he swung open the gate and held a torch aloft, throwing flickering illumination through the cell. When the light touched the cripple's eyes, Wolf's blood turned to ice, for standing before him was not the sorcerer he'd heard so much about but his old friend, the boy he thought had lost his life on the rocky shoals beneath the cliffs of Abergwynn.

"I knew you'd come," Cadell said in an even tone. "What took ye so long, Ware of Abergwynn?"

"For the love of Jesus. Cadell."

"Aye. 'Tis I."

"What happened to ye—where've ye been?"

"We have no time for this."

"Let's go!" Jack said.

"Aye," Wolf said, grateful that his old friend had survived. He wasted no time, but opened the cell. "Right now, we must leave." He unchained his old friend, then slapped a small dagger into his hand.

"I use not weapons."

Wolf's eyes met Cadell's in the darkness. "If we escape without battle, praise God. But if we run across anyone who wants to kill us, please, do them the honor first."

"Come!" Jack yelled. "We've lost too much time." He had gagged and bound the guard and now tossed the frightened man into Cadell's cell. Slamming the door shut with a distinct clang, he led them up the slippery stairs.

The air became clearer and Wolf, holding on to the hilt of his sword, breathed deeply. Within minutes, they'd ride through the gates of Dwyrain and into the forest. Once back at the camp, he'd start looking for Megan, sending his men out to the villages and keeps until he found her. Cadell could help . . .

And what then, Wolf, his mind sneered. *What do you plan to offer her? The life of an outlaw—a man with no castle, no house, his only possession a sword? Or are you willing to give up your freedom?*

Pale light filtered through the open door, and Jack stepped cautiously out of the tower. Wolf was behind him, his eyes searching the bailey for Tom and Robin, who were nowhere in sight. They might have been waylaid trying to raise the portcullis in the gatehouse. Or . . . the hairs on his nape raised and his fingers tightened over the hilt of his sword. The castle was still as death. Stepping onto the packed mud near the door of the tower, he began to sweat in the cold mist.

"Wolf! Watch out!" Jack's voice cut through the silence,

then there was the clang of steel striking steel. Swords clashed, ringing through the bailey.

From the corner of his eye, Wolf saw a glint of metal, a silent, swift movement near the side of his head. He ducked, spinning fast, sword drawn, as a battle ax cleaved the air and sliced heavily into the earth. The ground shuddered.

Wolf rolled onto the balls of his feet, slicing around him as men, 8 or 10 of them, ran, swords drawn, from the shadows. Within seconds, they'd surrounded the doorway of the tower. Bloody Christ, what had gone wrong?

Tom and Robin were both with the soldiers, their wrists lashed, their faces pale as the moon. Blood ran from one of Robin's nostrils and caked his lips. Tom's eyes were round with fear, blood staining his tunic.

Jack spun and struck, but a huge man swung a mace and it caught Jack midsection, sending him to the ground with a sickening thud.

"Halt, outlaw!" a gravelly voice ordered as a soldier lunged at him, and Wolf's sword was swift, severing the man's arm and sending him reeling. With a hideous roar, he fell against the tower wall, blood spurting and spraying as he slid down the stones. Another man, big and burly, rounded on Wolf, only to feel Wolf's blade slash him through the ribs. As a third came at him from behind, he whirled, intending to draw blood.

Bam!

Pain exploded in his brain and he fell to his knees.

Thud!

Another blinding jolt of pain. Wolf cried out, dropping his sword. The world tilted. His head slammed into the dirt, the stars and moon spun wildly. He tasted his own blood, and suddenly there was nothing.

Megan woke with a start. Heart pounding, she sat bolt upright. *Wolf!* Dear God, she'd been dreaming of him, touching him, feeling his skin upon hers, his lips brushing her eyes and throat and breasts, when suddenly he'd jerked, like a puppet on a string, his body wrenched from her. She cried out and the battlements and walls of Dwyrain came into her view.

'Twas only a dream, she told herself and tried to slow her

racing heart, but she couldn't shake the feeling that Wolf was in trouble, that he needed her. But that was silly. Restless, she crawled out of the tent Hagan had staked out for her, and walked to the stream. A sudden chill turned the marrow of her bones to ice and she rubbed her arms.

Pausing at the stream, she heard the sound of wings, the rustle of feathers, as a huge owl landed on the bare branch of a willow tree over her head. She swallowed hard and remembered seeing such a bird with the sorcerer when he'd predicted trouble at Dwyrain, then again in the woods at the camp with Odell, and now here.

The owl stared at her with round, unblinking eyes that caused another shiver to race through her blood. He didn't settle down, his head never lowering into his neck, and he flapped his great wings several times, as if straightening his feathers. She tried to ignore the winged creature—he was probably resting from the hunt—but she felt his eyes upon her and thought that his presence could only be a sign, and not a good one.

What had old Rue said so long ago? That the creatures of the forest had a sense unlike those of man, that the beasts could smell trouble before it appeared, feel a storm before it broke, sense the movement of a fire before the smoke had met human nostrils?

The horses were close by and she saw her notched-ear jennet resting at her tether, one hoof cocked in slumber. 'Twas quiet in the camp, aside from the gentle snoring of the man who was supposed to be tending the beasts.

Praying she was not making a huge mistake and inviting the wrath of another baron when Hagan awoke, Megan stole to the horses and untied her mare. The horse awoke with a snort. "Shh," she murmured, knowing she was inviting doom.

But because of Wolf, she could wait no longer. As sure as the moon rose in the sky, there was trouble at Dwyrain, and she, as the baron's eldest daughter, had to return.

Cold water splashed over him in a wave and Wolf coughed and sputtered, his eyes opening slowly, his head thundering in pain. He didn't remember where he was or how he'd gotten there. A second after he saw the smooth leather shoes and gold braid of a surcoat, he lifted his eyes farther to find his old enemy Holt standing before him in the inner bailey. There were people everywhere, the sun was rising through a gray fog, and geese, ducks, chickens, and children scrambled out of the way of the new, imposing ruler of Dwyrain.

"How dare you," Holt said. One of the guards hauled Wolf to his feet and he stood, between two burly men, swaying. Stripped to only his breeches, he tried to stand on his own and failed. His muscles flexed as a blast of northern wind cut through the bailey, chasing the last hint of fog. "How dare you sneak into my keep and try to steal one of my prisoners? Did you not think my soldiers were told to watch and wait, that your coming here was inevitable?"

Even in his pain, an insolent smile curved Wolf's lips. "How dare you presume to be baron?"

A glimmer of recognition flashed in Holt's eyes and Wolf knew he'd struck a sensitive nerve.

"Ewan chose me as his successor."

"Was that before or after you started poisoning him?"

Holt's fist crashed into Wolf's body, the metal studs on his gloves cutting into Wolf's flesh. "Impudent whelp!" he roared, then, as if realizing dozens of pairs of eyes were upon him, Holt drew in a long, ragged breath. "Bring him to my chamber," he growled.

"What about the others?"

"Leave them to rot for now. They'll hang later."

Surcoat billowing behind him, Holt stormed up the steps of the keep, and Wolf was half pushed and shoved behind him. He caught several men's eyes, and their expressions varied. The carpenter, Tom's father, gritted his teeth against his fury, the armorer slid Wolf a knowing look, several soldiers spit as Wolf was hauled roughly through, and milkmaids and laundresses looked upon him as if he were an amusement. An old woman, weathered and gaunt, crossed herself, though her piety seemed forced.

"Move!" one of the guards ordered as he elbowed Wolf forward.

On shaking legs, he followed Holt up winding stairs, past rush lights that cast shifting gold shadows upon the walls, and into the lord's chamber. A fire roared at the grate and tapestries draped the walls. Above the curtained bed, the horns and antlers of beasts the lord of the manor had felled in years past were mounted proudly.

As the guards held Wolf, Holt sat in a huge chair. A page brought him wine and dates, which he plucked at as he stared at his enemy. "Where is my wife?" Holt asked, a vein throbbing across his temple.

Wolf managed a sneer. "Have trouble keeping her?"

With a motion of one finger, Holt gave a silent command to the guard and a fist, hard-knuckled and bare, crashed into the side of his face. Bones crunched. Blood sprayed. Wolf's knees buckled, but the sentries held him upright. "Why is it you stole her from me?"

"Know you not, Holt?" Wolf asked. "Do you not remember me when Tadd of Prydd had his way with the fisherman's daughter in a village east of Prydd?"

"I remember not. . . ." But his voice faded and his jaw grew tight. Clearing his throat, he glared at Wolf.

"Now," Holt said, dismissing whatever thoughts chased through his evil mind. "Let's start again. Where's my wife?"

"Go to hell."

Holt's lips flattened over his teeth. "Hell? Interesting that you should bring it up, because I think, when I'm through with you, you'll wish you were there." Rubbing the stubble on his jaw, he said to a thick-bodied knight, "Throw him in the dungeon, but not in the same cell with his friends. Torture him slowly, until he tells us what we want to know. When he finally confesses, see that all the rest of the prisoners—the damned sorcerer, the two who rode with this cur, Jack, and Tom, the carpenter's son—feel the noose tighten around their necks."

Wolf felt sick. Because of his love for Megan, he'd brought Robin and Jagger to their deaths.

Another flick of Holt's finger. A fist splintered Wolf's nose and the world swam again. Wolf felt as if he were drowning, but before he slid beneath the balming waters of unconsciousness, he sputtered, "I'll see you in hell, Holt."

Holt shuddered at the words. Why would this man not break? How deep was his need of vengeance for a woman who had been raped . . . a woman Holt did not remember? "Take the Judas to Ivor and see that his tongue is loosened,"

Holt commanded, his nerves jangled. How could one man, beaten and battered and half dead, dare defy him?

Holt had felt a rush of ecstasy when he'd heard that Wolf had been captured in the north tower. Finally, his luck had turned, and he planned to prove Wolf for the traitor he was. There had been too much gossip in the castle, too much speculation that Megan had not been found because she didn't want to be located, that she'd taken up with her abductor and willingly slept with him, that she was dirtying her marriage vows and laughing at him.

Holt's stomach turned at that thought. True, he'd not been celibate since his wife had been stolen from him, but with his vexation, he'd needed some comfort. Nell had willingly provided her lush body to him, but it wasn't enough. Even when Dilys was forced to watch them couple to add to his delight, 'twas an empty union. As he'd gazed down upon Nell's freckled and gap-toothed mouth, it had been Megan's face he'd seen and he had nearly tasted her total and complete surrender. He wanted to mount her like a stallion and trumpet in primal lust that she was his and his alone.

Except for the outlaw. If the cur of the forest had bedded her, then Holt planned to cut off each of Wolf's balls slowly, drawing out the process and savoring the gelding of his enemy.

He finished his wine and met his guards in the chamber deep beneath the north tower that Ewan, the fool, had rarely used. Wolf was deep within the bowels of the keep, spread-eagled upon the floor, still unconscious. More icy water was used to awaken him, and when his eyes blinked open, Holt stood before him.

"Now," he said, "let's begin again."

Wolf felt as if a thousand destriers had trampled upon him. Every muscle ached and his bones felt as if they'd splintered from his joints. Pain, deep and feral, pounded on his body and he was aware that he was in a dark, fetid chamber surrounded by Holt and his men. A huge fire burned bright in one corner, a boy fanning the flames with a bellows.

Holt reached for a long-handled clamp with his gloved

hand, and using the tool, dug in the flames until he found a coal that glowed like a red eye in the night.

"You will tell me where my wife is," Holt said, advancing slowly, the red ember menacingly close to Wolf's face.

Wolf raised his head, and mustering his strength, spit on the toe of Holt's boot.

Rage sparked in the new lord's eyes. "So that's the way it is, eh? Fine. You're a fool, Wolf, and I brand you as such." With that he dropped the coal onto Wolf's back. White-hot pain seared into his body as flesh singed and burned. Wolf convulsed and bit down on his tongue. They could burn him, slice him, set the beasts of the forest upon him, nearly drown him, but never would he betray Megan.

"Lord Holt!" a soldier cried as Wolf struggled with consciousness.

"Not now. I'm busy!" Holt walked to the fire again, his wicked weapon in his hand.

"But, m'lord——"

Spinning fast, Holt pinned the soldier with harsh, unforgiving eyes. "I said——"

"'Tis the lady Megan," the soldier announced, his gaze moving from Wolf's singed back to Holt's face.

Wolf swallowed to keep his stomach contents from spewing from his mouth.

"What of her?"

"She's here, m'lord, at the castle gates, and she's demanding to be let in!"

❊ *Fourteen* ❊

"So my wayward bride has returned!" Holt's eyes gleamed as the winch was turned and the portcullis grated open. Dressed in a crimson velvet surcoat befitting a king, Holt was surrounded by soldiers holding torches and drawn swords. Though he forced a smile, disapproval edged his mouth and brought deep furrows to his forehead. A dozen accusations sizzled in his eyes—questions Megan didn't want to hear or have to answer.

Astride the bay, Megan shivered but refused to show any sign of weakness. Fear could never be her companion, for courage was her shield. This keep, with its familiar stone walls, tall watchtowers, and wide battlements, was her rightful home, the castle she was to inherit once her brother, poor Bevan, was pronounced dead. Squaring her shoulders, she stared straight at the husband she loathed. "I needs speak with my father," she said, bracing herself for the ugly truth.

"Well, that's a bit of a problem, you see." Holt glanced from her and shook his head slowly. Despair burrowed deep in her soul and she knew before he spoke a word that the old crone had been right. "Baron Ewan passed on a few days ago, I'm afraid."

Megan thought she'd steeled herself, but when the dreaded words rolled so easily off Holt's tongue, her insides turned to jelly. A mind-numbing wave of grief washed over her, extinguishing the solitary flame of hope that had burned so brightly in her heart. *Oh, Father,* she silently cried, *I abandoned you. Had I returned sooner, mayhap I could have forestalled your death.* Swaying upon the mare's back, she grabbed the saddle's pommel, blinked for a second, and fought the tears that blocked her throat.

Dawn was breaking over the walls of the keep but the joy she should have felt at returning to her home, the castle where she'd grown up, withered away. Father, mother, brother, and baby sister, nearly everyone gone. Only Cayley remained, and that thought brought her a ray of happiness. At least she was not alone.

Do not forget that you carry Wolf's child in your womb. You will never be alone or without one you love. She took a small bit of comfort in that thought.

"I've upset you," Holt said, with feigned remorse as he lifted a hand to her, and the sun, fettered by a thin layer of clouds, offered some illumination to the winter-cold castle. "I'm sorry about your father's death—'tis a tragedy." Holt motioned to her horse, and receiving the unspoken command, one of his men, Elwin, a gangly youth who nearly tripped over his own feet, charged forward and grabbed her mount's reins. The thin straps of leather slipped through her fingers and she silently cursed herself for letting down her guard.

"Come in, wife, and warm yourself."

'Twas time to set matters straight. "Make no mistake, Sir Holt, I'm not—nor will I ever be—your wife!"

"Did I not hear you vow in front of God, country, and everyone in this keep that I was to be your husband?"

"'Twas my father's bidding. He's gone. I no longer have to try to please him."

"Too late, Megan," he said without the slightest inflection as his jaw turned to granite. Determination flickered in his gaze and Megan knew more than a moment's fear. This man—heavily muscled and ruthless—was not about to be denied. "Surely you've not forgotten that the priest married us, and by the law of the land, as well as that of the church, you are now and for the rest of your days bound to me."

She didn't move, but the words crashed over her, echoing through her brain over and over again, like a monk's damning cadence. "Come, Megan," Holt said with a hard, unforgiving smile as he motioned for her to climb down from her mare. "You're tired and need rest. I trust you were able to elude the outlaw who ransomed you."

Feeling like Judas, she nodded woodenly, telling herself not to think about Wolf and her love for him, that if she pushed him to a far corner of her mind, the pain in her heart would lessen. She could never be with him as wife to a husband—not that he would want that—nor could she be his wench, not as long as she was married to Holt. Bitterness crept into her soul and she prayed for an end to a marriage that had never begun, a marriage that should never have existed. Her heart belonged in the forest with the outlaw who wore the name of the beast of the night. Though she'd tried to turn her mind against him, to pretend that he was nothing but an uncivilized rogue, a criminal who hid in the woods and preyed upon innocent travelers, she couldn't. She loved him far too deeply. 'Twas her curse.

Holt was staring at her and she forced the image of Wolf's handsome face from her mind. "Has . . . has my father been laid to rest?"

"Aye. This morn. In the chapel cemetery."

Pain ripped through her, as she was unable to say goodbye or see again the man who had sired her, taught her to ride and shoot a bow and arrow, the man who had taught her to look for the finer points of a horse, and, in the end, thinking he was doing what was best for her, insisted she marry Holt. Heart heavy, she said, "I need to visit his grave and speak with Cayley."

Holt's eyebrow quirked upward and he smiled, opening his hands to her. "Then come into the keep. She's not been well and—"

"What?" Megan's head snapped up and she stared at Holt. Her pulse pounded a dread-inspired tempo. Cayley was the last living member of her family. Nothing could be wrong with her. Nothing!

"'Tis true," he said, frowning thoughtfully. "Since your father's death, the lady has been beside herself and the physician knows not if 'tis something within her or only her grief causing her so much pain."

"For the love of Jesus, take me to her," Megan said, her

own sorrow forgotten in the thought that she might be able to help her sister. Every muscle in her body ached from days of riding without much rest, but she needed to see the one remaining member of her family. Though they'd often fought as children, she and Cayley were close and had shared many a secret between them.

Dismounting in one swift motion, she was grateful her legs held her, for she wanted not any help from Holt. Though 'twas early, the castle was coming to life with the approaching morning. Peasants, soldiers, and servants alike began to cross the bailey, and she smiled at the faces she recognized—the baker and miller, wheelwright and ale conner. Boys of every age lugged firewood, sacks of grain, and baskets of stones. Girls, too, were busy gathering eggs, tossing seeds to the chickens, carrying laundry to the creek, or checking the eel traps in the pond. Water was being drawn from the well and the farrier's hammer was already clanking against his anvil.

"Hey, look! 'Tis the lady!" one of Cook's helpers, who was hauling a side of venison, said.

"'Tis!" Nell, this time, carrying a pail of milk.

"Wonder what 'appened to her with that outlaw?" the miller's wife asked.

A giggle. "'E was a handsome devil, 'e was."

"Look at her. Wonder what she's thinkin'? Poor lass, losing her father while she was gone."

"Lady Megan!" Rue cried out, and Megan smiled as she spied her old nursemaid. Never had there been a kinder-hearted soul than Rue. Plucking her skirts upward so the hems would not become soiled, the old woman started across the bailey, but at a signal from Holt, one of the men detained her.

So this was how it was going to be.

"Come, Megan, Cook will fix you something warm while you see to Cayley. Mayhap you can make her feel better," Holt said, and Megan caught the unspoken messages being exchanged among some of his men. Something wasn't right in the castle, and 'twas more than her father's death that caused the eerie feeling to settle upon her.

But she had to see her sister.

As she hurried across the bent, frozen grass, her stomach rumbled at the smell of smoke mingling with the scent of sizzling meat. A side of pork roasted on a spit over an open fire, turned by a dog rigged to the contraption as it ran in circles.

Chapel bells pealed softly, reverberating in Megan's heart and reminding her of her mission to untie herself from this unwanted marriage. Father Timothy hurried across the bailey and Megan stiffened. She trusted not his piety or his words. "Welcome, m'lady," he said with a worried smile. He'd become thinner since she'd seen him last and his air of superiority was missing this morning. "'Tis sad news you've come home to."

"Aye," she said, nodding.

"The lady needs her rest," Holt said swiftly while clamping possessive fingers over Megan's forearm.

"Of course." Timothy nodded, but his eyes never left Megan's face. 'Twas as if he was trying to silently speak with her. "I've said the Mass for your father and I prayed that you or your sister would have been there when he was laid to rest. 'Twas a pity he had no family at his bedside near the end or at his burial—"

"No family? But Cayley . . ." Dread strangled the words in her throat while Holt glared at the priest. ". . . was she too ill to attend Mass?" she asked, fear and suspicion mingling in her mind. Had Holt deceived her? "Do not tell me that my sister is on her deathbed."

"Oh, no, I only meant that she wasn't in the chapel during Mass when your father—"

Holt coughed loudly and the fingers tightened over her arm. "Excuse us, Father," he said, "but the lady is tired from her journey and we've not had any time together as husband and wife." His voice was soft and filled with suggestion. "You understand."

Timothy blushed. "Aye—"

"Wait!" Megan whirled on the hated man who was her husband. "Why would Cayley not attend my father's funeral Mass?"

"She was not here," Holt admitted.

"Where was she?" Megan's heart blood turned to ice.

Something evil was happening here at Dwyrain, something she didn't understand, something that involved her sister.

"Lady Cayley left."

"Left?" She turned to the priest so quickly that a gust of wind caught her hood and tore it from her head.

Father Timothy stared at her for a heartbeat, cleared his throat, and nodded. "Aye."

Holt scratched his upper lip. "I did not want to worry you—"

"So you told me she was ill?" Megan spat. Vile, treacherous man!

"She was kidnapped by a prisoner who escaped. A big yellow-haired brute who used her as a shield as he made his way out through the gates—"

"Bjorn?" Megan said, her mind spinning in restless worrisome circles as she recalled him at the outlaw camp. Shaking her head, she said, "Nay, he would not . . ."

"He was desperate," Holt inserted, shooting a look at the priest as if to stop any disagreement from the man of God. "He and the other man—"

"Cormick," Megan said under her breath, unable to hear over the painful hammering of her heart.

"—aye, they tried to escape. The one you call Cormick was killed in his attempt to flee the castle, but the other used Cayley as his hostage and was able to elude my men."

"Liar!" she said, feeling revulsion as the earth shifted beneath her feet. Not only was her father dead, but Cormick, gentle, gruff Cormick, as well. Because of Holt. "Bjorn would never use another's life to save his."

"So you know him well?" Holt was not pleased. Several deep clefts appeared in the skin between his eyebrows.

"Aye, and he's a good man, a—"

"Criminal. Wanted by the law. A robber, thief, pickpocket, murderer, or rapist, most likely. Your precious criminal is no better than the scum of the earth."

"No, Holt, methinks you alone retain that honor," she argued, thankful that her sister was free from the rein of terror that was sure to ruin Dwyrain and everything Cayley held dear. *Run, Cayley,* she silently thought, *run fast and never return!*

Holt's jaw clenched and the fingers around her arm dug deep into her flesh. "So my wife has come home only to defy me."

"And annul the marriage."

Holt laughed. "Christ Jesus, you be a saucy tart! 'Twill never happen." He leaned closer to her, his voice low and rough to her ear. "I've waited long for you, wife, but tonight the waiting ends and I will get you with child. Then, not even God Himself would dare break our union."

A wave of sickness climbed up her throat. She could never give herself to this cur who wore her father's robes, stole his keep, and lied through his teeth. "What do you want of me? You have the keep!"

Holt eyed her reflectively. Hesitating a second, he touched her hair and sighed. "'Twas true, as well you know. I wanted the castle and the wealth that was Dwyrain, and I worked close with your father so that he would choose me as his successor, but that wasn't enough, Megan. I wanted you as well." She could hardly believe her ears. His voice was firm, his chin set in determination. "I hoped that you would care for me, that you would agree to become my bride."

She tried to step away, but his grip was harsh, and as he drew her closer, the tip of his tongue swept over his thin lips. "Since you defied me and rejected my courtship and proposal, I wanted you more than ever."

"Why?"

His grin stretched into a seductive leer. "Because, dear wife, the taming of you will be that much sweeter."

Without thinking, she slapped him. The sound of flesh striking flesh echoed through the bailey. A woman gasped. The priest crossed himself and all work ceased. The farrier stopped pounding, the carpenters stayed their hammers, even the windmill quieted.

Holt's expression changed from leering seduction to rage. "That," he said through lips that barely moved, "was a mistake."

Two soldiers stepped forward as if to take her off his hands. Every eye in the keep turned in their direction. Holt's patience was stretched to the breaking point. "Careful, wife, or our joining will be rougher than you might wish."

"You sick, lying bastard! You told me that Cayley was ill, that you were taking me to see her!"

"A small deception, I'm afraid. I did not want to worry you."

Her eyes narrowed. "What would you have done once I was in her empty chamber?"

"Detain you."

"As you would a common prisoner?"

"You leave me no choice," he said with measured calm, "for you said yourself you do not think of me as your husband. Until I can convince you otherwise, you will be locked in your room and—"

"Nay, m'lord," Father Timothy interjected. "You cannot jail her as you would a traitor."

"She'll have her own room, food and water, a guard at her door, and be allowed visitors of my choosing—treated much better than those held captive in the north tower." Yanking on her arm, he half dragged her toward the keep.

Megan felt like a fool. She dug in her heels, trying to stop him, knowing that dozens of curious eyes were cast in her direction. The men and women who watched her being pulled into the keep against her will, would they help her or damn her for not living up to the forced promises of her wedding day? "Nay," she cried, "unhand me!"

Holt's face changed from a mask of determined impatience to one of leashed, ugly fury. "Tell her," he ordered the priest, anger creasing his words. "Tell her she is my wife."

Father Timothy fingered the cross at his neck. His eyes, once so superior and condemning, now held only pity. "'Tis true, m'lady. Your marriage vows are sacred."

Despair threatened her and she turned her gaze upon the man with whom she was doomed to spend the rest of her life. "Would you want a wife who loves you not?"

Holt stopped dead in his tracks and whirled on her. "Love?" he repeated. "What in the name of Christ has love got to do with marriage?"

"Everything!" she cried.

"Megan, Megan," he said, clucking his tongue. "What happened to you in the forest to make you think that love is so important? I never took you for such a fool—" His words stopped suddenly and his eyes narrowed as if a great understanding had come to him. "Wolf," he said, his teeth grinding together. "You did not come here to flee him," he said, his nostrils flaring in silent rage, "but to find him."

"I—"

"Everything that was said, about you leaving with him willingly, about your giving yourself to him like a common whore, 'twas true," he said venomously, as if wounded to his very soul. Then, as if finding an inner strength, he spat and said, "It matters not."

She tried to jerk her arm from his deadly grasp, but he only tightened his grip and pinned her hand behind her back, forcing her to face away from him and stare at the carpenter's hut, where a platform and scaffolding was half finished. "Merciful God," she cried, realizing that the structure was a gallows, nearly finished. "What is this?"

"For your friends," he said. "Wolf, the sorcerer, a boy and man who rode with him, and the traitors in the castle."

"No," she said and thought she might be sick. The skeleton of the gallows swam before her eyes and her knees buckled, but Holt's firm grip kept her upright. "You cannot," she cried and panic raced through her blood, thundering in her brain. "Nay, nay, nay!"

"'Tis true enough," Holt said. "They all will hang. I was only waiting until one of them told me where to find you, but now that my willful wife has returned, there is no need to delay the event any longer."

"Holt, please," she begged. "Please, do not send them to their deaths."

"'Tis too late to bargain, m'lady," he said, smiling at last. "They'll be hanged tomorrow at sunset, every one of them, including the leader of the outlaws—your precious Wolf."

Awaken.

The voice sounded odd, as if it were spoken from a great distance.

Ware of Abergwynn, awaken and I will heal you.

Wolf opened an eye and sucked in his breath. Gritting his teeth, his body clenched from the pain, he held his tongue. For the first time in his life, he welcomed death.

She is here. Lady Megan has come searching for you.

What? With every ounce of strength he could summon, Wolf struggled to a sitting position and found himself in a hideous, smelly cell deep in the dungeons of Dwyrain. His head ached wildly, the pain behind his eyes was intense and blinding, and his back stung as if it were on fire.

"'Tis over," he said, though no sound came from his voice.

You cannot give up on her.

Megan. His heart ached at the thought of her, her warm, golden eyes, easy laugh, and wild curls. The few hours of bliss he'd had on this earth were when she'd been with him, giving of her body and her spirit. His throat ached, but not for water. Nay, though he was thirsty, 'twas not for drink. If only he could see her before his spirit left this earth.

You will only die if you so wish it, the voice reprimanded again, and finally his head was clear enough to understand that Cadell, the sorcerer, was speaking to him through his mind—or was it that he was addled himself?

For the love of Christ, look at me!

Wolf raised his eyes and his gaze connected with the intense, outwardly serene stare of the magician. *Now, friend, pay attention, for I will heal you and you will be strong again, but for our plan to work, you must pretend to be weak and feign that you are near death. Not even Megan can suspect that you be whole; elsewise, all is lost.*

"'Tis lost already."

"Say what?" the guard asked, looking up from his post.

I've never thought you were a coward, Ware. Prove me not wrong! Lady Megan's life depends upon you.

Gritting his teeth and closing his eyes, Wolf inched himself across the cell. Through fetid rushes, scraps of bone from previous meals, rat dung, and spiders, he forced his battered muscles and broken bones to move. Each bit of space he crossed felt as if it lasted forever, but he set his jaw and decided that if he was going to leave this earth, he'd do it while trying to save the woman he loved.

The thought jolted him, for he'd vowed never to love another woman, not after giving his heart to Mary and watching her be destroyed. Now, years later, he'd fallen for another woman, a beautiful, headstrong baron's daughter who had married his worst enemy, and his actions had started a chain of events that might cost Megan her happiness as well as her life.

Nay, he could not die with her death on his hands. If there was a way to save her, he'd find it, no matter what the cost.

That's better, Cadell intoned without words. He stretched a hand through the bars and clasped Wolf's frail fingers with his own strong hand. *Heal, friend.* Cadell closed his eyes and a warmth the likes of which Wolf had never felt before swept from the magician's body to his. *Be strong and you will see your beloved Megan again.*

"I demand an audience with my husband!" Megan yelled, the word tasting foul on her tongue as she pounded on the door. "Do you hear me, guard? Fetch Lord Holt, for I needs speak with him!" She'd been deceived and locked in her chamber for nearly a day. In that time she'd slept fitfully, prayed constantly, and eaten only a bite or two of the food sent her way. She was allowed to speak to no one but the guard. Not even Rue was permitted to visit her.

She'd waited, standing for most of the day upon a stool to look through the window and watch as the gallows was constructed. Every thud of the carpenter's hammer drove a nail of fear deeper into her heart. She'd heard snippets of gossip from the laundress and milkmaid as they'd passed under her window. Not only were Wolf, Jagger, and the sorcerer to be hanged, but young Robin and a boy named Tom—the son of the man building the hated structure—as well. But the builder did not slack in his work, and the horrid wooden structure was taking form.

"Did you not hear me? I demand to speak to Lord Holt!" she cried again, pounding on the thick oak of the door until her knuckles began to bleed.

"I heard ye, m'lady, but the baron's out for a while."

"Then am I not in charge of the castle?"

There was a soft laugh on the other side of the heavy oak beams and Megan leaned uselessly against those imprisoning timbers. "Lord 'Olt, 'e said ye'd try somethin' like this. Nay, Sir Connor is in charge while the baron's out 'unting."

"Hunting?" she repeated, feeling the horrid talons of

defeat swipe at her courage. *Holt is out hunting while Wolf and Robin are doomed to breathe their last breaths?*

"Aye—oh, ye do 'ave a visitor."

With a clank of locks and the scrape of the heavy bar being lifted, the door opened and Father Timothy, a look of vast superiority pinned neatly on his face again, swept into the room on a cloud of pious pomposity.

"Please, m'lady, if you would pray with me," he said, his voice cold and distant, "for your husband has pointed out to me that you may have sinned in the days since your capture and you may need to confess." He lifted his eyes to the sentry still standing at the open door. "This is private," he said, "between a woman and her God."

"Aye." Crossing himself, the sentry scooted quickly out of Megan's chamber. The bolt slid into place.

"I have nothing to confess."

"On your knees," Father Timothy commanded in a rough voice. "Fold your hands and pretend to pray, so that if the guard opens the door, 'twill look as if everything is right. Now, listen, I care not about your confession, nor about your sins."

Falling to her knees, she wanted to believe him, but this man had lied before, his piety second only to his own needs.

"Cayley did not leave the castle as Holt would have you believe. Nor did your father die quietly in his sleep." Solemnly, in the cadence of a chant of prayer, the priest unburdened himself, telling of his part in Cayley's escape, Holt's murder of Cormick, his torture of Wolf, and finally, the sorcerer's claim that her father was sent to his grave early by the man who was her husband. "He is a fiend, the very spawn of the Devil," Father Timothy admitted, "and I placed my trust in him. I was a fool and God is punishing me. As part of my atonement I helped Lady Cayley flee, and I will do my best to see that your marriage is annulled."

She should have been relieved but she was stricken by the depths of Holt's treachery.

"Alas, I cannot save you from your husband unless you, like Cayley, leave and give me time to speak to the abbot and the bishop on your behalf."

"I cannot leave," she said firmly. As long as Wolf and

Robin were alive, she would stay and try to help them. "But if you need atone, then help me find a way out of my chamber so I can visit the prisoners."

He shook his head. "'Tis impossible. The guards have instructions."

"You are a man of God. Surely you can convince a dull soldier that 'tis the will of the Lord that I visit the poor wretches in the dungeon, as part of my duties as the baron's wife."

Sighing, he glanced to the window and shook his head, as if seeing, in a distance visible only to him, his own ruin. "I'll try," he said, rising from the floor and crossing himself. At the door, he spoke with the guard, who argued with him for a few minutes, then left, only to return and argue again. Megan heard only parts of the conversation, but it had to do with the soldier's doomed soul and the will of God. Father Timothy was adamant that God wanted the lady of the manor to visit the prisoners, to speak with the men who had kidnapped her and to, in good Christian manner, forgive them before their black souls left this earth.

Eventually, after many words and much debate from the dullard who stood by her door, Timothy was allowed to take her to the dungeon as long as the guard himself joined them.

Megan steeled herself for the worst. Though she'd never been to the prisons of Dwyrain before, she knew they were cruel cells that were built to hold only the most dangerous criminals and traitors to the baron. Her father used the dungeon rarely and she trembled inside as she followed the priest down the staircase and outside the great hall. A rush of wind tore at her cloak and brushed her cheeks with its icy breath. Shivering with dread, still she smiled at the people who greeted her, the steward and tailor and a farmer who had sold sheep to her father.

Inside the north tower was worse than she'd feared. Aside from reeking of a foul stench, the stairs were dark and uneven. The prisoners were held on the lowest level, the same dark hell where they'd been tortured, according to the priest, a place she'd visited only once as a child on a dare from her brother Bevan.

Clutching her cloak, she followed the priest to a guard

station and the surrounding cells, small rooms with walls of rusted bars.

Wolf lay within one cell, his back to the door, and her heart, traitor that it was, soared at the sight of him before she saw the new welts upon his shoulders, the bruises showing beneath his dark skin, and the fresh scars of burns where he'd been tortured. The contents of her stomach, meager though they were, threatened her throat, and she swallowed hard as she made her way to the cell door.

"Let me inside."

"Nay." The guard on duty shook his head. "Father Timothy, these men are not to have any visitors."

"'Tis the lady of the manor. She is here only to see that the prisoners are treated fairly."

"But—"

"Hush, man!" Megan ordered, taking Timothy's cue. "Elsewise I'll report to my husband that I was mistreated."

Wolf's head rolled her way. His eyes, once bright, were glassy and vacant. *Oh, God, no! Let him not be in pain. Help him, please!*

"'Tis Holt's wife," he sneered, his voice gravelly and foreign.

"Wolf!" she cried.

"What is it you want?" he snarled with no trace of kindness—no hint of the gentle man hidden deep beneath his hard exterior. His eyes were feral and slitted; he appeared a beast she didn't recognize.

"I—I—wanted to know that you were treated well."

His laugh was a ruthless bark. "Your husband's hospitality, m'lady, leaves much to be desired."

"Why are ye speaking to her so?" Robin, in the next cell, demanded. "Lady Megan, we were worried about you. We tried to find ye for fear—"

"The lad's addled with fear," Wolf said in that same hoarse, cruel whisper. "And half in love with ye. Stop it, boy, the lady's a married woman. The new baron is her husband."

Something deep in her heart withered. "Why be you so cruel?"

"'Tis my way," he said, and for a second she thought she

saw another emotion flicker in his eyes, a pain she didn't recognize, but it was fleeting, and when he stretched to his feet and limped slowly to her, her heart tore open. How had she thought he might ever love her? The shackles on his feet chinked as he moved and his face was tight, his lips flat, his gaze steady and hate-filled. His grimy fingers circled the iron slats of his cell and she reached forward to touch him, only to have him draw away. "Return to the keep and leave us in this hellhole, woman," he said, his lip curling in disgust at the sight of her. "We need not your pity."

"I'm tellin' ye, m'lord, he acted as if the sight of her disgusted 'im, as if he couldn't bear to see her," the guard told Holt. "'Twas wicked he was to her. Father Timothy he stayed on, asking for confessions, offering to pray with the prisoners, but they turned their backs on 'im as well."

"And the lady?" Holt asked, suspicion still pounding through his brain. When he'd heard that Father Timothy had disobeyed him and had taken Megan to the dungeon, he'd been furious, but now, upon the second guard's word, which was as strong as the first sentry's, he felt some sense of relief. Was it possible that the outlaw had at least a shred of honor and hadn't stolen Megan's virtue? Or was he protecting her? Or did he actually loathe her?

As Holt sat in Ewan's recently vacated chair in the great hall, with one boot propped on the hearth and the servants scurrying through the keep to see to his every need, Holt felt a second's peace.

The hunt today had been rewarding—a doe and one fawn, though the other wounded yearling had escaped, its trail of blood leading nowhere. Now, it appeared that his stubborn wife might not be tainted, and he so loved to enter a virgin. Lifting his mazer to his lips, he sighed. "You were speaking of my wife," he said, savoring the word. Marrying Megan had given him this keep, and aside from the pleasures of her body, which he planned to soon sample, his new-found wealth was gratifying.

"Aye, she's been askin' to see ye," the guard proclaimed.

More good news. He'd been patient with her, hoping she would see that there was no use in resisting him, but he could not wait forever.

"Bring her in." As the sentry hurried up the stairs, Holt clapped his hands and felt immense satisfaction when a page, his eyes round with fear that Holt wasn't satisfied with the performance of his duties, listened in trembling silence, then retrieved another cup of wine.

Life, indeed, was good.

Within minutes, he spied Megan walking slowly down the stairs and he couldn't help the small catch in his heart at the sight of her. She was beautiful, with her bright, ale-colored eyes and quick smile. The bridge of her nose boasted a few freckles and her thick hair curled in russet-colored waves. She'd dressed in a deep blue tunic and amber mantle and looked as if she were truly the mistress of the keep. One day she would bear him strong sons and beautiful daughters, and if only he could teach her to rein in her wicked tongue, she would be a good companion for him.

"'Tis said that you want to speak with me," he ventured, waving toward a chair and sliding a cup of wine across the table toward her.

"Aye," she said, and he waited until at last she muttered, "m'lord."

"What is it you wish to discuss?"

"The prisoners," she said, hitching her chin upward in defiance and refusing to take the seat he offered. Nor did she show the least inclination to pick up the cup of wine. Willful. Stubborn. A woman who would be a challenge in bed.

"I heard you went to visit them and were not well received."

"Let them go."

He laughed. Surely she was joking, but the serious expression on her small face convinced him otherwise. "They are criminals and needs be punished."

"Because I was stolen from Dwyrain," she said. "But I've returned."

He ran his finger around his mazer thoughtfully. "How can I be assured that you will stay?"

"You have my word," she said without the slightest hint of hesitation. "Did I not return when I had the chance?"

Lifting a shoulder and mindful of the servants who were within earshot, including Nell, who was taking her time polishing the candleholders while pretending not to listen, he said, "Aye, but how am I to know that 'twas your first attempt at escape from the outlaw?"

"It wasn't. But I was caught every other time. The last time, I took the leader's destrier."

Holt laughed. "That must have stolen the piss from him."

"Unfortunately, it was stolen by the farmer who found me and took me to the nunnery."

"Aye, the nunnery that was far from Dwyrain. It appeared you were not returning here so much as fleeing," he said, watching for any hint of reaction in her smooth features.

Her eyebrows drew together. "Aye, 'tis true, but I could not chance riding to Dwyrain without the outlaws catching up to me, for 'twas what they expected."

"So you want me to believe that you led them on a wild chase that took you to the nunnery."

"Believe what you will, Holt. Know you that I did not come to be your wife willingly. I wanted you not. But now"—she turned defeated palms to the ceiling—"I cannot pretend to love you or even care for you, but . . . I . . . I am willing to be your wife day and night if you let the prisoners go free."

He laughed again and this time felt a mite of joy. "Silly girl. Why would I agree to this? You are already my wife. You will do what I say, eat what I tell you, sleep with me when I want you, hold your tongue when you disapprove, and bear my children. This you have agreed to do."

"Not willingly. I'll fight you every step of the way."

"But if I release the prisoners?"

"I will be your servant."

He nearly choked on his wine. "Ah, Megan, a fine liar you be, but I think no man would ever be your master." The thought caused his blood to heat a bit, and seeing her standing before him in her tunic as blue as midnight, color high in her cheeks, her lips quivering slightly, he could barely restrain himself.

"'Tis a deal I wish to strike with you, Holt."

"And you'll promise to do anything I ask?" he jeered.

She closed her eyes and her fingers clenched into tight fists. "Aye," she agreed. "Anything."

Twirling the stem of his mazer in his fingers, he considered her proposition. Was she sincere? The skin drawn tight over her nose and the lines around the corners of her lips convinced him, and had she not always been true to her word? Firelight gleamed against his silver cup. 'Twas pleasant to think her malleable and fearful of his power. If he agreed, he would finally have her where he'd wanted her—under his thumb and groveling to do his bidding.

Unless she was lying.

"You will not argue with me?"

"On my word."

"You will lie in my bed and give me sons?"

He watched her swallow. "As many as God allows."

He couldn't resist seeing how far she would go. He'd been humiliated in front of his men and 'twould be good to get a little payment in kind. Since he was made to look the fool by her capture and rumors of her ardor for the damned outlaw, Holt wanted her to taste what it felt like to be utterly mortified.

"What if I wanted to bed you in front of some of my men—or mayhap share you?"

"Dear God," she cried in dismay, her face flushing with color, her eyes blinking wildly.

"Well?"

She bit down hard on her lip, drawing blood. "Aye," she consented and faltered a bit as if she were about to keel over.

"So tell me, Megan," he said, unable to push aside the horrid thought that had been nagging at him ever since she made her first request. "Do you love the outlaw so much that you would suffer complete shame and indignity to save him?"

She hesitated, but when she opened her eyes to stare at him, he was awed by the strength in her gaze. "I've said I would do what you ask. Why I do it is of no matter. Now, Lord Holt, will you spare the men?"

"Each one but Wolf. The other men, including the boy and traitors in mine own castle, will be allowed their freedom, but Wolf must remain in the dungeon. His sins of kidnapping, traitorous insubordination, and murderous intent must be atoned for." She nearly lost her balance, but leaned against the table for support. "Wolf's punishment will be an example for those who dare think they could defy me. The gallows, though they are nearly finished, will stand for a week, as a reminder of what happens to those who betray me. Then, at week's end, he'll be hanged by a rope until he's dead."

"You cannot do this!" she cried, her calm exterior cracking and tears of genuine fear filling her eyes. "Holt, please, I beg you . . ."

"'Tis no use."

"But—"

"Hush! 'Tis done," he said, his lip curling in disgust when she revealed how much she cared for the forest thug and his motley band of thieves. "Guard!" he called, then turned his anger to Megan. "Prepare yourself, m'lady, for I will come to your bed tonight. Rest now."

She started to protest, but held her tongue.

"So you be a smart girl. Asides," he said with an ugly chuckle, "your friends will go free. Except, of course, for your beloved, doomed Wolf."

❧ *Fifteen* ❧

"So where were ye for the years we thought ye dead?" Wolf asked, eyeing his friend through the iron slats of the wall separating them. "You never once sent word to Garrick or Morgana that you'd survived the fall."

"Aye, nor did you," Cadell reminded him.

"I had reasons."

"As did I."

Cadell stared up at the small hole where a breath of fresh air sometimes filtered into the dungeon. "Nearly drowned and broken I was when I washed up on the shore. An old woman, one the townspeople called a witch, Fiona of the Hills, found me. There was barely a breath left in my body, nary a hint of life, but she took me in, healed me with her spells, herbs, and runes. I remembered nary a thing, my mind was near gone, but in time most of it returned. By then, 'twas years and many miles later."

"So how did you come to be a magician?"

"Again, 'twas Fiona. She saw that I had the gift, as did my sister Morgana, and my grandmother, Enit. Fiona was a patient woman and childless; she was grateful to find one who could be nurtured and taught. She showed me how to use what the gods had bestowed upon me."

"And you became a sorcerer."

"So some say."

"You can heal."

"Sometimes."

"But not yourself? You still are lame."

Cadell stared deep into Wolf's eyes. "'Tis wise to remember we are only people, even those of us who have been given special powers."

"So you stay crippled by choice?" Wolf asked.

"'Tis not so bad."

"Cadell, 'tis nonsense ye speak!"

"Shh! 'Tis time." Cadell's gaze shifted to the stairs and Wolf felt it, that tiny rush of air stirring through the cells before the first scrape of a boot was heard. "Holt approaches." With a twisted smile, Cadell turned his attention to the staircase and his lips moved not, though his words reached Wolf as surely as if he shouted. *Do not forget, Ware, ye are injured so badly ye may not survive.*

Like an emperor visiting paupers, Holt strode through the shadowy caverns that were the dungeons of Dwyrain. His mouth was compressed against the foul air, but he carried himself as a conquering king and walked steadily, only to stop in front of Wolf's cell. Four soldiers stood behind him, their hands on their weapons as if they expected the prisoners to attack through the bars.

"Lord Holt!" the jailer exclaimed, jumping to his feet from the stool where he'd been nearly napping. "I knew not that ye'd be visitin' the prison."

"Be still!" Holt ordered as his eyes slitted in the darkness and settled on Wolf. "The lady has bartered for your pathetic lives."

Wolf's nostrils flared and his muscles strained. Glaring at his captor through the bars, he prayed for one more chance to place his bare hands around Holt's neck and strangle him until the bastard could not draw a breath. Megan, sweet Megan, would be better off widowed. "Bartered with what?" he snarled.

"Her subservience." Holt's smile was smug and Wolf's insides turned to ice.

Megan? On her knees before this lying, murdering cur? Never! Not as long as there was a breath of life in his body.

Holt studied his fingernails for a second, as if thinking. "She cares about your flea-riddled hides. Because I want to please my wife, I listened to her pleas, but granted not everything she wanted. 'Twas my decision, as an act of good faith, Wolf, that I would release everyone but you."

Wolf felt a second's relief. At least those he'd dragged into his personal mission of vengeance would be safe. But there was Megan to consider. He could not allow her to spend the rest of her life living as Holt's doormat.

"The traitors will be banished, of course, and they will be freed one day at a time to prevent them from banding together and plotting against the castle. But you, Wolf, will hang for your treason."

Wolf felt no fear and managed a smile. He was about to tell Holt that he'd meet him in hell, but Cadell's unspoken voice called to him. *Hold your tongue, Ware. Do not mock him. Play the victim.*

The thought was revolting. "I cannot!" Wolf announced, and Holt laughed.

"But you have no choice. You'll swing by your neck until it breaks or until you can no longer breathe. Either way you'll be dead."

Wolf rolled onto the balls of his feet, ready to lunge.

Stop! Remember, you are weak and ill from the beating and the torture of the coals against your skin. Do not give him the advantage of seeing that you are healed, or all will be for naught. If ye care for the lady, Wolf, pretend that ye can do nothing to help her—that the bastard has nothing to fear from you.

"I'll not—"

She is with child, Ware. Your child.

"What?" he cried, and Holt laughed.

"Are ye daft, Wolf?" Motioning toward the dingy cells, Holt said, "Has being locked away stolen yer mind? I blame ye not. 'Tis not easy to be a prisoner, is it? The mind sometimes leaves us."

Gnashing his teeth in frustration, Wolf pretended to try to lunge at the bars, only to fall to the floor as if in great pain. With an agonized whistle, he dragged air through his teeth, then cursed Holt roundly. "Go to hell, you sick bastard."

A child? Megan was with child? Was it possible?

'Tis true.

"Why did ye tell me not sooner?" he demanded.

"He's gone mad," Holt said, clucking his tongue.

'Twas not necessary and should be something a woman tells a man, but I had no choice.

Wolf closed his eyes. A baby. His child and Megan's, and she was now married to Holt. His fists curled into balls of frustration and he pounded uselessly on the grimy floor. He had to protect her and their unborn child. Nothing else mattered, not even his own life.

"Save your strength, fool." Holt laughed. "You'll need it when the hangman comes for you. Now, you, magician, leave this castle tonight and never return. 'Tis banished ye are, and I have guards posted outside the walls of the keep. They have orders to kill ye on sight if you come anywhere near Dwyrain." He glanced to the connecting cells and said, "This goes for the rest of you. If any of my men spies your faces again, 'twill be the last time."

Wolf, determined to defy Holt and steal Megan from Dwyrain again, watched as his enemy turned and hastened from the dungeon, his bodyguards following after him like trained dogs. "Trust him not," he warned Cadell, but the sorcerer was smiling to himself, as if he alone knew all truths.

"Worry not about me. 'Tis your own skin that is in danger."

Holt cared not about his own life, but he'd fight the very Devil himself for Megan and the baby she carried.

Riding through the gatehouse with the magician tied and bound on the horse behind him, Connor decided Holt was a fool. Not only had the big outlaw—the one he'd heard called Bjorn—escaped with the woman Connor had planned to seduce, but now Holt was letting his prisoners leave the castle unharmed, or so it was to appear. The magician's well-being was for show because some of the peasants and servants—aye, even the soldiers—had begun to believe that the man had mystical powers, and Lady Megan had demanded his release.

'Twas Connor's mission to kill the wizard once they were far from the view of any of the sentries who might still be scouring the woods for Lady Cayley and her captor.

Glancing to the dark sky, Connor cursed his luck. He'd given what small amount of trust he had to Holt, and the man had deceived him. While playing dice and drinking too much ale, one of Holt's bodyguards had admitted to hearing the new baron conversing with the priest about marrying Cayley off to Baron Rolf of Castle Henning. The thought was disgusting, even to Connor, for Rolf was a withered old man, blind in one eye, who took pleasure in the torment of others—not that Connor didn't understand the old man's needs, but Rolf was past his prime, with a limp cock and a thirst for killing his wives, or so 'twas rumored. Connor could have accepted this, but the fact that Holt had lied to him by promising him Lady Cayley, then planning to barter her to a rich baron, was too much.

Mayhap it was time to deal with Holt.

A fine mist seeped from the ground, rising upward as Connor turned into the woods and stopped beyond a copse of oak, where a small clearing was surrounded by trees, ferns, and brambles. "Here," he said, hopping easily to the ground. His quiver pressed between his shoulder blades and he thought that killing a crippled man was not much sport. He would rather have had a shot at Wolf or one of the younger, agile prisoners—Robin or Tom—but Wolf was sentenced to hang and the boys were locked in the dungeon.

Why not kill Holt for betraying you, his own mind said to him—or was it his mind? He felt a shiver like tiny footsteps crawl down his spine.

"Get down," he ordered, and pulled roughly on the man's tied hands. The cripple toppled to the ground, lost his footing for a second, but managed to scramble to his feet, such as they were.

Connor slid an arrow from his quiver and hoisted his bow. "Run!"

No.

God's eyes, he hadn't said a word, but Connor had heard the answer clear as a bell. Perhaps 'twas his mind playing tricks on him again. His hands weren't as steady as they usually were as he drew hard on the bowstring with the arrow. "Move, sorcerer, and ye've got a chance."

And your soul will rot forever in the depths of hell.

"Say wha—?" Connor jerked as if someone had struck him. This time he was certain it wasn't his own mind chiding him. Nay, but the prisoner hadn't moved his lips nor used his voice. 'Twas as if the sorcerer had talked to him mind to mind.

He looked over his shoulder, half expecting another to have joined them. What kind of devilment was this man conjuring?

Go on, kill me if you can.

"For the love of God, I will!" he said, nearly pissing in his breeches.

Overhead, through the rising mist, came the sound of great wings flapping wildly. An owl, the same huge ruffled-feathered bird who had landed on the prisoner's arm the night he'd been recaptured, settled onto one of the cripple's shoulders.

"So ye've found me, Owain," the magician said in his calm voice. He turned his haunted eyes to Connor and the soldier felt a shiver cold as death crawl through his bowels. "Give Holt a message," the cripple commanded, spreading his arms wide, his wrists no longer bound, as the mist, like a thick curtain of fog, began to rise from the ferns and grass surrounding him. "Tell him that the Devil wants his due."

The forest became engulfed in the icy haze and Connor let his arrow fly. He waited for the scream, or the sound of running feet, or the angry flap of huge wings, but silence greeted his ears and the fog was suddenly thick as Cook's tasteless pea soup.

"Where are ye?" he called, striking out after the sorcerer, assured that he'd stumble across the man's corpse. "Hey! Where are ye?" He walked across the clearing thrice before stopping to scratch his head and fight the dry fear that had settled in his mouth. His arrows never missed; his aim was straight and true. A split second before the mist rose, he'd had the sorcerer in his sights, but . . . Then he realized that not only had the man disappeared, but so had the owl and both horses as well. Without a sound, they'd been swallowed by the forest.

Unnerved, he whistled sharply, hoping his mount would respond, but there was no answering whinny, no snort of recognition, no pawing of a hoof against the forest floor. Nor was there any other sound. The shrouded woods were completely silent and he heard neither the call of a winter bird, the scramble of some rodent hurrying through the bracken, nor the whir of a single insect's wings. No breeze rustled the dry leaves and no water splashed over stones in a nearby creek. 'Twas as if he were truly alone on the earth, and for the first time in years, fear—as dark as the middle of a winter night—bored deep into Connor's black heart.

Walking backward, he expected the sorcerer to appear and kill him on the spot, and when he reached the edge of the clearing, he turned and ran, not knowing which direction he took and not caring. He knew only that if he was to escape with his life, he would have to run as far and as fast as his feet would carry him.

"Well, I'll be jiggered!" Odell's smile stretched from one side of his craggy face to the other as Bjorn rode into the shifting circle of light thrown by the campfire. "Find us, did ye?"

"Where's Wolf?" Bjorn demanded, blowing on his hands in an attempt to warm them, then motioning for Cayley to urge her horse forward and join him. He searched the faces of the men, looking for the man who had sent Cormick to his death.

"Ain't 'e with you?"

"Nay."

"But he and Jagger and Robin left days ago to find Lady Megan and collect the ransom. Leastwise, that's what he claimed!" Odell's grizzled face squinched and he scratched his bald head thoughtfully. "Where's Cormick, and who's the woman?" he asked as if suddenly suspicious. "Ye know the rule."

"Aye, and I had no choice but to bring her," Bjorn said, hopping lithely to the ground before trying to help Cayley from her saddle. She would have none of his assistance and he held up his hands as if in surrender and allowed her to dismount. Rubbing the kinks from his shoulders, he was grateful to have finally found camp and the men he knew and trusted. Women, especially rich women, were trouble to deal with and difficult to understand. He wanted to despise this headstrong blond woman he'd been forced to ride with, but he'd found, as they'd spent so many long hours together, that she'd proved herself stronger and quicker witted than he'd ever thought possible. "This, lads, is Lady Cayley, Megan of Dwyrain's sister."

"Another one!" Odell rolled his eyes as if searching for divine intervention.

Bjorn took the time to introduce each man, but Odell was impatient.

"Tell us all everything," Odell demanded as Peter saw to the horses. "Sit down by the fire and I'll get ye somethin' to eat, but tell us what happened."

The strips of eel and shanks of rabbit were far overcooked, but it had been long since Bjorn had eaten. As he gnawed on a rabbit bone, Bjorn told them of his capture, Cormick's death, and his escape with Cayley. The men were grim-faced throughout and in the end, they voted, by throwing their knives into the fire, to seek vengeance for their comrade's death.

"Holt will rue the day he killed one of us," Odell crowed.

"Aye," Heath agreed, the skin beneath his beard stretched tight. The thirst for vengeance glinted in his eyes.

As the men swapped stories about how they intended to find Wolf and kill Holt, Bjorn watched Cayley from the corner of his eye. She wasn't repulsed by the outlaws' promises of revenge. She ate heartily and without complaint.

When she was finished, she eyed each man, opened her mouth to say something, then closed it decisively. Bjorn swallowed a smile as she licked her greasy fingers, then wiped them on her mantle. She was a pretty one, though spoiled, and she'd been far less trouble than he'd expected. But her tongue—how she could give a man a lashing with it!

"I had trouble findin' ye," Bjorn admitted as Heath passed a jug of ale. Bjorn took a long swallow. The brew was bitter, but he was grateful for a draft and drank his fill before wiping his mouth with his sleeve. He handed the jug to Cayley, who licked her lips and seemed about to decline. Then, gaze fastened to Bjorn's, she hoisted the dirty vessel to her lips and took a swallow, only to end up coughing so hard she had trouble catching her breath and nearly dropped the jug.

"Careful!" Odell warned.

Tears streamed from her eyes, spilling on red cheeks. "What *is* that?" she asked.

Odell sniffed, offended. "'Tis me own brand of mead."

"'Twill burn out yer insides if ye're not careful," Peter said.

"Even if you are," she said, struggling with her voice.

"I don't see ye passin' the jug too often without takin' more'n yer share, Peter," Odell grumbled, his pride wounded.

"Shh. 'Tis of no matter." Bjorn glanced at Cayley. "The lady is fine. Mayhap she'd like another sip."

"Later," Cayley said, her voice a raspy whisper, and she patted her chest with the flat of her hand.

"Good." Bjorn couldn't hide the amusement he felt as she tried to regain her composure and hide the fact that her face had turned crimson. "Now, we must find Wolf. Since he's not returned, he's at the chapel waiting for our return, or on the road, or at Dwyrain."

He's in the prison, Bjorn, where you were once chained. Bjorn turned swiftly, reaching for his sword as he saw the crippled sorcerer step into the golden shadows of the campfire. A speckled owl sat on his shoulder and he held the reins of two fine horses in his hands. "Hagan of Erbyn has a small army of men that we can join," he said, the men staring at him as if he were the ghost of some great Welsh warrior. "The lady left him and rode day and night to Dwyrain. His soldiers moved more slowly but they will reach the gates of the castle soon." No one had heard him approach, nor had they heard the sound of his horses' hooves.

"God be with us, ye've got that flappin' beast with ye!" Odell exclaimed, leaping backward at the sight of the sorcerer and his winged friend. The bird's head swiveled to pin the wiry man in his wide-eyed stare. "Owl stew is what ye're good for, and nothin' more! Git!" Odell waved his arms at the bird, but the owl only settled in and gave a soft hoot. "Bloody Christ, just what we need!"

The magician heeded him not. 'Twas as if he hadn't heard

a word of Odell's chatter. "Wolf needs our help. If we hurry, we can join Hagan of Erbyn's army and try to save him." The sorcerer somehow locked his gaze to that of each and every person gathered around the fire. "If we do not come to his aid—and soon—I fear that he, Robin, Jagger, and those in the castle who have been his spies will surely die."

"Jack?" one man asked.

"Aye."

"Anyone else?"

"Yea," the sorcerer said sadly. "The Lady Megan as well."

"'Tis time to collect my part of the bargain." Holt swayed slightly as he glanced over his shoulder to the hallway. Leaning against the doorway, he said, "Leave us be, guards—I want no one to disturb us." Then, weaving, he entered her chamber and closed the door behind him.

Dread clamped around Megan's lungs. Throughout the gloomy day she'd watched from her window as the gallows was finished, nails pounded into place, a thick noose swinging ready from a crossbeam. The thought that Wolf would lose his life on that monstrous scaffold turned her stomach, and now, facing the man who was her husband, the self-proclaimed baron who had ordered Wolf's death, she recoiled. "All of the prisoners have not been released."

"'Tis only a matter of time." He fumbled with his belt and she smelled wine souring on his breath. "You and I, wife," he said, his eyes finding hers, "have wasted too much time already."

"Nay, I—"

His head snapped up and his lips turned bloodless with rage. "Do not dare defy me, wench, for we struck a deal and you, if you want to see any more of that sorry lot of prisoners released, will do as I say."

She bit down hard on her tongue rather than telling him to fly straight to the portals of hell. A breeze swept through the half-open window, rattling the shutters and causing a stir in the fire. Amber coals glowed brighter and flames crackled.

"Or would ye rather see the young one—Robin, I think

he's called—hanging from the end of a rope? Is that what ye want, his death on your head?"

"He's but a boy," she protested, knowing that Holt had her cornered.

"And a traitor to Dwyrain." His jaw grew tight, his countenance unforgiving. Fury flared his nostrils. "Now, Megan, test me no more." His belt dropped to the floor, the buckle smacking the stones with a heavy chink. She jumped. Oh, God, this was really going to happen. She would have to lift her skirts to this . . . this monster she detested. Frozen for a second, she watched as he tossed his surcoat onto the foot of the bed and began working the laces of his mantle. "Did you hear me, woman? If ye do not strip yourself of your clothes, I'll do it for you and I'll make you watch while not only Wolf but his band of thieves and Judases are killed one by one!" With a final tug, the mantle fell free and dropped to the floor.

Megan's heart beat in fear.

Advancing upon her, his eyes gleaming bright with the reflection of the fire, Holt stretched out a hand and ran one long finger over the slope of her jaw. Her skin crawled and she fought the urge to slap the damning hand away. What did it matter if he touched her tonight or later in the week? She was doomed to lie with him, to pretend that the child within her was his progeny. She had no choice if she was to protect Wolf's babe, but she'd never been the kind of woman who let her fate be decided for her. For as long as she could remember, she'd been vocal and demanding about what her life should be. Her independence had been her undoing in the end, and her father, deciding she could not make the right choice, had betrothed her to Holt.

Now her enemy of a husband bent closer, the stench of consumed wine with him as he pressed his lips to her cheek and neck. Her skin prickled in revulsion and she couldn't imagine the torture of letting him bed her.

Could she lie with him night after night? Nay! 'Twas unthinkable, but she had only a few days and then each of the prisoners would be released. If she allowed Holt to think that she enjoyed him, that she couldn't wait to be with him, there was a chance he would no longer lock her in her chamber. He might even remove the guard from her door. If he were duped into believing that she'd accepted her lot as his wife, he might not have her watched so closely and she would be allowed to roam the castle freely. She knew more about Dwyrain than anyone within the castle walls, for she and Bevan had, while growing up, explored every staircase, attic, loft, and cellar. If given a tiny bit of freedom, she could find a way to release Wolf.

She had allies, she thought, as Holt's hand reached for the tie holding her tunic over her breasts and his hot breath feathered across her collarbones.

Father Timothy, and surely the carpenter, the nursemaid Rue, and others loyal to Ewan. Surely the outlaws would come for their leader, and Hagan of Erbyn was due to arrive on the morrow unless he, infuriated with her for deceiving him and stealing away into the night, had returned to his family.

The tunic opened and she shivered with loathing. "That's better," he breathed against her skin before looking up and pressing hot, insistent lips to hers. She couldn't kiss him back, but neither did she push him away. His tongue slid into her mouth and she nearly gagged. *Please God, no!* she silently screamed as his weight pressed her down to the bed. Tears burned behind her eyes as he stripped off her clothes, ripping them in his hurry, dropping them onto the floor by the bed along with his own tunic, breeches, and purse.

With great effort, she closed her eyes and pretended that she wasn't in the room, that what was happening to her body had naught to do with her. His hands were rough against her breasts, tweaking and pushing them, giving her no pleasure, and when he slid his knees between her own bare legs she scooted upward on the bed, as far from him as she could get.

"Do not try to escape from me, wife," he ordered. "'Tis time to give up your virginity."

Oh, God, soon he'd know! There would be no blood, no ripping of her maidenhead. Then he'd realize that she'd been with another man. Surely he was not so stupid that he would not discern who that man—the father of her child— was. Eventually, he would know the babe wasn't his.

Holt growled into her ear, "I have waited long for this, planned for it, dreamed of it, been more than patient since you arrived at the castle. Taking your virtue will be more satisfying than killing your brother—"

She gasped and cried out.

"'Tis true," he admitted drunkenly, his tongue loosened by wine. "Your brother as well as your father. Neither would hurry to his grave fast enough." With a belch, he laughed, and Megan wanted only to do him harm.

"I detest you!" she spat, giving up her plan to dupe him and play the willing bride. She could never, would never . . .

He clucked his tongue. "I would have done anything for this time with you," he said and she spat up at his face.

"Get off me!"

"Too late. Now, wife," he said, rising above her, his white, naked body poised between her legs, "watch as I make you mine."

She stared up at him, but she would not touch or caress him. One of her arms was flung over the side of the bed and her fingers touched his garments, the velvet and leather and . . . something metal. Her fingertips scraped the hilt of his knife.

A gift from God. She licked her lips as her fingers wrapped over the carved handle.

"Now and forever, Megan of Dwyrain, ye belong to me!"

He thrust forward. Her fingers wrapped around the weapon and with a swift shifting of her body, she brought up the knife and plunged the wicked blade deep into his side.

Blood sprayed the bedclothes.

Holt let out a hideous, timber-rattling roar. Rage and pain contorted his features. "I'll kill you!"

"Go to hell, you murdering beast!" Megan squirmed away as Holt tried to reach for the knife that stuck beneath his ribs.

Rolling off the bed, she grabbed her chemise and landed near the fire and basket of logs. She had to get out of here. Now! Escape!

"You'll pay for this," he charged, but was sweating and breathing hard. Stumbling to his feet, he yanked out the knife. More blood splattered. Holding the dripping weapon, he dove forward. She sidestepped his attack and he fell on the floor with a thud and a pained grunt.

"'Tis Wolf I love," she said, wanting to wound him, to make him feel some of the pain she felt now that she knew that he'd taken both her brother's and her father's lives. She threw her chemise over her head.

"The thief."

"But not a murderer."

"He killed Tadd of Prydd." Holt was struggling, his arms levering his torso upright. Blood ran from his side. "Now, you are my wife and—"

"In name only," she said, as she gathered up the rest of her clothes. Holt's skin was pale, but as Megan tossed on her tunic and backed toward the door, he sprang to his feet with renewed strength.

"You'll regret you ever crossed me, woman." He thrust at her with the knife and she spun away, knocking over the basket of firewood. Small logs rolled free.

"Keep far from me!"

"Not until you beg for mercy."

Without thinking, she snatched up what had once been a branch and heaved it at him. He ducked, but the corner of the log caught him on the edge of his jaw and sent him spinning into the wall, where he cracked his head on a crucifix hung near the door. Megan, certain she'd killed him, dropped a second piece of oak and stumbled backward. "Oh, God, please help me," she cried.

He groaned and lay still.

Never before had she taken a life, and though she hated Holt with all her heart, she'd never truly believed that she'd have to kill him. She nearly retched, but told herself to keep going, this was her chance. Grabbing her mantle and boots, she stepped over his bleeding body. Fingers fumbling, heart pounding, she threw on her mantle, pried the knife from his fingers, and bolted for the door. It opened without a sound and soon she was in the corridor for the first time in days.

"God be with me," she whispered, thankful as she locked the door behind her that Holt had dismissed the guards.

The air in the corridor was cool. The rush lights flickered

dimly, casting shadows against the walls, but Megan's steps were sure. She'd grown up in this castle and knew connecting routes to back stairs and seldom-used passages. Walking barefoot and noiselessly, she slipped unseen through the hallways. Most of the castle was asleep—only a few nodding guards stood their posts—but Megan hurried down a curving staircase, through the gallery, past a door leading to the priest's quarters, and finally down another set of steps to the kitchen.

A cat lurked near the door, but it only watched with amber eyes as she stole outside where the moon, not quite full, bathed the bailey in its silvery glow. The gallows, with its noose swaying softly, loomed like a huge, ungainly beast, casting a horrid shadow over the grass. In her mind's eye, Megan saw her beloved Wolf swinging from the hangman's rope, and she sped forward, past the evil structure and the pillory to Rue's hut.

Quietly, she tapped on a window until it was opened by a sour-faced Rue, who grimaced as if she were about to give whoever was bothering her a tongue-lashing.

"Megan," she said in surprise, "come in, come in." Within seconds, the door was open and Megan threw herself into the nursemaid's outstretched arms.

"'Tis worried I've been. Holt, he would not let me visit ye and I feared . . . oh, Lord, child, don't worry about what I feared." Her small hut was warm, a banked fire radiating heat. From the rafters hung bundles of herbs that Rue had collected and had suspended to dry.

"I've not much time," Megan said, her words coming out in short, wild bursts. "I killed Holt and now—"

"Killed him?" Rue crossed herself. "What were ye thinking, child? The punishment for murdering a baron is—"

"—what he deserved. *He* killed Father *and* Bevan. He admitted as much to me." She was suddenly shaking, her teeth chattering as she talked, the cold in her soul deep and mind-numbing.

"There now, lass, worry not about it. What is it ye want from me?"

"I want to know who is loyal to my father, who would rise against Holt's soldiers; and then I need a disguise, for I'm going to set Wolf and the rest of the prisoners free."

"Holy Mother," Rue said, her face wrinkling in concentration and worry. "Think ye it's wise to—"

"I killed Holt!" Megan said again. "I have no choice."

Rue nodded and rubbed her hands, with their big knuckles, together nervously. "Many in the castle despise Holt, but would they take up arms against his men? I know not." Shaking her head, she said, "There is Ellen, Tom's mother; she would do anything to free her boy, for she's certain that Holt will make him hang from the very structure her husband built."

"She has many children—boys," Megan said, "I need one of their—George's, as he's near my size—his tunic and breeches."

"His clothes?"

"For my disguise, of course."

"Oh. Of course." Rue looked more worried than before.

Megan rattled on. "And I'll need someone to go with me to the dungeon."

"Yes."

"And more—I'll need my own guards posted to warn me of any soldiers approaching."

Rue bit her lower lip and grabbed both of Megan's shoulders in her long, bony fingers. "Ye should have been the baron, ye know, if the king would allow a woman to rule. Ye'd be as good a ruler as your father and far better than Bevan would have been." Tears sprang to her old eyes. "Ewan, proud he'd be of ye."

"Aye, but we have not time for this now," Megan said, her throat growing thick with the sorrow she held back. "Hurry!"

"Come. We'll talk with Ellen," Rue agreed, reaching for the door. Before she stepped into the bailey, she turned and her face softened. She touched a hand to Megan's crown. "God be with ye, lass."

"Halt!" the guard commanded as he heard the sound of footsteps on the stairs. "Who be ye?"

"'Tis only me, Ronald, and me helpmate Stanley," a boy answered, and Wolf recognized the voice as belonging to one of the peasant children whose job it was to bring down buckets of food and water as well as empty pails in which he and the other prisoners were supposed to relieve themselves. Stanley was younger, with a pockmarked face and a stutter that was so difficult to understand, he rarely tried to speak.

"'Tis late ye be," the guard said with a yawn. There was an edge of suspicion to his voice.

"Aye," Ronald replied. "Cook fergot to give us these buckets of slop earlier."

"Could not it have waited 'til morn?" The guard was on his feet to greet the boys. A nervous man, he'd been watching Wolf most of the night, as if he expected some plot to set him free. The sentry was a big man and one who had sworn to Holt that there would be no attempts at escape under his watch. Too many times lately had a prisoner tried to flee. To strengthen his words, he was heavily armed with two daggers and a sword lying unsheathed upon his table.

"Ye'd have thought morning would be soon enough," Ronald agreed around a yawn as he and his friend set the heavy pails on the guard's small table. "But ye know Cook. 'Waste not, want not,' 'e's always preachin'. Worse than Father Tim, he is."

The guard chuckled. "Right ye are about that, boy." He motioned toward the cells. "Come, we'll feed the animals, then we both can get some sleep."

Wolf felt something in the air, a breath of breeze laden with a familiar scent, and his heart jolted as the boy Stanley turned and faced him. Amber eyes held his for an instant and his throat was suddenly tight with fear. Megan! What was she doing here? She'd only get herself killed! Frantic, he shook his head quickly, trying to discourage her. Whatever she had planned, she should not be risking her life or that of their child.

"'Ere we go," the guard said, starting with Jack's cell. "Come, huntsman, for some of the leftovers." Keys jangled loudly, rattling Wolf's nerves. The rusted cell door squeaked open on old hinges. Wolf's heart thudded as slop was poured into a bucket on the floor. Did the others not know? Were they not ready to ambush the guard?

Wolf had never been a man of strong faith, but now he

prayed to God and watched as the small trio moved to the next cell. *Robin's* cage. Holy Christ, the boy would surely recognize her and blurt her name, and everything would be lost. Sweat ran down Wolf's arms as he saw Robin meet the silent boy's eyes and his mouth drop open, but before the guard noticed, he fell into a squatting position next to the pail, staring at its unappetizing contents as if starving. To the next cell, Tom's, the guard and his helpers moved, and now Wolf could see her plainly, a few wayward strands of mahogany hair poking from her cowl, her small upturned nose. How much she appeared as she had at the camp when he'd tried to disguise her female curves from his men. His throat went dry and love beat wildly in his heart.

Wolf's mind screamed for her to be careful, to forget her plan, whatever it was, that 'twas not worth risking her life for his, but he held his tongue and as the cell door swung open, he was on the balls of his feet, every muscle in his body strung tight. As "Stanley" poured the slop into his pail, the guard watched him. "Be careful," he said. "This one—Wolf, they call him—is truly a beast and would gladly rip out both yer throats, but he's calmer now, in pain from the beatings he's been given."

"Is that so?" Ronald asked, and Megan, in her disguise, feigned tripping over the pail, sending slop everywhere.

"Oh, son, look at the mess ye've made! Bloody Christ!" the guard reprimanded.

Reacting by instinct, Wolf caught her and felt her body close. She clutched his hand but for an instant, leaving a small knife in his fingers.

"Come on, ever'body out!" the guard ordered. "Wolf, 'e won't get to taste any of Cook's fine—"

Wolf leaped onto the man's back.

"Hey! Stop!" He whirled and Megan, grabbing a bucket from the floor, slammed it against the guard's big head as Wolf plunged the knife into the man's shoulder. They fell against the cell walls, rattling the bars, the guard starting to yell.

"Say a word and I'll slit your throat!" Wolf promised, his blade at the sentry's thick Adam's apple as he still rode the burly man's back.

"He—"

The blade pressed closer and blood oozed. The sentry's voice suddenly failed him.

"That's better," Wolf said as Megan lifted the man's keys from his belt.

Within seconds, the guard was bound and locked in Wolf's cell, the other prisoners released. The weapons—two buckets, two knives, and a sword—were distributed as they headed for the stairs. "This was foolish," Wolf reprimanded her in a low whisper.

"I could not let you die."

God, how he loved her! "So you risked your neck and that of our babe?"

"How—how did you know?" she asked, and a small smile tugged at the corners of his mouth. Was she not the most beautiful woman in the king's lands?

He glanced at her abdomen covered in tattered clothes and placed his hand over her flat stomach. "Cadell—the magician—he told me."

Her fingers folded over his and he melted inside. "The sorcerer is Lady Morgana's lost brother?" she asked in wonder.

"Aye, but let us not tarry. I will tell you everything once I have killed Holt and we have fled Dwyrain." Reluctantly, he turned to the task at hand. They were not yet free of the walls of the dungeon.

"Do not worry about Holt," Megan said, and then crossed herself in the dim, flickering light. "He's dead."

"Dead?" Holt hardly dared believe his good luck.

"Aye," she said and he felt her shake. Her golden gaze was troubled, her chin jutted out defiantly.

"*You* killed him?"

"'Twas either that or share his bed."

Wolf's heart warmed for this woman. He held her close for a second, then brushed his lips over hers. "'Twould have been all right," he said, reassuring her. "Nothing is worth your life."

She shook her head vigorously. "Nay, I could never—"

"Let's go!" Jack growled.

Jagger, carrying a knife in one big hand, agreed. "Aye, there's time for talk later. Now listen, Robin, Jack, and me—we'll take care of the guards in the gatehouse. You,

Wolf, and Megan and Tom, get the horses from the stables. We'll open the gates as soon as we see you with the beasts."

Wolf nodded. 'Twas as good as any plan they could conjure without more time. "We'll meet in the shadow of this very tower."

Without another word, they hastened up the stairs. At the door, Wolf motioned for everyone to wait. He stepped into the moon-washed bailey first, the guard's sword at ready. As his foot touched the ground outside, he whirled lithely, but no one accosted him, and aside for a few sentries positioned as they ever were in the watchtowers, the castle was quiet.

Was it possible? Could Holt be dead, slain by his wife, and no one in the keep be aware of his death? His heart leapt at the thought, for finally he and Megan could be together—as man and wife. If she were widowed, he could surely ask for her hand. Though she had killed Holt, Wolf was certain Megan would be acquitted of any crime and he . . . he would give up 'living as a criminal in the forest, if only she would be at his side.

He motioned to Jagger and the prisoners split into two groups. Jagger, Jack, and Robin, pressed close to the stones of the bailey wall, hid in the shadows as they hurried toward the gatehouse. Megan, Tom, and Wolf crept into the stables and, sliding through the half-open door, spoke softly to the animals as they chose six swift horses.

Despite their caution, several nervous stallions whinnied noisily. "Damn it all to hell," Wolf muttered under his breath.

A bleary-eyed stableboy opened the door. Wolf set upon him, his sword at the lad's throat. "You'll say nothing," Wolf commanded in an authoritative whisper.

"Nay, nay, nothing!" The boy gulped. "Wolf, is it?" Even in the partial darkness, Wolf noticed the youth's face lit in admiration. "Can I come with ye? I've fancied meself an outlaw for a long time now."

"'Tis not as glorious as you may think," Wolf said, hoping to discourage the lad. How many boys had he met like this one who thought living the life of a criminal and outrunning the law was a grand adventure? Had he not thought the very same?

His attempts to dissuade the boy were in vain.

"I'd be a good thief," the lad insisted.

"We must be off," Tom said, but the stableboy wasn't finished.

"Ian's me name, and I've stolen from the baker and armorer and poached in the baron's woods and not been caught," he boasted.

Foolish youth! Wolf remembered the guard who had complained of his son getting into trouble. 'Twould be better if he left the boy here, but he had no time to argue. "I wouldn't be bragging of your crimes," he reprimanded. "Now, hush. Come with us if ye will, but understand that if ye be caught, ye'll hang."

"I won't be," he said with the confidence of youth.

"Then keep these beasts quiet and come along!"

They led the horses from the stables, and with Ian along, the horses quieted and were less nervous. Wolf's heart was drumming, his nerves stretched tighter than a dying man on the rack, dread inching up his spine. Surely their escape wouldn't come so easily. Everyone in the castle had suffered Holt's wrath when Cayley and Bjorn had stolen their freedom, and certainly the guards would be doubly vigilant, on the lookout for another attempted break from the dungeons, rather than feel the sting of Holt's anger.

The wind was chill and moist, promising rain, though no clouds blocked the moon, the castle silent except for their muffled tread. Their breath fogged in the night. Freedom was so close . . .

Silently they approached the gate, but the portcullis hadn't been lifted.

Wolf sensed trouble. There had been more than ample time to winch up the iron gate. Holding Megan's small hand in one of his, he silently prayed. The fingers of his other hand tightened around the hilt of his sword. Something was wrong. Looking upward, he scoured the battlements and towers, but nothing appeared amiss.

Come on, come on! Jagger and Jack were strong men; winching up the gate would be no trouble.

Unless they'd been caught.

Unless even now they'd been taken prisoner again.

Dread thudded through his brain.

"Well, well, well." Holt's voice, deep and foreboding, rang through the bailey.

For the love of God, no! Whirling, sword ready to cleave anyone who should try to thwart him, Wolf found his old nemesis, not dead as Megan had vowed, but very much alive and standing proudly upon the gallows as he glared pointedly at Wolf and Megan. His voice was deadly as he said to the sleeping castle at large, "If it isn't my murdering wife and her outlaw of a lover trying to flee!"

❈ Sixteen ❈

"Now, Wolf, outlaw of the forest, you die," Holt announced with some difficulty, and Megan's heart turned to stone. They were doomed, and the glint in her husband's eyes warned her that he would extract his revenge upon each and every one of them. Absently, she touched her abdomen, to the low spot where her baby was growing—so innocent, so perfect. She could not endanger this fragile life.

"Let's kill him," Tom muttered under his breath.

"Aye," Ian said.

Wolf shook his head. "Not yet."

'Twas idle hopes. Lurking in the shadows were soldiers who had been hiding in the towers, behind the hayricks, under carts. They came forward with bows strung tight and arrows aimed at Wolf's heart. *Oh, love,* Megan silently cried, and her mouth was suddenly dry with fear.

The horses, sensing danger, fidgeted, pulling tight on their reins, whinnying and snorting, but Wolf held them firmly.

Holt was not finished. Swaying slightly, standing as if with great effort, he said, "Before I send you to hell where you belong, you pathetic outlaw"—he ran a hand over the fresh wood of a support beam of the gallows—"you'll watch each of your men die, one by one. Now!" He snapped his fingers and grimaced in the pale moonlight.

Megan shivered, not from the cold of the wind that blew past the thick stone walls, but from the despair gathering in her heart, the fear that she'd never see her beloved Wolf again. "Please be with him," she murmured to a fierce God who, she sensed, had abandoned her this night. "Save him and my child."

Sentries in the watchtower opened the door of the gatehouse and pushed their captives into the bailey. Jack, Jagger, and young Robin shuffled forward, their eyes blindfolded, their mouths gagged, their hands tied in front of them.

Megan's legs threatened to give way, and had it not been for Wolf's strong arm supporting her, she would have swooned on the frozen grass of the bailey.

"For the love of Jesus, what's going on here?" Like a mother hawk swooping from the heavens to save her chicks, Father Timothy, robes askew and billowing behind him, ran barefoot across the bailey. He blinked rapidly, as if fighting to maintain his courage as he shoved his way through the armed men. "Lord Holt, I beg of you, do not shed any more blood!"

"And why not?" Holt demanded, his jaw tight, his skin pale as death. "These men and my own dear wife are traitors of Dwyrain." A dark bruise and bloody cut discolored the skin above his eye, yet the wounds Megan had inflicted hadn't been mortal, and though he was not as strong as he had been, he appeared to be able to survive. "The outlaw turned my bride against me."

"Nay, Holt, you did that yourself," Megan said boldly, finding her courage and pushing off Wolf's restraining arm to step forward to face the man she'd thought she'd killed. All the pain and suffering was her doing, and she would willingly sacrifice herself if only Wolf and his men were allowed their freedom.

"Stop!" Wolf shifted quickly, dropping the horse's reins and throwing himself between her and the soldiers' arrows. "Do not be foolish," he said under his breath, but Holt heard the command and laughed.

"Isn't that touching? The outlaw and his would-be murderess of a lover! Who would have thought that there was such devotion between criminals?"

"'Tis not God's will that innocent people die!" Timothy proclaimed, his lower lip trembling nervously.

"Innocent?" Holt said with a lusty laugh as he slowly

climbed down from the raised floor of the gallows. Grimacing in pain, he repeated, "Innocent? Did ye not hear that my lady tried to kill me, first with my own knife and then with a piece of kindling? Believe me, priest, no one here is innocent this night."

His stride faltered a bit as he strode across the trampled grass. His steps were not firm, and he was still pale as death. A crusted bruise was beginning to show over his temple, where a vein throbbed in anger. "You!" he said, his voice echoing through the castle and in Megan's heart. His eyebrows slammed together and his lips were bloodless and flat against his teeth, his eyes hot coals as they found hers in the night. "You, wife, come with me. We have unfinished business."

"If you want her, then you must kill me first," Wolf invited, his voice smooth as glass.

Megan's heart sank. "Nay!"

"Gladly." Holt's grin was pure and intense evil as he unsheathed his sword. "Why wait?"

"No!" Frantic, Megan tore herself from Wolf's possessive grasp. "Nay, do not kill him," she cried, the ugly thought too horrid to bear. "I'll go with you. Willingly." Tears filled her eyes, and despite the knowledge that she was inviting her own doom, she turned to Wolf and stared into his blue eyes one last time, searing their image into her mind for all eternity. She felt a deep rending in her soul and she fought the urge to break down. Tears streaming from her eyes, her fear suddenly abated, and she sniffed, lifting her chin and refusing to weep any more. In a choked voice, she vowed, "I will love you forever, Wolf."

A muscle worked in Wolf's jaw. His fingers clenched until his knuckles showed white over the handle of his sword. "As I love you, Megan," he said, his voice deep with conviction. "Until the day I die."

"Which will be soon," Holt announced. "Spare me the pitiful scene."

Megan's heart caught. She heard not Holt's scorn, only that Wolf had said that he loved her. She would carry that sweet drop of heaven with her to the grave.

With a howl, the brutal wind swept through the bailey, moaning eerily, as if God himself were watching Dwyrain and voicing his disapproval. A cloud crept over the moon as Holt stalked up to the outlaw.

Wolf's eyes narrowed savagely on his enemy. Fearless, he ground out, "Harm her, and I swear that I or my very ghost will hunt you down like the filthy cur you are, find you wherever you cower, and rip out your throat."

"Bastard!" Holt's fist crashed into the side of Wolf's face. Pain exploded behind Wolf's eyes and Holt nearly stumbled with the effort. "Take him away," he snarled at his men. "Haul his pathetic hide and the rest of the traitors to the dungeons. I want a dozen of you to stand guard. There will be no escape! Not this time. Do you hear me?"

When no one answered, he clenched his fist. "Do you?"

"Aye, m'lord," a fat knight agreed anxiously, his Adam's apple bobbing in fear.

"They'll be hanged at dawn, and everyone in the castle, every man, woman, and child, from the oldest crone to the newborn babes, will witness how I deal with those who betray Dwyrain and deceive me." Yanking her roughly, he pulled Megan toward the great hall, and though he had lost blood, he was strong, his grip punishing, his strides long.

"Lord Holt, wait!" a sentry in the watchtower shouted, his voice ringing over the commotion that erupted as the doors of several huts began to swing open. Men and women, bleary-eyed and confused, filtered into the bailey.

Holt stopped dead in his tracks and turned, his head uplifted in harsh fury. "What?"

"There are men outside the gates," the sentry yelled.

"Who?"

Megan had to fight a glimmer of hope.

"I know not." Cupping his hands around his mouth, the sentry yelled down to those on the outside of the portal, "Who goes there?"

"Damn it, man," Holt thundered. "I care not if it's the bloody king! Can't you see I'm with my wife?! Leave them be 'til morning!" Strong despite his wounds, he headed for the keep and hauled Megan with him.

"M'lord!" Again, the priest tried to intervene. "Please, Holt, listen to me. As God is my witness, you must not kill these men, nor harm this woman."

"As God is my witness, you and your false sense of piety bore me, Timothy. You are a traitor." His eyes swept the crowd that was beginning to gather and gape. "Yes, the good priest has betrayed me," he said to his subjects, "as many of you have, and I will not—will never—allow any kind of insubordination." He snapped his fingers.

Hiss! Thwack!

The priest screamed in pain as an arrow pierced him from behind.

Megan gasped in horror.

"Oh, Jesus, Lord, forgive me of my sins!" Timothy fell forward, first to his knees and finally onto his face.

Someone in the crowd screamed. A horse reared and lashed out with its hooves and Holt sneered at the blood staining the priest's robes. "Now I suppose he can speak with God more easily."

"You brute!" Reeling away from him, Megan dove toward the fallen man. "Father Timothy, oh, Timothy—" she said, cradling his head. "Call for the physician or Rue!"

"Leave him be!" Holt commanded as the doctor pushed through the crowd. Reaching down, he jerked Megan to her feet. "Weep not for the priest."

Wolf lunged, but was restrained, and Holt laughed at his futile efforts while Megan again fought tears and fury that such horrors had happened in her beloved Dwyrain.

Groaning, the priest lifted his head and began chanting prayers. Blood spread over his robes, and the bottoms of his bare feet turned upward, showing calluses and corns in the shimmering moonlight. "Make an example of him as well," Holt ordered. "When he's bled to death, gut him and mount his head over the south tower."

"Father, take me now," Timothy prayed.

"Nay!" Megan ordered, whirling on Holt. "You are a fiend!" To the soldiers, she commanded, "I'm mistress of this castle, and I say you let the prisoners go free and see that Father Timothy is seen by the doctor and—"

Slap! Holt's hand connected with her face, sending her spinning. Pain blinded her. Blood slipped from her lip. She started to fall, but Holt caught her before she hit the ground and in one swift motion, hauled her over his shoulder.

The earth swayed and heaved and she caught a glimpse of Wolf, lunging forward, trying to reach her, screaming something she couldn't hear as she pounded on Holt's back and kicked. His laugh was brittle as a leaf in January, and several burly soldiers restrained Wolf.

"You'll find out what happens when a woman defies me," Holt promised, limping and swearing as he carried her up the stairs to the keep. She pounded on his back and kicked wildly, hoping to land one of her blows in his wound, but he shifted his weight so that she could not draw any more blood.

"Bastard! Fiend! Dirty son of a—"

"If you do not want to see your traitor of a lover killed right now, you'll stop!" Holt growled, and she quit moving in an instant. She bit her tongue in her efforts not to scream at him, but she knew she would never accept her fate.

Desperation clawing at his soul, Wolf watched in silent agony as the woman he loved was torn from him and hauled up the stairs of the keep to be raped by the man she'd wed. Rage thundered through his blood, pounding in his brain, nearly blinding him.

Holt's soldiers dragged him roughly toward the prison, but as Holt's hand connected with Megan's cheek, Wolf roared in fury. Pivoting sharply and snarling, he flung off the men restraining him as if they were stuffed with down.

"Hey, what the bloody hell—"

Wolf snatched an arrow from a guard's quiver, then rammed the deadly tip deep into the man's neck. As the soldier squealed and bled, Wolf snatched his sword and began swinging.

Jagger, though blindfolded, heard the sounds of battle and threw his considerable weight at his guard. He sent the man reeling, tore off his blindfold, and with his wrists bound, leaped upon his captor, snapped his neck in his powerful hands, and grabbed the guard's sword. "Now, men!" he yelled.

Jack and Robin tore off their blindfolds. Tom kicked a guard in the shin and Ian reached to the ground, found rocks, and hurled them at a horse's haunches. A destrier neighed in fear and tore through the crowd. Other beasts followed, scattering soldiers and peasants.

"Bloody hell!" one soldier exclaimed.

"Don't shoot. They be the baron's best stallions!"

"For the love of Christ!"

"Watch out—" another guard shouted as he reached for the reins and was knocked to the ground. Screaming in tortured agony, he was trampled by heavy, frightened hooves.

Still swinging the sword wildly, Wolf yelled to the soldiers attacking him, "Those who swore your fealty to Baron Ewan, rise against Holt and his army, for 'twas he who killed the baron and his son!"

Tom ran for the gates as Foster yelled, "'Tis true! I heard Sir Holt bragging after he drank too much wine!" Several other voices took up the battle cry and joined forces with Wolf. Swords crashed. Arrows zinged. Wolf ducked and saw an attacker running at him, crossbow aimed at his heart. Throwing himself to the ground, he rolled, and before the man could realign his weapon, Wolf's sword sliced his legs. Tumbling to the ground, the guard writhed in agony. Wolf tossed the loaded bow to Ian.

Tom, swinging a mace he'd grabbed from a fallen guard, inched his way backward toward the wall and finally disappeared into the gatehouse. Soldiers fought their own. Peasants found weapons and joined the battle. Blood stained the grass of Dwyrain.

Wolf swung his stolen sword, slicing anyone who came too close as he made his way across the bailey to the keep, to Megan.

With a loud grinding of gears, the portcullis opened, spilling a small army of men into the bailey. Swords unsheathed, they entered with a piercing battle cry and the thunder of hooves. Swords clattered and clashed and horses screamed. Some of the new arrivals were dressed as soldiers bearing the colors of Erbyn, while the rest were those loyal to no baron, members of Wolf's bloody band of thieves. Odell and Cadell rode side by side, but Wolf's heart stilled when he thought he spied another man, one afoot, creep through the open gate.

Connor, whom he'd heard a prison guard say had not returned after escorting Cadell away from the castle walls, was within the keep again.

Hagan's voice rang through the bailey. "Put down your weapons or make ready to die!"

"You die!" a man loyal to Holt said, only to be cleaved by Robin's piercing sword.

Arrows hissed through the air, and Wolf, running swiftly, turned his thoughts to Megan and the man who was defiling her as he dashed up the stone steps of the great hall.

He was met by peasants and servants racing from the keep, awakened and drawn into the bailey by the sounds of battle. Throwing on clothes, grabbing torches, pokers, swords, and knives, they hurried to defend Dwyrain as Wolf slunk through the dark hallways, as he had once before when he'd started his quest to kidnap Megan, the very journey that had sealed her doom.

Continuing ever upward, running along hallways, opening doors, his eyes scanning each chamber as his heart thudded in fear of what he might find, Wolf stole through the castle, his sword drawn, his mind and body relentless in his search for the lord's chamber and the woman he loved.

Megan swallowed hard against her fear and inched her chin up a notch as she leveled her gaze on Holt.

"You lied to me, wife," he said, circling her as she stood at the foot of the bed. The window was open and the sounds of clanging metal, screaming voices, shouts, and frightened cries of horses seeped into the room. *Wolf, oh, love, please be safe. Take Robin and flee for your life!*

Holt's nostrils flared and he fingered the hilt of his sword as he pointed the deadly blade at her face. "You bartered for the lives of those loyal to Wolf, then you went against your own word." So many memories she had of this, her father and mother's chamber, so many happy thoughts, now destroyed. "You tried to kill me, Megan." Clucking his tongue, he shook his head. He was pale, the wound in his side leaking through his tunic, his head bruised, but he was strong enough to frighten her. "I could have forgiven you, except for the fact that you gave your heart to a vile forest creature and then stabbed me, hoping for my death." His eyebrows lifted in accusation. "'Twas a mistake, I'm afraid. There was a time when I wanted you to reign beside me, to be mistress of my manor, to bear my sons. Now, I only want to force you onto the bed and mount you, then let you whore for my soldiers before I cut out your traitorous heart."

Her mouth turned dry with fear, her insides cold as the death that would surely be hers, but she squared her shoulders and glared at him. She'd not die without a fight. As long as she was alive and there was a breath of life in her body, she would fight this heathen murderer.

"Strip," he ordered, but his attention was averted as he heard the rattle of chains, grind of gears, and a thunderous battle cry scream through the window. "Oh, for the love of Christ, what now?"

"Could it be that your men have turned against you?" she taunted, and he whirled on her again.

"Take off your damned clothes, woman!"

She didn't move. Defiantly, she stood.

"Did you not hear me?" His mouth was tight against his teeth, his eyes blazed with fury.

Without a sound, she disobeyed, and a vein in his temple began to throb.

"Foolish woman! You have no power over what I do. You will do as I say or I will call for the boy Robin to be brought here. I could start by cutting off his fingers one by one, or his toes, and you could hear him cry in pain and beg for mercy while he bled on the rushes. Or if that be too unpleasant, you could take off your bloody clothes for me *now!*"

Trapped like a cornered dog, she had no choice but to follow his commands. *Dear God, be with Wolf and the rest of his men. Save them.* Closing her eyes, Megan reached for the ties of her mantle. *Pretend it isn't happening,* she told herself. *'Tis only your body. He will never lay claim to your heart.* She lifted her mantle over her head.

She stopped, and his eyes flashed in the dark room. "Keep going," he said, his voice uneven. Though she didn't want to notice, 'twas impossible not to see the swelling in his breeches as his cock rose in anticipation. Revulsion filled her throat as she untied the ribbons of her tunic and tossed it off. Standing only in her chemise, she shivered.

He motioned with the sword again. "Your underclothes as well, m'lady. Christ, you are beautiful," he said almost in reverent awe as she lowered her chemise and stood proudly before him. Refusing to cover her breasts or the thatch of curls guarding her legs, she waited. "Come forward," he ordered, and 'twas all she could do not to leap at him and try to scratch out his eyes, but 'twould be futile and others would suffer.

Stopping short of him, she didn't move when he set the long blade of his weapon between her breasts. "Now, m'lady," he said, breathing in short, shallow gasps. "Kneel before me as you would your king." When she hesitated, he growled, "I'll bring up the boy," and slowly she fell to her knees. "Unlace my breeches."

Oh, God, no, she silently prayed.

"Do it now, Megan," he said, his voice rough, the pointed end of his tongue rimming his lips, "and do it slowly."

"Sweet Jesus, you cannot ask me to."

"Guard!" he yelled. "Send for the boy—"

"Do not!"

"Then unleash my cock, whore, or see the boy suffer, and if that is not enough to convince you, I'll bring your precious Wolf up here so that he can watch me bed you."

"Nay—"

"And each of my most trusted men will stand in line, waiting and watching for their turn to lay you any way they so wish, and you will service them while the outlaw looks on."

I'll die first, she thought, and decided that she had no choice but to do as she was bid, for though she would go willingly to the gates of hell rather than suffer the humiliation and degradation that Holt conjured, she could not take her child's life. *Be strong, Megan.*

As she reached upward and touched the leather of Holt's breeches, she caught a glimpse of movement from the corner of her eye. She dared not look too closely and pretended interest in the task at hand. Holt closed his eyes and groaned in ecstasy.

The door inched open and Wolf, blood running from a cut in his forehead, rushed into the room. "Run!" he yelled at Megan.

Holt's body jerked. His eyes flew open. Megan ran to the door, and Holt, seeing his enemy's reflection in the blade of his weapon, hoisted his sword high as he swung it round, facing the door. He slashed the air with his weapon, his eyes centered on Wolf. "Die, you bloody bastard!"

"Only if I take you with me!" Wolf said as he swung a bloodied sword at the new baron, twisting from the blows of Holt's weapon. Too late. The sharp blade sliced into Wolf's arm. Blood sprayed the chamber. Megan screamed, and with her horrified eyes trained on the two men reeling, parrying, lunging, and swearing, she stepped away, closer to the fire, searching for something, *anything*, to use as a weapon.

"This is for Mary, the fisherman's daughter!" Wolf cried as he jammed his sword into Holt's thigh. Holt roared in pain, but struck with his sword, slicing through Wolf's tunic.

"Tadd raped her."

"Aye, but you held her down, did you not?"

Oh, God, they were both going to die! She found a stick used to tend the fire and lifted it, only to have the slender wood cleaved by Holt's sword and her feet knocked out from under her. "You, too, will see the end of this earth," he promised her, spinning to meet Wolf's thrust. Desperate and mindless of the fear, Megan held on to the short end of her stick, and on her knees, stretched upward, plunging the cleaved stake into the wound at Holt's side, the wound she'd inflicted earlier. Holt bellowed like a wounded bull.

"Jezebel!" he roared, but fighting the pain, swiped his weapon at Wolf. Swords clanged, bodies fell against her. Megan, struggling to her feet, lost her balance and fell. The room spun, rush lights glittering wildly. Wolf and Holt locked swords as the rush-strewn floor came up to meet her.

"Megan!" Wolf cried.

Her head slammed into the stones and her body crumpled. The room temporarily went black as she felt a sharp, hard pain deep inside, a tearing, but she bit down against the agony and tried to save Wolf.

"Stay back!" Wolf commanded. He swung fiercely, cutting Holt on the ear.

With fire in his eyes, Holt rushed forward.

Wolf grinned with vengeance and held his sword aloft. "Now, you die, bastard!"

Men rushed into the room and Megan thought that they were Holt's men until she recognized the sorcerer, Robin, and Hagan of Erbyn. Her heart soared for an instant.

"'Tis over!" Hagan ordered.

"This is still my castle!" Desperate, Holt grabbed Megan, one arm locked around her waist, the other holding his sword outstretched as he used her naked body as his shield. "Leave me be, or she dies!" he screamed.

She kicked him hard in the shins, her heels screaming with pain, but he didn't let go, and to Megan's horror, Connor stepped into the room, a crossbow in his hands. "Everyone step away!" he ordered in a voice as cold as the depths of a bottomless well.

"Thank the saints!" Holt said, his legs unsteady. He shoved Megan aside and approached his knight. His smile faltered as the flat-eyed man watched him. "It's been days since you took the prisoner and . . ." His gaze wandered to the sorcerer and his words stuck in his throat for a second. "Where have you been, Connor?"

"To hell and back." The soldier's eyes narrowed and he let the bolt of his weapon fly as Wolf reacted, hurling his sword at his enemy, the blade driving deep through the muscles of Holt's chest to pierce his dark heart. The crossbow bolt gored Holt in his gut. "This is for lying to me about Cayley, you pig. I know you intended not to give her to me."

"Bloody God, no!" Holt cried out, falling to his knees as he stared blindly at the man who had defied him, and fell into a useless heap, where he surrendered his last rattling breath.

Megan held a fur coverlet she'd snagged from the bed over her body, but she couldn't move. Determined to stand, she closed her eyes, tried to rise, but was suddenly weak. Deep within she felt a rending, and her head spun. She blinked hard.

"Get that mess out of here," Hagan ordered.

"'Tis over," Wolf said, gathering Megan into his arms. He was warm and strong and . . . another sharp pain gored her. She bit down on her lip and couldn't stop the tears in her eyes, for Wolf was safe, she was alive, and . . . and . . . oh, dear God, no . . . the baby!

Wolf buried his face in the crook of her neck. "Love, oh, sweet, sweet love," he said, blinking against tears as he lifted her into his arms and carried her down the hallway. He kissed her head, her throat, her eyes, but she couldn't move, couldn't speak, because she knew as he laid her on the bed in her chamber that she was losing his baby. Silent agony tore through her, blinding her, extinguishing the light in her soul.

"Megan?" His voice came as if from a distance. "Megan."

"'Tis gone," she said and felt the rush of blood between her legs. "Wolf, please listen . . . the babe . . ." Deep racking sobs rose from her lungs, and then he understood.

"'Tis all right, rest," he said, lying beside her, refusing to let her go. He pulled the blankets over her and held her close, whispering into her hair. Outside, the sounds of battle quieted, but deep in her heart, Megan felt a pain more desperate than ever before. "I will be with you forever," he vowed, but she hadn't the strength to believe him. As she closed her eyes and drifted into sleep, she knew that she'd lost their child, their precious babe, and even Wolf's love couldn't fill that gaping hole in her heart.

The sorcerer came later.

Wolf stood at the window of her chamber, and while Megan lay half in and half out of consciousness, Cadell laid his hands upon her and shook his head. "'Twill be difficult, friend, for the babe's life has barely started and is slipping away."

"I know, I know. Damn it, would you try?" Wolf muttered through a jaw clenched so tight it ached. The wounds he'd sustained while battling Holt were nothing compared to the agony ripping through his soul. 'Twas as if the Devil himself were chasing through his heart, laughing at him, mocking him, for 'twas he who'd brought this pain to his beloved Megan, he who got her with child, he who inadvertently, while slaying Holt, had nearly killed his own unborn babe.

"Leave us," Cadell ordered, and the candles near the

bedside flickered as the great owl who was the sorcerer's companion landed in the window and stared inside.

Reluctantly, Wolf walked through the corridors of Dwyrain, past chambers where the wounded were being tended, through the kitchen, where Cook was attempting to start the morning's meal, and outside to the bailey, where bodies were being hauled through the gates to the graveyard.

"So there ye be, ye black-hearted cur," Odell growled as, bartering with the armorer, he spied Wolf.

"What now, Odell?"

The grizzled outlaw picked his way over the spilled blood to stand below Wolf on the steps. "Ye sent Cormick to his death and nearly took Robin and Jagger as well."

"Aye." Guilt would forever be Wolf's companion. In the distance, the sun was just beginning to rise, sending pale rays through the mist that clung to the cold ground. "'Twas my mistake."

"All for a woman," Odell reminded him, and spat upon the ground.

"For the woman that will be my wife."

"We have rules—"

"Should they not be bent for Megan?" Wolf growled, reaching for the front of his old friend's tunic and clenching the rough fabric in his fingers. "'Tis sorry I am about Cormick. Could I, I would trade places with him, but it cannot be."

Odell's mouth opened and closed and Wolf, realizing that he was close to strangling the man, let him go. "I'm giving up the band," he said as Holt's standard was lowered from the flagpole and the old colors of Dwyrain flew once again, for now Megan was truly mistress of this keep.

"Leave us?" Odell paled. "But—who will lead us?"

A cold smile played upon Wolf's lips as he watched Bjorn order the men about, telling the soldiers what to do with the wounded and commanding the carpenter to tear down the rigging for the gallows. "Bjorn will be your leader," he said, and strode down the steps to meet his friend.

"He's not happy with you. He was almost killed as well," Odell said, rotating his neck like a chicken eyeing a fat bug and rubbing his throat.

"Aye, Odell, I know. You needs not screech at me like a fishwife, now do you?"

Bjorn dusted his hands as the last of the dead were carted from the castle. "Wolf," he said, his eyes showing no trace of emotion. "We needs speak." His gaze moved pointedly to Odell, but the grizzled old outlaw didn't budge.

"I'm not movin', if that's what ye're askin'."

"I'm leaving the band," Wolf announced. "And I want you to be its leader."

Bjorn rubbed his jaw. "'Tis your group of thugs."

"Aye, but they need a new leader."

"Why?"

"'Tis time." Wolf sighed. "What say you?"

A corner of Bjorn's mouth lifted. "I know not if 'tis an honor to be the leader of so foulmouthed and ill-tempered a group."

"Well, I'll be jiggered. If ye won't be the new—"

"I'll do it," Bjorn said.

"'Tis thanks I owe you," Wolf said, glancing to the window of Megan's room, where the owl was perched and blinking against the winter rays of the sun. "You saved my life and that of those in the castle."

Bjorn shook his head. "As ye saved mine years ago."

The two men clasped hands and Odell spat in disgust as the men Wolf had been close to—Heath, Peter, Robin, Jack, and the lot—came to shake his hand, forgiving him for the death of Cormick.

"The lady," Robin asked, his cheeks reddening a bit. "How is she?"

The pain in Wolf's heart was great, but he said, "She'll be fine, Robin lad. She'll be fine."

He only hoped it wasn't a lie.

Hagan's troops left on the third day and Cayley, sitting in for the absent baroness, was in charge. She was young and pretty, but stronger than Wolf had ever thought possible, helping tend to the sick and wounded while dealing with the squabbles of some of the peasants and ensuring that the castle kept running.

The only time Wolf wondered about her strength was

when she said goodbye to his band of thugs, for she appeared to be fighting for self-control, and as Bjorn and his ragged group filed through the gatehouse, she bit her lips and dashed aside tears that had formed in the corners of her eyes.

Elsewise, she was an able and caring leader. She spent hours with Megan, sitting with her, praying for her, and ordering the servants to care for her.

Cadell had done what he could, and Megan, bedridden, was still with child. But the days stretched long and she was tired, her face pale, worry shining in her beautiful ale-colored eyes. Wolf didn't leave her side. While Rue and Cayley tended to her, he'd turn his back and stand at the window, but as she regained her strength, he stayed with her. 'Twas as if he was afraid she might slip away again.

'Twas nearly a week before she seemed alive again. There was color in her cheeks for the first time since the battle, and she smiled at him.

"The baby?" she asked, biting her lip.

"Cadell and Rue did everything they could," he said, frowning, "but you lost a lot of blood."

"Oh," she murmured, the pain in her heart inconsolable.

"But the flow—it stopped on the second day—and if you can keep yourself in bed, there's still hope." But she saw the doubt in his eyes. He was trying to give her hope when there was none. *Oh, sweet, sweet baby,* she silently cried, but pushed the painful thought aside.

"Tell me . . . Holt?"

"Is dead."

That much she vaguely remembered, though the days were lost to her and one was like any other. She knew not how much time had passed, nor did she care. "Many of his men were slain as well, and Cayley has not punished their wives or children, but kept them here."

"Is she a wise ruler?"

"Very." Wolf sat on the corner of her bed and held her hand. "Connor is in prison and Father Timothy is staving off death, though 'tis a miracle."

As he talked, Megan tried to shake off the shroud of guilt that had been her cloak ever since feeling her unborn baby's precious life begin to slip away. She'd dreamed of the child, as she had of Bevan, sweet little Roz, her father and mother.

"Cadell has returned to the forest, though he will visit, and Jovan the apothecary is in the dungeon, for 'twas he who gave Holt the poison that killed your father."

"So much treachery," she said and closed her eyes. Wolf placed his arms around her and held her fast against him.

A week passed before she had the strength to rise and walk on shaky legs to the window. The cold breath of winter touched her face as she looked into the bailey and saw that the hated gallows had been destroyed, the timbers broken apart, to be used for firewood.

Wolf had been dozing in a chair he'd brought in. Though he'd held her often during the day, at night he'd refused to lie in her bed, insisting that she needed her rest and knowing that her body and mind needed time to heal. He roused and smiled as he saw her on her feet.

"The lady arises, eh?" he asked, stretching in the chair.

"Aye."

"And how're you feeling, Mistress of Dwyrain?"

"Better."

His blue eyes gleamed and a shock of black hair fell fetchingly over his forehead. "Well enough for a wedding?"

"A wedding?" she repeated. "But whose—?"

"Our wedding, love," he said, standing and circling her small waist in his arms. "The priest, he swears he's able to perform the ceremony. All we need is a willing bride."

"Father Timothy is still recovering."

"Aye, but Hagan rode to the abbey and located another man—Brother Something-or-Other—to help Timothy. He's ready."

"Are you?" she asked, touching his rough cheek with her fingertips.

His smile was warm, his eyes sincere. "I've been waiting for you all of my life, Megan," he said, his lips brushing lightly over hers.

"But your life as a—"

"What? A criminal? An outlaw?" He let out a soft little chuckle. "'Tis over. Bjorn is the leader now."

"So you're ready to settle down here?"

"At Dwyrain?" He shook his head. "Nay, m'lady, I think we need a new start, and long ago my brother promised me a small portion of land with its own keep. 'Tis time to take him up on his offer. If you'll agree to be my wife."

Her heart was suddenly full and she pressed a soft little kiss to his lips. "How could I deny you?"

"You couldn't." Lifting her off her feet, he carried her to the bed and fell with her on the rumpled coverlets. "'Tis too early yet for me to show you how much I love you, m'lady, but when you are well and truly healed, I will take my time pleasuring you."

"Mayhap I'm healed already," she teased and sighed as his lips found hers.

"When you are, woman, we will have another child," he promised, "and 'twill be the first of many."

"*How* many?" she asked.

He laughed and the sound echoed off the rafters of the chamber. "As many as you want, Megan. As many as you want."

Snuggling close, she wrapped her arms around the rogue who would soon be her husband and whispered into his ear, "I think we've already started."

"What—?"

"I know not, but the bleeding's stopped, and I . . . I feel that the babe is still with me, that somehow Cadell saved that small soul."

"Megan," he said, shaking his head. "'Tis too much to believe."

"Trust me," she said and placed a kiss at his temple. "Do you not know that I love you, Wolf?"

"Forever?"

"At least," she said with a giggle.

"And I love you, woman," he vowed. His lips found hers in a kiss that touched her soul and promised a lifetime of happiness for the lady and her outlaw.

❋ *Epilogue* ❋

Father Timothy sprinkled holy water on the infant's forehead and said a soft prayer over the rising wail of the tiny babe. When the prayer was finished, Wolf accepted the small bundle from the priest's trembling hands, and to his wife's surprise, planted a kiss on the shock of fine red hair. "You be a loud one, son," he said before handing the baby back to Megan.

"And strong," she said as she greeted their guests, those who had attended little Cormick's christening, for the child had indeed survived, despite the deep rending she'd felt in her womb and the fear that she'd lost him.

Throughout the chapel were the people she'd grown to love and trust: Robin, now much taller; Odell; one-eyed Peter; Cayley; Bjorn; and Cadell, the sorcerer. Even Lord Hagan, Lady Sorcha, and Bryanna joined them, as did Morgana and Garrick of Abergwynn. Morgana, tears in her eyes, stood with Cadell, her brother, and would not let go of his sleeve, as if she expected him to disappear from her again.

While little Cormick squealed unhappily, the guests filed out of the chapel at Dwyrain, where she and Wolf had made their home during most of the past year while waiting for the birth of their child. Cayley was ruler of the castle, and between her and Hagan of Erbyn, all Wolf's sins had been forgiven. Now, 'twas time to return to Abergwynn and to a small keep not far from the castle.

Wolf wrapped an arm around her middle, and urged her toward the steps of the great hall.

"I'll be there in a minute," she said, and while he led their guests into the keep for a feast, Megan hurried through the gates of the castle and up a small hill to the cemetery. As the October breeze swirled her skirts, she laid a small bouquet of flowers from the christening on her father's grave. Finally, Ewan was at peace with his beloved Violet. Bevan's grave and a small one for Roz were nearby. "I miss you," she said, "I miss you all, but Father, finally, at last, I'm married. As you wanted."

"And happy?" a voice boomed behind her. Turning, she spied Wolf, his hair catching in the wind, his face as rugged as the great hills of Wales.

"Where's Cormick?"

"His aunt Cayley was cooing to him when I left."

"She needs a babe of her own."

"First a husband."

"Who would marry her?"

"A man more stubborn than she."

"Is there such a bullheaded man in all of Wales?" she asked, laughing, and the merry sound carried on the wind.

"Now, wife, you didn't answer my question," he said, advancing upon her. "Are you happy?"

"Oh, nay, Wolf, can you not see I'm miserable?" Again, she laughed.

"As miserable as I am."

He circled her waist with one arm and tilted her face up with his free hand. Cool lips brushed over hers.

She eyed him in the afternoon sunlight. "You're not an outlaw any longer. All charges against you were forgiven."

"A pity," he said with a cynical grin.

"So now you're an honorable man."

"Is that what you believe?" He kissed her again as a great owl flew above them and disappeared into the forest. His smile was wicked and a glimmer of seduction appeared in his eyes.

"I believe a part of you will always be a thief and rogue."

"'Tis true," he agreed, and her heart raced a little as he kissed her lips again. "But only for you, m'lady, for I plan to steal your heart over and over again."

CHAMBER MUSIC

MUSIC

A Novel By

Doris Grumbach

FAWCETT CREST • NEW YORK

CHAMBER MUSIC

THIS BOOK CONTAINS THE COMPLETE TEXT OF THE
ORIGINAL HARDCOVER EDTION.

Published by Fawcett Crest Books, a unit of CBS Publications, the
Consumer Publishing Division of CBS Inc., by arrangement with
E.P. Dutton, a division of Elsevier-Dutton Publishing Company,
Inc.

ISBN: 0-449-24271-4

Printed in the United States of America

First Fawcett Crest Printing: March 1980

10 9 8 7 6 5 4 3 2 1

For SHP

—*sine qua non*

ACKNOWLEDGMENTS

Chamber Music is fiction, not biography. Its three major characters are based, vaguely, upon persons who once were alive, but most of the details of their lives are conjecture and invention.

Some real persons, musicians, teachers, and actresses of the early twentieth century, appear in these pages in somewhat changed chronology. The Maclaren Community is imaginary and bears no relation to places it may resemble.

Two such real places, Yaddo and The MacDowell Colony, gave me working time and space for this book. I thank them both.

> ... Who may this singer be
> Whose song about my heart is falling?
> Know you by this, the lover's chant,
> 'Tis I that am your visitant.

JAMES JOYCE, *Chamber Music*

CHAMBER
MUSIC

Part One

BEGINNINGS

I have decided to write this account because, long as my life has been, it has given me no opportunity before this to say what I wish to put down here. Perhaps the time was not right to do it before.

When I was young, and even into my middle years, a scrim of silence surrounded what really happened in our lives. If there was talk, it was quiet conjecture about the little discreet adulteries, the attic madness, and the pantry drinking of our friends and neighbors. Rumor and gossip were conveyed in whispers. Secrets were surely no better kept than they are now, but they lived quietly, under the breath. They never appeared in public print or were reported by professional gossips on the air waves. They were confined to the inner coils of the private ear, a foot away, perhaps, no farther. We closeted our secrets, or forgot them. This we called decorum, and we lived securely under its warm protection.

But now the Maclaren Foundation, which I headed for so many years, almost fifty by now, wishes to have a permanent record of Robert's life, and mine. Ours together, to put it more exactly, and mine alone with the Community, after his death. The government has become interested, they tell me, in "the arts." There is a chance that, with its financial help, in some place, the Community will be restored to life.

My initial reluctance to accede to their request is a matter of personal habit, I suppose. I am an old woman born in the last quarter of the nineteenth century, with all that decent age's love of a calm surface to our society. It was then the custom to have a regular, uniform pattern to our lives, to present the historian with only those facts which would contribute to an orderly picture.

So I am not equipped to write a confession in the modern sense. Whether what I remember here will be useful as a record to the new Foundation I cannot say. I am of an age not to care, almost ninety. My hearing is defective, my bones seem to lie upon each other like dry kindling, my skin falls away in slack little pinches of flesh. I am dry and brittle,

I strain and break easily. Rarely any more do I insert my two rows of teeth; few persons bother to visit.

I write this description of myself not because I want pity—who pities the very old?—but to explain my unaccustomed openness in this account. I have nothing to lose that extreme old age has not already taken from me, and no time to gain. The way the world thinks of me may well change, but even that, if it happens, I will not survive. The Foundation promises me that it will be some time before the history of the founding of the Community can be completely collated and that it has no plans to publish it. I will not be here to witness the astonishment of the reader. I am comforted by the realization that there is no one I know alive to be surprised at me.

For the representation of truth, old age is a freeing agent. No one should write of her life until all the witnesses and acquaintances, family and lovers, are dead. In addition, it helps to outlive the mode of one's time until it has changed beyond recognition. Then one is left alone with what was. The wrinkled, spotted hand writes of a time out of the memory of everyone alive but itself. So what one tells is unavailable to verification or correction.

I write this, then, because I am freed by my survival into extreme old age, and because I write in the air of freer times. Whether this air is entirely salutary, whether

the old must of chests, of closets, bell jars,
and horsehair sofas is not a better climate for
the storage of the private life, I do not know.
But I tire very quickly these days and must
speak openly, for once. I am now free. Extraordinary for me, and for one of my time,
I intend to put down extraordinary truths.

My birth coincided with the year of the Centennial Exposition in Philadelphia. In May
my parents traveled for two days down from
Boston to be present at the great crush when
the Brazilian emperor Dom Pedro and General Grant opened the fair. Later in the week
my father pushed my mother, who was seven
months pregnant, in a wicker chair to see the
Corliss engine, a gigantic 1,500-horsepower
structure that seemed to him to represent the
promise of the future. He took her past the
English paintings and the Italian sculpture
in the huge Agricultural Hall, remarking on
what a strange name it was for a place housing such cultural treasures.

My mother remembered it all. Over and
over she told me of the wonders she had seen.
Later, in New York, she purchased a number
of pieces of furniture made in the manner she
had seen at the fair. They were of bent wood,
rockers and a sofa of profoundly uncomfortable contours, as I remember. She told me
about a gigantic grapevine, twelve thousand
feet in all, which had been brought from

southern California and replanted outside the Horticultural Hall. She and my father sat under one of the great arms of the vine, resting from the effort of traversing the long narrow halls of the art exhibit. They drank cold water from the Temperance Fountain and ate soda crackers given out at the Adam Exton of Trenton, New Jersey, exhibit. As a child, in bed at night, I heard so often about the two white whales that P.T. Barnum had placed in a tank forty feet high and wide and brought on a special train to the Exposition.

My childhood was composed of these stories of oversized glories. I believe that summer was the zenith of my mother's life, alone with my father, before I was born, in the presence of great marvels. My father at that time was full of plans for their future and mine. He thought it might be possible to apply the principle of the Corliss steam engine he had seen in Philadelphia to the automatic operation of knitting machines, which at present were worked by hand and by foot pedal in his small mill. But he died suddenly when I was nine without accomplishing that difficult reduction.

My mother was bereft. She sank down into a grief I have never since seen take such complete possession of anyone, the absolute despair of a mourner for a beloved husband. The Centennial became united in her mind with early love, her memory coalesced the Corliss engine with her proud, handsome, inventive husband. She paired my birth, I think, with the great umbrella of the Santa Barbara grapevine. Perhaps I, too, have symbolized that time, for the bentwood sofa is still downstairs in the music room, or at least it was the last time I was able to go there.

I grew up always living alone with my mother, regretting in a mild way the loss of my father but not mourning his absence as she did for the rest of her life. I remember his smells, of mustache wax, of the leather of his gloves and hatband. I can still smell his hands as he held me, the odor of acrid coke, the material with which he tried to power his experimental engine. He carried a cane topped with a silver knob. At my level, close to that knob, I could smell his hands and the oiled wood and the polished silver of the cane. He remains in me through the solid scents of his manhood. I cannot recall his voice. His face must have been too high and too often turned toward my mother and away from me for me to remember his eyes or the shape of his nose. His pictures show his mustache curling in a small thick arc around his upper lip, a waxed brush whose smell has followed me for eighty years: that, the bentwood sofa, and the memory of my mother's mortal loss of love.

After his death my mother's only interest was in my future. Left with a little money invested, through the advice of her brother,

who was a clerk with J.P. Morgan in New
York, in railroad stocks, she still dressed me
well. She had educated herself in the fiction
of romantic novelists and learned from them
that a presentable-looking daughter was
usually marriageable. I read her little collection of ladies' novels when I was fourteen,
recognizing that the fanciful inventions about
life they embodied were only wishful. All the
same, I entered into them all. I cared very
little about taffeta skirts and full-bodiced,
lace-edged shirtwaists, soft, high-buttoned
kid shoes with small, high heels and felt at
the tips, elaborate coiffures that required an
hour's construction each morning and another hour of reconstruction in the evening.
But I submitted to them all because my
mother's interest and future were involved,
as well as my own. I was her investment, the
promise of her old age, and had I rebelled it
would have meant the end to her hopes for
our security.

My only rebellion was music. I had often
watched and listened while a school friend
practiced the piano. I pleaded with my mother
for the use of a little of the money she had
put aside each year for habiliments. I wanted
to learn to play the piano, that noble, for-
midable instrument, to stroke those soft ivory
strips, each with its slight lip, and the
rounded edges of the black keys. The beauty
of the piano bench which opened upon paper
music collections, the fine, deep string-and-

felt odor that came from the piano's interior
as the harp-shaped cover was raised, the ease
with which the stick fitted into its hold, the
lovely, easy machinery of it: I loved it all.

Mother, who was tone-deaf and oblivious
to every sensation but her grief, finally
agreed. The lessons began in a tiny studio on
Dartmouth Street, not far from Commonwealth Avenue where we had our rooms. I
had no piano on which to practice, my mother
being of the conviction that we had very little
room in which to put one, "very little" being
for her a relative term. She remembered
clearly the wonderful Steinway pianos she
had seen at the Centennial, where William
Steinway had filled his exhibit with inlaid
instruments, a piano decorated to represent
the Parthenon, a delicate grand piano mir-
rored to look like the furniture at Versailles.
She could not conceive of a piano that was
small and upright and still able to perform
properly. The large open spaces in the sitting
room, almost devoid of furniture, for we
owned very little, had to kept free for breathing, she said. She believed that the fresh air
in most rooms was consumed by the plush of
sofas, the linen covers of chairs, the mahogany of side tables, and the porous, colored-
glass panels of lamps.

I was delighted to go to my lessons, and to
walk the long blocks every other day to practice there. I started when I was eleven and
continued, almost without interruption, until

I was seventeen. Mrs. Seton, my teacher, had been a Peabody, it was said by my mother to her acquaintances, as if to excuse by lineage her adult indulgence in harmony and composition. A *Peabody*. I never understood what that emphatic, raised-tone designation, which always followed Mrs. Seton's married title, always after a pause, implied. Was it a connection to the Salem family, or was there a connection to the Philadelphia musical persons? I never knew, or even heard from her, if that *was* her maiden name, for she was a woman given to gestures, not speech.

I remember that my lesson was at three on Friday afternoon. Mrs. Seton would open the door for me, bowing her head and smiling her slow and then quickly obliterated smile, wearing her hat. I don't remember ever seeing her bareheaded.

After she had smiled her greeting, she would lock the door behind me. I would start up her narrow brown varnished stairs, hearing as I went the sounds of the other two locks being turned. The last, a rolling bolt, took much doing and I was usually in the music room before she managed it. Her floors always seemed freshly varnished and the leather of my soles stuck a bit to them, making a sucking sound. The room was small, windowless, and dusty—every beam and cornice of that room comes back to me even now—just large enough for her upright piano, her wicker chair placed to the left of the piano seat, and a lamp, its squat gold base nudging the metronome that peered down at me like a tirelessly blinking eye.

At lessons she always sat, her face shaded by a large, broad-brimmed hat. The hat perched on her head evenly, as though she were balancing it, while she played passages in the pieces she was teaching me. She apparently never felt the desire to explain. Her method was to illustrate how notes should sound, her long, delicate fingers hardly lifting from the keys. Accompanied by the undeniable force of the square-set hat, her playing took on a didactic power that I could not withstand.

Mrs. Seton would gesture to me to be seated. When I was settled, a ceremony which, in the first years, involved arranging a stack of *Century* magazines under me to raise me to the proper height, she would point to the piece of music I was to begin playing. I was expected to extract it from the pile, open it, smooth it carefully, and wait. Using an ivory corset stay, Mrs. Seton would then point to the place where she wished me to begin. I would play. Her disapproval (very often it was disapproval that followed my efforts) would be indicated by a light tap on the back of my right hand (or the left: whichever was the greater offender) with the long, supple stay, not to hurt but to arrest. My hand would freeze—and lift. Hardly pausing, Mrs. Seton would then raise the stay to the music, point-

ing with the sharp tip to the mistaken staff.
Wrong: one tap at the place, begin here,
again. Two taps were hard to bear. They sig-
nified despair at my repeated stupidity and
begged for my close attention the next time
I attempted the passage.

I was puzzled by her unbroken silence. Did
it suggest a distrust of the spoken word, a
faith in gesture and facial expression as more
direct, less open to ambiguity than speech?
As I think back, I assure myself that she must
have spoken at times, perhaps to greet me
when she let me in for my practice hours.
Surely she had addressed my mother, but
never that I can remember did she say a word
to me during a lesson, or to fellow pupils
whom I whispered to in a corner of the room
at her teas. To each of us she gave thirty-five
minutes of her expressive pantomime. We
learned to play Schubert and Schumann correctly, or at least as well as her indicative
fingers holding the stay, the dismayed bend
of her head backward, could suggest to us.
We heard no words of praise. She would nod
yes two or three times, emphatically. For me
that was almost enough.

I put all this down about Mrs. Seton of
Dartmouth Street, her unbroken silence,
her triple-bolted door, because it was in her
sitting room that I first encountered Robert
Glencoe Maclaren, to whose life I was for so
long to join my own. I remember the occasion,
perhaps because all of Mrs. Seton's gather-

ings were occasions. Twice a year she invited her pupils to visit her, to meet each other and a few of her musical friends. We came in response to tissue-thin, pink-paper invitations sent to us through the mail. Somewhere downstairs, I think, I still have one of them I saved. It measures about six inches square and is folded in half over her minuscule spidery writing. It reads:

Come at four. Tea. Biscuits. Friends.
Amelia Seton

There was no provision for refusal. The delicate invitation had the weight and strength of a command. No address was included, on the theory, I'm sure, that only those who knew the way were invited, and the exact day seemed somehow to have been known to us.

Some years later, Robert, who was one of the "friends" she proposed to serve with tea and biscuits, told me that Mrs. Seton had never changed her dwelling. Her elderly parents had brought her as a young child with her upright piano to those rooms. Mr. Seton, of whom I knew nothing, had come to live there upon their marriage, I later learned, and had died soon after. Just before the Great War, my friend Elizabeth Pettigrew told me, Mrs. Seton died in her sitting room. She suffered a stroke when she was alone and lay there, it was conjectured, for three nights and three days unable to rise from the figured rug. Had she *then* used her voice? I wondered. Pupils who came to her door found it locked (three times?), there was no answer to their knocks, and so they went away. She was found by a neighbor who had grown curious about the continued darkness in the upstairs music room and broke a window to find her. Her body lay straightened like the stone effigies on tombs in Westminster Abbey, her eyes opened upon a final silence. Only her hat was misplaced. It lay some distance from her head, having been knocked away by her fall, I believe.

On that earlier afternoon of which I write, I arrived at Mrs. Seton's door at precisely five minutes before four, knowing well that she could indicate her displeasure at late arrival by keeping her heavy, red lids down over her eyes long after it would be expected she would raise them to look at you. I feared that canopied look and rarely came late. She herself opened the door for each guest. On feast days like this she wore her broad straw hat with a velvet band encircling the brim and ending in streamers down her back. She followed me up the stairs into the sitting room, her light step making me feel in contrast, oafish and leaden.

Mrs. Seton disappeared into another room, presumably to get tea and biscuits for me. There were of course no introductions to the other persons already standing about. The

young man standing next to me holding his
cup carefully said, "You must be Caroline
Newby."

"Yes."

"I'm glad to meet you at last. Mrs. Seton
speaks often of you. My name is Maclaren.
Robert Maclaren." He laughed a little. "Robert Glencoe Maclaren. My mother calls me
Rob."

"Yes. How do you do?"

That is all I can remember we said to each
other that day. I remember thinking: He
must be very polite, or perhaps prevaricating.
Surely Mrs. Seton had never *spoken* of me to
him or to anyone. I watched him as he moved
around the room, admiring his fine head, his
russet hair, his thick brush of a mustache
that sat upon his lip like—like my father's,
I thought. Yes, he looked very much as I remember my father looked, even to his ears,
which seemed to pinch his head tight, his
thin, almost arrogant nose ending so abruptly that it displayed the black dashes of
his nostrils. He seemed foreign, somehow,
perhaps because of the soft, low collar of his
shirt. In those days men in Boston wore tall,
stiff collars whose corners turned out neatly
over their cravats. Perhaps it was the European look of his suit, which was made of a
very heavy cloth.

I watched him put his cup down on the top
of Mrs. Seton's glass-doored bookcase in which
she kept small busts of Mozart and Meyer-

beer. He opened his jacket and then unbuttoned his vest. I remember these actions so well because, watching him, I decided he must be a musician or perhaps an artist: his discomfort in his suit of clothes, his restlessness as he moved around from one side of the room to the other. Finally he sat down on the green settee and talked quietly to the man already comfortably settled there, to whom I was never introduced, only to rise again to greet a pupil standing awkwardly at the side of the piano. I recognized the pupil, a gangly, pimpled boy impelled, I decided, by his ambitious mother to wear the uniform of the prodigy: black silk tie, bowed extravagantly at the base of his collar, and velvet knickers. We had passed each other once or twice at the end of my lesson and the start of his, but we never spoke, Mrs. Seton's reluctance to express the simplest greeting having been communicated to her pupils. I remember comparing the pupil's awkwardness to Robert's grace, to the ease of his laugh, the tone of his low voice: their *suitability* to the room, to the occasion, rising over the unappetizing dry soda biscuits and the blushing boy juggling his tea and his velvet tam.

I was seventeen that year. It must have been 1893, if indeed I am right in thinking I was seventeen. In the late summer Robert and I met again, walking in the Common. He tipped his hat to me and smiled. I felt an unaccustomed rush of pleasure in my face, in my breast. He said he enjoyed our meeting at Mrs. Seton's tea and then he laughed. At the memory of the tea? I wondered, flooded by the charm of his shy smile, as the leash on which he held his huge collie circled my long skirt, pulling it tight to my legs.

"What is his name?" I asked, unable to think of anything more intelligent to say, and untangling myself from the leash.

"Paderewski, I call him. After the pianist I very much admire."

"Have you been at his performances?"

"Once. In Stuttgart, when I was studying there."

"Piano?"

"Yes, and composition. I'm returning to Europe in a month or so, this time to Frankfurt, to continue my studies with Carl Heymann and Joachim Raff."

He smiled a beguiling, gentle, self-deprecating smile as though to indicate the vast gulf between him and the great teachers at the Hoch Conservatory. I could say nothing to this impressive itinerary, I whose musical horizons were limited to the windowless room on Dartmouth Street, to the hatted Mrs. Seton's mimic instruction. I remember staring at him: he seemed a paragon, almost supernatural, a man of the world with talent, free to travel, to study, to leave the little parks and tightly housed streets of Boston for the wide, ancient avenues and noble panoramas of Germany. I yearned for this conversation, full of revelations, to go on.

He took my arm. "May I walk along with you?" he asked, already in step with me, the collie marching slowly ahead of us both, at the end of his taut leash.

"Mr. Maclaren, do you ever think of conducting?"

"I would be pleased if you would call me Robert, or better, Rob."

"Thank you. I'll call you Robert."

"Thank you. I'd like to conduct, of course. I'd like to conduct my own work best of all."

"That seems to me the best one could hope to do, to compose music, and then to direct its performance."

"To me as well. Control, that is what one would achieve."

Our conversation on that occasion, as I recall, was formal and exploratory. He asked about my music and I told him, worrying as I did about the disparity between my small pianistic trials and errors and his great plans, that I hoped someday to accompany a singer, or perhaps to play duets, purely for my own enjoyment.

"Of course. Does your family support your ambitions?"

I told him about my dead father, and my mother whose life had closed too early, perhaps even as she sat, pregnant, enfolded in my father's love, at the foot of the great vine at the Centennial Exposition, my mother whose time was now lived in the twilight of that year, a light diminished with each disappointed day. "I'm afraid I am her only interest," I said. He smiled a concerned smile and shook his head. He said, "I recognize that condition. My own mother must resemble yours. She took me to Paris to study when I was fifteen, leaving my father and brothers behind in Boston. She told Professor Marmontel, when she had me play for him the first time, that she had recognized what she called my genius when I began to have lessons at eight. And so she has, you might say, invested herself in me ever since."

"Is she still in Europe? Waiting for you?"

"Yes," he said, "in Frankfurt."

We walked and talked together for more than an hour. It began to turn to dusk. I reminded him of my waiting mother, he said he would walk my way, we laughed together at Mrs. Seton's idiosyncrasies, he told me she had worn a hat during *his* few early lessons with her. By the time we arrived at my house I thought I knew a great deal about him. I felt he liked me, and I knew, without a single doubt or hesitation, that I loved him.

Three months later we sailed for Germany, leaving Paderewski with friends of Robert's, for the time being. Our engagement had been brief and somewhat perfunctory, only long enough to calm my mother's fears that I was rushing precipitously into the unknown, as she put it, when Robert asked her for permission to marry me before he returned to Germany.

"I will take good care of her," he said. "Some day I will have more money than I have now, I feel certain, and then Caroline will want for . . . very little." I think he started to say "nothing" but corrected himself, feeling no doubt that it was presumptuous to prophesy too much for his talent.

My mother agreed. She was willing to offer her aloneness to my success in marrying this charming and promising musician with an aura of foreign places clinging to his haircut and his unusual suit. She made no demands on us for the customary wedding. Indeed, she seemed too distracted and weary to plan and execute such an event. We were married before a city magistrate who was a friend of Robert's father. His brothers, Logan and Burns, were his best men, Elizabeth Pettigrew accompanied me, and Robert's father was a witness. But the titles were honorary, for the legal ceremony was very short. We took our guests to the Carlton for a late breakfast.

It was curious: my mother did not attend. It seemed to me she did not wish to leave, even for an hour, her abiding conviction that her life was at an end, especially for the predictable optimism of a wedding ceremony, especially for mine. So I took on a new person, and a new name, out of her presence. Not having witnessed the event, she appeared not to believe, or not to wish to believe, in the fact. Her letters to me in Frankfurt were always addressed: "Miss Caroline Newby." She spoke in her letters as though I were bearing the strangeness of a foreign country alone, warning me of the dangers in the streets at night for an unaccompanied young girl. She sent abroad small packages of Boston tea, and English biscuits in tins, even long leather gloves with buttons at the wrists against what she imagined to be the bitter cold of Germany's black forests.

My letters to her that year, I am sure, spoke of Robert, his hard work and long absences from home while he studied and practiced at the conservatory. I wrote to her about his great delight when he played his first concerto for William Mason, a favorite pupil of the great Franz Liszt, who praised him warmly and predicted a great success for him in the future.

My mother's replies to me, which came ever more infrequently in the first year abroad, gave no sign that she had received my news. She wrote of the terrible dampness of Boston that had begun to invade her bedroom. She was certain she detected mold in her shoes. If it grew there so easily it must certainly have fastened itself upon the lining of her lungs, which ached with every breath she took. She described the constant ringing in her left ear, which she believed had begun when a doctor had removed the wax from it and inserted in its place a tiny bell that rang whenever she moved her head.

Robert was amused by the fancies in her letters. "Poor woman," he said. "It comes of having too little to do in her life. Strange ideas take hold and grow in such emptiness."

I laughed with him, wishing at the same time that I had been able to fill her life more amply. Sixteen months after we sailed from the United States her letters ceased. I must confess I stopped writing to her. I felt no concern, thinking her silence was a pique, or another aberration, like the mold, like the bell in her ear.

But it was not so. She had succumbed completely to her imaginings. A wire arrived from the Massachusetts General Hospital addressed to "Miss Caroline Newby care of Robt. Maclaren," informing me that my mother had died two weeks before, in hospital, of pneumonia. The details came later from Elizabeth: my mother had pulled her bed as far as it was possible to do into the closet, and gone to sleep with her head in what she hoped (I believe) would be a culture of mold. True or not, water had filled her lungs and killed her.

The city authorities wrote to tell me she had been buried, decently, they said, in a public field in Belmont. Robert was appalled and

wanted to send money to have her moved to
his family's plot. But somehow we never did
it. There was not enough money at the time,
and after a while it began to seem natural
that she should rest, finally, as she had lived,
among the anonymous of the city.

Elizabeth wrote to assure me that she had
rescued some of my mother's furniture from
the public sale. She had put it in the attic of
her family's house. I was grateful that the
bentwood sofa, particularly, had not gone to
strangers.

It was accepted as reasonable that Virginia
Maclaren, Robert's mother, would not be
present at the wedding. After all, she was
abroad, the trip back would have been, to the
Scots mind of her family, a needless expense,
even a foolish one for so short a ceremony, so
meager a celebration.

We met for the first time in Frankfurt in
the rooms Robert and his mother had occupied in the Praunheimer Strasse before our
marriage. Robert had wired her that he was
bringing a wife. As we leaned against the
ship's rail, or walked the deck of the *City of
Paris* in the morning sun, he told me a little
of her life dedicated so entirely to his welfare,
of her constant worries for his health, her
concern that he keep his feet dry and his
hands soft.

I listened, watching the sea for whales or any sign of life in what seemed to me, at almost eighteen, a vast, anonymous, and ancient burial ground for armadas of ships. I had never crossed an ocean before. I had known of the Atlantic only from the Boston wharves where its grandeur was reduced to a series of brackish inways between piers, swirls of shallow water, full of the spill of ships.

I was frightened by the hugeness we were traveling over and, when it stormed, *into*, so frightened and sick that I was excessive in my relief and joy at landing and finally reaching Frankfurt alive. I remember, and still burn with shame when I do, that I threw myself into Virginia Maclaren's arms when we met, without waiting for evidence from her that she wished to engage in so intimate and enthusiastic a greeting. We parted almost at once: I felt a gentle but insistent pressure on my shoulder and withdrew my impulsive self from her arms. "What a surprise, Rob," she said.

"Why, Mama?" He accented the last syllable of that word in a way I had never heard in America. "I cabled. You knew I had married Caroline. The twelfth of November it was. You never answered the cable."

"Yes. I had the cable. *That* was the surprise, Rob. How long have you known ...Caroline?"

"A few months. What difference does that make?"

While they talked, through, around, and over me, I stood between them and looked at my mother-in-law. She was a small, very tight woman with a solid, bosomless body, like a cork. Her bodice and skirt seemed pasted to her tubular trunk; her dress was wrinkle-free and taut. At the very tcp of her head her red-brown hair, the color of Robert's, was coiled like a spring, making her seem a little taller than she was. Still she did not come to Robert's chin. She had a way of directing her words into the far corner of a room, never looking at those to whom she spoke, not even her beloved son. This curious distance gave her statements, as well as her questions, the force of edicts. It did not matter that she spoke in English to German shopkeepers (she felt it unpatriotic, she once said, to learn a foreign language); they responded with alacrity to what they took to be her commands.

From that first day I knew that she considered Robert guilty of desertion in marrying me. She had left her home, her children, her husband, her beloved Boston, afternoon teas, evening socials and concerts, to live in a barbarous country for the sake of his genius. Now, in his twenty-second year, a fully trained and maturing musician, he had deserted her. Her bitterness burned in the deep

creases that crossed her forehead, kept perpetually red the lobes of her ears and the
triangular tip of her small, furious nose. Only
her eyes, which never lighted on any object,
were gray and calm, like the horizon that
they perpetually sought out, the color of haze
or fog.

Robert did not seem to be disturbed by his
mother's anger. "For a while, at least, until
I can earn some money, Mama, we should
like to stay with you."

His mother looked as if she had been asked
to give lodging to the wife of Tom Thumb
whom Barnum was at that time exhibiting
in the capital cities of western Europe. "That
is of course possible, if you wish, Rob," she
said, looking into the distance. Robert went
to bring in our cases and the trunk. She ush-
ered me into a small hallway.

There is no other way to write of this. I
must put it down directly. My mother-in-law
pointed toward a huge room, almost the size
of a Boston ballroom. Its ceiling was very
high and beamed with what seemed to be half
oak trees. At one end, mounted on a platform
up three wide wooden steps, was a mammoth
bed, as broad as four ordinary beds and covered with a yellowing lace spread. The canopy
was of the same lace and draped down over
the four posts, each one as thick and tall as
a tree. I had never seen a bed of such pro-
portions. It might have been a ship from a

fairytale book—perhaps Timlin's *The Ship That Sailed to Mars*. It was the size of my entire bedroom in Boston.

I stared at it. "If you are staying here, this will be your room," she said. "Your bed."

Stupidly awed, I said, "But this must be your room. I wouldn't want to..."

"It was," she said, "mine and Robert's. Now it will be yours."

That night, huddled in a corner of the cold field of coverlets and comforters, I erred again. Young and badly frightened, I needed refutation of the strange vista of their lives that his mother had opened to me. "Did you share this...room with your mother before I came?" I asked him. I was afraid to say "bed."

At first he did not answer. His silence told me I had made a mistake to question him. He moved farther away from me and lay still, his arms folded under his head, his russet eyes taking light from the dying fire at the other end of the room. He stared at the canopy.

"Yes." Then he closed his eyes and slept or seemed to sleep. I lay awake, filled with fear of the great expanse of blackness outside the four posts, and inexplicable terror for the future.

So we three lived together. Mrs. Maclaren

made the sewing room into a small bedroom. Robert left very early each morning for the conservatory and returned after seven in the evening for his supper. I spent my mornings trying to practice on the grand piano in the drawing room, feeling Virginia's resentment across the distance from the sewing room where she preferred to sit in the morning, staring at the barren tree outside her window, sometimes sewing or doing her needlepoint.

Often, in my cold misery (Germany in the winter is cold and dark and without hospitality even toward its native inhabitants, it seemed to me), I took walks along the formal, square blocks of the city, so different from the unpredictable curves of Boston. One could not get lost in Frankfurt. Its rectangles were too regular. After I had walked around one and come back to my starting point, I would have a hot chocolate and pastry in the Hotel du Nord, I think it was, and then walk around the rectangle in the other direction.

In those two years my days were filled with music and silences, transplanted, I would often think, from Mrs. Seton and her music room. I stayed away from our flat as much as possible, walking the streets of the city, visiting its museums, going to afternoon concerts. I made no friends and missed Elizabeth and the few I had in Boston. In those years— I don't know how it is now—Frankfurt had beautiful parks and I would walk there on pleasant days, wishing we had brought Paderewski with us to accompany me.

Only once do I remember Robert walking with me. He was very quiet, his head bent slightly to one side as though he were listening to sounds pitched so that only he could catch them. He seemed happy, he seemed to be enjoying the absolute peace of those woods. Later in that year he wrote a pianoforte piece called *From a German Forest*. Then I knew something of what it was he had heard in the silence of the woods that day: the grave low sounds of the wind as it stirs leaves and twigs, moving around amid the Indian pipes and mosses at the foot of great trees, and its high, rhythmic whirrings in the top branches, interrupted at irregular intervals by the cries and pipings of birds.

We were short of money, but I wanted very much to find rooms of our own. So Robert acquired two pupils, whom he preferred to instruct in the practice rooms of the conservatory. One wet afternoon (did it rain every afternoon in Germany or do I only remember it so?) I took the long walk to the school, thinking Robert and I might walk home together, at seven, his usual hour. The matron in a front room somewhat reluctantly directed me to the practice room on the second floor where he was giving a lesson. I went up. The door of the room I had been sent to was ajar, and I looked in. I saw Robert bent earnestly over a young woman seated at the piano, one of his hands lightly on her shoulder, the other poking at a place in the music before them both. She nodded and began to play. He stepped back, bending his head in his customary way, to listen.

Then I saw, standing in the shadow in a corner of the room, a slight young man whose extraordinarily white face was luminous in the dark space. He seemed to be listening intently, but his eyes were on Robert, not on the young lady who was playing. He watched Robert so closely that his whole body seemed pointed toward him.

I don't remember why it so disturbed me to see Robert doing what he said he had to do so that we might be able to afford separate quarters, and the young man (another pupil?) watching him from the shadows. There was surely nothing improper in what I saw. But my discomfort kept me from staying there to wait for him that evening or from inquiring about the young man in the corner. Never again did I return to the conservatory except for the night of the farewell party for Robert. Now I took walks in other directions, resting on the aged wood benches in the parks, on the stone slabs in the art galleries. I learned a little café German so I could speak, hesitantly, to waiters and to the amiable guards in the rooms of the museums. I can hardly remember the pictures I studied day after day, but I remember well my loneliness, my

sense of being held in the solitary confinement of stone buildings, surrounded by un-
peopled forests and empty oceans, always,
everywhere, alone.

Robert would take his mother and me out
to dine on Saturday evenings, every Saturday
evening. I remember the heavy dinners in the
restaurant we frequented in the Jahnstrasse,
the blood-thick brown gravies over slabs of
brown meat, the heavy, dark beer, the
weightlessness of the fine strudel held onto
the plate by full-bodied apples. I would leave
the restaurant almost anchored to the sidewalk by the food. Robert would suggest we
"walk it off," and we would: he two or three
steps ahead, walking lightly and fast, my
mother-in-law and I following a little behind,
all three of us silent and shielded from each
other by our resentments and the leaden sed-
iment of the long dinner.

Sometimes now, in wakeful moments in
the long nights of my ninetieth year, I go
back to read in a small black leather notebook
I kept during our time in Frankfurt. There
was no one for me to converse with so I occupied myself with putting down my thoughts,
what I heard talked about, what I noticed:

October 18

Yesterday the rain slanted so oddly that, as

*it entered the gutters, it made no splash,
merely met and joined the waters already
there—is this called confluence?—as though
flowing downward from another, higher
stream.*

November 2

*Robert says that the piano's wondrous lim-
itations ought to impel the composer to write
for full orchestra. In those effects, the strings
of the piano have been plucked out and
mounted on panels to be bowed. The hammers
have been amplified into percussion. Only the
winds are not derived from the eviscerated
innards of the pianoforte.*

November 9

*Robert is a handsome man. His thick red
hair is parted carefully in the center, making
him look freshly barbered, mother-tended,
neat. He has all the graces of a young, confident, and talented man. His quiet humor is
always turned first upon himself. The red of
his irises seems a ruddy reflection of a glowing
mind, stirred not by persons but by determination to know more. Why, then, does he not
seem loving?*

December 7

V Mcl—hers is a maternity which freezes from love and burns with hate, which consumes what it hungers for, not food but the nearby spirits of family and other persons, which dies slowly when deprived of the bed of its son.

December 18

Europe seems elderly to me, covered with hoar, learned, sly, selfish, an octogenarian who resents the sight of his American great-grandson who is youthful, vigorous, vital, and full of boundless hope.

January 9

Where is natural music, the real music of the world, to be found? In woods, among low banks of ferns, at the spindly tops of birches, in reeds at the edge of ponds, under the lift of ocean waves, and around the edges of its spume. Below one's feet passing on ancient bricks laid for roads. Between the folds of organdy curtains blowing into sun-rooms in a light wind. Under the eaves of an old house during a storm which dispossesses the swallows.

January 14

*A story Robert told last evening: in Paris
in the conservatory in 1887 there was a pupil
named Claude Debussy. His elderly professor,
Antoine Marmontel, was stiff and severe,
rigid and Prussian. He preferred the smooth,
effortless playing of Robert to Claude's abrupt
and choppy performances. Claude was somewhat younger than his fellow pupil. He
breathed raucously when he played difficult
passages so that his nasal noises intertwined
themselves with the harmonies. He panted
loudly in order to emphasize strong beats.
When he performed at the conservatory he re-
sembled a snorting steam engine, so everyone,
including Professor Marmontel, despaired of
him, predicting a dim platform future for the
clangorous young pianist.*

February 5

*Robert recalls the time when his teacher,
Carl Heymann, returned from a successful
tournée of Paris, London, Copenhagen. He
seemed to his students no longer a teacher now
but a performer, an elevated personage, an
example of the polish and assurance such a
journey and such acclaim give to a man. He
seemed mysteriously now to be capable of anything. Robert said he played the classics as*

though they had been written by men with blood in their veins.

March 9

Robert's red mustache has grown. It droops at its corners. Gravity is pulling it down, it fills the whole area of his face between his nose and lower lip, burying his upper lip, crossing his face with color. Now he brushes his hair upward in the imperial German fashion. But his pink and white skin is of the American type. Professor Joachim Raff calls him "the handsome American."

April 1

The Maclarens are proud of their Scots ancestry. They talk of it as though they had never made the oceanic migration to New England. They still salt their American speech with dialect from Scotland; their true patriotism is to the older country.

May 14

The death of Raff, the death of Liszt a few years ago. Robert wonders why he stays in Europe any longer. He has discovered there are no appointments for an American in Eu-

rope. Würzburg has turned him down, the
conservatory here considers him too young for
Heymann's post. That redoubtable old man
has begun to lose his mind and is to be made
to retire. Poor Heymann—often he plays the
same piece again and again and again, some-
times for an entire day, and always the theme
from Spontini's Olympia Overture. *A few*
days ago he sat seemingly fastened to the
piano and the piano bench. He has to be lifted
up and led away to his bed each evening.

I reflect now on what I wrote in those long-
distant German years, my interior dialogue,
my rehearsal of what I heard Robert say, of
what I thought. Sometimes I wrote in an effort to understand Virginia Maclaren's quiet
decline, or to record my desperate, lonely reflections, my talk to myself alone.

Virginia Maclaren began to grow visibly
thinner. The solid cork of her body lost its
firmness, her neck, a peg that had held her
block-like head erect on her rigid shoulders,
became ragged, bent forward, her chin often
almost resting upon her chest as she sat in
a chair in the evening working at her em-
broidery hoop. A strange weakness of her
spine was diagnosed by doctors in Berlin. I
never believed she was physically ill. I thought
she wanted her eyes to sink down from the
distances they once sought, to the floor. The
strength in her neck and in her spirit began
to weaken from the day I came to live in Eu-

rope. Everything gave way in her: the almost youthful, well-corseted stocky body, the sure posture of her head, her will to stay alive to witness her son's success.

Once, coming home early on a rain-drenched afternoon—I had been caught in the sudden downpour and was wet through my cape to my dress so that it clung unbecomingly to my legs—I stopped in the entranceway to remove my sodden shoes and cape, trying to make no noise, as my mother-in-law often rested in the afternoon hours. For some reason I remember my hat that afternoon: the black feathers, dyed egret, I think, that covered it like birds in flight, smelled dank, like crows submerged in a cistern. There was no sound of life anywhere in the long string of rooms in which we lived. I went to my room to change, passing the closed door of the sewing room.

The door to our room, too, was shut. Odd, I thought, because my New Englander's concern for the proper airing of bedchambers during the day always compelled me to leave it open. Opening it, I saw my mother-in-law stretched out on the bed, her face buried in Robert's pillow, her shoulders shaking although no sound could be heard. One of her hands seemed to be under her lower body, which moved convulsively, up and down, up and down over the hand. Her thin, violet-colored morning dress showed me the outline of her moving back, her legs, her shoulders, her knees, dug into the softness of the bed. She looked as I imagined Christ might have looked from the back of the cross, still alive and moving, a woman in an agony of grief and sexual passion, crucified upon a coverlet.

I tried to back away. She heard me, sat up, saw me, and brushed her wet eyes with her sleeve. "And now you spy upon me," she said, her voice hoarse.

"Oh, no, I did not know you were here."

"I know, I know. There is no place left for me. You heartless Caroline Newby. You have taken it all." She climbed down from the bed's great height, down the steps to the floor, looking like a toy, a dwarf beside the treelike posts. Her eyes blank and unseeing, she went past me into the hall. I wanted to follow her, to take her head in my hands and kiss her suffering face and tell her that I had taken *nothing*, that her son gave almost nothing to me and surely seemed to desire nothing from me. I wanted to tell her what I had learned, that he belonged only to the secret music in his head, or perhaps to his young lady pupils or to his watching friend, but not to me. In the enormous bed in the great bedchamber she had had as much of him as I, or more than I because she had had him at the beginning and, I still believe, had taught him the arts of maternal love and mature passion, had loved him as only a mother, hardly ever a wife or a mistress, can love, with the hands that caressed his infancy, the lips and tongue that tasted the sweat and new odors of his puberty, the avid eyes that knew his contours from their first appearance, watched the curl about the ear turn to sideburns and reach down to become a beard.

I wanted to tell her how deeply I envied the love between her and her son, how I had never learned to love my recently deceased mother in this way, how my mother had never loved me, my mother who, like Virginia Maclaren, had not come to our wedding, to whom, too, I had always been Caroline Newby.

But the long hall lay between her room and mine. Her heavy door was shut, the words she had spoken still hung like smoke in the air. Her beloved son, who was also my husband: all that stood in the way. I stayed where I was in the bedroom and closed the door. We never spoke directly to each other again.

How do I put down on this paper my feeling of inadequacy, so profound that it began early in my marriage to Robert and lasted until his death downstairs? I felt there was no way to charm a man so charming himself, or to interest a genius who heard only the higher treble notations of significance, while I stumbled about on the low notes of the bass clef. Or to console his mother, a woman bereft of her lover.

The night Robert and I first made love (of this subject I do not enjoy writing, yet I have set out to be open, so I must put down what

I have felt, or not felt, not alone what I have seen and overheard) in the berth of a stateroom aboard the *City of Paris*, the act, which I had virginally dreaded, was over quickly. Robert was listless and tired, he told me what he was about to do to me as though he were a physician calming the fears of a child with a description of surgical procedures. I felt nothing under his demonstration but sharp pain and hot blood on my inner thighs. He fell asleep heavily while I tried to dry the blood from myself and the sheets of the berth without waking him. A week later—we made love again. This time it was my suggestion that we do so. I was curious to know if I had healed. I wanted to feel the rush of pleasure I had been led to believe (from the occasional confessions of my Boston friends) was customary.

I did not. This time, and in the growingly infrequent sexual encounters Robert and I had in the next two years, I felt nothing except mild satisfaction in serving what I considered to be his need. Never did I think of my lack of ardor as a failure in him. Always it was I who seemed deficient and inadequate, without beauty and charm, ignorant of the subtle guiles that awaken and sustain masculine desire. And then, after those two unsatisfying years, we rarely made love again.

I have often speculated: Why did Robert look upon me so kindly in the Commons that day and decide to marry me, I who looked

mouselike, murine, perhaps even birdlike?
"You are such a *little* girl," my mother had
said hopelessly, in that age of proudly buxom
women equally endowed in the bustle area.
"You remind me of a starved heron," my
friend Elizabeth once said, meaning it to be
a purely descriptive phrase, not cruel, I am
sure. My hair was, as it is still, without de-
finable color, as though it had very early begun to rehearse for its inevitable whiteness:
a thin, weak-brown shade. True, my hands
and feet were small, and that was fashionable
and called, often, aristocratic, but my reach
at the piano keys suffered from this. Robert
once said that my hands were not practical.

Why, then, did he choose to turn Miss Caroline Newby into Mrs. Robert Glencoe Maclaren? Because it was suitable, practical, for
a young composer to have a wife? A man who
hoped some day to have a chair of music at
a university or a post as principal of a conservatory: should he not have a wife?

Or, I wondered, could it be that Robert was
seeking to unlock the maternal prison? With
a wife beside him he would be free at last,
and yet hardly, as it turned out, tied to me.
Once Robert's natal bonds were cut, he floated
free, wary, careful not to form another emotional attachment as exhausting and lengthy.
We two were bound to each other by law. But
beyond that, we were bound by air, we lived
in the common ozone of his indifference, his
eternal politeness and charm, his passion to

write music, perform it, listen to it, and, as
it was to be later in Boston, to walk compan-
ionably in the parks in the evening with me
on his arm and Paderewski, now growing
heavy, walking beside him on a slack leash.

Inadequate as I felt to his needs and to the
larger realization that he needed far less of
me than I of him, still, often, he wanted me
present. I may have served his desire to establish himself as a family man, trustworthy
and solid, in the world's eyes. I suited his
arm, I occupied a chair in his sitting room.
I learned from his mother to keep an orderly,
clean, and attractive house. I had, he often
said, a way with servants. I *knew* food and
was rapidly learning about wine. I took up
very little room, being birdlike. The Steinway grand, newly arrived from Hamburg,
was a larger, more decorative and significant
addition to the display of his life than I.

We had been living in Germany for more
than two years when Robert decided it was
time to return to America. His musical future
was there, he now felt. He said his education
was over, smiling as he spoke, saying he
hardly *felt* educated, in his self-deprecating
way—and still, think of what the favorite
pupil of Liszt had said of him! It was time to
leave the world of student trials for the proof,
to move beyond his tutors and masters in order to carry out their instructions.

We made our plans to depart, booked three
passages on the *Servia* and arranged for the

shipping of our household and the careful crating of the new piano and the great bed. In the first flush of optimism about his future, Robert thought of buying another piano to be sent to America but was restrained by the cost and by the reminder that William Steinway now had offices and showrooms for his instruments in New York.

But at the very last, Virginia Maclaren would not come with us. She would not leave Germany. Robert tried to reason with her. I said, "You are so far from people, from your family." She shrugged, saying they did not need her. "My husband is dead, my sons are grown." I spoke of her friends. "I have friends no longer," she said, "here or there."

"Robert," I said, playing what I thought to be the strongest card. To that she said nothing, searching the floor with her eyes, looking up at Robert only briefly. He seemed to have grown taller as she shrank. "You would not wish to live so far from us, would you, Mama?" he asked. I remember clearly the strange tense he used: indefinite, conditional.

Again she raised her eyes from the floor to look into the distance. "Yes, I do. As far as it is possible to be. I no longer wish to live near anyone. Not even you, my beloved Rob. I wish to be alone, to live alone, without reminders of the past."

"But the shipping. The packing. We've arranged to have all this furniture sent back."

Her eyes strained into the distance of the

hallway that led to her sewing room. She gestured with a sweep of her arm that took in the whole series of rooms. "I want none of this, to live or die among. I will acquire new objects of my own. Don't be concerned about that."

Even though I heard what I took to be theatrical coloration in her sentences, it was a dreadful time for me. But Robert seemed unaffected. He said nothing more, considering the matter peaceably, satisfactorily, settled. He helped his mother find a flat on Neuleystrasse which was already furnished. He supervised all the packing of her personal belongings.

From all the furnishings she had brought with her from America, and the others she had gathered in Paris, in Stuttgart, in Frankfurt in the years she and Robert had lived together in those cities, she took with her only a small needlepoint-covered pouf on which she had rested her feet in the sewing room. Its area was the size of a lady's handkerchief, its pattern that of two mourning doves, their heads tucked into each other's breasts, their feet a pattern of entwined twig-like toes.

On the last day before our sailing, Robert took his mother's arm and guided her toward the door, carrying her coat and parasol, for the short walk to her new home. I could not bear to watch. It was like being present at a human sacrifice or forced to witness a hang-

ing. She stopped, reaching to peck at my chin,
because Robert said as she walked silently
to the door, "Aren't you going to bid Caroline
bon voyage?" Her kiss was as dry as dust, her
lips too parched, I thought, to feel my burning
skin. I was consumed with embarrassment
and pity. I know she hardly saw me as she
bade me farewell. I was not present when she
said good-bye to her son.

We came home in June of '96. I can see us
still, standing at the rail in the wind, watching the tugboats pull at the *Servia*, edging it
with their great hawsers toward the pier.
With one hand Robert held the high felt
crown of his hat. With his other he worried
at a sore on his lip, trying in his nervousness
to work off the scab with his nail.

A cool wind cut across New York harbor.
I remember thinking it was a new-world air,
brasher and fresher than the ancient heavy
air of Frankfurt we had just left. We watched
the miniature waves of the Hudson River lap
the white sides of the ship. Robert put his
hands down on the rail and bent over to listen, I suspected, to the suspirations of the
water. I knew he was listening for a pattern,
a melody, even a refrain. I heard none, only
the irregular gasps and smacks of tame harbor water.

The ship made its slow bend to the right,
seeming to lean into the wind, nudged into

its docking position by four insistent tugboats
on its left side. The wind died as the maneu-
ver cut the ship off from the river. Almost at
once it became very warm, with the hot
breath of the shore and the land.

I knew Robert was absorbed and nervous,
not from the intricate motions of bringing a
great ship to berth, but by the uncertainty
of his future, by his already forming nostalgia
for the securities of his life abroad. For him
the present never existed, which was perhaps
why I never seemed to exist for him. I
watched him pat his hat again, saw that the
work of his nail on his lip had produced a
small trickle of blood. "Good Lord, Robert.
Your lip is bleeding. You've been picking at
it again."

He licked his lip, smiling a little as though
he were pleased at the taste. Perhaps he was
making a small physical addition to the pain
he was feeling, to the fear of coming home to
America, to Boston, compounding dread with
blood. "Will it take us long to come through
customs, do you think, Robert?"

"I don't know. Burns took me through last
time. Even so, it was two hours before I could
start for the hotel."

I tried to think how I could make the passage from the ship to the hotel easy for him,
in place of his brother, whom we had not informed of our arrival. Robert was unable to
manage such journeys, often following crowds
in the direction they flowed, forgetful of his

own. Sometimes I wondered if he thought
everyone was going to his destination.

The gangplanks were lowered. They re-
sembled three parallel tongues reaching toward the shore. We followed the crowd to one
of them. Once down and on the pier, I felt the
first assault of the depression that was to
afflict me all that first year back in Boston.
Robert had come home to promise, I to more
of my married life as it had been lived in
Germany: a maker of late suppers, a duster
of piano keys and the lowered lid in the off
hours when they were not in use, a solitary
visitor to galleries and concert halls in the
afternoons.

Still, the moment of stepping ashore at the
foot of New York's towers was exciting. There
was the chance that much might change now
that Virginia and the conservatory were left
behind. Robert might turn his eyes toward
me, *see* me, might erase my sense of insuffi-
ciency with his love and notice. Now that we
were home in our own land, he might open
a little of his handsome European surface to
my deep American love for him.

A few steps from the end of the gangplank
we were met by a strange young man who
seemed to have been waiting for us. He introduced himself to us as a reporter from the
Boston Transcript, come to New York, he
said, to interview the returning native son
back from his European success. He wore a
straw hat with a wide red-and-white band,

and a white-and-blue—striped jacket that had suffered in the June heat of New York. There were semicircles of dampness under his arms. His forehead was wet. I saw Robert draw back from him a little.

"Have you lived in Germany very long?"

"For some years," Robert said, in the clipped Germanic diction he had acquired abroad. He sounded precise and curt, as though the interview had already gone on too long.

"Study there, did you?"

"Yes, of course."

"Performed on the piana too, did you?"

Robert looked at me helplessly. The new-found patriotism of his return seemed to be slipping away in the presence of this reporter's callow American ignorance. I gestured toward the trunks and grips, now piled neatly under a cardboard sign that said *M*. "Perhaps we should get into our line for the customs inspector," I said.

"Just a few more questions here, sir. Knew some of the greats, did you, over there in Paree?"

"I was in Paris only a year. Debussy was a fellow student there. We both studied under Savard."

The reporter, I saw, wrote down *DE-BOOSIE* carefully in his notebook and then asked, "Where did you go then? Vee-enna?"

"To Frankfurt, Germany, where I studied with Carl Heymann and Joachim Raff."

I spoke up quickly to fill what threatened to be a long silence while the young man struggled with the proper names. "Mr. Maclaren's compositions were highly praised and encouraged by William Mason, a protégé of Franz Liszt," I said, to prevent Robert's leaving rudely.

The straw-hatted young man wrote on his pad *LIST* and something else I could not read. "And now what are your plans, sir?"

"To compose and play, and perhaps to teach, in Boston."

"Well, good luck to you, sir. And to you, ma'am. Excuse my dumbness. I'm—this is not my regular beat. Know nothing about music myself. City side of the desk is my place. Just happened to be in New York, so they asked me to come by."

"Quite all right." We walked away, toward the letter *M* and our luggage.

An astonishing metamorphosis of this conversation appeared in the *Transcript*, signed by what I took to be the young man's name, E.P. Duckworth. It was full of rhetoric and an invention of which I had not thought him capable after hearing him speak. The news report said that "the composer and his wife, Caroline, had lived abroad for some years, he studying and composing a great deal of music of which the composer Franz Liszt had been very admiring. A friend of Robert Maclaren's, interviewed in Frankfurt, said of the couple that 'their union, perfect in sympathy and closeness of comradeship, was nothing short of ideal.' " He continued (I am quoting now from the newspaper account, which I still have in a scrapbook and which I will lay here in this account): "Their life in Frankfurt was characterized by an ideal serenity and detachment. It was a time of rich productiveness for Maclaren, who is now only twenty-four, and it is to be expected that his return to his homeland will be marked by further steps toward the great promise of his talent. His lodgings will be in Boston, where he and Mrs. Maclaren will reside on Mount Vernon Street. There he will accept private pupils. His *First Piano Suite* will be performed in November in Chickering Hall."

A felicitous editor, I imagine, had turned Robert's bluntness, a reporter's ignorance, and Weeks's friendly blindness into tribute. I do not wish to seem critical or ungrateful when I say that this magical process, this kind of transmutation, was to occur again and again in Robert's biography. Admirers of his charm and his music created the myth of him that has remained to this day. The descriptive mode used for writing about him has always been euphemism—until the very end, and after his death, when critics, conductors, and students began to be critical of what they called his extreme romanticism. They were to comment upon the small scope of his work; the sentimental impressionism (I am using their terms, not mine) of his later compositions. But not yet: at this time about which I am writing, only panegyrics were written about him. The *Transcript*'s article was the beginning.

The house we rented in Mount Vernon Street on Beacon Hill was narrow and three-storied. It looked out at back on a small, lovely shaded garden, and had a very large room suitable for a music room, two small sitting rooms, one for each of us, and two bedrooms. We reclaimed Paderewski from the friends who had boarded and overfed him in Robert's long absence. He had lost his lean look and become lazy and slow in his movements. He loved to lie in the garden and to be taken for short walks around the gardens on Commonwealth Avenue. Delighted to have him back, Robert took him out for airings every morning, and then returned him to his banishment in the garden when he went upstairs. Robert could not bear to work with any motion or breathing in the room. Paderewski disliked being put out, but he learned to be patient, to lie under the plane tree until Robert, finished with a long day of composing and lessons, would come for him again in the early evening. They walked together while I talked to our supper guests, if we had them, or supervised the food if we were to be alone. Only on weekends was the routine broken, when Robert went out to perform with the Symphony, or with the Kneissel Quartette, or to play at Chickering Hall in Boston.

Or, on Sunday evenings, we very often went to concerts, to hear Robert's work played, for it was beginning to have a vogue and could be heard quite often there and in other cities. I remember when *Lear and Cordelia* was played for the first time by the Symphony Orchestra. Artur Nikisch was to conduct it. He came by to call for us that evening. We took a hansom cab together to the Music Hall, it must have been, since I don't think the orchestra had as yet moved into its new Symphony Hall. Nikisch, Robert, and I had met in Leipzig; Robert and he had become good friends. This evening was the first time in a long time, almost since the farewell party, that I had seen Robert so animated. It was not because the Boston Symphony was going to play his work but because someone from the past—a friend from his beloved Germany—was there in his Beacon Hill sitting room.

I doubt if either Robert or Nikisch knew I was present. We entered the old Music Hall through the back door, I somewhat behind the two of them, and they in a transport of delight in being together again. Robert had his arm around Nikisch's shoulder. It was much like a reunion of fellow army officers who had once been stationed on the same foreign post, or college classmates come together after a long absence.

I went to my seat, and Robert joined me there. When Nikisch came to the podium I noticed how much alike he and Robert looked, with the similarity that seemed to characterize most men of their age and European training and class. Except for his beard (Robert never adopted the European habit), Nikisch had the same short, middle-parted hair, the same thick, curving mustache, the same absorbed look. They belonged to a close fraternity of artists—of men—which I had learned about in Frankfurt and from which, because I was a woman and a very minor musician, I felt eternally excluded. There *were* women musicians we had known in Europe—Teresa Carreño, who played Robert's *Second Piano Suite* in Wiesbaden, and a Miss Adele Margolis in London who performed two movements from his first suite. Robert wrote grateful notes to the two pianists, but he made no efforts to meet them: in the fraternity there was room only at a distance for women.

I had always thought that a *perfect union* (so the *Transcript* happily termed it) was the result of spiritual and intuitive harmonies, an intellectual fidelity, so to speak. If this were achieved, one could then enter into the highest harmony, which was physical love. In this day it is thought to be the other way around, but I had never believed that. Robert and I had almost no physical love, and never, it seemed to me, had it come at the culmination of the other unities, always as a sudden thought, a remembrance of conjugal duty. For neither of us do I think it was a great pleasure, certainly never for me. Indeed, I was not to know the joy of that pleasure of which so many speak and write until much later and in another way...

Robert occasionally performed his duty as meticulously as he walked his dog, parted his hair, trimmed his mustache. But at the end of a long day, I knew his energy was very low, his interest elsewhere, his physical prowess used up. We lay in the great bed, which we had transported safely and crammed into an upper chamber of our thin New England town house. We rarely touched; he slept stretched out straight on his side, unwilling to lose his rest by contact, as solitary in his sleep as he was in his waking hours, a man who lived almost entirely within himself. Every month when I had my female visitor, as we used to call it, he would move to the couch in his studio, offended, I think, by the unmistakable odor, which the strips of rag I wore could not disguise. His nights and days were designed to shield himself and his art.

Or so I then thought.

I have mentioned the farewell party given Robert by his fellow students and his pupils before he left the Hoch Conservatory, two evenings before, as I recall. None of the women students came, perhaps because of the lateness of the hour. It was at nine o'clock. I was the only lady among twelve or thirteen solemnly suited men standing about the room, wineglasses in their hands, talking together, Robert in the center, laughing often. I was introduced to a number of persons I had not met before. Professor Heymann came over to speak to me when I seemed to be pushed to the very edge of the animated groups. He took my arm and moved me over to speak to a pale-faced young man who was also standing alone. I remembered him at once as the young man I had seen in the shadows of Robert's lesson that day. "Mrs. Maclaren, may I present Churchill Weeks," the professor said. "A very good pianist. This is Robert's wife, Caroline."

Churchill Weeks stared at me. His brows were so heavy over his deep-set eyes it was difficult to see them clearly. His face seemed almost sickly in that studio light. He took my hand, raised it a little, and bent stiffly over it, in the German way, without kissing it. "I am honored, Frau Maclaren. Your husband is my very dear friend. I shall miss him very much."

I was astonished: tears streamed down his face. I was startled, for I had not seen his eyes, I did not know he was crying. That was all he said for a long moment, and then he went on, "You must pardon my display of feeling. I am an American—my home is in

Milwaukee—and it is hard to stay on here—alone." He turned and left the room.

Walking back toward the Praunheimer Strasse, I asked Robert about Churchill Weeks. "Is he always—so emotional?" Robert seemed reluctant to talk about him. "He's—a musician, a composer. Very sensitive."

"Have you been friends long?"

"We have known each other since we came to Frankfurt at almost the same time."

"More than two years, then?"

"Yes, it must have been. Somehow it does not seem that long."

"Why did I never meet him before? Why did you never bring him home?"

Robert made no reply. We walked for some time in silence, the usual climate of our walks. Silence was more characteristic of him when we were together than the sound of his voice, low and pleasant as I remember it being to friends. After a while he said, "I enjoyed the party. It was good of them all to have it for me. They're very kind friends."

I managed to bury the memory of Churchill Weeks's pale, wet face until the letters began to arrive, not long after we had settled into Mount Vernon Street. One morning the postman handed me three thin letters in blue envelopes as I walked out to do the day's shopping. Robert was cloistered in his studio upstairs where he had breakfasted alone in order to begin work early. All the letters were from abroad, and in the left-hand corners

read: *Weeks/Jahnstrasse 76/Frankfurt/
Deutschland.* I went back into the house and
climbed the stairs to deliver the letters. I first
knocked on Robert's door and then went in.
He was standing beside the piano, his head
bent over a manuscript page of music, both
hands resting on the lid. He had not heard
me enter.

I did not want to interrupt, knowing how
intently he was listening to the sounds in his
head as he often did, even in company, and
always when he was alone with me. I went
out, closing the door quietly behind me, and
left the letters for him on the reception table
near the downstairs entry. On the way to his
walk later, with Paderewski, he will find
them, I thought.

That night we were to sup late. Robert was
still in his studio, engrossed in his new *Woodland Songs*, which he had told me he hoped
Carl Faelton would play in his recital in New
York next season. Robert came to supper and
ate in silence, wiped his mustache carefully
with his napkin, folded it, and then for the
first time turned his eyes on me, with that
weary look he always had at the end of a long
day of work, close to the end of his patience
with himself and with me, for some unknown
reason. "I found my mail very late this afternoon. Does it not usually come earlier?"

"Yes, about nine-thirty, usually."

"Why didn't you bring it up to me?"

"I did, Robert. You were working. I didn't wish to disturb you."

"You might have offered me a choice," he said in a small, angry voice.

I was aghast. No household crisis or sudden personal disability, nothing, had ever before been sufficient cause for Robert to be interrupted. But Weeks's letters...

I must now write frankly, perhaps more frankly than I am sure the Foundation wishes me to. For the fact was, those letters from Churchill Weeks were love letters. I must be pardoned for the venial sin I committed: I read them. It happened this way. A few days later another thin blue envelope from Germany arrived. This time I carried it at once to the music room. Robert took it, smiled his quick, charming smile, thanked me, and turned away to read it. I remember thinking how his smile had shrunk, from the wide grin I first noticed at our meeting in the park until now: it had become abbreviated, a token, a quick gesture like a handshake, the remains of a smile. Then it was gone and one was left, *I* was left, that is, frozen rather than warmed by it.

That afternoon Robert went to a rehearsal. I watched him from an upper window as he turned the corner into the avenue and then I went quickly into the music room. With me I took a duster as pretense. The room was meticulously neat—Robert could not work

unless it was—but the surfaces were somewhat dusty and I began to stir the dust about.
Under a pile of music paper near the back of
the piano I saw a light blue color. And while
only Paderewski watched my shameful act,
I read Weeks's letters.

What shall I say of them? They were written in an agony of love such as I had never
in my life been witness to. Weeks told Robert
of the pain his departure had caused him, of
the illness he had suffered for two months
afterward, of his slow recovery during which
his only thought was to see Robert again, to
hold his beloved head in his hands once
again, to take strength from *his* strength.
Was it at all possible that Robert was planning a summer return to the Continent, since
he, Weeks, would not be free to come to Boston? In a cribbed, uneven script that seemed
visible evidence of his distraught state, he
asked:

*When shall we two be together again, my
beloved friend? For the old talk, the old making of music together, four hands at the same
keyboard, four hands and two mouths and our
whole beings engaged in the same loving act.*

These words, as I have here put them down,
were etched into my memory and are still
there. Often now I do not remember what day
it is, or what dinner was served to me last
night, but the words of Churchill's letter I

have never forgotten. Other parts of the letters were sprinkled with Scots phrases, for Weeks claimed his ancestry was like Robert's and seemed to affect the Scots language as part of his own. He called Robert an *auld farran*, he blamed himself for being a *bluntie*, sometimes a *blunker*. He felt alone and melancholy—*leefulane* and *ourie*—he sent his *lock o' loo* to his fellow *pingler*. Some I did not know and had to look up in the large Webster; I had never heard Robert, the proud descendant of Scots, use one of them. It must have been their private language of love, kept for those burning letters.

I returned the letters to the place I had found them, feeling deep guilt for having allowed myself to be driven to such an act. Of course I know nothing of Robert's answers to those *cris du coeur;* were they, too, sprinkled with loving dialect? But Robert wrote, I know. Once I saw a letter, addressed to Weeks, before Robert carried it himself to the postbox on the corner during one of his walks with Paderewski. In the late evenings I would see him writing, I seated across the room knitting or reading (never writing: to whom would I have written? surely not to my mother-in-law, who would not have responded, I felt sure), Robert holding his writing desk on his lap.

As he wrote he would rub his lower lip thoughtfully. The sore I had first noticed tended to heal and then to appear again be-

cause, I always thought, in his nervousness
and unease, he would rub his lip, returning
the little eruption to life.

What was I to do with this discovery, except to recognize what I thought at the time
might be one explanation: there was a deep,
unfathomable alliance among men of talent
which involved them wholly, making it impossible for women to enter their consciousness except in a curiously negative way. Remove our services, our presence as helpmeets,
and our absence is remarked upon. Our physical support restored, we sink back to the
outer limits of their awareness.

But admission to the alliance? I have never
seen it granted, except as a chivalric courtesy
uttered for the moment—Shall we join the
ladies?—After ample brandy and smoking
and the serious talk was exhausted. The next
half hour would be spared us for polite small
talk, women's subjects.

Perhaps, I tried to tell myself, the letters
were an extension of all this, with the added
exaggerations and emotional excess natural
to creative persons who thought and wrote
in the romantic tradition. In one of Weeks's
letters there were quotations from Heine and
Goethe. My imagination supplied mottoes
from Tennyson and Victor Hugo in the replies
Robert must have sent to his friend. Once I
came upon Robert standing with his foot on
the grill in front of the fireplace, his face red-

dened by the flames, reading Tennyson's poems, saying a line or two aloud, to himself.

Our life went along evenly. The only change was Robert's increasing success and recognition. Those were good years to be in Boston, to be a young American composer. We began to read, in the musical columns of the newspapers and in the journals, praise for Robert's compositions, which were played with increasing frequency by pianists in New York, in Philadelphia, in San Francisco. The Symphony Orchestra in Boston, now under a new conductor named Emil Paur, played his work often. Poor Nikisch had gone back to Hungary after three years in Boston, a disappointed man who told us one evening at dinner that he had tried without success to come to terms with the men of the orchestra. But they had resented his demands for rehearsals over and above the ones they felt reasonable. Nikisch had invited Robert often as a soloist; Paur did, too, even increasing the number of appearances he offered him in a year.

Robert traveled to other cities on the invitation of conductors, one of whom, Anton Seidl, I think it was, told the *Evening Post* that he considered Maclaren the first great American composer. Robert returned from that trip glowing at the phrase, almost a prophet in his own time and country, he quoted Seidl as having said, with his tight shy smile to Elizabeth Pettigrew, who had been visiting with me while he was gone those weeks. Later, Philip Hale was to say almost the same thing in the magazine *Music*.

Elizabeth congratulated him. She had always admired him. Now, from the distance of her spinsterhood, I was able to tell, she regarded him with awe. She had a way of rising whenever he entered the sitting room, as though he were of a priestly caste. I think she found it very difficult to sit in his presence. But I don't think he noticed, or noticed her at all, thinking of her, I felt sure, as an occupant of my spare time who did not, fortunately, impinge upon his.

The unaccustomed glow in his face after that tour turned into a fever almost immediately upon his return. At first he denied its presence. Finally he was too sick to insist upon its absence and took to his bed, lying inert and hot, refusing to allow me to call a physician. "It's the body's way," he said. For three days he slept, long and feverishly. I brought him meals and sat on the edge of the great bed while he tried and failed to eat. He said his throat was too sore.

"Shall I read to you, Robert?"

"I think not, Caroline. I don't mind the silence. Sometimes it's a pleasure to hear nothing but what comes into my head from the temperature, can you believe it?"

I tried to be playful. "Would you care to hear some early Maclaren, like *Petits Morceaux pour Piano*?" In the dressing room off the bedroom was an upright piano on which I used to play a little now and then, quietly, so as not to disturb Robert.

"Thank you, but I think not."

"Some Liszt, perhaps?"

"No, no, thank you. It will sound odd, but I think I have begun to avoid listening to music, except my own when I must, so that I won't be in danger of using it when I begin to write."

I remember his weakness during that time but, more, his new, acquiescent agreeableness. We seemed close to each other, because illness brings the nurse and the patient into an anxious union and because, as it does many men, his illness frightened him. He seemed willing to be nursed and tended to. But not doctored. The rash that covered his body worried me—could it be scarlet fever? But after a while it receded. I was converted to his view that home care and bed rest were adequate doctors. In two weeks the fever and the rash disappeared. Even the little red shiny herpes on his lower lip healed finally and never returned.

Our closeness in that September: I cannot forget it. Robert would allow no visitors, wanted to hear no music. We talked together, as always, very little. But I felt pleasure in being able to spend my days in his company, crocheting, I recall, the large afghan for the couch in his music room, stopping now and then to fetch tea or soup for him, or watching his face as he slept. I slept on the little couch in the guest room so that I would not disturb his nights. When the afghan was half finished he recovered enough to walk about the room, and into the dressing room, where he would play small pieces, sometimes only fragments, on the piano, first humming gently, and then following the sound of his voice with music on the piano from the store in his head he had apparently collected during the fever.

At the end of the third week he dressed slowly and went downstairs. I could hear the fresh snap of long sheets of staff paper as he turned them impatiently, the runs of trial notes on the piano. For a few days he allowed Paderewski to lie in the room with him during the morning as he worked, an admittance that delighted the loving old dog, who worshiped him in somewhat the same way Elizabeth did. But the slap of his tail and his occasional strolls about the room between naps began to irritate Robert. He was expelled to the garden and never again, in the time of his life that remained, was he granted that privilege.

I took heart from that interlude. It made me hopeful that we could find paths to each other that might wipe out my loneliness. The year that followed was near the end of our time in Boston. One day in October—a beautiful fall full of cool sunlight and the little gusts of air that made life on the old Hill and along the paths of the Public Gardens so pleasant—Churchill Weeks knocked on our door at teatime.

Settled in the sitting room, munching on cookies and drinking cup after cup of tea, he told us of his plans. He had come home to begin his American career as Robert had done before him. You will remember that in those days European training was thought to be essential for an American musician. He said he was on his way to Milwaukee, where his parents lived. We spent the time of dinner and the early evening hearing tales of life at the Hoch Conservatory, of the students Robert and he had taught, of their teachers, some now dead, others about to retire.

I was content to sit on the edge of those hours of talk that night, providing the coffee and schnapps they both liked, listening to the talk that moved so easily between the two old friends. I was content because I had realized at their first moment of meeting that time and distance had transformed Weeks's feelings: the strength and passion of his professed love for Robert, in the letters, had weakened or died out entirely. They sat at a distance from each other, having seemed to choose chairs to effect this, and their voices were loud and forced, as though they were giving instructions to a class or lecturing to a club.

Weeks was attentive to me, ascertaining my comfort in the small chair I had chosen, twice offering to surrender his upholstered armchair to me. I began to like him, to forget about the anguish his person, even at a distance of three thousand miles, had caused me. I asked him if he would care to stay the night and he accepted gracefully, with no hesitation. "It is very good of you to think of it."

"Not at all. You're an old friend. We're both pleased to see you again."

But Robert said nothing. He seemed nervous, rubbing on his lower lip in his old way. After his illness of September his energies were low in the evenings. He excused himself to go early to bed. Weeks seemed disappointed but showed no surprise at his departure. "He looks very tied. It must have been a severe illness."

"It was. And as usual he refused to have anything done for him, anything professional, that is. He waited it out, as he likes to say. But he's much recovered now."

"I see, yes. And you're looking very well."

"Thank you. And you." It was true. His pale skin had been colored by his ocean voyage, he looked sturdy, healthy, and somehow, American. The Berlin cut of his coat could not disguise his country look.

"I am about to be married," he said. "I wanted to tell you both, but Robert went up before I was able to."

I took a deep breath and relaxed in my

hard chair, almost unable to say anything to this news. "You can tell him in the morning. I'm so pleased for you. To someone from the conservatory?"

"No. The daughter of my mother's close friend. The three of them visited me in Germany last year. We've been in correspondence ever since. The wedding is to be at Christmas in Milwaukee. Do you think you and Robert could come?"

"Surely," I said, very quickly, and then checked myself. "That is, yes, of course we would both love to, but I must consult Robert about his schedule."

"I'll send you an invitation in plenty of time to arrange for it."

I showed Weeks his room. On my way to ours I felt light-headed, almost giddy, uplifted by his news. Now I believed it all to be a sick fancy. The letters did not exist or they were merely literary exercises, romantic jokes exchanged by the two men. Robert was asleep when I came to bed. I lay awake for some time thinking of how time, by means of its simple accumulation, had wiped out the apprehensiveness that had lasted so long. Weeks left the next morning before Robert was awake.

Robert worked very hard in the next month, to catch up, he said. Because money was still a problem for us, he took on a third pupil, a boy of eleven named Paul Brewster whose self-taught prowess was almost miraculous, said Robert. Now three pupils occupied his afternoons, always the best hours of his day. He kept his mornings, in which he was usually very slow to start, for composition, and in those hours he worked with such concentration that he abandoned his walk with the collie, taking him out only in the late afternoon. Paderewski had grown very old since our return from Europe; his still stately gait was now very slow and deliberate. This satisfied Robert, who was weary from working for nine hours before the walk. I would sometimes come up on the two old companions ambling along the paths of the park, Robert dazed and self-absorbed, Paderewski looking back at him every now and then.

We made our plans to take a Pullman room on the *Twentieth Century* train to Chicago and then on to Milwaukee for Churchill Weeks's wedding. I had persuaded Robert he ought to go. But in the end we did not do so. In early December Robert had a letter from his mother. It was a stiff, formal, strange letter:

I wish to tell you, Rob, that I feel very close to the end of my days. I am now almost always bedridden with what my physician has called a disease of the heart. My feet and ankles swell badly at times so that I am unable to walk at all. I would not concern you with this but my physician has issued a warning to me, advising me to communicate with my relations in America so that I will not be alone in a last illness which, he says, may well be imminent. I am not writing as he suggested, for I wish no company now, having had none in the last years. But it seems wise to convey to you the warning he has given me so that you will have had notice.

Your mother,
Virginia Maclaren

Much disturbed, Robert booked passage for himself on the first ship sailing to Wilhelmshaven, the *Kaiser Wilhelm der Grosse*, I think it was. We were not in a position to afford two passages, he said. I agreed: Virginia Maclaren needed Robert unaccompanied by his wife. Two days before he was to sail, a cable came for Robert from the coroner of the city of Frankfurt informing him of his mother's death. Sometime later a long letter arrived from an attorney-at-law describing the contents of Virginia Maclaren's will. Her husband having predeceased her, she left her small estate from him to her sons Burns and Logan. To her youngest son, Robert, and wife, Caroline, were to be given her personal effects and her clothing. To the Hoch Conservatory, with her gratitude for the fine training it had given to her son, the composer Robert

Glencoe Maclaren, she gave all her books and
the manuscripts in her possession of his early
works, including the one most dear to her,
Opus 3, *Barcarolle pour pianoforte,* dedicated
A ma chère maman.

Boston was growing too much for Robert. He
talked often of finding a quiet place in the
country in which to live and work. I still loved
the city, having renewed acquaintance with
some of my school friends, visiting the Mu-
seum of Fine Arts with them and with Elizabeth, lunching often in the downtown shops.
I went each week to the Boston Public Library, where there were afternoon lectures
on the most recent books. Sunday mornings
Elizabeth and I went to the Unitarian church
together.

But Robert was restless because of the demands upon his time. He became increasingly short with his pupils, especially with
young Paul Brewster, who was advancing so
fast that it seemed to me to be in direct dis-
proportion to Robert's patience with him.
Robert always referred to him as Master
Brewster, suggesting by the designation that
he was far too young for opinions, of an age
only to listen and then do as he was told.

I must tell you more about him. Paul had
been coming to Robert for some months when
we decided to find a place in the country.
Working as hard as he did, Robert had lost
weight. In the first three months of that year

he had gone on tour, performing, lecturing, conducting his work and the music of his admired European masters, Liszt, Mozart, Beethoven. He came home exhausted from these trips. On lesson days he would lie on his couch through most of the morning, write almost nothing, storing up his meager supply of energy against the arrival of the precocious Master Brewster.

Paul Brewster at eleven still dressed as a young boy, in dark knickers, a silk shirt, a black silk tie. Twice each week, accompanied by his mother, he came to our door. When I opened the door to their ring, his mother would dip into a small curtsy, as I had not seen it done since the peasant women in Germany, greet me in a language I did not understand, and then disappear.

Robert told me she was Hungarian. Paul was her only child. In her eyes she and her son were sentenced to exile living in the United States until the time came for Mr. Brewster's firm to send him back to Budapest, where they had met and where Paul was born. To her, Boston was a tomb, a cell, a cage, she had told Robert, who understood enough Hungarian for those words. Having arranged for Paul's lessons, and unburdening herself of these few details of autobiography, she made no other explanations. Her sole function became the delivery of the small genius, her son, to our house, and his retrieval an hour later.

In that year, because of Paul's avidity and skill, Robert sometimes instructed him far longer than his allotted hour. The boy seemed to consume the music he was given. His small, thin, tense, accomplished fingers were capable of performing extraordinary feats for one so young, his memory was perfect, his understanding of what he was doing almost that of a mature musician. I worried, not about him, for I hardly encountered him at all and knew all this only through Robert's weary reports of him at our late suppers, but about Robert, whose fatigue grew with the boy's virtuosity. No longer did he stand to give his lessons but had moved a wicker chair from another room into the music room, a chair that reminded me, when first I saw it there, of Mrs. Seton's.

Many afternoons, through the closed door of the music room, I heard Robert's sharp, angry voice, reproaching Paul for a mistake, I surmised, since I was not able to hear the words. His voice would maintain the same tone after the repetition of the long passage, which to my ear was played brilliantly. Robert would find some small matter to carp about, the boy would play the music again with verve, with greater accuracy, although, not having discerned the initial error, I cannot be sure of this. Again Robert's voice would cut across the last notes. Often I went downstairs and out into the garden so that I did not have to listen to Paul replaying the same passage, the same rejected perfection followed by the same unreasonable anger.

After all this time I no longer can remember how prepared I was for what happened. But I did wonder: Would the boy complain to his mother so that she would take him away from Robert's lessons? Would Robert completely lose control of himself at the boy's undeniable talent and send his pupil away?

It was not to be either of these suppositions. In the spring of that year, and just after Robert had returned home exhausted from his tour, Paul arrived alone for his lesson. He had been caught in a sudden rainstorm. His eyes red, his nose running, he stood, coughing, on the landing. His coat dripped water, his thin face was apologetic, his shoes full of water. The boy seemed afraid to go to Robert in this state, and yet there was little I could do for him except to insist he remove his shoes. I gave him a pair of Robert's old slippers, many sizes too large. Coughing and shuffling in the slippers, he knocked on the music room door and went in.

I took the sodden shoes down to the kitchen to try to dry them. So I missed the explosion. Paul had been ill with a cold, he had apparently told Robert: "I did not practice yesterday. I hope you will understand that..."

The ceiling above me shook. Something heavy had been—thrown? dropped?—to the floor. I heard a crash, and then a desperate, thin, child's voice cry: *"Stop!"* I went up the stairs as quickly as I could, hiking up my skirts to facilitate the climb. The door was ajar. In a fury such as I had never thought him capable of, Robert, in his shirt sleeves, stood in the center of the room, holding the fire poker above his head. Paul was crouched on the window seat, his face drawn and white, his mouth open in a mad, terrorized grimace. All his small, even, sharp teeth showed. "Robert, what *is* it? What are you doing? Stop that. Put it down." Commands and entreaties poured out of me in one long line of sound.

Robert looked at me, dazed. Then he sat down, almost as if he had collapsed, onto the piano bench, dropping the poker at his feet. He put his head into his hands. I started over to him, but I was too slow. The boy had jumped toward Robert from his crouched position on the window seat, like a small spring released into the air. Before I could stop him he had crossed the room, stooped down, opened his mouth, and dug his teeth into the flesh of Robert's upper arm.

Robert sprang to his feet. "My God! Let *go!*"

Paul Brewster appeared for a few seconds to hang by his teeth from Robert's raised arm, the cloth of Robert's shirt bunched into his mouth. Robert went on screaming, the high, thin sound flowing from his mouth like sickness. His other hand slapped at the boy, trying to make him let go. I held Paul's mad head in my hands and tried to pry open his teeth, which were like small pointed stones. His mouth was lined with foam. I felt it wet my hands.

Finally, it seemed an incredibly long time, but finally he let go when Robert's blood filled his mouth. He coughed, gagged, turned his head away, and vomited into the cave of the piano. Robert sat down heavily on the sofa, holding his bloody wound. I knelt down beside him. Robert had stopped screaming. The only sound in the room was Paul, spitting and retching. "Don't move, Robert. I'll send the maid for the doctor. You must have a doctor."

Behind me I could hear Paul staggering toward the door. He mumbled something but I could not make out what it was. I had no desire to stop him, I wanted him out of the house. At that moment I never wanted to see the beastly little boy again.

That day and night hang like bats in my memory, black and unmoving. Robert stretched out, inert on his sofa. The doctor I sent for came at once, inspected the wound, looked troubled. Robert's whole upper arm was now a furious blue-black color, with red teeth marks outlining the edges of the gash.

"May I have a look at the dog that did this?"

"It was not a dog."

"*Not* a dog?"

"No," I said. "A boy."

"Good Lord!" The doctor examined the wound again. He gave Robert several white papers of powder to take with warm water at intervals through the next days, washed the area again with alcohol, and shook his head. "There may be infection. One never can know. We will watch it. Rest," he said sternly to Robert. "I'll be back in the early morning."

Rest! Robert was so shocked that I could not persuade him even to leave his sofa for his bed that evening. His eyes closed, his wounded arm resting on a pillow at his side, he lay without stirring, refusing dinner, refusing to move at all to another room. He had been assaulted in every corner of his being, I believe, his whole system was affected, the insult was to his spirit as well as to his arm. For he told me the next day that all of his body ached, his head, his back, his knees and ankles. He was very thirsty, he said, his tongue felt burned, his throat cut and raw, but swallowing cool water hurt. The second night he moved painfully to our bed. He would not allow me to lower the lamps or to close the shutters and drapes. He seemed to be afraid he might be attacked again in the dark. Did he think the mad boy still crouched in a corner of the room? And the wonder of it! He wanted me to sit beside him while he slept.

His sleep was stony. He never moved, he breathed so lightly that once I bent over to see if he was still alive. By morning I was exhausted. Robert still slept his torpid, motionless sleep. I sent the maid to Elizabeth to ask her to come and relieve me, after the doctor had been there and assured me there was no fever and no infection: "It's healing very well," he said. "I'll look in at him again this evening." Because I did not wish to disturb Robert, I went to sleep in my sitting room, feeling somewhat of an exile, on my mother's bentwood sofa, covered with the afghan I had just completed.

The days that followed: Elizabeth and I and the doctor, together and separately watching over Robert, entreating him to return to his work if only for an hour or so a day, to see a pupil for a short lesson, to come to the dining room for dinner, to take a walk with the dog. And he, refusing, lying collapsed, white, as if wrapped in bonds of unforgiveness; hardly speaking, his sickness not of the wound (which healed quickly) but of the mind, the whole organism. He lost weight, his nightshirt hung upon him, his energy, almost his will to live, seemed gone.

The doctor came every morning to dress the wound. At the end of a week he whispered to me that he was no longer needed, that I could do what he was doing for a few more days and then the bandage would no longer be necessary. "No reason for me to come again, unless there is a change, and then you can send for me."

I hoped the doctor's permanent departure

would persuade Robert of his recovery, but I remember that his invalidism went on long after that. He refused to leave his bed. I had his music room completely rearranged, the ceiling painted, the paper redone, and the piano taken apart on the premises, without moving it, and cleaned by two men from the Steinway plant. I kept him informed of each stage in the transformation and the cleaning, but it did no good. At last he confessed to me, it was not the room, but the boy, the *boy*. Whenever he thought of returning to the room he saw Master Brewster crouched there, waiting to spring at him. He could not bring himself to go back into that room. I realized then that we had to find other lodgings.

Elizabeth and I visited agents in the area and spoke to them about a farmhouse to rent for the summer. I was given lists of houses to visit in New Hampshire, in northern Massachusetts, and in the upper part of New York State. We hired a touring car for the day and visited the places closest to us, without success. Some of the houses offered were in bad disrepair, others too expensive, and still others inaccessible for a couple without a motorcar. Only at the end of our search did we venture to New York.

The day we found Highland Farm, as it was later to be called, is still vivid to me. Elizabeth and I set out in the early morning to take an omnibus to the train depot, Robert being cared for by our maid in the few days I planned to be away. A block from our lodgings we almost collided with Mrs. Brewster. She looked discomposed. In her poor English, which I barely understood, she explained that she had been on her way to call on Robert and me, to tell us how mortified she was at what had happened between her son and Maestro Maclaren. From her random, rambling words, some of which were in Hungarian, I gathered that Paul had told her only that there had been a bad argument, so serious that he could not return for lessons. "Terrible. Terrible, I am so sorry for it. He too, he will not now touch the piano. He gives it up now, he tells me, never again to study. Can you believe?"

Her eyes filled with tears; she clutched at my arm for understanding. I nodded, and at last brought myself to ask, "How is Paul? Has he recovered from his cold?"

"His cold? Yes, from that, but from his other sickness, no. That will never go."

"His other sickness?"

"The fits, the grand mal, the seizures. Since he was a small baby, and always now, the doctor says."

Shaken, I bade her good-bye and said I hoped she would find another teacher for her talented son. I mentioned that his shoes were still in my kitchen, but she did not seem to hear. On the train to Saratoga Springs I thought of the two musicians, the thin, epileptic boy and the weary, sick maestro who fought with each other, locked together in a mortal madness born of the passion and the weariness of making music.

Part Two

THE FARM

There was no transition. From the first day, Robert loved the house I had leased. He settled into his quarters at one end of the rambling farmhouse and began at once to work. Some of his best music was to be written here. The house stood at the edge of a large farm property, seventy acres of lovely woods and meadows. The original fields, which had once been cultivated, now were almost returned to high weedy places where insects and bees lived and where new birches and maples were beginning a wild reclamation. Our privacy was absolute, the quiet, after Boston, so *loud* that at first we both had to grow used to it.

Everywhere there were fine walks into our own woods. Yet we were not isolated, for the village of Saratoga Springs lay at the foot of our property. Often we would walk into it in the evenings, stopping at the fountain to sip the ugly-tasting, sulfurous, healthy waters. At the center of the village were two large, quite splendid hotels and many small shops which filled to overflowing with visitors in the summer. In August another wave of visitors occupied the great houses on the outskirts. Then the streets were filled with motorcars and horse-drawn carriages as these late arrivals, the fashionable families from Newport and New York, Philadelphia and Baltimore, Charleston and Boston, visited and dined with each other, went to the races, gambled, took the baths, and drank the curative waters.

We had moved to the Farm in May. Our first summer was a delight. We enjoyed the bustle and confusion in the streets after the silence of our Farm, the cosmopolitan air the little village took on instantly with the warm weather. Mingled with well-dressed and sporting person were strange, black-suited, long-haired, ringleted Jews from the East Side of New York who lived for the summer in the boarding houses near the baths. They came, we were told, to drink the sulfur waters they regarded as a valuable diuretic for washing away the winter's accumulated interior impurities.

In August the racetrack became the center

of the village. Everyone, except the Jews, whom I never saw near the track, traveled up Union Avenue for the afternoon sessions. From our veranda (we never went to the races) we could hear the roar of people in the stands as they cheered the takeoff of the horses. And afterward, the paths near us were crowded with persons on foot, on bicycles, on horses, in their new open motorcars, coming away from the race grounds, returning to their hotels, their rented houses, their elaborate homes. It was a colorful, exciting, and somehow open and free place to be after the formal confines of Frankfurt and then Boston.

When the summer was over, we asked the agent to renew our lease for the next full year. In October, Robert wondered if we could afford to buy the property, if indeed it were available for purchase. I made inquiries and found to my delight that it was. "But all this property, Robert. How will we care for it?" I had been remembering the neglected state of our tiny backyard square of grass and shrubs on Mount Vernon Street.

"More to the point," he said, "how will we pay for it all?" His concern for money was theoretical, general. It was I who kept the bank records, the family accounts, saved what I could, recorded the payments for his compositions from orchestras and choral groups, paid the month's bills. He was right to be concerned, however, because now, alas, there were no pupils whose fees might have helped the year's income.

I visited the Saratoga Springs Savings Bank and found its president eager to lend the well-known composer and his wife money to acquire property near his village. Everything we had saved went toward the purchase of Highland Farm. I resolved, as Robert and I signed the ownership deed, that I would find a way to buy the property outright for Robert's protection and security, to pay off the huge mortgage somehow.

After one long winter at the farm, I came to realize that I had romanticized the village from its summer pleasures. Its vitality and interest departed with the summer visitors. Most of the shops closed, and the park band, the bathers, racing enthusiasts, and solemn, pale Jews departed for the cities, taking the life of the village with them. The paths and roads were deserted. Highland Farm was engulfed in oppressive, almost ominous quiet. The silence of the red woods and the yellowing fields was extended into our own almost soundless house.

I found myself alone, more alone, it seemed, than I had ever before been in my life, in a strange place, a large, quiet house, with Robert estranged from everyone by his music. He had resumed his usual schedule. Rarely did I see him before evening, except to take him his late-morning coffee and roll, and his tea in the afternoon. Then, as it had been in Boston, he sat with me at dinner still in the grip of the music he had written during the day, a silent audience to it, his head on one side in its customary listening position. He ate everything served to him, automatically, without seeing or tasting it, I think. Often I would chat desperately to fill the void. He listened politely but rarely responded. He was not rude, I would not wish anyone to think that, he was merely not present.

Guests came from Boston, from New York, even from the Continent, to call upon Robert. I always invited them to stay to dinner, often to stay the night, for the trains to New York and Boston were hard to reach in the evenings. We still did not own a motorcar: Robert felt that we would spend too much time motoring guests if we acquired one. At company dinner, Robert would rally briefly, speak of the world of music as it filtered through to us in the papers, and of his own work. But always, near the end of the meal, his small store of goodwill exhausted, he would sink back into apathy.

It was too late for me to regret the move to the Farm. We had the house and the large acreage. Robert seemed content. I resolved to try to build upon the long silences by going back to my own music. Fortunately, I thought, the house was large, I could practice at one end without disturbing him.

I can now clearly recall the pure, heady

pleasure of that return to serious study. An incentive presented itself, by accident. I discovered one day, when I stopped at the town library to borrow my week's reading, that the librarian had, briefly, sung with an oratorio society in New York. "I am Miss Milly Martino," she said, for that was how she always referred to herself. She learned I was Robert Maclaren's wife, and then she said, "I know so well who your husband is." She told me about her meager musical training, she apologized for it: "I studied voice with a lady in Glens Falls," she said, "a lady who sang at one time in the chorus of La Scala Opera. I left there to go to New York for a while, and then came to work in Saratoga Springs. Since then I have worked alone, at the piano—I do not play very well—with whatever music I can find in the library collection. There is not much."

I see Miss Milly Martino as I write, although it is more than half a century since those winter evenings we played and sang together. She was a strangely shaped, buxom little person made of two great balls of flesh, one upon the other, almost like the snowmen children used to love to erect in the front yards. Her warm, soft-fleshed, well-corseted form I was to see reincarnated, I imagined, many years later in the person of the great soprano Rosa Ponselle, whom I met only once. Miss Milly Martino was much like Ponselle in her rounded contours, her heavy arms and legs, her full red lips and black bright eyes, her shiny black hair. Often I think how close her voice might have come to Ponselle's: ripe, controlled, supple, lovely. Her back, too, was so fleshy it made her look almost humped, a sadly prescient shape, for in later years she had to retire from her post as town librarian because of a disease she had which was later named for its discoverer, Parkinson.

But not yet. I worked hard at the piano after I met Miss Milly. My fingers slowly began to regain their old dexterity, and my love of the piano as a sensual, satisfying instrument, soft and pliable to the touch, returned. Suddenly there seemed not enough time to accomplish all I wanted to do. I walked down into the village to tell Miss Milly Martino I thought we might try an evening together. "It must be at your house," she said. "I unfortunately have no piano now."

"Of course. At our house. Tonight?"

"Delightful. I shall be there at eight."

"A singer from town is coming here tonight. I will try to accompany her," I told Robert at dinner. "Fine. Fine," he said, absently. I don't think he heard what I'd said, for his custom was always to respond to the announcement of a plan with words like that: "Good, good. Fine, fine."

We worked well together, Miss Milly Martino and I. Her soprano was expressive and superbly controlled. Pressed, it could achieve extraordinary power and heights. It seemed to grow, expand, and rise without losing the delicate grain and texture of her middle range. She said she loved above all else to sing Mozart, so that first evening we began with *Così fan tutte*, Dorabella's recitative and aria. My confidence in being able to accompany her increased when I realized her grasp of the subtleties of the music, the firmness with which she attacked the little runs and slips of "Ah, scostati! paventa il tristo effetto." Since moments during my final year with Mrs. Seton I do not remember feeling such delight at being able to achieve with my fingers what my mind told me should be done, at falling back, acknowledging by my diminuendo, by the quiet tones, her right to soar out and over them, as though her voice had triumphed over my accompaniment as well as its own origins and limitations.

At nine o'clock Miss Milly gathered together the music we had been doing. "I must start back before it gets too late. It is quite some distance from here."

"Where do you live?"

"On Phila Street. You go down the hill, and then two squares over from Union Avenue. I board with the Seeleys."

"You have a beautiful voice. I so much enjoyed what we did tonight."

"And I. You play very well."

I walked with her to the door, urging on Paderewski, who had reluctantly agreed to come along, with my knee. The ailing old dog hated to be told to leave the house or the hearth. His trips to the outdoors to perform his bodily needs were always at my prompting. Indeed, at times I remember lifting him over the sill of the front door to help him out.

Miss Milly Martino admired the dog. She asked how old he was, and I told her not so old, really, but he seemed to have gone into middle age when Robert left him behind to return to Europe, and then moved into premature senility upon his return. She thanked me for allowing her to borrow the Mozart score. We arranged to have another time together on Wednesday of the next week. I waited at the open door, watching her start off down the Farm road, the road the town was later to name and register as Maclaren Road, and then I pulled Paderewski back into the house. I held his thick hair at his neck; he was so big, I so small, that my arm almost rested on his back. I was happy, with a new music-filled happiness, and the feeling of pleasure at having found a congenial, talented friend to share it with.

I remember another thought on that evening in November in the year that marked the start of a new century: it was possible to commune with the slow-breathing, warm, soft-haired body of an animal like Paderewski, even to feel his response to one's own contentment. I have had dogs since but none who so perfectly accepted my state of mind as compatible to his, perhaps because his age had made him patient and slow. I wanted the pleasure of that evening to remain, to dally in my head as he lay beside me. I was still able to feel the physical thrill that always rises in me as I listen to the perfect placement of a soprano voice.

When I closed the door behind me, I found Robert in his velvet house coat standing in the hallway, his fists clenched at his sides, his usually pale face red with fury.

"Never again, do you hear?"

"What is it, Robert?"

"The noise. That . . . that screeching. I could not think. I could hardly hear my own playing. There is to be no more of that in this house, Caroline."

He seemed overwrought, on the verge of tears. I took his hand. "Come to bed, Robert. It's late. I had no idea we were so—loud. Next time we'll be quieter. I thought you had finished your work long since."

The next Wednesday was cold and rainy. The fall had turned abruptly to winter, the ground was white and treacherous with the first freezing rain. Much of that day I worried that Miss Milly Martino would not make it across her two squares to Union Avenue and then up the hill to our road.

But she came, the score under her arm wrapped in a piece of oilskin and with it another score from the library, so that we would each be able to read, she said. Her broad felt hat and her coat dripped with rain, her men's overshoes were buckled tightly to her heavy feet. She seemed to be delighted to be back at the Farm. As she took off her wet clothing she told me she had practiced all week and thought she "had" the scene we had started "by heart."

On our way through the house to my sitting room I said, "Tonight we must try to keep our sounds low. Sometimes my husband works late and he is easily disturbed by any sound when he is composing."

"Of course, *of course*." I remember that her high sweet voice almost squeaked with awe. "I've never met him or even seen him. But once I played some of the short pieces of the *Woodland Songs*. Everyone in the village thinks it is a great honor to have him living near by."

We settled ourselves. I began to play the first bars of the aria "Smanie implacabili"... softly. Miss Milly started her "che m'agitate entro quest' anima" in a light, subdued tone. Then, apparently transported by the aria she loved, by the lovely absurdity of Dorabella planning to go mad for the rest

of her life, she struck the high G flat, showing
the Eumenides how to scream with all the
force of her absorption with the music. My
admonition was forgotten. Accurately, elevated, she carried the aria along in that in-
tensity, the music demanding another G flat
and then a third. She was note-perfect: her
flights between were triumphant, she sang
with her whole voice, gaining in power and
lyricism, showing me by the movement of her
sparkling black eyes how much she had
learned during her week of practice.

Robert flung open my door so hard it hit the
sideboard with a crackling sound and swung
back almost into his face. He waved it away.
His voice was shrill.

"Out. Out. Get out. No more of that . . . noise.
Out." His finger pointed at Miss Milly Martino's shoulder, then prodded it as she tried
to move across the room out of his way to
where her overshoes stood. I was afraid he
was going to strike her, but still I could not
move. I sat frozen on the bench. Never do I
remember feeling so angry and so impotent.
I wanted to shield her from this undeserved
indignity, to assure the uncertain, frightened
woman who was stumbling into her damp
india-rubber galoshes and now struggling to
put on her coat, that her voice was beautiful,
her high notes pure joy to listen to as well as
her effortless movement from one phrase to
the next. But I could say nothing. Her mouth

was clamped tight with terror. She scurried about the room, frantically gathering up her things. Immobilized by embarrassment, I could not intervene for her with Robert.

He stood to the side to let her out of the door. She pushed past him, saying nothing. Seated still, I felt as though I was leaving with her, accompanying the heavy, rubbery, clumping sounds as she padded the long length of the halls to the front door, fumbling with the lock—I don't think there was any light in the front hall in those days. Then the snap, the sharp clasp of the door closing behind her, the little click of the lock: I heard it all from the piano bench.

Robert had gone when I returned from my motionless trip to the door with Miss Milly Martino. He had turned down the gas lamp over the piano. I listened again, now to *his* slippered feet crossing the hall to the stairs that went to our room. I remember I sat for some time by that darkened piano, crying from frustration and chagrin. I closed the cover to the keys, thinking how stern and rigid those ivory keys appeared which in my girlhood had seemed soft, endearing, pliable.

The expulsion of Miss Milly Martino was never spoken of by me or by Robert. Of course she never returned: I believe she was badly hurt by Robert's treatment. I wanted to invite her to come again while he was away on tour, but somehow I never did. Sometimes I would

encounter her behind the oak counter at the
library when I called for my week's reading
matter. But we never referred to that evening, not even on the afternoon two weeks
later when I gathered my courage to return
the copy of *Così fan tutte* she had left behind.
Both of us, I suspect, were embarrassed by
our memories of that terrible evening and
preferred to stay safely on the subject of the
weather, the latest indignities to library cop-
ies by schoolchildren, and summer visitors,
whom she always called riffraff.

A few years later I saw that she tried to
disguise the growing palsy of her hand by
holding her right wrist with her left hand as
she stamped the date on the library card. But
often she could not manage to insert the card
into its tight little pocket at the back of the
book. The townspeople, who had grown fond
of the quiet, cheerful, fat little woman, would
reach out quickly to perform the task for her.
The library's withdrawal records became il-
legible. Dates were stamped at perilous slants
one on top of the other. Friends of the library
took up a collection to help Miss Milly retire.
I recall that I requested the Maclaren Foundation to send a contribution.

But I never heard Miss Milly sing again,
and after her retirement I never saw her. In
a few years, she went to stay at a boarding-
house for the sick where, a friend, Sarah
Watkins, reported to me, she was a sensible,

cheerful patient. Even after her faltering head had to be held at the chin by a broad scarf attached to the uprights of the chair in which she always sat, she could be heard, on occasion, singing snatches of what my informant said she took to be opera.

The first five years of this century: I must tell you about them in summary, because I confess the details have amalgamated in my memory into one continuous year. Robert wrote much, and well, in those years. He was awarded honorary degrees, his music was praised in the columns of *Music*, the *Courier*, in the English *Musical Times*, and in the large city newspapers. He was away often in the spring and the fall, playing and conducting his work with orchestras in New York, in Boston, in Charleston, and as far west as Cleveland. He would return tired out by the long railway trips between cities, for he was unable to sleep in the Pullman cars. Twice he went abroad, but I did not accompany him: the fees offered him for concerts were not sufficient to allow both of us to travel.

But during the long, hard New York State winters at the Farm we were alone together, except for the dog and the groundsman, Edward Collins, who kept our paths and roads clear, and the maid from the village, Ida, who came to do the household chores. Robert followed his usual routine rigorously, seven days a week. I "kept" the house, as we used to say, and prepared a lunch (Robert ate no breakfast and made his own cup of chocolate at six in the morning when he started his work), which I left at his closed study door. After my own lunch I rested and then walked into the village, to the greengrocer's or the butcher shop, which remained open in the winter, and sometimes to the bake shop if Ida had not made enough sweet rolls and cakes to satisfy Robert's passion for such things.

Yes, the days I was able to fill. I made a friend, by chance, the wife of a retired Hamilton College professor. She was about thirty, I think, fashionable, alert, and charming to look at. She loved to talk. I must confess I had grown hungry for talk. In our long conversations in her house in the afternoons over tea, I felt a comfortable connection to the trivial, friendly world I had thought I had lost during my life with Robert. I enjoyed listening to Sarah Watkins, for that was the name of the second wife of Professor Gordon Lyman Watkins. I felt ill at ease only when I became aware of my own lack of contribution to the talk.

Sarah would rattle on in her light-headed way, often humorous and sometimes wry and regretful, about her days—and her nights— with the Professor, as she usually referred to him. My days and nights, indeed, years, were composed of solitude and stillness. I had little I could add to her absorbing narratives. Awake, Robert and I lived at opposite ends of a large house, so that the sounds of my housekeeping, my "puttering," as Robert called it, would not carry into his study. He could not bear to hear talk before he began his day of composing. He said it sent him off in the wrong direction, colliding with and dispelling the usable silence of the early morning. In that silence, he said, he found the beginnings of melodies.

Sarah's confidences were about her husband's habits and practices, his failings and wrongs to her. She had no discretion; she never seemed to feel she owed him any loyalty, and perhaps I was wrong in so openly relishing her revelations about him. But I was lonely. I needed her chatter and her friendship, so I listened, feeling that her strange stories filled the void in my life.

As I came to think of him (seldom was he present in the afternoon room when I was there; usually he was in the shed at his woodworking bench), he was a fool, a figure of fun who, I imagined, fumblingly tried to love his younger wife and to live with her peacefully despite his elderly habits. He hoped to content her with mild caresses, with the bristling, wet brush of his heavy gray mustache on her cheek. Holding her teacup in one hand, she would lean across to me, making circles in the air with her slender fingers:

"The Professor likes me to come to bed in my chemise. He plays endlessly with the ribbons, he rubs them and fondles them. He touches my ... my ... bosom through the cloth. Never underneath, isn't that odd? His hands are roughened now from all the woodworking he does. His nails are so long they curl over the edges of his fingers. I can feel them through the cloth."

I would listen, wondering why she brought these details of the private bed into the sunny room, while I ...

"The Professor likes to stroke me with his tongue. He uses it in the dark as we lie together, in all the chambers of my ears, and in other places which I cannot mention."

I would wait, adding nothing, having nothing to add. Then, perhaps feeling that she had gone too far, revealed too much, she would change the subject and tell me about his hobby, which was carving birdhouses for the gardens and the lawn.

"I understand about the birdhouses with small openings for wrens and little cups for hummingbirds. And the roofed, gabled residences he makes for orioles and cardinals. And the special apartments which he says mourning doves and even owls prefer. But now I think he's gone quite queer: he's made an enormous wheel, the size of a wagon wheel. He made our gardener mount it flat on the roof, for storks. Storks!" she would scream in her light, charming voice. " 'Pelicans, too, and flamingos will be made to feel welcome there,' he tells me, 'and anhingas.'

"He lectures me about birds. 'Do you know,' he tells me, 'that some birds migrate a thousand miles and others only a few hundred feet? So,' he says, 'we must be prepared for the long-distance traveler, like the stork, as well as our friends from Watertown, Lake Champlain, and Bellview Street in Saratoga Springs.' "

All the trees around the Watkins' house, every gable and portico and porch, were hung with accommodations for birds. Professor Watkins, who taught classics before his retirement, had turned his entire attention to a concern for such housing. He told Sarah that often he lay awake thinking of the homeless bird, forced to sleep standing up on its fragile, twiglike legs for lack of a proper resting place. He mourned the apparent homelessness of the grouse: "Think of the grouse, with its heavy feathered feet. It must need a specially soft floor for its domicile." And so he built an elegant, ground-level cabin, lined with plush to spare the grouse further pain.

Professor Watkins' hands had hardened and split at the finger tips. His palms were crossed with healed cuts and rubbed places. The same capable hands that provided for the hotelling of birds turned feeble and foolish when they approached the lightly clad body of Sarah in their conjugal bed.

I write of this not because of Sarah. What, after all, is Sarah (and her curious husband who gave his whole time to the happiness of birds) to the point of my narrative? I write of this because it was to gossip, to such confessional afternoons, that I turned to escape the soundlessness of Highland Farm. Intimately involved in this way with the curiosities of Sarah's life with her husband, I could, for the afternoon, with tea and little cakes on the table before us, escape the blank pages, the empty saga, of my own existence.

Sarah did not always chatter on so, indifferent to her listener. Many times, I am sure, she must have asked how Robert behaved toward me. She waited for admissions from me about my satisfactions, shall we say, the "transports of delight" as they were termed in the fiction of my day. But I could not bring myself to describe the void, the great bed in which Robert and I lay like strangers, his exhausted back to me, his skin seeming to shrink from any contact with me. My life touched his only through the food I prepared and we ate together in the evening, through the accounts and records I kept of his earnings and our expenses, in the hundreds of letters from his admirers and musical friends to which I responded at his direction.

It might be thought—indeed, I have seen

it written somewhere—that the woman who is unawakened to the pleasures of the body, for which she has only uninstructed hopes, feels no physical need or lack. She is said to live in peace with her ignorance and her unfulfillment because she does not know what fulfillment is; nuns in convents are said to be endowed with such good fortune. I know this not to be so. Even Sarah's indelicate little disclosures to me about the Professor's small, feckless, ineffectual doings in their bed awakened warm rushes of feeling in me. There were regions in my body, bird-thin to the eye, arid and meager, that seemed to come alive when I heard about the Professor's fumbling with Sarah's ribbons. Just as, reading of the passionate embraces of men and women in the lending library's novels, of heroines' heaving bosoms as they felt the arms of their lovers around their shoulders, the touch of their fingers, I would respond hotly. My heart would pound. In my thighs, in my chest, at the small of my back there would be sensations I could not explain: warm, exciting, secretly wet.

Why do I write this foolishness? Why do I break now the reserve of three-quarters of a century, except perhaps to insert into the recounting of the history of that five-year span a few of the unspoken and unrecorded details of the heart and the spirit? It is hardly enough to know that a woman was born and lived and married and, in time, died. It seems somehow important to record, beyond the vital statistics, what she yearned for and was refused, what she imagined and did not realize.

And while I am writing of Sarah, and her one-sided confidences in those static, holding years: how many truths of the secret lives of women are lost to history in the still, social afternoon air that hovers between two women as they reveal the small singlenesses of their sex, the behavior of their husbands as lords, as lovers? Quickly said, revealed in a breath, in low tones, even whispers, such special truths are quickly buried and forgotten. And yet they hold more valuable human reality for the searcher after truth than the dates of history and the narratives of the lives and deaths of kings.

I may have told Sarah that I longed for children when she told me she did, but none had come. But I'm certain I never revealed that, since the time of his first serious illness in Saratoga, Robert had no capacity for the conjugal act. We had believed that illness to be a kind of pox, because of the terrible rash. When the scaly patches formed on his back and legs, I finally persuaded him to have the doctor inspect it.

Robert saw him alone in his offices: it was not the pox. The Saratoga Springs physician, Dr. Holmes, did not really know what it could be, Robert reported to me after the examination, but he prescribed a smoothed lump of sulfate of copper to be applied to the afflicted areas. I rubbed them carefully (painfully for poor Robert), but it did no good. Some of the areas became ulcerated and oozed a rank yellow pus. The doctor instructed me to apply a yeast poultice. On the worst places I placed, again at his instruction, a pack of crystals of acetate of soda. Robert would cry out in pain at these applications.

"What is it?" I asked the doctor on the one occasion I was in the examining room with Robert, who had grown weak and nervous under the ailment and could hardly walk alone.

I noticed he looked at Robert speculatively. Robert shut his eyes, and then the doctor said, "It is very hard to say." But the strange rash receded, taking with it his old, occasional desire for me and some of his thick, dark-red hair, which came out on his pillow and his shoulders in broom-like segments. It seemed to me he showed more concern for his loss of hair than for his connubial failure.

None of this did I tell Sarah. Even to myself I have not rehearsed these elements of my marital life, until now. Because to the musical world Robert was a much beloved figure. But this public man, this famous man, was important also to me, who needed private love so much. His indifference and discontent with me seemed at the time of no great moment beside his fame. He was renowned, a talented musician, "a composer of genius," many critics had already written. My contributory existence and auxiliary services, like my small, thin physique, were of no account in his light. History must be full of such alliances between famous men and their satellite, serving wives. Their true persons and their inner lives are rarely known or described in the painful and almost faithless detail I have given here.

And Sarah would go on and on with her logorrheic talk: "He spent this morning making special food for his warblers (although, he said, peregrines were said to be fond of it, too), roasting bread crumbs in the baking oven, and then mixing in the seeds of pumpkins. When I tried to enter the kitchen he told me I would confuse his recipe, so I left him alone. I'm sure he prefers his birds to me. I think he would like to live in a house under the eaves with them if only he could construct one large enough to hold them all.

"One died early this morning. Apparently its neck was broken as it flew head-on into the multiple apartment dwelling that hangs from the back roof. It lay on its side on the floor of the veranda. It was a finch, I think (I don't know the birds well, and I was afraid to ask Gordon). Its purple head was turned entirely backward as though (Gordon said) it had been examining its past in its last moments: a classical bird. Its beak was red with its own blood. The Professor wept and sat still on the veranda all morning looking at it and would not pick it up to dispose of it, and its blood sank into the wood. I sent the maid to him and he told her, politely, mournfully, to go away. I think he's quite mad.

"Did I tell you that last summer he discovered there were pigeons living in our attic above the maids' quarters? The maids said they would not stay if they were not removed. But the Professor lectured them, told them the pigeons had come there to find a shelter against the neglect and cruel treatment by the villagers, who find them dirty and offensive and try to poison them. Once I found him on the stairs climbing to the attic carrying a loaf of freshly baked bread and one of my down pillows. He said, 'They are nesting.'

"They are still there, although in the winter they seem quieter. One maid left in August, saying birds over her head frightened her. The other two, I think, have grown used to the rush of wings and the scratchings of feet and beaks on the boards above their heads.

"Flight. That is all he now talks to me about. *Mad!* Only organisms capable of flight are entirely alive, he believes. Walking creatures, weighted to the earth, are half dead, their feet turned and moving one after the other down into the full, dry dirt of the grave. 'Flight,' he says, 'is life, the climate and reminder of eternity, of ascent, not deathly descent, of triumph over the Fall. Not until men fly,' he says, 'will they be immortal. Some insects and birds are without mortal restraints. I have studied them, day and night. I know.'

"Nastily, I asked him about the dead finch, despising him and his madness and wanting, I suppose, to hurt him, to strike at his crazy creed.

"He never listens to me, he never hears me. He doesn't answer."

I go on too long about Sarah. But her stories about the Professor (who died peacefully in his sleep, I remember, at the age of eighty-six, long after Sarah had drowned in Lake George, thrown from a boat during a storm, they said) occupied and entertained me in those years. She introduced me to the life of the town, and through her I made friends with a few wealthy summer residents who came for the races: Anne Rhinelander, Cecily Lorillard, the Leland sisters, Emily Chisolm. They were later to form the core of the Maclaren Foundation, from which the Community grew. I have always been grateful to poor Sarah for that, and pitied her for her ripe, charming middle age wasted upon an aging, obsessed husband. I have always held to the private belief that she drowned herself, went downward into the cold blue water of Lake George to escape the Professor, or to provide him with further proof of his aeronautical metaphysics. But of course I do not know.

On the thirtieth day of August, 1904, Paderewski died. I will never be able to eradicate the memory of that day.

He was twelve years old, but for him it was extreme old age. He seemed to have come to it long before his appointed canine span. His sight had almost gone under the weight of cataracts in both eyes, we were told. His last months were noisy. His body was subject to attacks of ague. During them his trunk would shake, and his tail, independently agitated, would thump hard against the bare floor where he always lay because he hated the heat and texture of our oriental rugs. Most of the day he slept, breathing heavily, each long, hard breath ending with a penetrating snort, often so loud that it could be heard in the rooms at the other side of the house.

His nights were sleepless. We were never able to discover what disease it was that aged him so early and drove him so inexorably into senility and sickness. Sometimes in his deep internal distress, he would hoist himself painfully onto his thin legs and withered paws and move about the dark house, walking almost blindly, stumbling into chiffoniers and chairs, sideboards, and piano legs.

What was he searching for in those black rooms among the lifeless dark furniture, down at the edges of the tasseled heavy drapes? Was it Robert, the young, brisk, charming man with loving hands and bright smile, the soft, cocked way of listening, the gentle, amorous voice? I do go on here unpardonably, but I, too, remember Robert in this way. He had long ago exiled the aged dog to my quarters because his heavy, long-haired pelt gave off an odor not unlike mold and was offensive to him. Paderewski's pounding tail and snores during the day were disturbing to his work.

I have said it was late August, a very hot summer noon. The air was heavy, oppressive, with the promise of rain. My rooms, so close to the eaves over the south end of the house, were warm; it was hard to breathe the thick, still air. I thought I would walk out into the woods that stretched behind the house. Deep within them were cool, pine-walled, and needle-carpeted pockets, almost small rooms, where I used to sit in the months of the heat to read.

Paderewski was asleep, as usual, on the stone floor before the hearth. I remember starting out, and then returning for a shawl to sit upon. I don't remember, but yes, I must have done so: I left the side door ajar. Robert was certain that I had. He told me I had become forgetful, and perhaps he was right. It was from being alone so much, I came to believe, and having no markers, no hitching posts, in the long silences for my memory to fasten upon. But I do remember I was gone two hours during the hottest part of the noon and after. When I returned to my room, Paderewski was not in his sleeping place.

I searched the downstairs, knowing he could not have climbed the stairs. Desperate to find him, I disturbed Robert in the only place I had not been, the music room. Robert was resting on his couch at that hour, his eyes closed. But he was not asleep.

"Of course he is not here," he said, sounding irritated. I knew he hated to be disturbed during the day. He once told me he listened in his head, during his afternoon rest, to what he had written that morning. But he was upset enough at Paderewski's disappearance to come outside in his shirt sleeves to help me search.

We walked around the house, calling his name. Never, until that day, had that tributary name seemed so unsuitable for a dog. To be calling for a renowned, middle-aged pianist in the steaming Saratoga woods: I felt foolish. But he was nowhere near the house. We started to walk down the long, dusty Farm road—the road that was later to be given Robert's surname by an edict of the town council. But I think I may have already written this.

We rounded the bend in the road from

which it is possible to see the avenue beyond. Coming toward us were two men, carrying on a board between them what we could tell at once was the bloodied fur and crushed head of Paderewski. They were evidently summer visitors. Their straw boaters, white duck trousers, and striped linen jackets marked them apart from the native men who rarely dressed this way in midafternoon. Robert ran ahead to them.

"What happened?"

"Is this your dog?" one man asked.

"Yes. Yes."

The man—we were later to learn his name was Henry Huddleston Rogers—his face troubled and solemn, said, "It was entirely my fault. Entirely. I did not see him standing in the road until the horses were almost upon him. I shouted. I tried to rein them in, but it was too late. I am entirely to blame. What can I say?"

Robert seemed stunned, yet ready to agree with the poor contrite fellow, I thought. I intervened: "No. Don't think that. He never leaves the house. He must have wakened and been confused by a dream, or something like that. He's never done this before. Usually I've had to half carry him out." I knew I was rattling on foolishly.

"Oh, be still, Caroline."

Robert pushed me aside. He lifted the dead dog from the board into his arms, staggering under the weight. Somehow he managed to turn and walk back to the house, bearing Paderewski in his arms.

The man who had not spoken tipped his hat to me and started back down the road to the avenue, carrying the blood-stained board.

Mr. Rogers said, "This is terrible. I wish I could do something."

In the distance we could hear the roar of the crowd. Down the hill at the track the first race of the afternoon must have started.

"I'm Mrs. Maclaren."

"The composer's wife?"

"Yes."

"Oh, I'm so terribly sorry for this. That must have been the ... your husband. This is terrible. Will you tell him again how sorry I am?"

"I will. But don't blame yourself. The dog was old and almost blind." I put my hand out. "Good-bye, Mr. ...."

"Rogers."

"Mr. Rogers. Good-bye."

I almost ran back. Robert had taken the massive burden into the house: the front door was open and there was a light smear of blood on the middle panel where he must have brushed against it. I found them in the music room. Robert had put the dog down on the top of the closed piano, where he lay, already stiffened, his blind eyes opened to a new dark, his once-handsome coat suffused and beaded with blood and dust. Around him the piano cover, at that time, I remember, a fringed shawl I had brought back from Frankfurt, lay in contrasting splendor to the mangled Paderewski. Already he seemed to have shrunken, a mass of confused hair, paws, ears. Only his fine long narrow aristocratic muzzle remained intact.

Robert insisted on keeping him there for one whole day. I was reminded of Professor Watkins and his finch. Uncharitably, I thought of how anachronistic his attention to the dead dog was: for several years he had not allowed the animal in that room. Robert did not work the rest of that day but walked about the room, his hands behind his back, circling the piano, his eyes often on the now redolent carcass. I mourned Paderewski alone in my room, remembering all the haptic pleasures of that silken fur, the firm softness of his long, sleek, sensitive head and ears and nose.

Robert was more silent than ever at dinner that evening, and I suppose I, too, was absorbed in my own grief. I was full of it, ready to break down at the thought of losing the companion of my solitude, my walks and rests, in all those years since Germany.

On the second day Robert called our groundsman, Edward Collins, to remove the dog. Edward had dug a grave on a grassy little hill at the far end of the property. He brought a wooden box he had made to convey the body in. Robert would not watch the removal and conveyance. He refused to see Paderewski buried. I followed the farm wagon to the grave and stood at the side of the small, deep trench as Edward put the box into it, covered it with dirt and placed squares of sod over the raw spot.

"Will we want a marker for it, ma'am?"

"I'll ask Mr. Maclaren tonight what he wishes done."

"Very good."

But somehow Robert and I never mentioned Paderewski to each other again. Ida told me she had been unable to remove the bloodstains from Robert's shirt even after three washings, so I gave the shirt to Edward, who seemed very glad to have it. Robert did not ask after it. The piano shawl had to be disposed of.

The grave was never marked. I walked often to the place after that. From it there was a lovely view of the Adirondacks to the west, and the wooded hills of Highland Farm on the other side. I thought Robert had forgotten the place—he rarely walked that way alone that I was aware of, and surely never with me. But he must have remembered it. For later, in a cubbyhole in his desk, Anna Baehr found a small piece of staff paper on which he had written:

Bury me on the knoll near my dog,
Paderewski

We did. Robert lies there now. We did not disturb the small box Edward uncovered when he dug Robert's grave. The granite marker, elaborate and imposing, was put in place by the Maclaren Foundation in the years when it had the money to do that sort of thing. It is imposing, with Robert's name and dates, and my name and birth date. Only the final date is missing. Soon it, too, will be chiseled into the stone. Then we shall both lie beside our dog.

The letter said:

> *The trustees and the President of Columbia University are pleased to inform you that the University wishes to bestow upon you the honorary degree of Doctor of Humane Letters at the Commencement on June 5, 1905,*

and went on to give the details of the time and the arrangements that would be made for the comfort of those to be honored.

Robert showed it to me at dinner one evening and wondered if he ought to go. "Of course you must go. It is a great honor. You will enjoy yourself, and it's been so long since we have been to the city."

"But, Caroline, so long a trip? How will we travel? How much time will we have to spend in New York?" He was full of anxiety, his voice so low I could hardly hear him.

"A week, perhaps. Oh, Robert, you will enjoy it, I'm sure. We can hear some music and visit the galleries. Some of your former pupils live there, and your friends, friends from Hoch and Boston. Churchill teaches at Columbia. We can see him. Oh, Robert, let's go."

I watched him struggle to decide. He seemed worn out and very tired: The dog's death has diminished him, I thought. His work, all the copying it required, seemed to take him longer and longer, he stopped earlier than he used to. More and more often when I came to call him to dinner I would find him stretched out on his couch, exhausted. Lately, he said, he would lie down to rest at three. When I came at six, he was still there, inert and half-asleep.

How old and frail he looked to me now! His hair was more gray than russet, and very sparse. After that strange illness it had never returned to its full, thick, youthful growth. No trace of the old, charming smile remained, for he never smiled now. Looking at him, I was reminded of Paderewski, for Robert was like him: prematurely old at thirty-three, spent and lusterless, a used-up man.

Our preparations for the trip took almost a week, the packing of the grips, the arrangements made for a landau to convey us to the railroad depot in Saratoga Springs, the purchase of our tickets. For Robert it would have been a wearying series of chores, so I spared him everything but his actual presence at the departure. For me it was a great delight.

The season was just beginning. The arriving trains were full of stylish-looking visitors. Outside the depot the roads were crowded with omnibuses, dogcarts, and phaetons waiting to take travelers to the Grand Union and the United States hotels. I remember that the bells in the depot cupola rang as a train approached or departed. Robert disliked the racket and cringed against the terrible noise, but I enjoyed it all: the bells, the sounds of cars and horses, the shouts of Negro porters, train whistles, all making a fine cacophony of active, alive sounds.

We took a Pullman room. But Robert hardly slept. I stayed awake with him while he went over and over his short acceptance speech. He was trying to commit the ten sentences to memory, but he seemed unable to do it. I felt an uneasy surprise at this, at Robert who, a few years ago, could conduct the Brahms *Fourth* and the Beethoven *Seventh* symphonies together in one evening's program without the scores.

In those agonizingly long hours, traveling through the dark state along the Hudson River, past the dim, sleeping river towns (for Robert would not permit me to draw the shades over the windows: he said he felt very

confined in the small room allotted to us), I
realized for the first time how much he had
failed. In our house at the Farm surrounded
by familiar objects and secluded by the custom and routine of our quiet lives, I had not
noticed, or perhaps I had not looked closely.
My own days and nights were of an unchang-
ing sameness which I must have extended to
his. Now in this unfamiliar, moving place I
could see how far down he had gone. Can I
be blamed for my blindness? When he was
sick he would not tell me until it was una-
voidable, as though there was a shame in
admitting to bodily weakness. And even
then, he resisted having a physician called
to see him. He must have hidden his symptoms and his debility to have grown so old,
so quickly, so soon.

I had written ahead. In the morning,
among the crowds of persons milling around
the Grand Central Station, we found Churchill Weeks and his wife, Catherine. They were
at the barrier to meet us, to arrange with the
porters for our baggage, to take us to our hotel, which on that occasion was the Chelsea.
Catherine, whom we knew only slightly, said
nothing. It seemed to me she found our arrival a trial, as though she were not accustomed to such heavy responsibilities. She was
a thin, neurasthenic, almost flat woman
whose body seemed concave at the front. Her
brown hair was pulled tightly back from her

thin face and fastened at the nape of her neck in the style of those days. She had the look of someone waiting always for something unpleasant to happen, always expecting a repellent flavor as she looked at her food. When she spoke to her husband her voice was sharp and impatient as though his very presence was an annoyance to her. Try as I might for Churchill's sake and Robert's, I could not like her.

In our rooms at the hotel Churchill said, "We'll leave you now. You must be tired from the long journey. Is there anything we can do to make you more comfortable before we go?"

"We are expected to lunch with the faculty at twelve sharp, Churchill," said Catherine, in her rough, edgy midwestern voice.

"Nothing. Nothing at all, thank you," said Robert. "You are very good." He spoke as though he had not heard the asperity in Catherine's voice, and perhaps he had not. His own voice was distant and weary. He smiled at Churchill his half-smile, his eyes lighting up as he looked at his friend. "We will rest and perhaps take a walk and wait for you to come."

Churchill had looked at Catherine as though he were preparing to strike her, but when Robert spoke, he smiled at him. For one moment, I thought, the old ineffable love seemed to hover in the air between them. Neither sharp Catherine nor birdlike Caroline was present to them.

Catherine stared stonily at her husband. I thought, What a strange marriage this is, without even the pretense of civility before others. Or perhaps I was oversensitive to the import of the looks they exchanged and to the overtones of her words, because my own marriage had no resonances except for the echoes of wordlessness. It must have been that.

They left us. Robert lay down on the bed and slept almost at once. I lay beside him, careful not to disturb him by my motion, listening to his almost silent breathing and hearing beyond the hotel windows (we were on the second floor, we never stayed above the second floor, because Robert was afraid of fire and so feared to sleep in a room on a higher floor) the continuous roiling sound of traffic on the street below, and the shouting, and the clanging of wagons and motorcars. I felt exhilarated to be in a city.

At six o'clock the Weekses returned, but Robert had decided he would prefer not to venture out for the promised dinner. So Churchill arranged with the hotel to bring to our room a lavish set of covered dishes on a moving table, a service I had never before seen provided for guests in America. I enjoyed it all hugely, as did Churchill, who talked a great deal to Robert of the pleasures of living in New York, of teaching piano and harmony

and composition in a university where an
academic department devoted to the study of
music had just been established. Robert smiled,
nodded assent, but spoke very little. I listened. Catherine, as I recall, said nothing.

The morning of Commencement Day was
beautiful, cool, and clear. We traveled by trol-
ley car along Broadway to Morningside
Heights and walked through the great gates
to the new Seth Low Library to meet the president, Mr. Nicholas Murray Butler. Weeks
was there with other faculty members from
the department of music. I was given a ticket
to the chairs set up at the foot of the library
steps. When I found my place, there was
Catherine Weeks. I sat beside her. She asked
after Robert's condition and seemed to wish
to explore the subject of his apparent ill
health (it is uncharitable of me, but I felt she
was the kind of sour woman who enjoyed the
spectacle of other people's misfortunes). But
before I was required to say very much, the
music—trumpets and horns—started. We rose
to our feet to attend the glittering procession
of garbed professors and students. Walking
near the head was Robert, looking pallid and
gaunt in his black academic mortarboard
with a gold tassel falling before his eyes. He
wore a handsome blue robe decorated with
the crowns of King's College, for so this uni-

versity had been named at its inception, I read in the engraved program handed to me when I entered. Robert's forehead was wet with perspiration; I was sorry he had insisted on dressing in his old but still fine German suit. He was going to be very warm up there, I thought.

I sat through the opening of the ceremony feeling very hot, too, for the sun was beating down on us at that hour. I felt uneasy for Robert. Always before, as I had waited in audiences for him to perform or conduct, I was confident, knowing well his perfect control, his quiet command of all his powers. But after the night in the railway car my confidence was shaken. How would he *do*?

At last—it seemed to me a very long wait in that hot sun—President Butler rose to read the awards of honorary degrees. I was delighted that Robert's was read first. The citation was glowing and effusive. "Robert Glencoe Maclaren is one of America's great composers. He has turned his excellent European training to the service of American music, American themes and subject matter. America's Orpheus, he has been called by one critic, and his future," read President Butler from a parchment scroll, "promises to be as distinguished as have been the short years of his already eminent career. He is a man whose thirty-three years of life are studded with world-recognized accomplishments."

I watched Robert, seated in the front row on the platform, as the president read. He was looking straight ahead into the audience, listening perhaps, but somehow I felt he did not hear what the president was reading. The president stopped, there was applause. Mr. Butler looked over at Robert, expecting him to rise and come forward. The audience applauded loudly, but Robert did not rise. I saw a professor seated behind him lean over to shake his arm and whisper something. Robert seemed to awaken, looked back at the red-gowned man behind him, nodded his head slightly, and stood up. Then, to my horror, he turned and walked away from where President Butler stood, making his way carefully toward the steps at the opposite end of the platform.

A murmur went through the audience. I could feel myself covered by a red flood of embarrassment and heat. What could I do? Nothing but sit on my camp chair and watch my poor confused husband wander in the wrong direction, away from his honor, in front of hundreds of graduates and parents, professors, and the president of the university.

President Butler was quick-witted. A vigorous man in his early forties, he had only recently taken over his eminent position. At that terrible moment he seemed capable of dealing efficiently with anything, even so eccentric a situation as this. He strode briskly the length of the platform, while everyone else sat, frozen. He reached Robert and took his arm just as he was about to descend the steps and leave the platform. He pulled him back, turned him around, and, with wonderful tact that made what he was doing seem normal ceremonial procedure, pushed him gently ahead, in the right direction, inching him toward the podium.

Robert then seemed to remember what it was he had to do. He reached into the inner pocket of his hot woolen suit and brought out the sheet of paper on which I had printed for him in large block letters the words of his speech. While the president discreetly sat down behind him, Robert began to read in his low, musical voice.

I relaxed a little, although by now my dress was suffused with perspiration and my handkerchief could no longer contain the moisture from my forehead and hands. No, I thought, it will be all right. Beside me, Catherine shifted in her seat. In my apprehensive state I took her movement to be a tart comment of some kind on what had just taken place on the platform.

Robert came to the last line. He read it slowly, distinctly. A low swell of applause began to grow on the platform and in the audience, but it died abruptly when Robert's voice went on. Dear God! I realized he had

begun at the opening sentence and was reading the whole first paragraph again! I was
overcome with horror, hearing the low murmur around me. I wanted to rush up to the
platform and rescue him, stop the solemn
proceedings and take Robert home to the
Farm where he would be safe from the world's
knowledge.

But again the clever president assessed the
situation quickly. He half rose from his seat
as Robert once again came to his final sentence of gratitude, and when it was horrify-
ingly clear that he was about to begin a third
reading, President Butler was at his elbow,
taking his hand firmly in his two hands and
shaking it, saying something to him very low
that I could not hear. Robert stopped reading
and turned to the president in confusion,
seeming not to recognize him. But he was
silent, at last. The audience was now enthu-
siastically applauding my poor oblivious husband, as the president led him back to his
seat while appearing merely to be politely
escorting him. How grateful I was, sitting
below in a bath of fright and heat, for the
president's intelligence and his quick thinking.

The rest of the afternoon I remember quite
clearly, for much of it I was now able to enjoy.
Luncheon was served in wicker baskets to us
and to the graduates and their parents and
friends. Numbers of persons shook Robert's

hand and asked him if he remembered them. To each he nodded, said "Yes," and smiled his weak, gentle half-smile. But I could tell he remembered none of them. He held my arm, or Churchill's, during the hour that followed the luncheon, acknowledging the faculty members who spoke to him of their admiration for his music. He nodded, giving them each a wordless, childlike smile, sweet and vacant.

No mention was made by anyone of the debacle on the platform. It seemed to have been accepted and forgotten, regarded as the eccentric, absentminded behavior of a genius. Only I knew better.

The Weekses had arranged tickets for us for a music-hall entertainment that evening. The variety show was a theatrical experience Robert had loved since a boy. Often he had spoken to Churchill when they were studying in Germany, and later to me, of a variety star he had seen in Boston, Della Fox, a wonderfully beautiful, plump, girlish singer, as he described her to me. By fortunate chance it happened that she had decided to return to the vaudeville stage, which was now very popular, during the weekend we were to be in New York. Churchill was kindness itself. He had obtained four tickets for Della Fox's third appearance, on Sunday evening, the evening of the Columbia Commencement, after her scheduled opening on Friday.

Robert was excited, awakened from the trancelike state he had been in during the ceremony by the prospect of seeing and hearing Della Fox again. We sat in midafternoon under the great elms on the campus, cooler now, with Churchill and Catherine. Robert was better. He talked more than he had since we left the Farm.

"I simply cannot wait. I remember, it must have been when I came back on a visit almost twenty years ago—could it have been that long ago, Church?"

"I think so, Rob. The newspaper account said she had been retired for almost twenty years."

"Twenty years! She was my idol, my dream, my ideal woman when I was, what was I? Fourteen? I must have been. She sang in a small but pure soprano. The *Police Gazette* called her 'la petite Fox.' Do you remember ever seeing her, Church?"

Catherine stared at her husband. He blushed, and then admitted gallantly, I thought, to Robert, that yes, he remembered hearing about Della Fox.

Robert went on: "I removed her picture from the *Gazette*. And my mother found it in my room and destroyed it. But I see Della Fox in my mind's eye so clearly. She is small and blond, very blond, with small blond curls. She dressed differently from the other musical stars of those days. They wore spangles, and pinched-in stays and tights. But Della wore a white satin man's suit—trousers and vest and jacket and cravat, even a white yachting cap with a small visor that sat jauntily on her curls. Her eyes were deep, sparkling blue, and she was delicate, very delicate, yet—yet full-bodied, do you know? Do you know what I'm trying to say, Church?"

Churchill smiled at him, ignoring what I took to be his wife's evident displeasure at Robert's nostalgic flights, for she was looking sternly, unsmiling, at her husband.

"She is magnificent, Rob, I'm sure. I cannot wait to see her."

Robert continued: "And I remember, as clearly as if it were yesterday, the song she always sang as she lounged against a table, with her leg thrown over it so the audience could see her ankle. Something like ... shady brook? Yes—'Shady brook, babbling brook, and now serenely mellow,' " he sang in his fine low tenor.

Churchill joined in. The two men sang the verses of the foolish little song to the end. People seated near us on the grass applauded and laughed, and the two men looked dismayed at having been so carried away. Churchill gracefully acknowledged the gentle applause by tipping his straw hat. Robert, flushed, looked away, but I could tell he was pleased. It had been so long since he had come out of himself, enjoyed himself in that way.

Then Churchill said, "One caution, Rob. I read in the *Sun* last evening that Della Fox's first two performances had to be canceled because she was ill. I'm hoping that won't be the case tonight, but we won't know until we get downtown to the theater and see if the bills are posted out front. But there are six other acts if she doesn't appear."

Robert was still transported into his past and did not seem to hear Churchill's warning. "She smoked, onstage! I can see her now, leaning back, reaching into her white jacket pocket for her little silver case, opening it, putting a cigarette into her mouth and lighting it. She breathed out a ring of smoke and looked at us all in the audience with those deep blue eyes, as though she dared us to disapprove. Never had I seen so—so seductive an act. She was charming, performing what was forbidden in full view.

"I see her still, standing there, her leg swung across the edge of the table—another charmingly illicit act—all that delicious femininity encased in that white suit, blowing smoke rings at the audience and singing. Della Fox..."

We all laughed at Robert—all but Catherine, who stared at the table during his elegiac reminiscence. In that moment he looked

almost young and eager. I could imagine him
reaching out with his hot boy's hand toward
a mythic goddess of incredible allure. It was
so good to see him like this again. I was impatient for the evening's entertainment.

We dined with the Weekses in their apartment on Fifty-seventh Street, a long, dull
meal with too many hot rolls and heavy
brown gravy for the beef. We finished with
pie made, it seemed, of leaden apples. (How
is one able to remember the details of un-
memorable meals such as this one? It must
have been the happenings of the evening that
fastened these trivial matters forever in my
mind.) At dinner Robert was quiet but pleasant. He watched Churchill carve the roast
most capably and pour the Médoc, admiring,
I could tell, his skill with the knife and the
cork. At one point, I remember, he hummed
"Shady Brook," and we all listened, and then
laughed.

There was much talk of the old days, in
Paris and in Frankfurt. Only once was there
a break in the pleasant tenor of the supper.
When Churchill mentioned their beloved
teacher Joachim Raff, rehearsing the details
of his sudden death, Robert's eyes filled with
tears that ran down his cheeks. Catherine
looked away while Robert searched his pockets for a handkerchief. When he could not
find it, Churchill passed his. We all waited

for Robert to regain control.

Churchill said it was time. We walked down Broadway to the Lyceum Theatre. For me it was exciting to see the city in the evening light, spread, unbelievably, upward, and glistening in the clear air. I held Robert's arm and felt almost gay and young again, wishing we could preserve the exhilaration of that evening, wishing we could recapture the pleasures of the early days when we walked together on the Common, with Paderewski encircling us with his leash and drawing us together...

The marquee that jutted out over the sidewalk was lighted. A small crowd of persons gathered under it. Churchill smiled with pleasure when he saw the bills posted on both sides of the door:

VARIETY PROGRAM

Great Star of Yesteryear

Beauteous DELLA FOX

Songs! Her Famous Repertoire!

SIX OTHER ENTERTAINING ACTS

Tonight at 8

Under the corner of the bill on the right
side of the entrance was a picture of Della
Fox in her famous white suit, looking much
as Robert had described her: a small, plump,
pink and white, full-breasted young woman,
jaunty and fresh-faced.

Our seats were close to the front of the
orchestra in recognition, I guessed, of what
Churchill had remembered of Robert's boyish
passion. I wondered if we were not too close.
We seemed to be seated almost directly above
three shabby-looking musicians in the orchestra pit, now trying out their instruments
in a peculiar cacophony.

"No. We'll see well here," said Robert. He
was in a state of high excitement. All his
morning's weariness and disorientation had
vanished. Like a child, he seemed hardly able
to wait for the curtain to rise. He applauded
when the musicians, now somewhat more together, began the notes of "Shady Brook."
The rest of the audience was quiet. Unself-
consciously, Robert clapped alone.

After a long introduction, which consisted
of a medley, I assumed, of Della Fox's "hits,"
the theater was darkened and a spotlight
opened upon the left side of the stage. The
curtain went up on a set vaguely designed to
resemble the interior of a dilapidated cabaret. The spotlight hovered uncertainly around
the wings, the music repeated its themes, the
pause, in which nothing happened, seemed

to stretch interminably. And then she entered.

I can recount what I saw that evening, for
my memory of it is still very clear. The white
suit, the white cap, yes, they were still there.
But stuffed into them, straining every seam
and thread, was a monstrously fat little
woman. Her great girth made her seem ab-
normally short. Once onstage, she hesitated
uncertainly, dazed by the bright light. Then
she wandered toward the center of the stage,
her small feet appearing too slight to bear all
that gross weight. She smiled at the audience, a foolish, idiot-child smile with her red
bowed lips minute in her huge powdered face,
and patted the white button at the top of her
cap as though to be sure it was still there.
Then she waved to the musicians in the pit
that she was ready to begin. That gesture,
grand and silly, gave away her state: she was
profoundly, completely drunk.

After two false starts, during which either
Della Fox or the little orchestra was out of
step, she began to sing. Her voice was tiny.
She sounded as though it were being squeezed
out of her mammoth chest, issuing from between her bubble-like cheeks. She forgot the
words, sang "la la de la de la" in their placce,
grimaced, fluttered her little fat fingers in
the dim air in front of her, and then tottered
over to the cabaret table at the right of the
stage.

Now the famous act, I thought. But it was not to be. Della Fox made a gallant effort to raise one great leg, packed tight into the trouser, over the corner of the table, but failed. Instead, still singing in her little high-pitched tuneless voice, a measure behind the pianist in the pit, she crossed her ankles and fumbled for the famous cigarette. The silver box gleamed in the spotlight. Trying gamely to open it, she dropped it and it struck the steps a distance from her. The little dance she did, half-bent from the waist, made it clear that she would not be able to pick it up.

I glanced across at Catherine Weeks. For the first time all day she was smiling. Robert's eyes were closed.

"Let's get out of here," Churchill whispered, leaning across both of them. We walked up the aisle. I could hear the boos, the whistles, laughter, and shouts of insults from the gallery. People were already ahead of us in the aisle, on their way to the box office, I was sure, to have their admittance money returned to them.

Robert stopped outside to look at the picture of Della Fox on the poster, at the tiny dimpled creature whose young innocent eyes sparkled even in the old, poor photograph. In her shining man's suit, smoke curling about her piquant face, she was indeed, as she had been all those years in Robert's memory, a lovely creature.

"We should have known. I should have known," said Robert. "How could it have been otherwise? All those years."

Churchill, looking as though he were responsible for the whole fiasco, felt he had to lighten Robert's spirits. "Well, Rob, look at us. We're not what we were, either, if you examine us closely."

Robert put his hand on Churchill's still black hair and ruffled it a little. "Perhaps so," he said in the absent way he had of talking of the past, "but I think you look very well, Church." He hesitated, and I wondered if he might be thinking of his lapse of the morning. "I'm more like poor Della Fox. Old. Forgetful. Decayed. All too soon." He paused. Then he took my arm in his accustomed way when he was tired, and said in a whisper that I'm certain only I heard, "Lost."

That was almost the last, perhaps even the last, of the good times, for him. In our few remaining days in New York we heard the Aeolian String Quartette at Carnegie Hall play one of Robert's early quartets, the third, Opus 12, I think it must have been. We walked about in Central Park, we dined at Rumpelmayer's with Adolph Burmeister and his wife. Adolph and Robert had been in Frankfurt together. Now Adolph played in the string section of the New York Symphony Society.

From that dinner we came back early to the hotel because Robert complained of an odd unpleasantness: "I could not eat my dinner because it is hard to move my tongue," he said. "It feels heavy, wooden." I believed this to be an excuse for the dull silence he had maintained with the Burmeisters at dinner, but I said nothing. We left New York the next morning, two days before we had intended. It was Robert's last visit to the city, his last trip any distance from the Farm, and, it turned out, the start of the last year of his life.

The trip home in the railway car was longer and more tedious than the one down. Robert was very silent, persisting in his claim to a sore, cumbersome tongue. I read a little, sampled the chocolates from Maillard's Candy Store that Churchill had given us upon our departure, and slept well in the berth above Robert. In the early morning I tried to distract him by reading to him from the *Sun* newspaper I had brought with me from the city. It was on the theatrical page of this newspaper that I learned that Della Fox had made no further appearances at the Lyceum after the one we had witnessed. She had been taken to Bellevue Hospital, the same night we saw her sorry performance, suffering from the delirium tremens of acute alcoholism. I did not convey this information to Robert, preferring to read the comments on a musical affair at Carnegie Hall on the same page. But nothing could take his mind away from his troubling, strange new affliction.

"My tongue burns," he insisted on that morning of our arrival at the Saratoga Springs depot. We came back at last to the Farm, tired out from travel, dusty and disheartened. I remember the heat of that summer, I remember the persons who called and were turned away because, I told them, Robert was working, or tired, or temporarily indisposed. I was able to visit with Sarah Watkins only occasionally when I could get away from the care of the house, the garden, and Robert.

If now I will seem to dwell too much on the unpleasant details of that last year, you must forgive me: but they continue to live in my mind, vivid as fire. Now more than ever I see that they seem to be an integral part of the story I have determined to tell.

I do not remember exactly when it was that I knew Robert and Dr. Holmes were not acquainting me with the nature of Robert's illness. I confess to feminine foolishness or, perhaps, human blindness. But I think that, more than these, it was ignorance. For his increasingly horrifying symptoms meant nothing to me until the Christmas Anna Baehr came to help me nurse him, when his care had grown too heavy for me. She was to inform me; until then I knew only that

strange and pitiable things were happening
to him.

In late September, Robert agreed at last to
go into the village to see Dr. Holmes. The
racing season was over, and the lines of ve-
hicles: the touring cars and phaetons, omnibuses and barouches that had conveyed visitors back and forth from the hotels to the
track and to the Club-house for gambling had
all vanished, and with them the pickpockets
and touts, the politicians from New York
City, and the theater actors and actresses
who played in Saratoga. I always enjoyed
reading all the details of that high life in the
local paper. The *Saratoga Union* reported
that the village was almost back to its normal
population; only a few of the fashionable and
wealthy families lingered on for some weeks
of the baths and for the cure of the waters.

It was widely believed in those days that
the hot dissipations of the summer, the "pace
that kills," as the *Union* put it, could be
cleansed from the system by sufficient doses
of the mineral waters of the Congress Spring.
In the late mornings, well-dressed men and
women walked in leisurely fashion from their
hotels toward Congress Park to drink agate
cups full of heavy, sulfurous water. Often the
men were portly and red-faced: one knew that
rich food and fine French wines from the
United States Hotel and the Grand Union
Hotel dining rooms, the late suppers at the

Club-house, had been taken heavily into their distended stomachs five times each day. Even at the racing clubhouse they ate and drank as they watched the races. In those years their wives never accompanied them to the races or to the gambling casino—such attendance was thought risqué and *fast*—but still, the ladies, too, seemed to grow heavy in the season. They resorted to the same purgative treatment as their husbands in the Saratoga springs before they moved on to Wiesbaden or Vichy in the fall.

The morning we drove to the village to see Dr. Holmes we were stopped by a little procession of strollers on their way to the Congress waters to take the cure. Our hired motorcar waited for them to pass before turning into Broadway. But then I saw the carriage behind the walkers, driven by the famous woman.

"Look, Robert. Do you know who that is?"

"Who? Where?" he asked. Then he said, "No. Who is it?"

The woman driving her carriage alone was what we used to call a spectacle. Almost larger than life, she was crossing the broad avenue slowly, a great peacock of a woman in a white carriage, a lavender parasol in one hand, the other holding white doeskin reins to her all-white horse. Her hips, ample and stately, completely occupied the whole seat of the carriage, as though it took that breadth to bear the broad, snow-white, almost fully displayed bosom above them. She was dressed (*swathed* was the word we used to hear for this) entirely in lavender. Her huge, large-brimmed silk hat was lavender, too, except for the brilliantly red roses on its brim, and she smiled from side to side of her carriage, the smile of a confident, famous, massive, but still lovely face.

"That's Lillian Russell, the actress, Robert. She's grown fat, but isn't she still beautiful, in her way? She looks—majestic."

Robert looked at her and did not reply. Perhaps he was thinking of Della Fox, wondering if obesity was the fate of all boyhood visions, of all great beauties. "Let's move on," he said to the driver.

"We can't pass. The driver can't pass. Everyone ahead has stopped to see her."

Lillian Russell's carriage was trimmed with solid silver. On her lap, erect and small, lean and haughty, sat her Japanese spaniel, his diamond collar, the *Saratoga Union* reported, having cost eighteen hundred dollars. It was altogether a wonderful sight to see. I have never forgotten it. The *Union* reporter wrote that Lillian Russell had grown grossly fat from gluttony. She was said to eat three whole chickens at dinner, to drink three bottles of French wine during an evening, and to finish with six cream desserts. But I forgot that as I looked at her, lordly and elegant, her enormous stays lifting her great bosom far into the space before her, shading the little dog in her lap. She passed the corner where we sat still waiting and came to the corner of the Grand Union piazza. Every man seated there, resting after the strenuous season, I suppose, rose to his feet as she passed, removing his hat, as though to acknowledge the progress of a queen or a goddess.

She had passed the Grand Union Hotel and was driving up Broadway when our driver was able to move our vehicle. I was still full of the vision:

"Robert, do you know, she refuses to stay at the Grand Union Hotel. I read that in the newspaper. Despite all its elegance."

"Why?" he asked thickly. His tongue was again troubling him, and I could tell he inquired only out of politeness.

"I think it's because of that sign."

On the registry desk of the Grand Union Hotel a notice read:

No Dogs or Jews Allowed

"She has that spaniel she is so devoted to. So, of course she stays at the Crumb House instead."

Dr. Holmes examined Robert. Then he came into the waiting room with him. "I want him to be seen by a colleague of mine, a doctor in New York. Dr. Keyes, Edward Lawrence Keyes, at the Bellevue Hospital in New York."

"I will *not* go there," said Robert to neither of us, into the air of the waiting room. "I will not go back to that city."

"You must, Mr. Maclaren. You must be seen. I am not certain of the new treatment for your—ailment. Keyes is a specialist, an expert. He is writing a book on—such matters. You must go to see him."

Robert refused. Soon after, it must have been a month or so later, fortune came our way. Dr. Keyes, visiting friends in Saratoga Springs for the famous fall display of color in the leaves, called upon us. There had been no change in the condition of Robert's mouth and tongue. If anything, it had grown worse. The one view I had of them made my heart pound with fear. He could eat almost nothing, he said, everything stuck to his tongue and in his throat. Now it was impossible to keep his desperate state hidden any longer. "Look, Caroline."

He opened his mouth. I looked. Clinging to the normal dark-red lining of the roof of his mouth were white mucous patches, ugly and dead-looking. His tongue was coated on all sides with thick, viscid saliva. Before he closed his mouth again quickly, sensing my horror at the hideous sight, I caught a foul, acrid odor and turned away without thinking, to escape the unpleasantness of it. I felt nauseated.

"Dear God, Robert. What *is* it?"

He shook his head. His eyes looked wild and terrified. Rarely in the days that followed did he speak, for his difficulty in moving his swollen, covered tongue and the pain in his cheeks and mouth made him avoid the slightest effort. Once again, on the evening before Dr. Keyes's arrival at the Farm (Dr. Holmes had sent word with the mail carrier of the imminent visit), I caught sight of the terrible thing he kept shut away in the diseased cavity of his mouth. At dinner, eating the warm milk toast I had prepared for him, he tried to cough and choked. I started to go to him, thinking to help him by pounding his back but he gestured me away. Then (Lord, how clear that moment is still to me!) he thrust his fingers into his mouth and pulled out a rancid, ropy mass of thick, oily, copper-colored saliva. It clung to his fingers, he could not shake it off, he groaned helplessly. I rushed to him with my dinner napkin, wrapping his foul-smelling hand in it. It was the beginning of my witness to his long and terrible dying.

The next morning Dr. Keyes was with him in his bedroom for almost an hour. I waited downstairs at his request. When he came down he asked me to be seated. He took the settee at the side of the hearth.

"Mrs. Maclaren, I must be open with you. Your husband is gravely ill. There is treatment, of course. We can assuage his symptoms, we can make him more comfortable in this—affliction. But, I must be direct with you, we cannot cure him. It is, sadly, too late. He should have been treated when this first appeared, perhaps ten or more years ago. I do not know that exactly—he will not say. But even then we could not have been sure. We knew very little about the treatment then. Now our method works often, not always. At all events, it is too late to apply it to him now. It would do no good."

"What is it, Doctor? What does he have? Does it have a name?"

I thought Dr. Keyes looked uneasily at me. "It has a number of names. Some have called it a blood disease, a disorder of the red corpuscles. Others see it as a disturbance of the nervous system, a brain disease. But whatever it is named, it starts and then recedes, appears and then rests a long while before it finally reappears with terrible virulence, as you now see it in Mr. Maclaren."

"I understand. Can you tell me if other . . . what else will happen?"

"That, too, varies with the patient. The liver may be involved—there may be the jaundice that comes of that. His tongue may ulcerate, then harden, and finally become almost useless. That will cause a great deal

of salivation, almost constant drooling which
he will not be able to control. You must—uh,
prepare in some way for that, with towels and
large napkins, perhaps even a capacious bib
of some kind. There may be bad swelling and
splitting of the lips from all the water, but
we can help that with mercurial ointment."

"Yes. Is there more?"

"His gums are now spongy, almost like a
soft cheese. There are large patches of fungus
on them, what we call noma: they are very
infected. So we may expect his teeth to—be
lost quite soon. Even now there is much
bleeding from the gums. The blood tends to
be caught in that thick saliva you may have
seen. His throat is similarly afflicted now,
and it will be worse. It will swell and cause
him much trouble swallowing. He may try
constantly to cough, or to vomit, with no re-
sults. This condition we can lessen: we cannot
stop it entirely."

"Dear Lord! How can this be? How long ...?"

"The worst part will be over in a few
months, I think. After that there will be inevitable weakness in all the limbs—and, I
must tell you, for most loved ones find this
hardest to bear, diminution of the mental faculties. He will be bedridden, but must be
helped into a chair each day for a short time
to prevent liquid from forming in the lungs.
He will require feeding and his bodily func-
tions will have to be cared for, for he will lose

control of them. Often he will be irritable and sometimes irrational in his demands and complaints. You must be patient."

I stared at him, I'm sure, all the time he was reciting these terrible expectations. "Can nothing be done? Something, there must be something to do for this—nerve or blood disease, whatever it is..."

"I do not believe so, Mrs. Maclaren. But of course there are other doctors you might wish to consult. There is a Dr. William Gottheil in Boston who has written impressively on this subject. You could—"

"No, no, that is not what I meant. I trust your experience, your knowledge, Dr. Keyes. But to know, so surely, that it is incurable..."

"I wish it were otherwise, with all my heart. But it is not. I can only say that..."

"Robert will die?"

"Well, yes." He stood up. He turned a wry smile toward me, but I understood from what followed that it was directed more at himself: "A fatal termination, we say. But he will die, and soon. Yes."

I find it hard to remember if I responded aloud to this frightful finality. I do recall the curious mixture of my feelings: profound pity for my poor sick husband who had still so much more suffering to endure, and pity for myself at the prospect of having to witness his torment. But grief? The stricken and furious grief of the wife about to be a widow?

I felt none of that, for wife I was only in a sense, and woman I had not yet learned to be.

I saw him to the door. His chauffeur waited outside in his motorcar. Dr. Keyes turned to me and took my hand in his.

"My dear madam. This is a very hard thing for you to bear. I am keenly aware of that. But I will instruct Dr. Holmes, who is very capable, in all the procedures I am familiar with and he will be able to care for Mr. Maclaren well. Upstairs I have left on his table some prescriptions for treatment of the mouth—tincture of benzoin, another compound for his throat. Dr. Holmes will know what to do, whatever happens, you may be sure."

"Thank you. I will call upon him, of course."

"One final matter. If it is at all possible, I suggest you employ a nurse to assist you, very soon. It will be increasingly arduous for you to move him alone—you are a very slight lady. And you will need to be relieved from the constant care, especially—ah, at the termination, when you will need professional assistance in many ways."

"Thank you. I will give serious consideration to that. Thank you again."

So Anna Baehr came to Highland Farm. Dr. Holmes knew of her when I inquired a few weeks later. He told me this young woman had nursed a dying old lady in Fort Edward, very capably and kindly, he told me, and if I desired he would see if she was still unemployed after the lady's death.

It happened that she was. I prepared a room for her near the pantry and kitchen. She arrived on Christmas Eve in the afternoon. We had never met—Dr. Holmes had made all the necessary arrangements. So I was unprepared for her youth. Somehow, her name sounded so Germanic, I pictured her as impassive, strong, stolid, somehow. But the girl who arrived at the Farm was twenty-five, she told me (I would have guessed twenty), and had been in nursing service in New York, in Albany and in Fort Edward, a small village north of us.

During the long evenings we spent together that winter of Robert's dying, while he slept, she told me a little about her life. I learned it only very slowly, for she was not communicative about herself. But I put it down here, all together, as I came to hear it over the years.

Anna Baehr's voice was delicate, low, and charming; her diction had the formal awkwardness of someone whose first language had been German. She told me her father was a doctor who emigrated to this country with his wife and two daughters; Anna was eight and Rosa eleven when they settled in New

York City. He died soon after, while caring for the sick of the East Side during an epidemic of smallpox. His widow, leaving her young daughters with a friend, a Berliner who had settled in New York's Yorkville section, took his body back to Germany and never returned.

Anna told me, "Rosa and I never understood it. She wrote to Frau Mundlein, she sent money, but she never came back to this country. We waited, thinking, any day, but she never came. Even when Rosa sickened with diptheria and then died. My mother wrote to me. She sent money to Frau Mundlein to pay for masses to be said, for proper burial in a Catholic cemetery in Queens after a low requiem mass.

"But she did not come.

"Five years ago, after I had been graduated from nursing school, I went to see her. I sailed on a ship, earning my passage by acting as ship's nurse. I found her living in a house just off the Kurfürstendamm under another name. She had been married again and had been afraid to write to me about it. Her husband was in the government. It was strange indeed: she never told him she had two daughters in America. She was afraid he would not marry her if he knew. For everything it was the same: she was afraid.

"Even when I came to Berlin she told me to meet her outside the house in a café. She did not want me to come to her house for fear her husband would come home unexpectedly. So I never met him. But after she and I had two meetings in that strange way I sailed back on the return passage of the same ship I had come on. She continues to write to me, but I do not answer. She is not afraid of letters, but I do not wish to be related to a mother through the mails."

The skin of Anna's face was tight and scrubbed, almost translucent. Her long hair, light and thin, shone with the luster of much washing. She wore it around her head in a pouf like a halo, the ends tucked away at the top of her head in a small bun. In the pictures I have of her that arrangement of hair now looks odd, but it was everywhere the fashion in those days.

The only strange thing about her looks was the color of her eyes. The irises were so pale they sometimes faded almost away into the white part. At other times, when she was distressed or ill or angry, they took on the color of slate. Her figure was full and ripe-looking, much like the young women I remembered seeing on the streets of Frankfurt who had full bosoms, slim waists, and then the opulence repeated in the hips. Next to her glowing youth, I felt old and withered. And so I was, in some ways. My body had never come to bloom. It was still pressed into the flat lines of my girlhood as though maturity, the rounded voluptuous flesh of a woman's fullness, was always to be denied to my sparrow's body.

By the New Year, Anna Baehr had settled in and assumed most of Robert's strenuous care. His sickness proceeded in all the terrible ways Dr. Keyes had predicted for it, as inexorable as a teacher following closely the syllabus for her subject. Anna had to make many trips by foot into the village to obtain the ointments and acids, the granules and powders for Robert's decaying mouth, the mercury in compound tincture of bark tonic for the lesions that had broken out at the edges of his eyes and at the back of his ears. She was always willing to take those long walks: she loved the out-of-doors and the exercise.

At her suggestion we had Edward dismantle the great bed, carry it piece by piece down the stairs, and reassemble it in the largest downstairs room, the drawing room. It became Robert's bedroom. Anna and I sat with him there or, when he slept, in the small morning room near the music room, which was now shut off to preserve the fireplace heat for Robert. She moved her bed into the breakfast room so that she could be close to him at night, and I slept on the sofa in my little sitting room on the other side of the drawing room.

All the old orderliness of the Farm, the

musical calm and routines arranged to protect the composer's need for quiet and solitude, disappeared. Highland Farm had become a hospital with a single patient and four persons—Anna, Edward, Ida, the maid who came every day from the village, and I to care for him. All the rooms that had fires for heat were made into bedchambers. The whole downstairs became one vast dormitory.

There was no place to receive anyone, and no time. Callers hoping to see the noted American composer, as they put it, were turned away. Only Dr. Holmes stopped regularly at our house on his visits to his patients outside the village. Robert's extensive correspondence with persons all over the music world ceased entirely. The letter carrier rarely came now. We laid in stores against the expected heavy snows of February and March, the horse and sled being used for such trips to the village. Already the roads had become difficult, almost impassable. Edward brought ice, water, and wood to the house every morning and evening, and shoveled paths as best he could.

Most people now alive have never known the frightening isolation of those upstate New York winters. The snow piled against the ground-floor windows and the doors, and froze there, making caves of the rooms downstairs. I remember how delighted we were on those rare occasions when the warmth of the

inside fires caused small spaces to melt outside the blocked windows. Then we could
glimpse the dim, thin light of wintry February mornings. All day and in the evenings,
fires were lit: even so, there were very cold
pockets and corners in the house. We used
the upstairs as little as possible. Lamps had
to be lit in the early morning and they burned
all day.

In those frozen days Anna and I were, as
I have said, cave dwellers, the cold outside
kept at a distance by our fires and our lamps,
and by the ceaseless activity of caring for
Robert. Our sense of enclosure and impris-
onment was part of the very air of the house.

Without Anna I could not have managed,
without her gentle, strong hands (the skin on
them, as on her face, was pulled tight and
shone with scrubbing) around Robert, putting him into his chair in the late mornings,
changing his gowns, cleansing him many
times a day with the prescribed powders obtained at the pharmacy: he could no longer
bear water on his skin. The sores were everywhere, on his feet and hands, on the bridge
of his nose so deep the bone was exposed, on
his forehead and at the nape of his neck, on
his palms and the red, diseased soles of his
feet. Anna patiently applied the ointments
everywhere, rubbing so gently that he did not
flinch at the application of her fingers. Sometimes this procedure took almost an hour in

the morning and again at night.

Anna sewed a thin, long shirt of gauze cloth for Robert to wear under his nightgown. This absorbed much of the odorous mercurial oxide and made the daily launderings of his bedclothes easier for Ida. And because the inunction had to be done to Robert's most private areas, Anna devised a flannel garment to serve as underwear, a large diaper-like structure. I see him still in those garments when I remember that winter: gaunt, weak, pale, his ulcerated head almost without hair, his gauze shirt hanging upon his bony shoulders, sitting in his armchair. He looked like a toothless ancient Byzantine saint one sometimes sees in icons awaiting martyrdom. Edward and I would lift him a little from his chair, while Anna slipped the flannel diaper under him. Then she would start the arduous application to his furious sores—in his parts. He cried while that was being done and tried to push her away, but she held his hand and went on with her task. By noon his treatment was finished. Anna would renew his bed—with this I could be of help to her—and then we would call Edward and return him to it.

Anna and I had our luncheon, which Ida prepared, in the kitchen. At three, after I had rested and Anna had lain down to read, she said, in her New Testament or her herbals (for she had chosen the place on the Farm in which she planned to plant a garden when the spring came), the relentless process started over again: the mouth-cleaning and tongue-scraping, the cleaning up, the unctions.

I remember only a few breaks in the routine. Once I thought Robert's long tristful hours of staring ahead of him as he sat in his chair, or lay open-eyed in his bed without seeming to see, might be made more pleasant with music. I opened the door to my bed-sitting-room and began to play, I think it was a small section from Schumann's *Country Suite,* a gentle, quiet work I thought might ease his nerves.

I had just started when I heard a sound. I stopped and went into his room. His head was sunk on his chest and he was crying. "Is it the music? Don't you want to hear the music, Robert?"

He shook his head no. Another time I played, very quietly, a little from his own music, the piano transcription of the "Maiden's Song" From the *Indian Suite #2.* I have always loved the graceful, melodic curves of that piece, the way in which the tenderness of the squaw toward her dying brave is expressed in the long, slow, ascending tones, followed by the despairing fall, the descent of an octave in gradual degrees into the total grief of the low notes.

But the sound of the song unnerved him, made him cry again. Voices in other rooms had the same effect: his eyes filled with tears when he could hear them. Only silence soothed him. We took to wearing carpet slippers in the house, even Edward, to spare Robert the sounds of our footfalls. —

So we existed through the months of that long winter, the heavy silence inside (except for the small, so-welcome pockets of easy talk between Anna and me), the covered-over frozen spaces outside intensifying it. Robert's illness took its ugly painful course, until the blessed time in the early spring when most of the terrible symptoms disappeared. But, like a country from which a plague has been lifted, he was left wasted, a shell. As his body cleared of its open sores and ulcerations, his eyes emptied and his body stiffened, becoming almost paralyzed, so that his bones seemed locked together, frozen stiff. His mouth was a black cavity, all his teeth having come out.

He no longer knew me, I am sure. He could not tell who it was, I or Anna, who fed and bathed and changed him. The vision of him as he was then is still with me: seated in his chair, his knees and shoulders covered with blankets, and on his lap the book he always wanted there, a large picture-book copy of *Mother Goose*. He would stare at the pictures for a long time, and then blink his eyelids rapidly or gesture with his fingers to let us know he wanted the page turned. Coming to the end, we would start turning the pages backward. The pages of the book became frayed and torn with our constant turning, but he never wanted another.

I saved that book. It must be downstairs someplace, perhaps in the drawing room where many of his books are still. I remember that the book often got wet, for the excessive salivation continued. Pints of saliva poured over his bottom lip, requiring constant wiping by one of us. Sometimes we were careless or too late, and Robert had drooled upon the book he so loved.

Postponed often by late freezes and icy March rains and snows, the full spring came finally to us. The windows were washed of their winter ice-grime and opened, ashes were taken from the fireplaces. Outside, bedding hung on lines to be aired of its sour winter odors in the spring sun. Everyone, Anna, Ida, Edward, and I, took heart at the warmth, at the sight of rich brown earth and the suggestion of buds on trees and bushes.

Everyone but Robert. He sat in his chair knowing nothing, suffering nothing of which we were aware (Dr. Holmes said he was experiencing no pain), unable to celebrate with us the end of the wearisome winter. For him the freeze went on: he was always cold, always shivering as he sat wrapped in shawls and blankets. Inert, silent, almost paralyzed, he became the still, inevitable hub of our household, the unmoving center of all activity, his welfare the point of our communal existence, like the statue of a deity, a Buddha.

But he was not there. The endless gowns and robes, blankets and shawls, shirts and towels that caught his excretions (by spring he could no longer contain his urine or his feces) and his saliva attested to his presence, but he was not there.

During the early spring evenings, Robert in bed in the next room, Anna and I alone in the little bed-sitting-room of mine, we played lotto. Anna taught me the game. When we tired of it, I taught her to play chess and dominoes and checkers. We usually played in silence. By that time in the evening we were both too weary for talk. I was occupied by the rules of the game and by the thought of Robert asleep in the next room. I didn't know what it was Anna was thinking, her almost colorless eyes fastened on the pieces and counters, until the evening she pushed the game away as we finished a round and said, "Where do you think, Mrs. Maclaren, he came into contact with it?"

So absorbed in the game had I been that I did not at once understand her.

"Contact with what, Anna?"

"His disease. This—luetic disease."

What was this word, *luetic*? I assumed it came from her medical training, a technical adjective.

"I don't think anyone knows. How does one

contract blood disease or diseases of the nerves like this? Dr. Keyes did not tell me anything about that."

Anna's eyes, I noticed, seemed to darken as she turned them, now suddenly slate-colored and fierce, upon me. "Do you then not know what it is, how it comes?"

"No, except for what I have said, what I have been told, about the blood, the nerves. No. I don't know what else there is. What do you mean?"

Anna breathed deeply, and then with her expelled breath she said, "Syphilis. Syphilis is what I mean. Mr. Maclaren is dying of syphilis in its final, tertiary stage. Dr. Keyes is a very famous syphilologist. That is why Dr. Holmes sent him to see Mr. Maclaren. Surely you knew."

I was aghast. Did I know? Did I suspect and refuse to let myself know? It is all so long ago now it is hard to separate what I knew or was later told, what I looked away from in my fear or was unaware of in my discreet, feminine ignorance. It has always been my way: did I closet the truth to delude myself or others? . . . But now I knew. Anna was incredulous of my innocence. She went on: "There is another thing I wish to say, now that I have said so much already. It is not only a terrible disease for him, but it can be communicated when two people—come together. Often it is—given to the other person."

My heart pounded. My hands were wet with sudden terror. "Do you think—are you saying I might have caught—his syphilis?"

"Of course, I do not know. Only a doctor can tell you that. You must be tested, examined by a doctor to find out. Sometimes the first signs are so slight you do not notice them. A small, hard sore on the side of the lip or even—I knew a man in the hospital where I trained who had a little sore at the edge of his finger, almost under the nail. That was all, the only sign."

I thought of Robert. How could he not have known earlier about himself? In time to be helped?

Anna and I had begun, unconsciously, I am sure, in those evenings and even in Robert's presence during the days, to use the masculine pronoun for him, not his name, and to refer to him in the past tense. He was the subject of all our sentences and the object of our silent, mutual concern. Our alliance began, it seems to me, not with us but with him, his needs, his past, his terrible present.

"He may have known and not said anything to anyone, not even to a doctor. You cannot tell. Or he may have requested his doctors not to speak of it."

That was how it all came out, after a game of lotto. Now I knew. There were questions still in my mind: Where did he contract it? When? From whom? Why had he not sought treatment? Did he know? Anna told me of the two stages that preceded this final one which his shame or ignorance or secrecy must have disguised and ignored. The pox, I thought...

I wanted to know so much. But there could be no questions from me, and no answers from him. He was no longer there. The talented son of ambitious Virginia Maclaren, the pride of Professor Raff, the beloved American composer, the respected conductor of symphonies, and the performer of great works as well as his own distinguished compositions, my husband: brought to this by bacteria, a spirochete (as Anna told me it was called), a minuscule germ of disease put into his blood by a sick person with whom he had—lain.

It was hard for me to believe: so much, brought at the last to so little. Paralyzed and demented, there he sat through the spring and summer, always smiling gently, his eyes fixed vacantly on the picture of a cow jumping over a moon.

Part Three

AFTERLIFE

Anna was a devout Catholic. Many winter mornings it was impossible for her to get to Mass in the village. She accepted with equanimity what she must have regarded as a deprivation. But when the spring thaw arrived she started out at five every morning for the hour's walk to the church in the village. She bundled against the cold, wore heavy overshoes, and wrapped her head, peasant-like, in a woolen shawl. She always managed to return before Robert woke and I had barely awakened. Her cheeks glowing from the cold wind, her eyes bright, she told me, in that low, charming voice that always caught my attention, that the reception of the eucharist renewed her spirits. I remember smiling at her rhetoric and thinking, It is as much the walk, the wind, the out-of-doors that she so loves.

At once, after returning from her three hours outside, Anna bounded about her room, airing the bedding, and then made her bed, straightening everything in the small space allotted to her. By the time I was dressed and had come into the kitchen she had changed into her gray shirtwaist dress covered with a white bib apron, the "uniform," she called it, which she always wore for work, and was breakfasting with Ida.

Sometimes I joined them, more often I ate alone in my sitting room, feeling the need to continue the foolish distance between me and those in my employ. But Anna's open, vital presence started every day for me: she was the one healthy, fresh thing in that wretched house of sickness. Her liveliness enlivened me and made bearable the relentless daily routines.

In the evenings, the arduous procedures for Robert being over, and he in his bed for the night, we sat in my little room, adjacent to his bed-drawing-room. When the games we played began to pall we often read. Now the fires were smaller. It was April and a little warmer in the house, so our evenings together lengthened appropriately: in the little room it might be described as being cozy.

Anna's reading was in the New Testament

or Thomas à Kempis' *Imitation of Christ,*or
sometimes in her *Gardener's Complete Her-*
bal. I recall I was reading *Middlemarch.* Now
and again we would interrupt each other's
companionable silences to read something
aloud. I loved her apologetic insinuations into
my attention, the sound of her soft voice with
its light echoes of her beginnings in the for-
malities of the German tongue. I learned she
was particularly fond of old wives' wisdom
about the weather, about growing things. "In
the Decay of the Moon," she read aloud, "a
Cloudy morning bodes a fair Afternoon."

I always laughed at these ancient super-
stitions, but she was very firm, very serious
about them. "You will see. Frau Mundlein
who raised me taught me these things. When
our garden flourishes in the summer, they
will be proven. You will see."

I in turn pursued the history of Dorothea
Brooke, reading aloud to Anna the wonderful
passage on her visit to Rome:

Our moods are apt to bring with them im-
ages which succeed each other like the magic-
lantern pictures of a doze; and in certain states
of dull forlornness Dorothea all her life con-
tinued to see the vastness of St. Peter's, the
huge bronze canopy, the excited intention in
the attitudes and garments of the prophets and
evangelists in the mosaic above, and the red
drapery which was being hung for Christmas

spreading itself everywhere like a disease of the retina.

It grew later, the lamps burned low. It was almost ten o'clock. Anna countered my rolling literary sentences with her stepmother's wisdom about the best state in which to plant turnip seeds. "How?" I asked.

"You should be unclothed."

"Unclothed? Why ever so?"

I thought she smiled, her brief, quickly erased, charming smile, but I could not be sure.

"It is quite sensible. If it is warm enough to be without any clothes it is then warm enough for the seed to be sown. I have heard it said that in one English county farmers sit naked upon the ground to plant their barley. This must be the same kind of test, don't you think?"

Naked. It was a word I had seldom heard spoken aloud in those days, let alone acted upon. Even my own body I rarely saw without clothes, for I was accustomed to dropping my nightgown over my loosened stays and chemise before removing them, from habit, I suppose, because my mother had shown me how the act was properly performed.

But when my gentle friend Anna said *naked*, I had a startling, unaccustomed vision: of *her*, stripped of her gray shirtwaist dress, her pointed black leather high shoes, her gray stockings—everything. In a manner I do not believe I ever thought possible for one woman to want of another, I wanted to see her so, *naked*, to see her breasts I could only sense from their deceptively bound contours under her dress. For in those days women were beginning to bind themselves as flat as possible if they were especially full in that area. Immediately I suppressed this desire, put it away from me, telling myself my emotion was curiosity. It had been so long since I had been close to live flesh. Like a child, I thought, I miss being held, warmed, comforted, and touched by the softness of another. This need, for a woman, I could in no way comprehend. Yet it was there, in that curious moment.

But always, the living-dead existence of Robert ruled every hour of my life. I felt the weight of emptiness at the center of my being that nothing and no one had filled—since when? When had the small spark of passion left to me from my girlhood, the reaching out, which I suppose is what passion is, died in me who had hoped so ardently for so much in life? I had placed my emotional faith in music, in love, in the handsome young composer who walked with me in Boston Common. When did it all disappear? When had love died in my marriage and the long loneliness begun? In Virginia Maclaren's cold, dark-paneled rooms in Frankfurt? In that practice room in the Hoch Conservatory of Music? In my surreptitious reading of Churchill Weeks's love letters from Germany? Somewhere. Because it *was* dead, or absent, or dormant, until the moment Anna Baehr said *naked* one evening and stirred in my heart a vision, a strange, ineffable hope.

After Edward plowed the garden for her, Anna did her planting. It was all accomplished according to her eclectic learning. At one end of the plot was an old stone wall. Against it she planted fruit trees, which she said might be espaliered some day when they were larger. Around the base of each newly planted tree she wound strands of horsehair, obtained from the track stables down the road from us. She lectured to me: "Out of season is when one must obtain them. The hairs are in great demand by upholsterers for sofas and chairs."

I was dubious about the efficacy of horsehair. My doubts met with Anna's usual, serious conviction: "Believe me. It will keep earwigs, slugs, and snails from the trees, because as they go up the stems from the ground they must pass over the points on the sharp hair. They will be mortally wounded." I shuddered at the prospect of a border covered with sick and dying insects. Anna smiled. "You will not notice. Quickly their carcasses become part of the useful soil."

In late April she waited, she said, for the waxing moon in order to plant the vegetable seeds. "Why?" I wanted to know. She was somewhat vague about her reasons but convinced it had to be so, that in the periods of a new moon there is likely to be more rain. So, oddly enough, it happened. It rained every other day until the first sprouts appeared. She seemed pleased and smiled indulgently at my surprise.

One morning while we were changing Robert's great bed I noticed that the small bun she had always worn at the top of her head was gone, the ends of her long hair being held in place with large combs.

"Have you been cutting your hair?"

"Well, yes. I needed it. This week I will be planting beans."

"Oh?"

"Yes. If you place human hair in the trench you have dug for the seeds it makes the bean stalks strong and tall."

These were the natural oddities, the lore I came to accept as truth. I learned from Anna that ordinary refuse was to be cherished and used. She saved banana skins to be placed beneath the surface of the soil around our lilacs, which then, I must report, later flourished and bore flowers as never before in any year. Our tea leaves nourished the three climbing rose bushes at the side of the house. And stranger still: Robert's now unworn and

outworn leather boots she would not allow
me to put into the dustbin. I was permitted
to throw away only the rubber soles and
heels. "These you can have back. I will bury
the uppers in the far end of the garden. When
they rot they will enrich the soil."

The garden flourished as Robert declined.
By summer all the flesh was gone from his
bones. Now he was inert and almost always
asleep, and caring for him was somewhat easier. Except to remain beside him when occasionally he awakened, and the thrice-daily
changing of his bed linen, there was little we
could do for him. He could not eat. He lay
still, like a stone, in the center of that great
bed, a burden for Edward to lift so that Anna
and I could roll clean sheets under him. Even
his opened eyes seemed fixed, staring, paralyzed in their sockets. His scanty hair had
turned completely white. "Only his heart,"
said Dr. Holmes, who now came almost daily,
"keeps him alive. It cannot be long now."

On August 31, 1906, in the cool of the late
afternoon, while Anna weeded in her garden
and I dozed in my chair beside him, he died.
He made no sound, there was no rattle of
protest in his throat, no gesture of his hand
seeking help. He died in his sleep, the newspaper reports said. But his sleep had been
almost a year long: he had died long before.
On that afternoon in August his heart stopped.

Anna discovered it when she came in from

the garden, smelling of the tomato vines she had been tying up with scraps of our silk stockings. She woke me gently, pointing to the still form.

"He is—gone. You must send for Dr. Holmes. To certify."

She knelt down at the side of the bed, crossed herself, and dropped her head in her hands. For the first time in my life I too knelt. I tried to pray for Robert, to say the childhood words to God that my mother had taught me: *hallowed be Thy name ... Thy will be done ... and forgive us ... and lead us not into temptation. ...* But nothing more than this rote would come, for (I feel I must now be honest) I could feel nothing as I looked at the still, white face of my poor husband but pity for his lost life, for his meager remains. And when I began to feel something, I realized it was pleasure at the closeness, the sun-warmed heat of Anna's soft skin, her arm against mine as we knelt together, the joy at being, for the first time in so long, adjacent to a glowing life.

I watched her as her lips moved. She had taken from her pocket a string of wooden beads. At that moment I wanted very much to be able to join in her worship, to find the proper words to say with her, to be united in her devotions. ... It was impossible for me. The deep emotional freeze in which I had lived for so long, the ice age of my heart, would take a long time to melt, even beside the glowing flesh and warm heart of Anna Baehr.

From where I kneeled I could see, out of the long window of the drawing room, the edge of one of the climbing rose bushes. I thought irreverently, I remember, how efficacious the tea leaves had been. The bush was bursting with flowers which crowded each other against the panes of the french door.

The funeral was simple, but still rather grand because of the persons who came, so many eminent people from the world of music. Many walked up from the village, and others came long distances by motor and by train from New York, from Albany, and from as far away as Philadelphia and Washington. My old friend Elizabeth Pettigrew, now married, whom I hadn't seen in many years although we often corresponded with each other, traveled from Boston.

Robert was laid out in the music room, dressed in his old performance jacket with brown velvet lapels which he had not worn in a long time. The funeral service was conducted in our drawing room, now restored to its former appearance, by the Reverend Edmund Whitehall, an Episcopal minister from Saratoga Springs, who had not known my husband at all. Robert was strongly opposed

to all churches, even refused commissions to
write liturgical music, and would not have
been happy with these high-church arrangements. But Father Whitehall had offered his
services out of his long admiration, he claimed,
for Robert's music, so I accepted his church's
established service.

We had to send for dozens of camp chairs
from the Grand Union Hotel to seat all the
persons who came. The whole downstairs of
the house was filled. Those at the greatest
distance from the drawing room must have
found it harrd to hear the eulogy Father
Whitehall delivered, but it was as well.

He had concocted it from newspaper clip-
pings and a biographical article in the *Musical Courier*. I remember only a little of it—
it went on very long—but I recall he reminded us of Rollo Walter Brown's phrase for
Robert, "a listener to the winds." He said that
Robert had composed the greatest piano son-
atas since Beethoven, that others had called
him the equal to Grieg, and that, like Grieg,
he was a miniaturist of great scope. He
quoted to us Robert's remark: "I never listen
to other people's music for fear of being in-
fluenced by it." This the Reverend took to be
a sign of Robert's great originality. He ex-
panded upon it at some length.

Anna and I sat on chairs close to Robert's
bier. We had been designated, together with
Robert's brothers, Burns and Logan, the chief
mourners. We both wore black dresses, and

the brothers had wide black armbands sewn
to their gray suits. What, who were they
mourning? I wondered. They had not seen or
communicated with Robert in years.

Everyone told me they admired the way I
bore my grief. "My dear Mrs. Maclaren," said
the Reverend, "you are holding up so well."
I felt saddened, but it was buried. It was
there, down beyond the display of tears. I
mourned my wasted life in Robert's service,
I grieved for his long absence from my conscious life, and mine, I think, from his. Only
the curious unbidden thought of Miss Milly
Martino at one point near the end of the service brought tears to my eyes. For what reason? I could not tell.

Perhaps thinking I was about to break
down, Anna put her hand over mine. I
grasped it tight and held it during the Reverend's long prayers, his last flights of fancy
as he painted the dead composer in the image
of a Parnassian god. I held her hand, thinking
of the frightened, sick, troubled man in whose
poisoned bloodstream spirochetes had raced
like demented ants.

On foot we followed the casket, which was
mounted, as Paderewski's had been, on the
board of the farm wagon, to the spot Robert
had designated. Anna had found his instructions for burial in his desk—have I written
this already? Edward climbed down, stiff and
sad-faced, self-important in his best clothes,

and helped the three undertaker's men lower the casket into the grave. My mind was not in control that day. I was at the mercy of sudden irreverencies. At one moment, for no reason, I wondered if anyone had thought to line the grave with human hair in order to promote luxuriant immortality.

I took Anna's arm for protection against my fancies. We walked back down the road with Ida and Catherine Weeks, somewhat ahead of the others so we could see to the luncheon. It was all over: his short life, his long dying, the end of so much that began in promise, came to short fame, and ended in premature decay, long before death. As we entered the house, for the first time without Robert as its central inhabitant, I felt desolate, lost, in the way he must have meant when he said "Lost" to me, that time after Della Fox. Without him, the hub of my empty life, what would become of me? of the Farm?

First to leave were the relatives, and then Elizabeth, who had to return to her husband. As soon as the luncheon was over, the Maclaren brothers bowed stiffly, said a few polite words to me—after all, I could expect no more; we had not seen each other since my wedding—and took their leave. But the Weekses stayed on with us for a few days. Churchill was quite tired out by his long sum-

mer of teaching just concluded, by the trip to
Saratoga Springs, and by his profound grief:
he cried throughout the service, clinging to
Catherine's arm. He touched Robert's hand
just before the coffin was closed and murmured, "Good laddie." For two days afterward he stayed in bed, Anna and Ida preparing him special invalid foods. I took him
his meals on a tray while Catherine visited
the baths. We were all still in practice for
invalidism. It seemed quite natural to be caring for someone.

"There are wonderful, healthful baths
there," Catherine told us upon her return one
late afternoon. "I think Churchill would benefit from them. The waters are warm and full
of minerals—sulfur, I think, which the attendant at the Ladies' Bath says is beneficial
for skin irritations."

"Does Mr. Weeks suffer from a dermati-
tis?" Anna asked politely in her professional
voice.

"My, yes. Just recently he has recovered
from a very severe rash, everywhere, but
mainly on his back. And the treatment was
terrible, almost worse than the rash. But the
doctor insisted on it."

"Treatment?" I asked, finding myself listening to Catherine for the first time. Often
in the past I was able only to make an effort
to appear to be listening to her cheerless,
ill-tempered conversation. Now she seemed

to be taking pleasure in the details of Churchill's affliction.

"Yes, he went daily for almost a month to
the doctor's office. Often I came with him and
waited while he had his treatment. Once I
went in with him. I watched while he sat bare
to the waist astride a special chair, his breast
pressed against its back. An attendant
squeezed a blue ointment from a large cap-
sule onto his back and rubbed hard with his
two hands; for almost half an hour. So hard
that at times the pustules would break and
spew out a yellow pus all over his hands.
Church was not permitted to wash the terrible ointment off. He put over it a gauze shirt
to wear under his clothes. Next morning he
had to return to have a mercurial bath in a
tin-lined tub, and then a hard alcohol rubbing, and then the terrible treatment all over
again.

"It was a terrible ordeal for him. It went
on for weeks, every day, even Saturday and
Sunday. Now of course he is somewhat better,
so I am wondering if these baths might not
benefit him. I should ask Dr. Keyes."

"They would not," said Anna curtly. "He
should not go to the baths here. He may communicate his illness to others. I knew of a
patient who abandoned such treatment because it was so unpleasant in order to travel
to the Hot Springs in Arkansas, but it did
him no good. It was very wrong of him to

interrupt the treatment."

Catherine seemed impatient at Anna's interruption of her triumphant (or so it seemed to me) recital of Churchill's symptoms and treatment. She told us no more, and next day they departed. Church seemed very quiet and depressed, by Robert's death, I supposed. His two days in bed had left him weak and shaky on his feet. He said he dreaded the prospect of another difficult year of teaching.

The house was quiet, almost eerily calm that evening as Anna and I sat in the drawing room, once again restored to its old appearance. We played lotto for the first time in many weeks. My mind, however, was not on the game, being full of questions: "What do you think, Anna, about..."

"About Mr. Weeks's rash?"

"Yes."

"Only a doctor would know properly." She was short, not wanting to talk, I thought, perhaps because she liked to win at these games and was distracted by my interruptions. "I cannot really say."

"But, the mercury...I remember some years ago, a similar rash that Robert...Could it be?"

"It could be another thing. One can never tell from a story."

"But Dr. Keyes. You said he was a physician only for..."

"Well, yes. Dr. Keyes. That, of course, is something."

Alone in my room, on the following evening, I wrote a letter. I did not sit with Anna, as usual, because I was writing to her and because of the disturbing nature of what I had decided to ask her:

My dearest Anna:

When you took my hand during the service for Robert, I knew. I do not understand how I knew, or what it is I now want. I think it is this: to combine what remains of my life with yours, if you are willing, to spend our time together in the understanding, the peace, the easy conversation, the companionship we have already shared to some extent. My feelings for you are confusing to me. I do not understand what it is I am feeling, or even what it is precisely that I desire. I had thought my life would be almost over when Robert died. Now I see it was over long before, in one sense. For suddenly I have had a vision of an afterlife for me, for us, where we will nourish and sustain and, yes, love each other, in a new way. We are bound together now in sympathy for each other. Will you stay with me?

Thine,
Carrie

I never gave her this letter. I kept it among my papers, and I put it here, in this record, to allow it to speak for itself. Immediately afterward I wrote a second one:

Dear Anna:

This is a large house, and there is much to do in it. You have made such a fine garden, you have been so good to Robert and me, that I have thought to ask you now: would you be willing to stay on, not as nurse or housekeeper, but as companion and friend to me?

Caroline Maclaren

Anna stayed. She didn't respond to me in words but simply went on with her constant helping, her activity in the house and in the garden, her gentle listening, and her comfortable talk. Her lissome, fine-boned, full-fleshed body hidden under the heavy dress and apron, she spent much time in the kitchen preserving the excess from the abundant garden harvest.

The time came to clear away the dead garden matter and to cover the area with leaves and bracken. In October Anna prepared the bushes for the onslaught of winter ice by wrapping them in coverlets of hemp cordage. Early each evening she would leave the house carrying two heavy watering pots: "It is necessary to spray cold water on the perennials and the bushes when there is a chance of frost. So that heat will be created by evaporation. This prevents frost-freezing."

My days and evenings were spent responding to the hundreds of letters of sympathy sent to me. Among the first letters to arrive was one from Henry Huddleston Rogers on

stationery that informed me he was
vice-president of the Standard Oil Company.
He had been in touch with Robert ever since
the accident with Paderewski. He wrote now
that he wished to do something in Robert's
memory: "What would you suggest?" Many
other letters came that posed the same question.

I began to give serious thought to some
kind of memorial for Robert. There was very
little I could do alone, the taxes and the mortgage remaining on the Farm being almost
more than I could pay at the moment out of
my meager widow's money in the bank. Late
that fall, I asked my faithful friend Lester
Lenox of the bank in Saratoga who had
helped us when we wished to buy the Farm
to come for afternoon tea. I also invited a
lawyer I knew in the village, Alfred de Wolfe,
my longtime acquaintance Anne Rhinelander (who was good enough to come up from
New York for the occasion) and Emily Chisolm, who traveled with her from New York,
and of course my old friend Sarah Watkins.

I had written to Churchill, thinking that
he, too, would wish to be part of the decision
about a memorial. In return I had a short
note from Catherine: "Churchill is ailing
again. He is confined to his bed, has a high
fever, and is at times incoherent. Tomorrow
there is to be a consultation among our doctors to determine the treatment." She could
not tell me the exact nature of his illness, as

yet, but she had been informed by one physician that it was a variety of blood disorder, severe but curable.

We six, and Anna, met in the drawing room. I showed them the letters I had just finished responding to, pointing out how many expressed a desire to do something. "What do you think should be done?" I asked.

Many possibilities were suggested: the award of a medal in Robert's name each year to a composer of great promise, a national competition for a scholarship to a European conservatory, the endowment of a chair of music at a university. It was Lester, as I recall, who first offered the idea of a foundation to establish a summer community for musicians and composers.

"I have given this idea much thought," he said. "It would be fitting, very fitting indeed, to honor his memory in this way. Also, while we are raising the funds to prepare accommodations for the young composers who would come to the Farm, it may be possible, at the same time, to find funds to pay off the remaining mortgage on the Farm. So Mrs. Maclaren's security, too, would be assured. And the memorial will be established for the young and promising. Of course, the village of Saratoga Springs will benefit from it as well."

Mr. de Wolfe was enthusiastic: "By all means. I am so tired of our town being spoken of always as a gambling place or a racing center—or worse. A community for musicians on the outskirts would be a great improvement."

There was general agreement about the advisability of the plan. So it came to be. Those present became officers and members of the Maclaren Foundation, to be so listed in the charter. All but Anna, who said she would help in any ways she could, but she did not wish to be "listed." Entirely fearless in the presence of slugs, snails, spiders, earwigs, and aphids, and in her encounters with snows and rough winds, she had no self-assurance or courage in a gathering such as this. I think Mr. de Wolfe and some of the others may have been relieved at her retiring nature, not knowing quite what to make of her presence, of my insistence that she be part of the plan. To them she was a nurse, a companion, now inexplicably raised to equality with her mistress and employer. But not to me.

This is the time to place in this account an explanation of what Anna Baehr was to me. If it is distasteful to the Foundation officers who will read this, it can always be deleted. Nowadays a relationship such as Anna and I had may be openly declared. Women who love as we loved are called freely by the name of the isle inhabited by the Greek poetess. They walk hand in hand, I am told, in daylight through the streets of the city and proclaim their sexual preferences in public.

In my time—that is to say, in my middle years, in the afterlife I was fortunate enough to be granted by a compassionate and broad-minded Deity—such choices were hidden under the discretion of conventional appearances. We made no public announcement of what was, after all, a private intention. Nor was there any need for ostentation. The world would not have sanctioned it nor, for that matter, believed it of me.

Nor would an open admission have made one whit of difference to what *was*. We were two women of disparate class, living together in a farmhouse on the outskirts of a small village. We were disguised by my condition: marriage and widowhood, and by what came to be regarded as my mission, my work, assisted by Anna, on behalf of the memory of my husband and her patient, Robert Glencoe Maclaren.

If there was irony in this it was not seen by anyone but me. It must never have occurred to anyone that my intense determination to establish a memorial to him was in inverse proportion to the love that had been lost between us. Often I puzzled over this. Then I came to see that I had devoted myself to his public image, his music, not to his person as I knew it. I came to understand my activity.

But this strays from what I wanted to say about my profound love for Anna Baehr. During that first winter we were alone together in the house. Ida had to be let go because I could not afford to keep her, and Edward came only irregularly to do the outside chores. Anna and I did everything together. I wooed her quietly (yes, *wooed* is the word, there is no other accurate one), hoping to find in her something of the passion I felt, not knowing if I might frighten her, as indeed I myself was frightened, by my advances.

Our compatibility was very great; we talked often and of everything, together. But I soon knew that was not enough for me. I must be frank in this, and it is difficult. My fantasy, my vision of Anna and me together ended in the great bed. I wanted to sleep with Anna in my arms, to be held in her arms in Virginia Maclaren's bed, the bed in which Virginia Maclaren had slept with her son, the bed of her son's long death, the one I now so insufficiently occupied alone. I wanted to renew those old, soft linen sheets—with what? I was not sure what I would do, what we could do. I wished only for Anna's closeness, her warmth, her womanly presence and fullness, the touch of her soft skin against my small, thin, cold bones, in the center of my enormous bed.

My suit went no further than the tenderness of my first tentative steps: my fingers on the nape of her neck when she came in from her tiring physical labor in the garden and complained of a little stiffness. The gratifying feeling of her muscles relaxing, her shy smile of gratitude when I had finished. My kiss on her cheek as we said good night and went to our rooms. And after a while, her return of my kiss, her warm lips on mine.

Then all at once, I needed to go no further, there were to be no other trials. One night as we kissed good night she moved close to me, reached to my bony shoulders with her strong hands, and pressed me to her. I felt no surprise, no awkwardness. There was no spoken prelude to that night, and no verbal aftermath. It was understood: we no longer went to our separate beds.

To tell you what we had together that night, and during all the nights and the days that filled the next twelve years: how difficult it is to find words to hold it all, to capture the quality of close, understanding comradeship, to place inexpressible love into public phrases. I find I think most readily in images. But then I realize how one-sided are these images of mine. I could not tell at the time, do not still know, if Anna would have used the same ones, or any at all. She was not given to figurative language.

I think of the first, soft spring rain: she was moisture to my dried roots. I think of the way a certain configuration of notes played on the flute, alone, above the muted sounds of a symphony orchestra, can bring tears to one's eyes. Anna was those things for me. I had known "life" before that night, known what it was to be alive and to be aware of the horrors, too often, happening around me. I knew that life had substance without possessing any of it myself. I realized my own body not as a subject but as an object. Because of Anna I began to know it intimately, because she had touched me, given me knowledge of myself, with her loving hands.

Anna was a quiet woman. Words, especially abstract words like *love* and *happiness*, came hard to her. She never explained her feelings, rarely even mentioned them. Only her hands betrayed the humanity that burned in her. I knew what she felt when she touched me in places of my body to which I had always been indifferent, had known about only theoretically.

I remember one very cold night when we sat as close as possible to the fireplace. The fire burned high and hard, but it still did not seem to warm the rest of the sitting room. Anna said it might be better on the floor. So we gathered our skirts about our legs and lowered ourselves to the hearth, making cushions under us of our petticoats and skirts.

Suddenly I was very warm. I felt the heat

invading my neck, my ears and armpits, almost piercing my skin. Anna must have felt as warm as I. She reached behind her neck and opened the little buttons that formed a long line down her back. I watched, marveling at her dexterity: usually we did each other's buttons. I wondered how she would manage those at the broad place of her back. She did. Then she reached to her shoulders and pulled her dress and the chemise beneath it to her waist, baring her full breasts, pale as snow. I wanted to touch them, to feel their extraordinary softness and warmth, but I waited. Her hands lifted her breasts toward me, I bent toward her and put my face down into their center. She took my head and held it there. I breathed the sweet warm odor of her skin, her glowing smoky flesh heated by the proximity of the fire.

It was enough, it was more than enough to compel us to our room upstairs, to the bed to which we climbed each night. Dousing the fire, we went upstairs. It was odd: for one of us to remove her dress, as Anna had done, was enough for us both. A single act represented two. The sensual pleasure we shared resulted, I have often thought, from the guesses we had made about ourselves and the answers we found in each other. Now I knew another like myself. My suppositions were confirmed.

I had discovered a strange thing about our love: when I held my breasts, thin and unsubstantial as they were, I was reminded of Anna's. I was touching her, re-creating the pleasures of contact with her on myself. To my inadequate self I assumed her lovely flesh. It was the very opposite of narcissism— it was metamorphosis.

I remember another time: in the early spring we were planting together, at the sunny side of the house, a place Anna had decided would be right for a wisteria vine. "It will grow over the edge of the porch in time and make a cool place to sit." The roots of the little plant were tangled. On our knees we both reached into the shallow hole to disengage them. Our fingers came together around the stem. We looked up and smiled at each other, holding hands in the fragrant soil surrounding the young roots of the wisteria vine. In such silent but telling ways Anna spoke to me. She used gestures, sudden affectionate motions that were both symbolic and at the same time concretely warm: these came easily to her.

To me, the world we had discovered together at first seemed strangely unreal. My long education in connubial behavior before Anna had been so different. Between us there was no flirtatiousness, as there is so often in the world of men and women. We had no struggle for dominance, we experienced no submissiveness. We were each dominant and each submissive when we needed to be. Sometimes I took her in my arms, sensing her need for comfort. At other times I wished to be held, helped, comforted.

One wet fall day, I remember, I was taken by a very bad attack of lumbago, as it was then called, while kneeling on the damp ground to plant bulbs. The pain struck so quickly that I could not stand erect. Anna helped me into the house. I hurt so badly, I was a child again. How long it had been since anyone handled my body so carefully, so tenderly. She rubbed ointment into my spine, her gentle, capable hands full of remedy and assurance. I lay in bed, still sore and very tired. She sat beside me on the bed. "You are a born nurse," I said.

"Oh no," she said. "I was not born a nurse. It happened, my decision to be a nurse, after my sister got ill, a long time ago. My mother was gone then, and we were living with Frau Mundlein. She was very kind, kinder to us than I can remember my mother to have been. Sometimes I think she might have been ... somewhat closer to us, but she was afraid, she once told me. Our mother might return and take us away and then she would feel a deprivation. She never kissed me or took me into her arms, and she kissed Rosa only once that I remember.

"Every day Rosa and I watched the post for word from our mother in Germany. One person on our street had a telephone, but Frau Mundlein did not. So we were able to tell ourselves that our mother called us often from across the waters but without an instrument there was no way for receiving her calls. We did not understand she was too far away to use such an instrument. Letters came frequently to Frau Mundlein containing money for our support. Frau Mundlein always read to us the sentence: 'Tell the girls I shall see them soon.'

"Rosa was very small for her age, very thin and pale. She was often sick and she recovered very slowly. I was in perfect health and never missed a day of school. Poor Rosa went to school very seldom. Frau Mundlein worked six days every week sewing shirtwaists in a factory near the East River. Often Rosa was alone in the house during the day, nursing her sore throat and the aches in her legs.

"Because of that I did not realize how sick she was when the diphtheria was in the city. Rosa was feverish and said her throat hurt her. She stayed in bed. When Frau Mundlein came home she made soup and milk toast for Rosa. That was all Rosa was able to swallow. I would get up in the night when she stirred in the bed beside me to get her water. She was always thirsty.

"But when she got very sick Frau Mundlein sent me to ask the doctor to come. We waited for him. It was two days before he climbed the stairs to our flat. He told Frau

Mundlein angrily, 'There are sick people all over Yorkville.' He could not see them all when they wanted him.

"The doctor examined Rosa for a short time (I thought) and then came out of our room and told Frau Mundlein that Rosa had diphtheria. He gave her some white papers of medicine and said 'Give her orange juice and weak tea.' He waited. Frau Mundlein said she would pay him next time. 'I'll come tomorrow,' he said, but he didn't come, not until it was too late and Rosa was dead.

"People were dying of the disease, I knew, and from the time I heard that was what poor Rosa had, I was frightened. It was shameful, I still feel a hot shame, for I was frightened, not for her, but for me. I was afraid to go into our room. I did not want to catch the sickness. So I slept on the sofa in the parlor. I put my head under the blanket when I heard her call in the night. Frau Mundlein got up to get Rosa water.

"Even when she called, 'Anna,' that last morning, my heart beat so fast from fear that I could not answer or go in to see her. I was afraid to look on suffering. I was afraid I would see death as it came, I was afraid of being sick and dying myself, I was afraid of everything. I could not bring myself to be near her.

"Frau Mundlein stayed home from work the day Rosa's fever went very high. She told me not to go to school and instead to fetch the doctor. I went gladly. He said, 'I will come when I can. New York is full of sick people.' I remember still, to my shame, that I walked very slowly away from his office. I looked in store windows. I sat on a bench in front of a cigar store and studied a painted wooden Indian with his raised arm, his fingers holding a tomahawk. I spent long minutes at the glass counter of the newspaper store on the corner deciding to buy a rope of licorice with the penny I had. I thought of visiting a friend who lived around the corner and then remembered she would be in school.

"All this time my heart was pounding, my lips were dry, my tight fists were wet. I was mortally afraid. I did not want to go back home to see the dying and to be there when it came.

"And so I wasn't. When I got home Frau Mundlein was sitting in the parlor, holding a handkerchief. Her face was red and wet. 'She is dead,' she said and cried. And I? I am ashamed to say, I was flooded with relief that I had not seen it. Afterward, yes, I felt sorrow for my sister, my companion and friend. And pity for her, and terrible guilt at my cowardice.

"The doctor came and wrote out a paper and gave it to Frau Mundlein. Again he waited. Frau Mundlein gave him two dollars. Two men came for Rosa with a stretcher. I stood in the doorway, watching them lift her from our bed. Before they covered her with sheet, Frau Mundlein leaned over and kissed her on the lips.

"It is the way I remember Rosa most clearly now: lying on the stretcher, her eyes closed, her small nose pinched in and blue, great black patches on her cheeks and her chin. And Frau Mundlein bending over to kiss her. I have never put the sight of it away, nor the guilty ache I was left with. The memory of me, huddled against the frame of the door, afraid, lingering at the store, always afraid.

"In high school I took science subjects so I could go on to a nursing school. I would not be afraid again, I thought. I would learn what to do for the sick and acquire courage so that in all my life I would not run away at the prospect of suffering and pain. Even if I could not stop it, I would learn to stay with it, to help, to be with the sufferer, as I had not been able to be with my sister."

The work of the Foundation went along very well in the ten years that followed, as the press and the public who have been informed of these matters know. Mrs. Rhinelander conceived of the idea of the Maclaren Clubs, somewhat like the Mendelssohn Clubs, all over the country. I, and others in the Foundation, traveled to all parts of the nation helping to establish these clubs. The plan was this: once a month members of the club would come together for the performance of American music by American musicians, and the proceeds, after expenses and fees, would come to the Community's scholarship and building funds.

I traveled much in those years, accompanied always by Anna. On occasion I played some of Robert's piano music, but more often I spoke to groups of interested men and women about his compositions and his life as a student, a conductor and composer. I became proficient in my omissions, after a while not even considering that I was promulgating an authorized version of his life in which only the surface detail bore any resemblance to reality. I was, however, entirely successful in my apostolate: articles and books, encyclopedia entries, and histories of music and musicians have accepted and made permanent, and still retain, my descriptions. Only here, now, when Robert's name and music have fallen out of the public memory and are known only to a few dusty scholars, do I fill in the blanks I left in those speeches to raise money in his memory.

The sums donated to our enterprise astounded me: one and one-half million dollars in the first three years, beginning with a most generous sum from Mr. Rogers, another from Dr. Butler and the members of the Columbia University department of music. All of Rob-

ert's acquaintances, the doctors who treated
him, musicians in the orchestras he had conducted, the publishers of his music, even dear
Reverend Whitehall, who had become my
good friend, all sent postal orders or checks.
Young men and women who had studied his
piano pieces when they were learning to play,
as well as eminent persons all over the musical world: it was most gratifying. With those
first years' contributions we were able to secure the future of the Farm by paying the
bank what was owed on the mortgage and to
begin to build the six studios in the woods we
had planned to house our young resident
musicians.

By the spring of 1911, I think it was, they
were ready for occupancy. I wrote to persons
I knew in the universities who taught music
(not so frequent a thing as it is now) asking
for the names of promising young persons I
knew in the universities who might want to
work at the Maclaren Community, as it was
formally titled in our chartered papers. One
of these letters went to Churchill at Columbia. It was some time before I had an answer,
and then it was not from Church but from
the chairman of his department. I include the
letter in this account for purposes of com-
pleteness:

Dear Mrs. Maclaren:
   I took the perhaps unwarranted liberty of

*opening your letter to Professor Weeks because
his widow, to whom it should rightly have
been forwarded, has returned to her home in
Milwaukee, where she has again taken up
abode. We are not in possession of her address
there.*

*The sad facts are these: Professor Weeks
died last summer after a long illness. He had
left the faculty during the spring semester before, suffering from a long series of afflictions,
to the liver, to the skin, and finally, I must tell
you, to his mental faculties. Regrettably, we
were forced to ask for his resignation. Mrs.
Weeks much resented our decision. She appeared before the department committee in
June to protest, claiming with some heat that
her husband was only temporarily ill and
would be well in time for the opening of the
fall semester. The doctors, she insisted, had
assured them of this.*

*It was our feeling, after observing Professor
Weeks's rapidly deteriorating condition during his last term of teaching, that this would
be impossible. Indeed, this judgment was,
sadly, borne out: he died during the summer
that followed from a heart attack, Mrs. Weeks
reported to us.*

*I hope you will permit me and my colleagues
to send our regrets to you, knowing of your
late, esteemed husband's long friendship with
Professor Weeks. Finally, I wish to say I am
sorry to have been the one to convey this news
to you. Apparently, Mrs. Weeks, in her grief,*

must have neglected to do so, and you must not have seen the short but respectful obituary printed in The New York Times.

> *I am yr. most obedient servant*
> *Lawrence Vandersee*
> *Chairman, Department of Music*
> *Columbia University*

I tried to find Catherine's address in Milwaukee, without success. I wanted to send her condolences. Not finding her, I had no place to mail my note. I have never heard from her and do not know if she is still alive.

Anna and I devised a routine for our six summer visitors to follow. They arrived in late May and remained, if they found the Community congenial, until early October. At first only male composers came to us. A few of them, oddly, found the life at the Community very hard. They were the gregarious fellows who could not withstand the long hours of enforced solitude. Our rules required that the days from early morning until evening must be reserved for creative work in the studios, alone. Some disliked the communal outhouse, which was cold at night and often inhabited by annoyances like spiders and mosquitoes. A few resented our communal approach to meals and other household chores. One man felt the lack of electric light in the studios was old-fashioned. We had hired a very good cook who came in mid-afternoon and stayed until dinner was prepared. So the clearing and washing after dinner was done by all of us together, to the dismay of a few of the young men whose talents had protected them thus far from close contact with domestic chores.

Professor Vandersee had enclosed with his letter a list of three names, graduates in composition now living precariously in New York, whom he recommended highly to me. One of them, a former student of Churchill's named Eric Anderson, was accepted for the first year.

Anderson was to prove our most faithful applicant and returnee. He was older than the others, in his late twenties when he started his attendance at the Farm, and had studied abroad as well as at Columbia University. He proved pleasant, willing, and surprisingly without the usual difficult temperament. His quietness was always welcome in the evenings, a little landing of silence in the midst of the general turbulence, the vocal excesses of the other, sometimes very arrogant, young men at our supper table. Anna and I were always glad when he applied to return for a summer and when the admissions committee, made up of established critics and composers, accepted him. Sometimes he played for us all in the evenings. The influence upon him of Robert Maclaren's music was evident: it was as though he had taken in from the air around him Robert's love of incorporating natural sounds in his melodies, his fondness for program pieces, his modest tunes and thin, delicate orchestrations. By the time the Great War began in Europe, Eric had become an expected part of our summer household as no other Community member ever was.

I can see him now, his six-foot-six frame bent over the piano keys, the lamp making his long blond hair, parted neatly in the center and reaching to his shoulders, even lighter, his huge hands wholly occupying the keyboard. He played Liszt with a kind of massive authority. He had his native country's light blue eyes. There was only one blemish to his blond handsomeness: a red mark, thin and salamander-shaped, which lay over his light skin from his eye to the corner of his mouth. Often he would sit with his hand over the mark, leaning on his elbow as he ate or listened to music. When he played, however, the scar darkened, although he seemed at those times to have forgotten it. The younger men called him the Quiet Swede. They appeared to resent his unusual reticence in the midst of all their racket and boisterous talk.

At the end of the summer of '15 we knew the war was close to us. That fall we had fewer applications for the next year. Many of the possible candidates, I suppose, were expecting to be called away to the army. But in May '16 Eric came with three others and we settled into a quiet summer before the inevitable turmoil of war.

I never knew quite why—it may have been the remnants of Europe that still lingered in Anna's speech and manners—but Eric found it possible to talk to Anna and to no one else. One night as she and I were in bed she told me he had said two periods of his life had been spent in sanatoria for the insane: once in Sweden when he was in *gymnasium* and again in New Haven, Connecticut, while he was studying music in New York. His illness was depression. When it came upon him he could not play or write or eat or move from his bed or his chair. The first time he had to be carried to the hospital and kept there for a year until gradually it wore away. "I am well now. It is six years since . . . I have been working very well since . . . that last time."

Only in Anna did he confide, as I have said. But even to her he would not say anything about his parents. "He is a solitary man," Anna told me, "who can not bring himself to talk about himself. He lives alone because he has lost his confidence that anyone else would accept his history or trust his present and future." But at the Farm his way of listening intently to the others made him accepted, especially, I had noticed, by Anna, who favored him when she served portions in the kitchen at supper. She always provided his lunch basket with extra fruit and the sweets he loved.

During the first week of October we held our customary party to bid the young men good-bye. The visitors brought the wine and we provided sandwiches and cakes. We always preceded the feast with some hours of performance. Eric was more silent than usual, preferring, when his turn came, not to play. He sat beside Anna on the love seat and twice I saw him bend over to whisper something to her. He ate a great deal—our small sandwiches always seemed to disappear into his outsized hands—and he smiled steadily, receptively, but made no contributions to the general hilarity.

The other young men were like children about to be given their vacation from school. They drank much wine, joked loudly with each other, and talked about how good it would be to return to New York for the beginning of the opera and concert season. They seemed glad to be finished with the long summer's work and solitude: but not Eric. As always, he was regretful and sad.

The party lasted until midnight. At half past ten I said my farewells. They were all to make their way to the village railway depot early the next morning before I expected to arise. Anna remained to close up behind the young men after they returned to their studios.

I must have fallen asleep quickly and slept for some time. The sound of a door woke me. I looked at the clock that stands in the corner of our room. It was two o'clock. Anna was not there.

I went to the landing, feeling panicked. She was coming up the stairs in the dark and seemed startled to see me awake. We went back to the bedroom together.

"Where have you been?" I whispered, although why I do not know. There was no one any longer I might disturb.

"Talking. Talking to Eric. He said he wanted—very much—to talk." She undressed quickly, came into the bed and stretched out as though she were very tired. I sat up, now wide awake, waiting for her to speak. Suddenly there was missing the accustomed, loving easiness between us, the way we moved together at the start of sleep to lie close, often in each other's arms, the sense of creature warmth and security we kindled between our two bodies as we touched, the wonderful way we were always able to converse about anything, everything. The room, the bed, my heart felt cold, a new twist of jealousy, the rattle of fear knocking on the panes of the heart.

"Anna. Do you, do you—care for Eric? You must tell me at once if you do." There was a silence. Anna pulled the quilt over her shoulders to her chin. I lay down a short space from her, barely able to see the dark outline of her head on the pillow. Only thin moonlight entered the room.

"No, Carrie. I don't care for him—that way. Not in the way I care for you. But he is a troubled, lonely man. He has no friends, he tells me. He needs someone to talk with, to hear about his fears and worries."

Immensely relieved, I reached across what had seemed a chasm in the bed between us and touched her hair. It curled tightly about her head. "Does he care for you, Anna?" She turned to me, and I realized the chasm had been of my imaginary making. Once more warmth returned to the bed.

"I'm afraid, yes. He does, Carrie. He wanted to tell me that before he left tomorrow. He says he has no hope, but he wants me to know, to think about him."

"Will you?"

"What?"

"Think about him?"

"Not in that way. I told him I would never leave you. But as a friend must think about another, of course I will. I said I would write to him in the winter. He is terribly afraid of the war, of America entering it, of being hurt or killed...."

Her voice drifted off. Almost at once I could hear her steady, deep breathing in sleep. But

I remained awake, staring in the darkness, somehow afraid of what could possibly happen. I slept very little that night.

That fall and winter, letters came regularly to Anna from Eric in New York. She read them all to me. They were frightened, depressed letters from a man alone in a studio on the Bowery in the bowels of New York (he called it that), trying to compose an opera on the theme of Oedipus, with no contacts with friends or fellow musicians. He had convinced himself, he wrote, that he must always stay indoors when it was light outside: "I must not be seen on the streets because my height, my strength, will call attention to me. I know the army has once said no to me because of my mental history, but I believe if they see me now on the street they will enlist me." He wrote that he went out only at four in the morning, when the wholesale markets in his section of the city were opening. He bought food and then raced back to his hole: "Literally, it is a hole," he wrote, "a basement from which I can see only the feet and lower legs of passersby."

Anna replied to him, composing her letters on the table in the evenings after we had finished our games, our reading aloud, our conversation. She showed me what she had written: "Do not stay indoors so much. It is bad for your spirits." She said she shared Eric's horror of the war, being rendered somewhat ambivalent by the call on her sympathies of her German and German-American friends and relatives. "Do not worry. The war in Europe cannot go on too much longer, perhaps we will not have to enter it, and then you will be safe. Are you planning a return to the Community in May? There will be a place for you. I will speak of it to Mrs. Maclaren."

Her letters were full of motherly negative commands: "Try not to stay so much within yourself... Never eat unwashed salad greens or fruit." Reading her letters, I thought, Now that Robert is gone, Anna is nursing Eric. But I said nothing of this to her. Our relationship was so good, so open, that it admitted only of truth-telling between us. I was not tempted to disturb the tenor of our days. Our love sustained me and, I hoped, her. It was a source of psychic reassurance and, yes, physical pleasure as well. So that the presence of Eric among her letters did not disturb me. She was so loving a woman that there was, within her nutritive spirit, room for more refugees than me alone. Together with Anna, I, too, worried about Eric.

That year, in April, the United States entered the war. Foundation members met to decide what to do about the Community and decided to open as usual in May despite the grave events. Anna and I volunteered to do our war work in addition to housekeeping for the Community. Evenings we worked in the

public library. Miss Milly Martino was no
longer there: by then she was retired because
of the trouble in her hands and neck. The new
librarian, a lady with the strange name of
Mrs. Osnas Fitz, opened the reading room for
war work in the evenings. Anna and I, with
the other ladies from the village, rolled bandages for the Red Cross and knitted, and "finished off" for other knitters, scarves and caps
and socks for our troops overseas. It was in
this way that it came about that we were
away, in the reading room of the library rolling bandages, when the fire started which
destroyed the Farm.

But to go back a little. The last summer of
the war, we had four musicians in residence,
not our customary six. For the first time one
of them was a woman, a most competent
young flutist and composer named Dorothy
Griffith who had come to the Farm to work
on a sonata for her instrument. We assigned
her the studio (Weeks, it had recently been
named) nearest the house so that she would
not have the long, dark walks home in the
evening that some of the other studios required of their occupants.

Eric had returned, and two other young
men were with us. One, from Massachusetts,
Gerald Foster, had lost a leg in childhood,
and the other, St. John Sterne (we called him

Jody), was weak in one eye and so was not called to the army. All four, for a wonder—usually we lost at least one the first week from restlessness or loneliness—found the Farm congenial to their work. They all got on well with each other, I thought, and with us when we saw them at dinner and during the evening musicales and gatherings.

The musicales were occasions of great pleasure to me. Sometimes, after the students had finished, I would play. Since the afternoon I went back to it, a year after Robert's death, I had regained my delight with the piano. The thick and oppressive quiet that filled our house during Robert's illness and, before that, my careful quiet so that he could compose undisturbed were ended, after what I had considered a decent interval of mourning.

Anna smiled at my "decent interval." I began to play *Lieder,* some pieces I had not looked at since my time with Mrs. Seton. To my great joy I discovered that Anna could follow the music and sing in a low, fine contralto. We began to study a song from Schubert's *Winterreise.*

There grows between accompanist and singer an unspoken bond. They signal to each other their readiness, and the accompanist plays the first note at the same moment as the singer begins. Between us there developed such a bond. I would hold my hands just above the keys. Anna, standing behind me, would place her hands lightly on my shoulders. At the moment I felt her touch I began, and so did she. Our understanding at these moments was complete.

Some notes were too high for her voice. But she managed the long ascent from "Manche Trän' aus meinen Augen" to the "Durstig ein das heisse Weh" with ease, only the final note giving her a little trouble. She would press my shoulder as she abandoned the attempt, and I would shrug and laugh. Then she would go on, to the long, slow, melodic descent to the end of that lovely song. I would applaud and she would blush. We were together in our amusement at our successes and our failures.

Always before, music had created a distance between Robert and me, a separation I served by my silence in deference to his greater accomplishments. With Anna it became collaboration, albeit an amateur one, and "in that union," as the Chinese sage who wrote the *Li Chi* said, "we loved one another."

That summer Eric found it hard, it seemed to me, to stay away from our house during the day. He would come to the kitchen at noon when Anna was preparing our luncheon and linger on one pretext or other. While I practiced in the afternoon I would see him from my window walking the road from his studio, cutting across the meadow to where Anna worked in the garden.

She always told me about his visits. Her

openness to me about every thought she had was consoling at moments when I had twinges of the old fear. A day in July came when she told me Eric had asked her if she would consider him as a suitor. He said to her: "I want very much to marry. I think I might conquer my sickness, my fears, if I were not so alone all the time. If I marry it can be no one but you, Anna. My thoughts are full of you, winter and summer. Can it be that you feel nothing for me?"

Anna said she told him she could not leave the Farm.

" 'Why not? You are merely a companion, a paid person. She could find another.'

"He took my hand—it was very dirty, covered with soil, and held it very tight. 'Let me go,' I said. 'It is more than that.'

" 'What do you mean, more than that? Security? I can make a home for you. I am publishing and being paid for my work now. True, not much right away, but once the war is over, orchestras will begin to play American compositions as never before, I am told. I love you, Anna. I have never loved a woman before, except my mother, who died when I was ten, in a fire. Her room, only *her* room, in our summer house on Long Island was struck by lightning. No one in the house but my mother died in that storm. She burned up alone, in her bed, while my brothers and I slept, and my father was in the city working.... And since then, no one. I've felt nothing for anyone, until now, for you.'

" 'I am sorry.'

" 'You feel nothing for me?'

" 'I feel affection and friendship. But love, no. I don't love you, Eric.'

" 'How can you be sure? Perhaps you haven't felt what love is yet.'

" 'Oh, yes, I know what it is. I have felt love.'

" 'For someone else? Another man?' "

She did not know what to say then, she told me. She hesitated, and then said, " 'No.' "

She turned back to her weeding. When she looked up again, Eric was standing a little way off, staring at her: "His face was red, Carrie. He looked—he looked unbelieving, as though he were suddenly remembering a dream—I don't know. He ran his hand through his hair and shook his head, again and again. Then he turned away and left."

"Do you think he understood?"

"I'm sure."

But Eric did not give up trying to be close to where Anna was. He held her chair, he always took the seat beside her at dinner, he followed her onto the back porch in the evenings when we all left the dining room and went out to witness the sunset. He sat beside her on the stone benches where we waited for the moon to rise and the stars to appear. His pursuit was sad and mute. Anna told me he did not speak again to her of love or require anything of her except that she not reject his presence close to her. He always asked her permission: "May I sit beside you? Do you mind if I walk with you?" His great size hovering over her must have been noticed by everyone, in the evenings, in the dining room, when we were all together. *I* noticed, and watched, feeling within me a little rough place like a ragged fingernail that irritated and troubled my mind. But of course I said nothing of this to Anna.

Our union had always been without descriptive words. We accepted without comment what we had discovered with each other by chance, the miracle of love. It may have been the irregularity to the outside world of our life together that kept us from talking about it to each other, even in private—I don't know—or it may be that there was no need for talk. A fitting vocabulary for such discussion did not then exist, or at least, if it did, Anna and I did not know any of its words.

Anna's kindnesses to Eric intensified because, she told me, "I feel so sorry for him. The least I can do is see that he eats and that his shirts have their buttons returned, and that Edward brings enough kindling to his studio against the early-morning chill."

Late in August we had our traditional Sunday evening picnic. It had been a beautiful day, almost an early fall day, and promised to be a fine evening. Dorothy Griffith, Anna, and I prepared the food hampers, and the men carried them to the elevated grassy area near the graves. The four young musicians seemed in very good spirits, wine was consumed quickly, we ate sitting on shawls, and watched the sun set over the trees. So when it happened no one was prepared for the violence in Eric's voice. In the course of a small joke she was making, Dorothy had placed her hand over Eric's, apparently (I did not see it but Anna thought she had), and Eric was enraged by the comradely gesture.

"Don't touch me. I dislike being touched. Why are you always touching me?"

Dorothy blushed deeply, rose to her feet at once, and walked away from us, down the path to Weeks Studio. One of the men—I don't remember which—went after her. The rest of us, surprised, gathered up the picnic plates and packed the two hampers.

Eric remained seated on the shawl, making no move to help us. He stared down, tracing the motifs in the shawl with a long finger.

"Anna, say something to him," I whispered to her as we packed. "Or shall I?"

"I think we should leave him be. He will be all right in a little while. It would embarrass him to be spoken to, I think."

Between us, Anna and I carried one hamper, leaving the other to be brought back later by the men. We said good night to Eric, who remained as he was, seated like a stone on the shawl, and did not answer. Once we had to put the heavy hamper down to rest our arms. I looked back. He was still there, but he was watching us, Anna and me, his light blue eyes looking almost red in the evening light. His hand was over the red blemish on his face, and he looked tragic, a giant child, seated on the ground in the dusk.

Edward drove us to the village for our two hours of war work in the library. He waited for us, and at eleven we started back.

We were near the Farm road when Anna noticed smoke on the horizon. I remember how I started at the sight, for the evening in town, all the women working together, had been so peaceful. Then we had been riding together on the seat of the farm wagon, feeling (or I know I felt, and I think she did too) the power of closeness, thinking our own thoughts. I will never know hers, but I was remembering Eric on the ground, his hand to his face, a human island of desolation, looking despairingly after us. Knowing? Did he know? I will never have the answer to that.

"Look," she said.

The sky was gray with smoke behind the house. Close to the horizon we could see flames. Edward thrashed at the old horse. By the time we pulled up to the front of the house, the hill behind it and the woods to each side where the studios were, were covered with smoke. We could see Dorothy Griffith and Jody running about with buckets.

"Get ours!" I screamed to Anna and Edward. "We can fill them at the garden pump."

"No," Anna shouted back, as though I were deaf. "It would be better if I go for help. To the Wrights..."

There was no telephone at the Farm—we had never wished to have one installed even when our neighbors had done so. But the neighbors to the north, Charles and Ellen Wright, had an instrument. Anna ran toward their place, disappearing at once into the night.

Her hair singed and smelling of smoke, Dorothy came up to me. Her hands were black.

"Are you burned, Dorothy?"

"No, no, but we cannot get to the other studios through the smoke. We don't know where Gerald is—or Eric."

"They may be on the other side of the fire and cannot get through to us."

Even had we wished to find them at once, we could not have. The smoke grew thicker as we stood helpless, watching it mount higher and spread farther to the side. Then I saw a small snake of flames moving along the ground. "The house, the house," I remember screaming to no one in particular. The house was now in danger. Dorothy, Jody, and

I began to splash water on the ground around it, on the walls and windows, everywhere. Our arms and legs grew weak from our repeated trips from the pump with heavy buckets.

The house was saved, not by our feeble efforts but because our neighbors, and then the fire wagons, arrived. The Wrights had telephoned at once: one engine and another equipped with a water pump came before the others could get to us on foot, while we were still wearily passing buckets to each other from the pump, now dousing the bushes and trees and grass near the house.

Anna returned with the Wrights, they took their places in the chain, and we were able to hold the little licks of flames away from the house until the firemen and their engines arrived. Their hoses were trained on the fire and the house itself. Little by little, the firemen moved forward into the woods, away from the house, their hoses creating massive yellow billows which rose above the charred trees.

Villagers, awakened by the smoke and by the fire bell calling for assistance, came to the farm and joined in the work. By the time the first light appeared in the sky I was too tired to do anything but watch—and pray.

Eric and one-legged Gerald Foster had not appeared. Anna was wild with apprehension. She ran from one fireman to another, plead-

ing, "Find the others. For God's sake, there
are two others back in there somewhere."

We were all so weary. We sat on the wet
black grass—Dorothy, Jody, and I—too tired
to raise our arms, to stand any longer, straining to see through the dense smoke, still
searching for signs of the others. We told ourselves they must have escaped to the back
road, they were now watching the fire from
the east side of the property, across the road,
worrying about *our* safety.

But when we found them, they were dead,
suffocated as they tried to escape the encircling fire, we surmised. They died alone, a
few hundred yards from each other. Gerald
might have been trying to reach Eric; he was
found stretched out across the footpath to
Eric's studio, face down in blackened underbrush, his wooden leg entangled in vines.
Eric had never left his studio. He had died
stretched in the ashes around him, his face
calm, his eyes closed. Only the red mark on
his face still looked alive and resentful. His
body was charred, yet his head had miracu-
lously escaped the fire.

The firemen and villagers worked all night
and much of the next morning to put out the
last little pockets of fire that kept breaking
out in the woods and fields. All six of the
studios, which we had so lovingly labored
over and constructed with such attention to
detail, were destroyed. Around each one the

faint, sour smell of burned pianos lingered for a long time. Twenty acres of our woodland were reduced to a naked forest of black stubs and sooty grass underbrush. Our fire pond, from which the firemen had pumped almost all its contents, was now a shallow dark cavity full of floating fallen branches and the black remnants of evergreen needles.

But we had saved the house. Like a magic island in an infernal conflagration, it remained untouched except by the pervasive smell and discoloration of smoke. By noon of the second day, Anna and I were able to enter it, to climb to our acrid-smelling bedroom and fall exhausted into sleep. Dorothy lay down on the couch in the drawing room, Jody on Robert's old horsehair sofa in the music room. The bodies of Gerald Foster and Eric Anderson were carried away to the funeral parlor in Saratoga Springs. We, the survivors, slept profoundly for almost fourteen hours.

Early the next morning—it was still dark—Anna and I, weary and very stiff, made our way downstairs to the kitchen to make some tea. The odor from the corner near the rear door reminded us that we had never unpacked the hamper. Before we boiled the water we thought it best to dispose of the decaying picnic remains. There, on top of moldering cheese and bread and decaying potato salad, was a folded piece of paper, addressed to Anna Baehr, from Eric Anderson. As she did with almost everything, she saved that letter. It was in her drawer among her handkerchiefs when she died. I put it here in this account:

Anna, my dearest:

I watched as you and Mrs. Maclaren walked away to the village. I understand, truly I do. I am writing this in my study which I need now to clean, by burning my score of King Oedipus. It is like my life: mediocre, and unlikely to amount to anything.

Burning is cleansing. Perhaps the fire will spread to the studio and then to me. I was burned once before, by my mother in an accident. She was very young, fifteen, and unmarried when I was born. One night she carried me to my crib and dropped hot wax, by accident, from a candle she was carrying in the other hand, onto my face. I was six months old.

Perhaps this fire I am planning will cleanse all that now seems vile to me: Dorothy's pursuit of me. The other men's childish silliness. You and Mrs. Maclaren. The whole idea of a memorial to her husband, the Community.

I don't wish you to burn, only be cleansed of—what? Please forgive me.

Eric

"He meant to burn us all—the whole Farm, the others, us, everything?" I cried.

Anna, still staring at the letter in her

hand, said, "No, I don't think he meant that. He was discouraged about his opera. I know that. The rest is just—wild declaration. It doesn't mean he would do it. The fire spread out of his control from the fireplace while he slept on his cot. . . . "

We never knew. I will never be sure. Sometimes I wonder if the spectacle of our love and the burden of his own goaded Eric to burn *my* Farm. Or was he gripped by a religious fervor, a command to destroy Sodom, to repay me for keeping Anna from him? Whatever, mad prophetic gesture or miscalculated accident, the Farm lay outside our blackened windows, a burned-out ruin.

Gerald Foster's body was returned to his family in Pittsfield, Massachusetts, I think it was. Eric was buried in our graveyard. His mother was dead, and there was no one else we knew about for him. Edward put a field stone at the grave's head and sank it into the ground. There is no name on it, but he is there, and I could identify the stone, if it has not sunk down entirely from view by now.

Three months later the terrible war he so feared was over. Anna and I spent Christmas at the Farm, the first one in many years, for ordinarily we would be traveling in winter, raising money for the Foundation.

What was there now to travel for? The desolation from the fire, even the remains of the studios in the woods, square flattened foundations, were now all mercifully buried by the snow, the idea of the Community, the memorial, buried with them. That Christmas, we were alone. We exchanged little presents. Together we cooked a simple supper on Christmas Eve. Anna prepared to go in the sled with Edward to the village for midnight Mass. I asked if I might join her.

Her face lighted. "Of course. It would be wonderful if you came."

The altar of the church was vivid with red poinsettias (I thought at once of Dorothea Brooke's disease of the retina) and smelled of newly cut evergreens. The Mass was sung in Latin by young boys, their high, sweet untutored sopranos sounding like the Sunday-morning bells I had heard in Frankfurt. The church was dimly lit with candles and a little electricity, still a novelty and a pleasure, for we had not yet had the house wired for it.

I loved the Mass that Christmas Eve of 1918. I loved the bells, the organ, the sweetish smell of incense, the scrubbed little blond faces of white-robed choir and altar boys, the solemn elevated expressions of the two priests who, Anna whispered to me, were "the celebrants." The procession of "the faithful" (the priest who delivered the sermon referred this way to the people in the pews, who had come long distances through the cold night and the snow) to the altar "to receive": that was the

way Anna described what she was doing up
there. She would often say, "Today, I received."

My Unitarian sensibilities, restrained and
intellectual, had not prepared me for what
was going on among "the faithful" as they
kneeled in their pews or at the altar rail. I
understood not one word, except for the sermon and the reading from the Gospel. The
heavily symbolic nature of the events escaped
me entirely.

But Anna was there beside me, her lovely
scrubbed countenance (a sister to the altar
boys, I thought) never turning from the se-
date pageant on the altar, her shining eyes
fixed on something she must have been wit-
nessing up there: I could not tell what. Outside, the wind rattled the stained-glass windows and rough snow puffs hurled themselves
against the walls and the doors, but inside
there were those serious, confident worship-
ers like Anna, glowing in the presence of
their God, the extraordinary concentration,
under the instruction of bells, of "the faithful."

Seated beside Anna while everyone else
kneeled, I tried to pray. I managed only to
think, The destroyed Farm, what shall I do
with it? Shall I start all over again? Will the
Foundation want to help to restore it all? Is
Robert's music still important enough to music lovers (who must have new favorites by
now) to appeal to them again in his name?

I floundered among questions vaguely directed to the Lord, but no supernatural answers presented themselves to me in that first hour of Christmas morning.

How do you pray? Do you command the Lord: "Grant me the time and the strength in which to rebuild, the Farm, my own life." Or question Him: "What do I do now?" Or petition: "Please, dear God, do not let me lose what little I have—the house, my friend, my love...."

The Foundation members met in early April, as soon as it was possible for those scattered persons to negotiate the roads. Anna had been called away that day by old Dr. Holmes. An unusual number of persons in the village were ill with influenza, the result of the hard winter and the change of weather, he said. He needed Anna's help with a family in which four of the young children and their pregnant mother were very ill. So she was gone when the members arrived. They knew of the fire, the damage—the newspapers had carried accounts of it, reporting that nothing was known of the cause.

Mrs. Rhinelander was curious: "Have you ever found out what happened?"

"No," I lied, "we never have. We came home from the village to find the whole woods ablaze. The chief of firemen guessed it might have been sparks from an unbanked late-

night fire in one of the studios. But we cannot
know for sure because all the studios burned
to the ground."

Lester Lenox gave us a dismal financial
report: "There would have been enough to
operate the Community for some time to
come, under ordinary conditions. But not
enough, by any means, to rebuild and refur-
nish. Prices are very high since the war. It
could never be done on what is in the bank
and what is invested."

We took everything into consideration on
that long afternoon. There was no way. I
heard in their voices a lack of enthusiasm for
rebuilding, I sensed their feeling that Robert
Maclaren's day had passed, and mine, and
the best that could happen was that I might
salvage enough to live on.

So it came to that. I did what they thought
I should. I agreed to sell most of the property,
all the burned acres, holding back only the
land surrounding the house and corridor behind it which led to the hill and the knoll
where the graves were. It was quickly sold:
the township of Saratoga Springs was anxious to have land on the outskirts on which
to build its storage sheds and to house its
road-building equipment. Later, years later,
the land was sold again, and subdivided. At
present, I understand, although I have not
been out to see it in some years, it has been
much built upon. Roads have been cut through,
there are power and telephone lines overhead

going to the small houses which have, thrusting out from their roofs, television antennas as high as trees. There is no sign, I am told, of what once was there, the studios hidden away from each other in beautiful woods, "an idyll," the brochure used to say, "for the exclusive use of gifted persons." Now even the graves seem to have sunk, like the gardens of Persia, below the much trampled ground of the subdivision.

There was still enough money, I learned, for me (and so Anna) to live on in the house. We would need to be frugal, but hadn't we always been? With Anna's garden and our preserving, and doing so much of the necessary work about the house ourselves, we would make out well. I felt no longer young when that meeting was held. I knew the members were right. I needed to rest, not to travel so much. Yet the thought of discontinuing Robert's memorial, abandoning the summer Community of young musicians, was disturbing to me. So I persuaded the members of the Foundation to continue its existence and their membership on it for a while, to keep the idea alive until we saw what the future held: "It might be that the day will come when it will be possible to start again," I said to them.

They left the Farm, relieved, I thought, to be rid of the heavy burdens of administering the funds of the Community and glad of my willingness to let it all go for a while. Lenox,

the Reverend Whitehall, and de Wolfe all
urged me to come into the village more often:
"Interesting things going on there now.
Wednesday book club, church fairs and suppers. A ladies' garden society, that kind of
thing," said de Wolfe, and I said I would try.
I remember thinking, No more spectacle. Lillian Russell. The baths closed down for re-
pairs. Are the waters still drunk by colorful
figures from New York, I wonder?

When Anna came back from her nursing
stint the next day, I told her what had tran-
spired. All she said was, "It is as well. Without Eric it would not be the same this year."
Her irises were almost white with fatigue. I
remember she went to bed at noon, having
had no sleep during her long night with the
sick children. No more was said about it.

Losing the Community made a difference
to my life, to my pretense, you might wish to
say, knowing now what you do of me, to my
pretense of devotion, to the apparent duty of
those years. True, to everyone I was Mrs.
Robert Maclaren, in the histories of music
(if indeed I did appear at all), in *Who's Who*
under Robert's long listing. But since his
death I had begun to be Caroline Maclaren,
the woman who raised quite large funds for
the Community by playing Robert Maclaren's music and lecturing about him at
fund-raising gatherings all over the country,
the administrator of the Community who
headed the table in the dining room during

the summer sessions. In a small way, I had become a person with a little authority.

With the Community gone, no, suspended, as I had insisted, the township of Saratoga Springs removed what it called "the musicians' haven" from its travel brochure in the summer of '19. The war over, the town had begun to look for the return of the old flood of summer residents and tourists. Reading that brochure, foolishly now it seems, I was flooded with regret, almost, I must confess, so depressed by the loss, by the end of my life's work, no matter how insignificant, that I hardly noticed Anna coming and going from the village at odd hours of the day and night, hardly heard her reports of the increasing number of persons stricken by the influenza. My depression closed my eyes to the signs, which must have been there, of her weariness.

The village had become an extended, crowded hospital. Never before in anyone's memory had an affliction spread so quickly and so lethally as the influenza of that year. It was no longer thought that the fierce winter was responsible, as Dr. Holmes had believed. Instead the theory now held was that the disease had been brought back from the front by young men who had survived the horrors of the trenches only to succumb in their beds, at home, having first communicated the germ, was it? spirochete? or what? to their families.

Anna insisted I stay away from the village.
She carried whatever we needed to eat from
the shops that lay along her path in her walk
home up the hill. We ate hastily and at odd
times. There were very few of our old long,
comfortable, and companionable evenings together. For the sick in town needed her. And
she did so well: she seemed to thrive under
the hard new discipline—she had been away
from it for a long time. The sense of service
brought the shine back to her cheeks and the
glow to her eyes.

There are persons whose vitality lies in the
performance of their duty, in their service to
others, which, I take it, is what duty really
means. There are many more such persons
than traditional history takes note of. We
have been well educated, we have read chron-
icles and biographies, plays and novels, about
rebels and revolutionaries, leaders of nations
and battalions, kings and great criminals,
theatrical stars and escape artists. But what
do we know of those whose pleasure in life
is service? The waiting classes, the pram
pushers, the burden bearers up the sides of
great mountains, the launderers of the sheets
of others, the seamstresses of our cloaks?

More than all those, there are the ones
whose hands distract the sick from their distress, who hold the frightened child they are
paid to care for against their breasts, who
comfort the dying while often the family

waits safely outside the sickroom, who cool
the distress of last moments. Anna was such
a person. She made Robert's last days bearable to him, and to me. In the village she
nursed the family of six, single-handed, until
the mother and two of the children succumbed and until the two other children and
their father recovered slowly and could leave
their beds, and until—it was almost inevitable—she contracted the terrible illness,
struggled weakly in her weariness against it,
crying out and rambling incoherently, blind
and deaf to me and to everything but the
ancient, mad, frightened world she rehearsed
in her head, and then died.

She was my friend, my companion, my beloved, she listened to me as no one, not my
mother or my teachers or friends and surely
never my husband, ever listened. She talked
to me, not often about herself but about me,
about us, and about others she loved. She
filled the silences of a lifetime for me. Even
at the end, as she lay in the middle of the
great bed, bathed in the rank sweat of mortal
sickness, red-eyed with fever, she talked to
me, even when Dr. Holmes was there and she
of course could not know that, was not aware
that we were not alone: "Travel together.
Should go to Germany. My mother. Alive
still? Don't know. Afraid, always afraid. Must

introduce you. So she knows about us, about me. Sees there is nothing to be afraid of in love. That I am her daughter. Even to her new husband. As I am your daughter. Your mother. Your husband. Your love."

I said in a low voice, "Shhh, Anna. Rest now, dear. Sleep for a while."

"Give her this powder when she is able to drink a little, Mrs. Maclaren." He put his silver tools away in his black bag and snapped the ends together. His face was very white. His reddened eyes looked strained and alarmed. He seemed eager to be gone. I wondered if he too was overtired, on the brink of the sickness himself.

"The Community dinners. When he talked and looked so long at me. To help him. To hold him close. Like a child. A son, a lover he wanted to be. Like Carrie. But hard to reach and frightened. Afraid like my mother. Wounded in the face. In the heart. Left alone. To the fire. We helped him not at all. How, Carrie? How could we help? I a nurse and not nursing. Died and was buried without the priest, without unction, without comfort. Burned again. Lying near the dog. Near the great man. He a boy and a man, without friends. I did nothing. Unspeakable crime."

She screamed. I held her, wiping the wet from her red, shiny face, kissing her damp forehead, paying no heed to Dr. Holmes. Was he still there?—I do not know—when Anna talked, raved, when I pleaded with her to stay with me, not to leave me in the dark, the loneliness from which she had rescued me.

I whispered to her, "I'm not afraid, Anna. Not of being alone. But of being without you. Stay with me."

But she didn't hear. She was out of her head, incoherent, almost out of time, on the point of leaving the bursting healthy life I had so loved in her. She had forgotten what she knew for certain, and in her delirium remembered only her doubts, her fears: "Know so much. The Foundation people. And Carrie. The great ones. The great man. How can I be with them?"

I said into her ear, holding her beloved head, smoothing her wet hair, "Love, you were with them all. Above them all. Out of all the world, my choice. I wanted you, I want you. Stay with me, love. There is no one else. Terrible loneliness without you, no one else. Not for me."

She could not hear me: "The long horsehairs. Long as you can find. They spawn eels. Good for the soil. Needed. In the garden. Long, long horsehairs."

But you know the truth already. At three in the morning—I remember that a full moon had just disappeared over the bend of the hill and the light in our bedroom disappeared— she woke and called, "Carrie?"

I moved from my chair, where I had dozed, to the bed.

"I'm cold."

"Anna, I'm here. I'll warm you." I went to
the cupboard for another blanket, a quilt,
anything I could pull out quickly.

When I came back to the bed she said,
"Carrie. Where is God?"

"God? What do you mean? The priest, do
you mean the priest? Do you want me to call
the priest?"

"Cold," she said. "God. Carrie."

And she died.

That was almost fifty years ago. (Can it be?
Sometimes I lose count.) That early morning,
in the darkened bedroom, Anna died. I have
never found a comforting euphemism for it.
She did not pass away, or leave this life, or
go to her maker. I cannot accept "She is with
God," which is what the priest who came the
next morning said. None of those things. She
died. She lay there, forever still. She turned
cold and began to stiffen. There in the great
Maclaren bed at three o'clock in the morning.
My love became a thing, a motionless per-
sonless strip of lifeless white matter.

I remember: I got into bed with her, lay
beside her, touched every part of her body,
as a student of sculpture would touch a classical statue to memorize its lines, to remember its curves and suggested softness. As long
as I am able to remember (forever for me),
her body will be alive in my mind, my eyes,
under my finger tips.

The light was up when I climbed out of the bed, dressed, and walked to the village to tell Dr. Holmes ("It must be certified," she had told me when Robert died) about Anna.

I felt nothing at first but the cold desertion. There would be no second resurrection for me, no third chance at life. I knew that. One is granted one great love if one is fortunate— and after that? Death while one is still in life. Endurance, waiting, survival, the slow, inexorable growth of a sense of loss and cruel grief until it floods the mind and drowns what is left of the self.

So it ended. It is an irony of my life that I have lived on for more than forty-five years, as the world would measure it. But to me the living time of my life came to an end long ago. Until Anna came, I had waited, prepared to be born. Life came, with her: the feeling that reached in to the bone and warmed it, the hours that were filled instead of passed through, the days I remember still, that swim in my memory, glow in my mind like phosphorescent fish. With her death, life for me was ended, but I lived on, a dead-live, half-woman, once again resembling the one who had lived so long with Robert, restored to the lonely solitary I had been during all the years of my marriage.

So. I have put it all down. I look back at the years since Anna's death and find it hard to remember what has filled the void. What have I done? I've waited—a long, still, terrible wait—to die. I've gone on living at the Farm because there was no other place I wanted to be or had to go.

Now and then I used to walk to the village—now a city, I must remember to say—to the library. I've read books, played music, listened to recordings, cleaned this house and then cleaned it again before it had a chance to grow dirty, sewn and repaired and darned, tended my garden—Anna's garden, at first—which now my visiting nurse tells me is weeds and dandelions. I've written a thousand letters, I would guess. Each day even now, I answer letters that come to me from musicologists, biographers, and historians questioning me about my husband, and about his friends in Europe, some of whom became very well known. Most of them are now dead.

Every day, summer and winter, I used to climb the narrow corridor between the house and the high knoll, to the graves, Anna's grave where she is buried to the side and below the great headstone that will be mine soon. I put a small stone at her head, with a cross and DUTY AND LOVE on it, and her beloved name and her dates. I used to take two bunches of flowers each week, one for display to place on Robert's grave, so that it would be seen by visitors, creating the illusion of a loving wife who faithfully remembered her husband all these years.

The other was a smaller bunch, a few wild flowers I would find as I walked to the knoll: meadowsweet and black-eyed Susans, violets and Indian paint-brush. Unshowy flowers for a discreet love, for my unremarked love who lies cold and silent, waiting, I believe, for me.

A new group, inheritors of the original Foundation, has written to me. It seems that the government of the United States has a plan to endow the arts. One of the places they are looking at is our old Foundation, the long-since abandoned Maclaren Community. Of course, all the land is long gone. We could not rebuild here on the original site without dislocating thirty homeowners and the out-buildings of the City of Saratoga street-re-pairing department.

But Lester Lenox's grandson, Alexander, writes to me, from the Saratoga bank. I put his whole letter into this account:

We are asked to present the National Endowment for the Arts with a complete proposal. Part of that proposal—the bank's part—will consist of a statement of the present condition of the Robert Glencoe Maclaren trust, as administered by this bank in conjunction with you. Our assumption is that, if the proposal for the revival of the Community should be accepted, upon your death you would as-

sign to the Foundation your rights to the estate.

A second part of the proposal will consist of a history of the Community. Of course, no one is better able to tell that story than you, Mrs. Maclaren. Are you willing? The committee from Saratoga working on the proposal (for of course we feel it would much benefit the city if we could reestablish it here) can provide you with a secretary who would come to the Farm if you would like to dictate the history, as you remember it. Here at the bank we have all the books and financial records. Should your memory of the facts fail at any point; we can check such matters as names, dates, and financial details for you.

But I have already told this: I rejected the offer to dictate to a secretary, deciding I would celebrate my ninetieth year with a final effort to donate to paper my inner life together with the externals already known. I would put it down in my own hand as a way, I think, of signifying, attesting to the truth by the witness of my handwriting as well as the force of my own words.

And the facts? I read back over this lengthy statement and I find I have included too few facts. But then, what are facts but the catafalque upon which one hangs all the memories of an emotional life, the sticking points of one's memories out of which events have long since fallen, leaving only what seems real: disappointments, despairs, rare intense joys, and even rarer loves. And finally, for us all, the omnipresent aloneness of our lives.

We are all alone and lonely, wrote that novelist Virginia Woolf, who drowned herself. And so it was for me, Caroline Newby, raised by a lonely, heartbroken mother, taught to play the piano by the wordless Mrs. Seton, affianced to a prodigy who first loved his mother and then a man, once and fatally (I have now come to believe) before his marriage to me, a wife caught in a joyless, dutiful marriage, and freed from it at last by the deadly journey of infection through the rivers of her husband's blood. And then, after discovering love, unlikely and unsuspected, in a woman who dispelled her loneliness, left behind by her death, more alone than ever before, deserted by the single point of light, the one glowing coal, in a long, cold, dark life.

The Foundation will say: What you have managed to remember is perhaps only partial and personal, biased truth. You have not given us Robert's truth. Surely it would have differed from yours. I would reply: True. He never wrote about his life. Or Eric's truth, Churchill's. Even Della Fox's and Virginia Maclaren's and my mother's. The others. Anna's.

But, at the last, I think, the historian's view always superimposes itself upon history. Out of a vast amount of available facts from an infinite acreage he chooses what fits his limited and single vision and writes one story. In this case, the story is mine alone. It is all I am able to know.

At the last (I say this often, I notice, because at my age everything points to the end) I know this has been useful, not to the Foundation or to Washington, but to me. Writing it, I have freed myself. I have gathered in what I value and what I have hated. What is here, after all, but a few persons indistinguishable from their inevitable tragedies, a few hopes and visions, many fears, a long waiting, and a profound, extraordinary love that has lasted in memory far longer than most living passions.

Asked to write the history of a man and an institution, I have managed to produce merely a sketch of the chamber of one heart. Like Robert, I see, I am a miniaturist.

In ninety years I have made no significant journeys, traveled nowhere except into the interior of a single spirit, my own. Conceived in the age of the Centennial's bentwood sofa, I lived an almost empty life into an overcrowded and hectic century. Like Professor Watkins' migratory birds, I was the one who flew not a thousand miles but a few feet.

The wisteria Anna planted now blooms outside my bedroom window. Her memory for me has grown, reached up, covered, and supported the rest of my life. During the cold winter Saratoga nights when I lie alone and afraid in the great bed, I remember her way of protecting our trees from insects, her assurance that their brittle little skewered carcasses would enrich the roots. I still cannot believe in a higher purpose or a kindly Providence that will unite us. So I wait for the time when my remains will join hers to serve the useful soil.

About the author

DORIS GRUMBACH, the noted literary critic, lives in Washington, D.C. She is a regular columnist for *The New York Times Book Review* and contributes book reviews and critical articles to a number of other publications. She is the author of two earlier novels, *The Spoil of the Flowers* (1962) and *The Short Throat, the Tender Mouth* (1964), and of a literary biography of Mary McCarthy, *The Company She Kept* (1967).

Isaac Bashevis Singer

Winner of the 1978 Nobel Prize for Literature